Pierre Souvestre, Marcel Allain

Fantômas: Action Thriller

OK Publishing 2021

Pierre Souvestre, Marcel Allain
Fantômas: Action Thriller

Published by

MUSAICUM
Books

- Advanced Digital Solutions & High-Quality book Formatting -

musaicumbooks@okpublishing.info

2021 OK Publishing

ISBN 978-80-272-7884-8

Contents

I The Genius of Crime   11

II A Tragic Dawn   17

III The Hunt for the Man   24

IV "No! I am not Mad!"   28

V "Arrest Me!"   34

VI "Fantômas, it is Death!"   38

VII The Criminal Investigation Department   46

VIII A Dreadful Confession   53

IX All for Honour   58

X Princess Sonia's Bath   64

XI Magistrate and Detective   71

XII A Knock-out Blow   75

XIII Thérèse's Future   80

XIV Mademoiselle Jeanne   84

XV The Mad Woman's Plot   87

XVI Among the Market Porters   92

XVII At the Saint-Anthony's Pig   96

XVIII A Prisoner and a Witness   101

XIX Jérôme Fandor   106

XX A Cup of Tea   109

XXI Lord Beltham's Murderer   112

XXII The Scrap of Paper   117

XXIII The Wreck of the "Lancaster"   120

XXIV Under Lock and Key   123

XXV An Unexpected Accomplice   127

XXVI A Mysterious Crime   130

XXVII Three Surprising Incidents   135

XXVIII The Court of Assize   140

XXIX Verdict and Sentence   144

XXX An Assignation   149

XXXI Fell Treachery   155

XXXII On the Scaffold   161

I
The Genius of Crime

"Fantômas."

"What did you say?"

"I said: Fantômas."

"And what does that mean?"

"Nothing.... Everything!"

"But what is it?"

"Nobody.... And yet, yes, it is somebody!"

"And what does the somebody do?"

"Spreads terror!"

Dinner was just over, and the company were moving into the drawing-room.

Hurrying to the fireplace, the Marquise de Langrune took a large log from a basket and flung it on to the glowing embers on the hearth; the log crackled and shed a brilliant light over the whole room; the guests of the Marquise instinctively drew near to the fire.

During the ten consecutive months she spent every year at her château of Beaulieu, on the outskirts of Corrèze, that picturesque district bounded by the Dordogne, it had been the immemorial custom of the Marquise de Langrune to entertain a few of her personal friends in the neighbourhood to dinner every Wednesday, thereby obtaining a little pleasant relief from her loneliness and keeping up some contact with the world.

On this particular winter evening the good lady's guests included several habitués: President Bonnet, a retired magistrate who had withdrawn to his small property at Saint-Jaury, in the suburbs of Brives, and the Abbé Sicot, who was the parish priest. A more occasional friend was also there, the Baronne de Vibray, a young and wealthy widow, a typical woman of the world who spent the greater part of her life either in motoring, or in the most exclusive drawing-rooms of Paris, or at the most fashionable watering-places. But when the Baronne de Vibray put herself out to grass, as she racily phrased it, and spent a few weeks at Querelles, her estate close to the château of Beaulieu, nothing pleased her better than to take her place again in the delightful company of the Marquise de Langrune and her friends.

Finally, youth was represented by Charles Rambert, who had arrived at the château a couple of days before, a charming lad of about eighteen who was treated with warm affection by the Marquise and by Thérèse Auvernois, the granddaughter of the Marquise, with whom since her parents' death she had lived as a daughter.

The odd and even mysterious words spoken by President Bonnet as they were leaving the table, and the personality of this Fantômas about which he had said nothing definite in spite of all the questions put to him, had excited the curiosity of the company, and while Thérèse Auvernois was gracefully dispensing the coffee to her grandmother's guests the questions were renewed with greater insistence. Crowding round the fire, for the evening was very cold, Mme. de Langrune's friends showered fresh questions upon the old magistrate, who secretly enjoyed the interest he had inspired. He cast a solemn eye upon the circle of his audience and prolonged his silence, the more to capture their attention. At length he began to speak.

"Statistics tell us, ladies, that of all the deaths that are registered every day quite a third are due to crime. You are no doubt aware that the police discover about half of the crimes that are committed, and that barely half meet with the penalty of justice. This explains how it is that so many mysteries are never cleared up, and why there are so many mistakes and inconsistencies in judicial investigations."

"What is the conclusion you wish to draw?" the Marquise de Langrune enquired with interest.

"This," the magistrate proceeded: "although many crimes pass unsuspected it is none the less obvious that they have been committed; now while some of them are due to ordinary criminals, others are the work of enigmatical beings who are difficult to trace and too clever or intelligent to let themselves be caught. History is full of stories of such mysterious characters, the Iron Mask, for instance, and Cagliostro. In every age there have been bands of dangerous creatures, led by such men as Cartouche and Vidocq and Rocambole. Now why should we suppose that in our time no one exists who emulates the deeds of those mighty criminals?"

The Abbé Sicot raised a gentle voice from the depths of a comfortable arm-chair wherein he was peacefully digesting his dinner.

"The police do their work better in our time than ever they did before."

"That is perfectly true," the president admitted, "but their work is also more difficult than ever it was before. Criminals who operate in the grand manner have all sorts of things at their disposal nowadays. Science has done much for modern progress, but unfortunately it can be of invaluable assistance to criminals at times; the hosts of evil have the telegraph and the motor-car at their disposal just as authority has, and some day they will make use of the aeroplane."

Young Charles Rambert had been listening to the president's dissertation with the utmost interest and now broke in, with a voice that quivered slightly.

"You were talking about Fantômas just now, sir — —"

The president cast a cryptic look at the lad and did not reply directly to him.

"That is what I am coming to, for, of course, you have understood me, ladies. In these days we have been distressed by a steady access of criminality, and among the assets we shall henceforth have to count a mysterious and most dangerous creature, to whom the baffled authorities and public rumour generally have for some time now given the name of Fantômas. It is impossible to say exactly or to know precisely who Fantômas is. He often assumes the form and personality of some definite and even well-known individual; sometimes he assumes the forms of two human beings at one and the same time. Sometimes he works alone, sometimes with accomplices; sometimes he can be identified as such and such a person, but no one has ever yet arrived at knowing Fantômas himself. That he is a living person is certain and undeniable, yet he is impossible to catch or to identify. He is nowhere and everywhere at once, his shadow hovers above the strangest mysteries, and his traces are found near the most inexplicable crimes, and yet — —"

"You are frightening us!" exclaimed the Baronne de Vibray with a little forced laugh that did not ring true, and the Marquise de Langrune, who for the past few minutes had been uneasy at the idea of the children listening to the conversation, cast about in her mind for an occupation more suited to their age. The interruption gave her an opportunity, and she turned to Charles Rambert and Thérèse.

"You must find it very dull here with all of us grown-up people, dears, so run away now. Thérèse," she added with a smile to her granddaughter who had risen obediently, "there is a splendid new puzzle in the library; you ought to try it with Charles."

The young fellow realised that he must comply with the desire of the Marquise, although the conversation interested him intensely; but he was too well bred to betray his thoughts, and the next moment he was in the adjoining room, sitting opposite the girl, and deep in the intricacies of the latest fashionable game.

The Baronne de Vibray brought the conversation back to the subject of Fantômas.

"What connection is there, President, between this uncanny creature and the disappearance of Lord Beltham, of which we were talking at dinner?"

"I should certainly have agreed with you and thought there was none," the old magistrate replied, "if Lord Beltham's disappearance had been unattended by any mysterious circumstance. But there is one point that deserves your attention: the newspaper from which I read an extract just now, *La Capitale*, draws attention to it and regards it as being important. It is said that when Lady Beltham began to be uneasy about her husband's absence, on the morning of the day following his disappearance, she remembered noticing just as he was going out that he was reading a particular letter, the peculiar, square shape of which surprised her. She had also noticed that the handwriting of the letter was very heavy and black. Now, she found the letter in question upon her husband's desk, but the whole of the writing had disappeared, and it was only the most minute examination that resulted in the discovery of a few almost imperceptible stains which proved that it really was the identical document that had been in her husband's hands. Lady Beltham would not have thought very much about it, if it had not occurred to the editor of *La Capitale* to interview detective Juve about it, the famous Inspector of the Criminal Investigation Department, you know, who has brought so many notorious criminals to justice. Now M. Juve manifested the greatest excitement over the discovery and the nature of this document; and he did not attempt to hide from his interviewer his belief that the strange nature of this unusual epistle was proof of the intervention of Fantômas. You very likely know that Juve has made it his special business to follow up Fantômas; he has sworn that he will take him, and he is after him body and soul. Let us hope he will succeed! But it is no good pretending that Juve's job is not as difficult a one as can be imagined.

"However, it is a fair inference that when Juve spoke as he did to the representative of *La Capitale*, he did not think he was going too far when he declared that a crime lay behind the disappearance of Lord Beltham, and that perhaps the crime must be laid at Fantômas' door; and we can only hope that at some not distant date, justice will not only throw full light upon this mysterious affair, but also rid us for ever of this terrifying criminal!"

President Bonnet had convinced his audience completely, and his closing words cast a chill upon them all.

The Marquise de Langrune deemed it time to create a diversion.

"Who are these people, Lord and Lady Beltham?" she enquired.

"Oh, my dear!" the Baronne de Vibray answered, "it is perfectly obvious that you lead the life of a hermit in this remote country home of yours, and that echoes from the world of Paris do not reach you often! Lord and Lady Beltham are among the best known and most popular people in society. He was formerly attached to the English Embassy, but left Paris to fight in the Transvaal, and his wife went with him and showed magnificent courage and compassion in charge of the ambulance and hospital work. They then went back to London, and a couple of years ago they settled once more in Paris. They lived, and still live, in the boulevard Inkermann at Neuilly-sur-Seine, in a delightful house where they entertain a great deal. I have often been one of Lady Beltham's guests; she is a most fascinating woman, distinguished, tall, fair, and endowed with the charm that is peculiar to the women of the North. I am very distressed at the trouble that is hanging over her."

"Well," said the Marquise de Langrune conclusively, "I mean to believe that the gloomy prognostications of our friend the president will not be justified by the event."

"Amen!" murmured the Abbé mechanically, roused from his gentle slumber by the closing words of the Marquise.

The clock chimed ten, and her duties as hostess did not make the Marquise forgetful of her duties as grandmother.

"Thérèse," she called, "it is your bed-time. It is very late, darling."

The child obediently left her game, said good night to the Baronne de Vibray and President Bonnet, and last of all to the old priest, who gave her a paternal embrace.

"Shall I see you at the seven o'clock mass, Thérèse?" he asked.

The child turned to the Marquise.

"Will you let me accompany Charles to the station to-morrow morning? I will go to the eight o'clock mass on my way back."

The Marquise looked at Charles Rambert.

"Your father really is coming by the train that reaches Verrières at 6.55?" and when he assented she hesitated a moment before replying to Thérèse. "I think, dear, it would be better to let our young friend go alone to meet his father."

But Charles Rambert put in his plea.

"Oh, I am sure my father would be delighted to see Thérèse with me when he gets out of the train."

"Very well, then," the kind old lady said; "arrange it as you please. But, Thérèse, before you go upstairs, tell our good steward, Dollon, to give orders for the carriage to be ready by six o'clock. It is a long way to the station."

Thérèse promised, and the two young people left the drawing-room.

"A pretty couple," remarked the Baronne de Vibray, adding with a characteristic touch of malice, "you mean to make a match between them some day, Marquise?"

The old lady threw up her hands protesting.

"What an idea! Why, Thérèse is not fifteen yet."

"Who is this Charles Rambert?" the Abbé asked. "I just caught sight of him the day before yesterday with Dollon, and I puzzled my brains wondering who he could be."

"I am not surprised," the Marquise laughed, "not surprised that you did not succeed in finding out, for you do not know him. But you may perhaps have heard me mention a M. Etienne Rambert, an old friend of mine, with whom I had many a dance in the long ago. I had lost sight of him completely until about two years ago, when I met him at a charity function in Paris. The poor man has had a rather chequered life; twenty years ago he married a woman who was perfectly charming, but who is, I believe, very ill with a distressing malady: I am not even sure that she is not insane. Quite lately Etienne Rambert has been compelled to send her to an asylum."

"That does not tell us how his son comes to be your guest," President Bonnet urged.

"It is very simple: Etienne Rambert is an energetic man who is always moving about. Although he is quite sixty he still occupies himself with some rubber plantations he possesses in Colombia, and he often goes to America: he thinks no more of the voyage than we do of a trip to Paris. Well, just recently young Charles Rambert was leaving the *pension* in Hamburg where he had been living in order to perfect his German; I knew from his father's letters that Mme. Rambert was about to be put away, and that Etienne Rambert was obliged to be absent, so I offered to receive Charles here until his father should return to Paris. Charles came the day before yesterday, and that is the whole story."

"And M. Etienne Rambert joins him here to-morrow?" said the Abbé.

"That is so —— "

The Marquise de Langrune would have given other information about her young friend had he not come into the room just then. He was an attractive lad with refined and distinguished features, clear, intelligent eyes, and graceful figure. The other guests were silent, and Charles Rambert approached them with the slight awkwardness of youth. He went up to President Bonnet and plucked up sudden courage.

"And what then, sir?" he asked in a low tone.

"I don't understand, my boy," said the magistrate.

"Oh!" said Charles Rambert, "have you finished talking about Fantômas? It was so amusing!"

"For my part," the president answered dryly, "I do not find these stories about criminals 'amusing.'"

But the lad did not detect the shade of reproach in the words.

"But still it is very odd, very extraordinary that such mysterious characters as Fantômas can exist nowadays. Is it really possible that a single man can commit such a number of crimes, and that any human being can escape discovery, as they say Fantômas can, and be able to foil the cleverest devices of the police? I think it is —— "

The president's manner grew steadily more chilly as the boy's curiosity waxed more enthusiastic, and he interrupted curtly.

"I fail to understand your attitude, young man. You appear to be hypnotised, fascinated. You speak of Fantômas as if he were something interesting. It is out of place, to put it mildly," and he turned to the Abbé Sicot. "There, sir, that is the result of this modern education and the state of mind produced in the younger generation by the newspaper press and even by literature. Criminals are given haloes and proclaimed from the housetops. It is astounding!"

But Charles Rambert was not the least impressed.

"But it is life, sir; it is history, it is the real thing!" he insisted. "Why, you yourself, in just a few words, have thrown an atmosphere round this Fantômas which makes him absolutely fascinating! I would give anything to have known Vidocq and Cartouche and Rocambole, and to have seen them at close quarters. Those were men!"

President Bonnet contemplated the young man in astonishment; his eyes flashed lightning at him and he burst out:

"You are mad, boy, absolutely mad! Vidocq — Rocambole! You mix up legend and history, bracket murderers with detectives, and make no distinction between right and wrong! You would not hesitate to set the heroes of crime and the heroes of law and order on one and the same pedestal!"

"You have said the word, sir," Charles Rambert exclaimed: "they all are heroes. But, better still, Fantômas — — "

The lad's outburst was so vehement and spontaneous and sincere, that it provoked unanimous indignation among his hearers. Even the indulgent Marquise de Langrune ceased to smile. Charles Rambert perceived that he had gone too far, and stopped abruptly.

"I beg your pardon, sir," he murmured. "I spoke without thinking; please forgive me."

He raised his eyes and looked at President Bonnet, blushing to the tips of his ears and looking so abashed that the magistrate, who was a kind-hearted man at bottom, tried to reassure him.

"Your imagination is much too lively, young man, much too lively. But you will grow out of that. Come, come: that's all right; lads of your age do talk without knowledge."

It was very late now, and a few minutes after this incident the guests of the Marquise de Langrune took their departure.

Charles Rambert accompanied the Marquise to the door of her own private rooms, and was about to bid her a respectful good night before going on to his bedroom, which adjoined hers, when she asked him to follow her.

"Come in and get the book I promised you, Charles. It should be on my writing-table." She glanced at that piece of furniture as she entered the room, and went on, "Or in it, perhaps; I may have locked it away."

"I don't want to give you any trouble," he protested, but the Marquise insisted.

"Put your light down on that table," she said. "Besides, I have got to open my desk, for I must look at the lottery tickets I gave to Thérèse a few weeks ago." She pushed back the roll top of her Empire desk and looked up at the young fellow. "It would be a piece of good luck if my little Thérèse won the first prize, eh, Charles? A million francs! That would be worth winning?"

"Rather!" said Charles Rambert with a smile.

The Marquise found the book she was searching for and gave it to the lad with one hand while with the other she smoothed out several variegated papers.

"These are my tickets," she said, and then broke off. "How stupid of me! I have not kept the number of the winning ticket that was advertised in *La Capitale*."

Charles Rambert immediately offered to go downstairs again to fetch the newspaper, but the Marquise would not let him.

"It is no good, my dear boy; it is not there now. You know — or rather you don't know — that the Abbé takes away all the week's newspapers every Wednesday night in order to read all the political articles." The old lady turned away from her writing-table, which she left wide open, conducted the young man to the door, and held out a friendly hand. "It is to-morrow morning already!" she said. "So now good night, dear Charles!"

In his own room, with the lights extinguished and the curtains closed, Charles Rambert lay wide awake, a prey to strange excitement. He turned and tossed in his bed nervously. In vain did he try to banish from his mind the words spoken during the evening by President Bonnet. In imagination Charles Rambert saw all manner of sinister and dramatic scenes, crimes and murders: hugely interested, intensely curious, craving for knowledge, he was ever trying to concoct plots and unravel mysteries. If for an instant he dozed off, the image of Fantômas took shape in his mind, but never twice the same: sometimes he saw a colossal figure with bestial face and muscular shoulders; sometimes a wan, thin creature, with strange and piercing eyes; sometimes a vague form, a phantom — Fantômas!

Charles Rambert slept, and woke, and dozed again. In the silence of the night he thought he heard creakings and heavy sounds. Then suddenly he felt a breath pass over his face — and again nothing! And suddenly again strange sounds were buzzing in his ears.

Bathed in cold sweat Charles Rambert started and sat upright in bed, every muscle tense, listening with all his ears. Was he dreaming, or had he really waked up? He did not know. And still, still he had a consciousness of Fantômas — of mystery — of Fantômas!

Charles Rambert heard the clock strike four.

II
A Tragic Dawn

As his cab turned by the end of the Pont Royal towards the Gare d'Orsay, M. Etienne Rambert looked at his watch and found, as he had anticipated, that he had a good quarter of an hour before the train that he intended to take was due to start. He called a porter, and gave him the heavy valise and the bundle of rugs that formed the whole of his hand baggage.

"Where is the office for forwarding luggage, my man?" he enquired.

The porter led him through the famous panelled hall of the Gare d'Orsay, and M. Etienne Rambert satisfied himself that his trunks had been properly registered for Verrières, the station at which he had to alight for the château of Beaulieu.

Still attended by the porter, who had conceived a respectful admiration for him in consequence of the authoritative tone in which he demanded information from the various railway servants, and who scented a probable munificent tip, M. Etienne Rambert proceeded to the booking-office and took a first-class ticket. He spent a few minutes more at the book-stall where he selected an imposing collection of illustrated papers, and then, his final preparations completed, he turned once more to the porter.

"The Luchon train," he said; "where is it?" and as the man only made a vague gesture and growled something wholly indistinct, he added: "Lead the way, and I will follow."

It was now just half-past eight, and the station showed all the animation inseparable from the departure of main-line trains. M. Etienne Rambert hurried onwards, and reaching the platform from which all the lines begin, was stayed by the porter who was laden with his baggage.

"You want the express, sir?"

"No, the slow train, my man."

The porter showed some surprise, but made no remark.

"Do you like the front or the back of the train?"

"The back by choice."

"First-class, isn't it?"

"Yes, first-class."

The porter, who had stopped a moment, picked up the heavy valise again.

"Then there isn't any choice. There are only two first-class carriages on the slow train, and they are both in the middle."

"They are corridor carriages, I suppose?" said Etienne Rambert.

"Yes, sir; there are hardly any others on the main-line trains, especially first-class."

In the ever-increasing crowd Etienne Rambert had some difficulty in following the porter. The Gare d'Orsay has little or none of the attractiveness of the other stations, which cannot fail to have a certain fascination for any imaginative person, who thinks of the mystery attaching to all those iron rails reaching out into the distance of countries unknown to him. It is less noisy than the others also, for between Austerlitz and Orsay the traction is entirely electric. And further, there is no clearly defined separation between the main and the suburban lines.

On the right of the platform was the train which was to take Etienne Rambert beyond Brives to Verrières, the slow train to Luchon; and on the left of the same platform was another train for Juvisy and all the small stations in the suburbs of Paris.

Very few people were making for the train to Luchon; but a large crowd was pressing into the suburban train.

The porter who was piloting M. Etienne Rambert, set the baggage he was carrying down on the footboard of a first-class carriage.

"There is no one for the slow train yet, sir; if you like to get in first you can choose your own compartment."

M. Etienne Rambert acted on the suggestion, but he had hardly set foot in the corridor before the guard, also scenting a generous tip, came to offer his services.

"It really is the 8.50 you want, sir?" was his first enquiry. "You are sure you are not making a mistake?"

"No," Etienne Rambert replied. "Why?"

"A great many first-class passengers do make a mistake," the man explained, "and confuse the 8.50 with the 8.45 express."

As he spoke the guard took the baggage from the porter who had remained on the platform, and the porter, after being generously remunerated for his trouble by M. Rambert, hurried away to look for other travellers.

"The 8.45 is the express, isn't it?" M. Rambert enquired.

"Yes," the guard answered; "it runs right through without stopping at all the small stations as this train does. It goes in front of this one and gets to Luchon three hours earlier. There it is on the side there," and he pointed through the window in the door on the far side to another train on the next rails, in which a number of travellers were already taking their seats. "If you prefer to go by that one, sir," he went on, "there is still time for you to change; you are entitled to take your choice since you have a first-class ticket."

But Etienne Rambert, after a moment's consideration, declined the suggestion.

"No: I would rather go by the slow train. If I take the express I should have to get out at Brives, and then I should be twelve or thirteen miles from Saint-Jaury, which is my destination; whereas the slow train stops at Verrières, where, by the way, I have already telegraphed to say I shall arrive to-morrow morning."

He walked a little way along the corridor, assuring himself that the various compartments were still quite empty, and then turned to the guard.

"Look here, my man," he said, "I am awfully tired, and I mean to get some sleep to-night; consequently I should like to be alone. Now where shall I be most quiet and undisturbed?"

The man understood. M. Etienne Rambert's enquiry about the place where he would be most quiet, was an implicit promise of a handsome tip if nobody did disturb him.

"If you like to settle yourself here, sir," the man answered, "you can draw down the blinds at once, and I dare say I shall be able to find room for any other passengers somewhere else."

"Good," said M. Rambert, moving towards the compartment indicated. "I will smoke a cigar until the train starts, and immediately afterwards I will settle down to sleep. By the way, my man, since you seem so obliging, I wish you would undertake to call me to-morrow morning in time for me to get out at Verrières. I am desperately sleepy and I am quite capable of not waking up."

The guard touched his cap.

"You can be perfectly easy, sir, and sleep without the least anxiety. I won't fail."

"Very well."

When his baggage had been stowed away, and his rugs spread out to make the seat more comfortable still, M. Etienne Rambert repeated his appeal, for he was an old traveller and knew that it does not do to rely too much upon the promises of chance attendants.

"I can rely upon you, can't I? I may sleep as sound as I like, and you will wake me at Verrières?" And the more to assure himself that the guard would execute his orders he slipped a franc into his hand.

When he was left alone, M. Rambert continued his preparations for the night. He carefully drew down the blinds over the door and over the windows of the compartment that gave on to the corridor, and also lowered the shade over the electric light, and then, in order to enjoy the last puffs at his cigar in peace, he opened the window over the other door and leant his elbows on it, watching the final preparations being made by the travellers by the express on the other line.

The departure of a train is always a picturesque sight, and M. Rambert leant forward inquisitively to note how the passengers had installed themselves in the two compartments which he could see from his coign of vantage.

There were not many people in the train. As a matter of fact the Brives and Luchon line is not much used at this time of year. If the number of passengers in the express were any criterion

Etienne Rambert might reasonably expect that he would be the only one in the slow train. But there was not much time for observations and reflections of this kind. On the platform for the express, which he got a glimpse of through the compartments, people were hurrying up their farewells. The passengers had got into their carriages, and the friends who had come to see them off were standing alone upon the platform. There was the sound of safety locks being fastened by porters, and the noise of trollies being wheeled along bearing articles for sale.

"Pillows! Rugs! Sweets! Papers!"

Then came the whistle of the guard, the shriller scream from the electric engine, and then, slowly at first but steadily, more rapidly as the engine got up speed, the express moved along the platform and plunged into the tunnel on the way to Austerlitz.

Meanwhile the guard of the slow train was doing wonders. Shamelessly resolved to assure perfect quiet to "his" passenger, he managed, without unduly compromising himself but yet without leaving any doubt about it in any mind, to insinuate discreetly that M. Rambert's carriage was reserved, so that that gentleman might count upon an entirely undisturbed night.

A few minutes after the express had gone, the slow train drew out in its turn, and disappeared into the darkness of the underground tunnel.

At the château of Beaulieu young Charles Rambert was just finishing dressing when a gentle tap sounded on the door of his room.

"It is a quarter to five, Charles. Get up at once!"

"I am awake already, Thérèse," Charles Rambert answered with some pride. "I shall be ready in two minutes."

"What? up already?" the girl exclaimed from the other side of the door. "Marvellous! I congratulate you. I'm ready too; I will wait for you in the dining-room. Come down as soon as you are dressed."

"All right!" the young man answered.

He wasted no time over his toilette, the more so because it was none too warm in his room, for at this early hour it was still quite dark; and then taking his light in one hand he opened his door carefully so as to make no noise, tip-toed along the landing, and went down the staircase to join Thérèse in the dining-room. The girl was an accomplished housekeeper already, and while waiting for the young fellow she had got a scratch meal together.

"Let us have breakfast quickly," she suggested; "it isn't snowing this morning, and if you like we might walk to the station. We have plenty of time, and it will do us good to have a walk."

"It will warm us up anyhow," Charles Rambert replied; he was only half-awake, but he sat beside Thérèse, and did justice to the preparations she had made.

"Do you know that it is very wonderful of you to get up so punctually?" Mme. de Langrune's granddaughter remarked. "How did you manage it? Last night you were afraid you would sleep on as usual."

"It was not much trouble for me to wake up," Charles Rambert answered. "I hardly closed an eye all night."

"But I promised to come and knock at your door myself, so you might have slept without any anxiety."

"That's so, but to tell you the truth, Thérèse, I was regularly upset and excited by the thought of papa arriving this morning."

They had both finished breakfast, and Thérèse got up.

"Shall we start?" she asked.

"Yes."

Thérèse opened the hall door, and the two young people went down the flight of steps leading to the garden. The girl had thrown a big cloak over her shoulders, and she inhaled the pure morning air with keen delight.

"I love going out in the early morning," she declared.

"Well, I don't like it at all," Charles Rambert confessed with characteristic candour. "Good Lord, how cold it is! And it is still pitch dark!"

"Surely you are not going to be frightened?" said Thérèse teasingly.

Charles Rambert made an irritable movement of vexation and surprise.

"Frightened? What do you take me for, Thérèse? If I don't like going out in the early morning it's really only because it is cold."

She laughed at him while they were crossing the lawn towards the out-buildings, through which she meant to get out on to the high road. As they passed the stables they came across a groom who was leisurely getting an old brougham out of the coach-house.

"Don't hurry, Jean," Thérèse called out as she greeted him. "We are going to walk to the station, and the only important thing is that you should be there to bring us back."

The man touched his cap and the two young people passed through the park gate and found themselves upon the high road.

It was still very dark, with just a wan reflection in the distance of the sky vaguely outlining some cloud-shapes to the eastward to give some promise of the day. There was no sound to break the silence of the fields, and as they walked briskly along Charles and Thérèse could hear their footsteps ringing on the hard surface of the frozen ground.

"It must please you awfully to be going to meet your father," said Mme. de Langrune's granddaughter half questioningly. "It is a long time since you have seen him, isn't it?"

"Three years," Charles Rambert answered, "and then just for a few minutes. He is coming home from America now, and before that he travelled in Spain for a long time."

"He was travelling the whole time you were a child, wasn't he?"

"Yes, always: either in Colombia, looking after his rubber plantations there, or in Spain, where he has a good deal of property too. When he was in Paris he used to come to the school and ask for me, and I saw him in the parlour — for a quarter of an hour."

"And your mother?"

"Oh, mamma was different. You know, Thérèse, I spent all the childhood that I can remember at the school. I liked the masters and had good chums, and was very happy there, and if the truth must be told I looked forward with anything but pleasure to the holidays, when I had to go to my parents' house. I always felt a stranger with them; my real home was the school-room, where I had my desk and all my own interests. And then, you know, when one is little one doesn't understand things much; I didn't feel having hardly any family, very much."

"But you loved your mother very much?"

Thérèse asked the question quite anxiously, and it was patent that she would have thought it dreadful if her companion had not had a real affection for his mother.

"Oh, yes, I loved her," Charles Rambert answered; "but I hardly knew her either." And as Thérèse showed her surprise he went on, telling her something of the secret of his lonely childhood. "You see, Thérèse, now that I am a man I guess lots of things that I could not have had even a suspicion of then. My father and mother did not get on well together. They were what you call an ill-assorted couple. They were both very good, but their characters did not harmonise. When I was little I always saw mamma silent and sad, and papa active and on the go, and bright and talking at the top of his voice. I half believe he frightened mamma! And then my father was constantly away, whereas mamma hardly ever went out. When a servant took me to the house on Thursdays, I was taken up to say good morning to her, and I invariably found her lying on a sofa in her room, with the blinds down and almost dark. She just touched me with her lips and asked me one or two questions, and then I was taken away again because I tired her."

"Was she ill, then?"

"Mamma always has been ill. I suppose you know, Thérèse, that three months ago — stay, it was just when I had taken my degree and went to Germany — she was sent to an asylum? I believe my father had wanted her to agree to undergo careful treatment of the kind long before, but she would not."

Thérèse was silent for a few minutes.

"You have not been very happy," she said presently.

"Oh, it was only after I grew up that I felt unhappy. When I was a little chap I never thought of how sad it is to have no real father or mother. The last four or five years it has hurt me, but when he came to see me once at school, papa told me he would take me with him as soon as I had taken my degree and grown up. Last October, after my examination, he wrote and told me to be patient a little longer, and that he was hurrying on with the winding up of his business and coming back to France. That gave me a hope which has brightened these last few months, and will also make you understand why I am so pleased this morning at my fathers coming. It seems to me that a new life is going to begin."

Day was breaking now: a dirty December day, with the light filtering through heavy grey clouds that drifted along the ground, hid the horizon, clung to the low hills, and then suddenly dispersed in long wisps driven by a keen breeze, that got up in gusts, and drove clouds of dust along the hard frozen ground.

"I have not been very happy either," said Thérèse, "for I lost my father when I was tiny: I don't even remember him; and mamma must be dead as well."

The ambiguous turning of the child's phrase caught Charles Rambert's interested attention.

"What does that mean, Thérèse? Don't you know if your mother is dead?"

"Yes, oh yes; grandmamma says so. But whenever I ask for particulars grandmamma always changes the subject. I will echo what you said just now: when you are little you don't know anything and are not surprised at anything. For a long time I took no notice of her sudden reticence, but now I sometimes wonder if something is not being kept back from me — whether it is really true that mamma is no more in this world."

Talking like this Thérèse and Charles had walked at a good pace, and now they came to the few houses built around Verrières station. One by one, bedroom windows and doors were being opened; peasants were making their way to the sheds to lead their cattle to the pastures.

"We are very early," Thérèse remarked, pointing to the station clock in the distance. "Your father's train is due at 6.55, and it is only 6.40 now; we still have a quarter of an hour to wait, and more, if the train is not punctual!"

They went into the little station and Charles Rambert, thankful for some shelter from the cold, stamped his feet, making a sudden uproar in the empty waiting-room. A porter appeared.

"Who the deuce is kicking up all this row?" he began angrily, and then seeing Thérèse, broke off short. "Ah, Mademoiselle Thérèse," he said with the familiar yet perfectly respectful cordiality that marks country folk, "up already? Have you come to meet somebody, or are you going away?"

As he spoke, the porter turned a curious eye upon Charles Rambert, whose arrival had caused quite a sensation two days before in this little spot, where with but few exceptions none but people belonging to the neighbourhood ever came by train.

"No, I am not going away," Thérèse replied. "I have accompanied M. Rambert, who has come to meet his father."

"Ah-ha, to meet your papa, sir: is he coming from far?"

"From Paris," Charles Rambert answered. "Is the train signalled yet?"

The man drew out a watch like a turnip, and looked at the time.

"It won't be here for quite another twenty minutes. The work on the tunnel makes it necessary to be careful, and it's always late now. But you will hear when the bell rings: that will be when the train is coming over the level-crossing; it will run into the station three minutes after that. Well, Mademoiselle, I must get on with my work," and the man left them.

Thérèse turned to Charles Rambert.

"Shall we go on to the platform? Then we shall see the train come in."

So they left the waiting-room and began to walk up and down the whole length of the platform. Thérèse watched the jerky movements of the hands of the clock, and smiled at her companion.

"Five minutes more, and your father will be here! Four minutes more! Ah! There it is!" and she pointed to a slope in the distance where a slight trail of smoke rose white against the blue of the sky, now clear of cloud. "Can't you see it? That is the steam from the engine coming out of the tunnel."

Ere she finished speaking the quivering whir of the bell echoed through the empty station.

"Ah!" said Charles Rambert: "at last!"

The two porters who, with the stationmaster, constituted the entire railway staff at Verrières, came bustling along the platform, and while the bell continued its monotonous whirring ring, pulled forward trucks in readiness for any possible luggage. Puffing portentously, the engine slackened speed, and the heavy train slowed down and finally stopped, bringing a noisy atmosphere of life into the station of Verrières that but a moment ago was so still.

The first-class carriages had stopped immediately in front of Charles and Thérèse, and on the footboard Etienne Rambert stood, a tall, elderly man of distinguished appearance, proud bearing and energetic attitude, with extraordinarily keen eyes and an unusually high and intelligent forehead. Seeing Thérèse and Charles he seized his baggage and in a twinkling had sprung on to the platform. He dropped his valise, tossed his bundle of rugs on to a seat, and gripped Charles by the two shoulders.

"My boy!" he exclaimed; "my dear boy!"

Although he had hitherto shown so little affection for his child, it was obvious that the man was making a great effort to restrain his emotion, and was really moved when he now saw him again as a grown young man.

Nor, on his part, did Charles Rambert remain unmoved. As if the sudden grip of this almost stranger, who yet was his father, had awakened a world of memories within him, he turned very pale and his voice faltered as he replied:

"Papa! Dear papa! I am so glad to see you!"

Thérèse had drawn tactfully aside. M. Rambert still held his son by the shoulders and stepped back a pace, the better to consider him.

"Why, you are a man! How you have altered, my boy! You are just what I hoped you would be: tall and strong! Ah, you are my son all right! And you are quite well, hey? Yet you look tired."

"I did not sleep well," Charles explained with a smile. "I was afraid I should not wake up."

Turning his head, M. Rambert saw Thérèse and held out his hand.

"How do you do, my little Thérèse?" he exclaimed. "You have altered too since I saw you last. I left a little chit of a child, and now I behold a grown-up young lady. Well! I must be off at once to pay my respects to my dear old friend, your grandmother. All well at the château, eh?"

Thérèse shook hands warmly with M. Rambert and thanked him prettily.

"Grandmamma is very well; she told me to tell you to excuse her if she did not come to meet you, but her doctor says she must not get up very early."

"Of course your grandmamma is excused, my dear. Besides, I have to thank her for her kindness to Charles, and for the hospitality she is going to extend to me for a few days."

Meanwhile the train had gone on again, and now a porter came up to M. Rambert.

"Will you take your luggage with you, sir?"

Recalled to material things, Etienne Rambert contemplated his trunk which the porters had taken out of the luggage van.

"Good Lord!" he began, but Thérèse interrupted him.

"Grandmamma said she would send for your heavy luggage during the morning, and that you could take your valise and any small parcels with us in the brougham."

"What's that? Your grandmamma has taken the trouble to send her carriage?"

"It's a long way to Beaulieu, you know," Thérèse replied. "Ask Charles if it isn't. We came on foot and the walk would be too tiring for you after a whole night in the train."

The three had reached the station yard, and Thérèse stopped in surprise.

"Why, how's that?" she exclaimed; "the carriage is not here. And yet Jean was beginning to get it ready when we left the château."

M. Etienne Rambert was resting one hand on his son's shoulder, and contemplating him with an affectionate, all-embracing survey every now and then. He smiled at Thérèse.

"He may have been delayed, dear. I tell you what we will do. Since your grandmamma is going to send for my luggage there is no need for me to take my valise; we can leave everything in the cloak-room and start for the château on foot; if my memory serves me right — and it is a very good memory — there is only one road, so we shall meet Jean and can get into the carriage on the way."

A few minutes later all three set out on the road to Beaulieu. M. Rambert walked between the two young people; he had gallantly offered his arm to Thérèse, who was not a little proud of the attention, which proved to her mind that she was now regarded as a grown-up young lady. On the other side of his father Charles made answer to the incessant questions put to him.

M. Etienne Rambert enjoyed the walk in the quiet morning through the peaceful countryside. With a tender half-melancholy he recognised every turn in the road, every bit of scenery.

"Just fancy my coming back here at sixty years of age, with a great son of eighteen!" he said with a laugh. "And I remember as if it were yesterday the good times I have had at the château of Beaulieu. Mme. de Langrune and I will have plenty of memories to talk over. Gad! it must be quite forty years since I came this way, and yet I remember every bit of it. Say, Thérèse, isn't it the fact that we shall see the front of the château directly we have passed this little copse?"

"Quite true," the girl answered with a laugh. "You know the country very well, sir."

"Yes," said Etienne Rambert; "when one gets to my age, little Thérèse, one always does remember the happy days of one's youth; one remembers recent events much less distinctly. Most likely that means, my dear, that the human heart declines to grow old and refuses to preserve any but pictures of childhood."

For a few minutes M. Rambert remained silent, as if absorbed in somewhat melancholy reflections. But he soon recovered himself and shook off the tender sadness evoked in his mind by memories of the past.

"Why, the park enclosure has been altered," he exclaimed. "Here is a wall which used not to be here: there was only a hedge."

Thérèse laughed.

"I never knew the hedge," she said. "I have always seen the wall."

"Must we go on to the main gate?" M. Rambert asked, "or has your grandmamma had another gate made?"

"We are going in by the out-buildings," the girl answered; "then we shall hear why Jean did not come to meet us." She opened a little door half-hidden among the moss and ivy that clothed the wall surrounding the park, and making M. Rambert and Charles pass in before her, cried: "But Jean *has* gone with the brougham, for the horses are not in the stable. How was it we did not meet him?" Then she laughed. "Poor Jean! He is so muddle-headed! I would not mind betting he went to meet us at Saint-Jaury, as he does every morning to bring me home from church."

The little company, Etienne Rambert, Thérèse and Charles, were now approaching the château. Passing beneath Mme. de Langrune's windows Thérèse called merrily up to them.

"Here we are, grandmamma!"

There was no reply.

But at the window of an adjoining room appeared the figure of the steward, Dollon, making a gesture, as if asking for silence.

Thérèse, in advance of her guests, had proceeded but a few yards when Mme. de Langrune's old servant rushed down the stone flight of steps in front of the château, towards M. Rambert.

Dollon seemed distraught. Usually so respectful and so deferential in manner, he now seized M. Rambert by the arm, and imperiously waving Thérèse and Charles away, drew him aside.

"It is awful, sir," he exclaimed: "horrible: a fearful thing has happened. We have just found Mme. la Marquise dead — murdered — in her room!"

III

The Hunt for the Man

M. de Presles, the examining magistrate in charge of the Court at Brives, had just arrived at the château of Beaulieu, having been notified of the tragedy by the police sergeant stationed at Saint-Jaury. The magistrate was a young, fashionable, and rather aristocratic man of the world, whose grievance it was to be tied down to work that was mechanical rather than intellectual. He was essentially modern in his ideas, and his chief ambition was to get away as quickly as possible from the small provincial town to which he had been exiled by the changes and chances of promotion; he was sick of Brives, and now it occurred to him that a crime like this present one would give him an opportunity of displaying his gifts of intuition and deduction, prove his quality, and so might enable him to get another appointment. After Dollon had received him at the château, the magistrate had first of all made enquiry as to who was in the house at the time. From the information given him he was satisfied that it was unnecessary to subject either Thérèse or Charles Rambert to immediate examination, both of the young people being much too upset to be able to reply to serious questions, and both having been taken away to the house of the Baronne de Vibray. It was, also, clear that M. Rambert senior, who had only arrived after the crime, could not furnish any interesting information.

"Tell me exactly how you discovered the crime, M. Dollon," he said as, pale and trembling, the steward accompanied him along the corridor to the scene of the murder.

"I went this morning as usual, sir," the steward replied, "to say good morning to Mme. de Langrune and receive her orders for the day. I knocked at her door as I always did, but got no answer. I knocked louder, but still there was no answer. I don't know why I opened the door instead of going away; perhaps I had some kind of presentiment. Oh, I shall never forget the shock I had when I saw my poor dear mistress lying dead at the foot of her bed, steeped in blood, and with such a horrible gash in her throat that for a moment I thought her head was severed from the trunk."

The police sergeant corroborated the steward's story.

"The murder certainly was committed with peculiarly horrible violence, sir," he remarked. "The body shows that the victim was struck with the utmost fury. The murderer must have gone mad over the corpse from sheer lust of blood. The wounds are shocking."

"Knife wounds?" M. de Presles asked.

"I don't know," said the sergeant uncertainly. "Your worship can form your own opinion."

The magistrate followed the steward into the room where Dollon had taken care that nothing was touched.

In its furniture and general arrangement Mme. de Langrune's room corresponded with the character of the old lady. It was large, and quietly furnished with old presses, arm-chairs, chairs and old-fashioned tables. It was evident that she had had no liking for modern fashions, but had preferred to have her own room stamped with the rather severe, yet very comfortable character of former days.

The whole of one side of the room was filled by the Marquise's bed. It was large, and raised upon a kind of dais covered with a carpet of subdued tones. At the foot of the bed, on the right, was a large window, fastened half open despite the keen cold, no doubt for hygienic reasons. In the middle of the room was a round mahogany table with a few small articles upon it, a blotting-pad, books and so on. In one corner a large crucifix was suspended from the wall with a prie-Dieu in front of it, the velvet of which had been worn white by the old lady's knees. Finally, a little further away, was a small escritoire, half open now, with its drawers gaping and papers scattered on the floor.

There were only two ways of ingress into the room: one by the door through which the magistrate had entered, which opened on to the main corridor on the first floor, and the other by a door communicating with the Marquise's dressing-room; this dressing-room was lighted by a large window, which was shut.

The magistrate was shocked by the spectacle presented by the corpse of the Marquise. It was lying on its back on the floor, with the arms extended; the head was towards the bed, the feet towards the window. The body was almost naked. A gash ran almost right across the throat, leaving the bones exposed. Torrents of blood had saturated the victim's clothes, and on the carpet round the body a wide stain was still slowly spreading wider.

M. de Presles stooped over the dead woman.

"What an appalling wound!" he muttered. "The medical evidence will explain what weapon it was made with; but no doctor is required to point out the violence of the blow or the fury of the murderer." He turned to the old steward who, at sight of his mistress, could hardly restrain his tears. "Nothing has been moved in the room, eh?"

"Nothing, sir."

The magistrate pointed to the escritoire with its open drawers.

"That has not been touched?"

"No, sir."

"I suppose that is where Mme. de Langrune kept her valuables?"

The steward shook his head.

"The Marquise could not have had any large sum of money in the house: a few hundred francs perhaps for daily expenses, but certainly no more."

"So you do not think robbery was the motive of the crime?"

The steward shrugged his shoulders.

"The murderer may have thought that Mme. de Langrune had money here, sir. But anyhow he must have been disturbed, because he did not take away the rings the Marquise had laid upon the dressing-table before she got into bed."

The magistrate walked slowly round the room.

"This window was open?" he asked.

"The Marquise always left it like that; she liked all the fresh air she could get."

"Might not the murderer have got in that way?"

The steward shook his head.

"It is most unlikely, sir. See: the windows are fitted outside with a kind of grating pointing outwards and downwards, and I think that would prevent anyone from climbing in."

M. de Presles saw that this was so. Continuing his investigation, he satisfied himself that there was nothing about the furniture in that room, or in the dressing-room, to show that the murderer had been through them, except the disorder on and about the little escritoire. At last he came to the door which opened on to the corridor.

"Ah!" he exclaimed: "this is interesting!" and with a finger he pointed to the inner bolt on the door, the screws of which were wrenched half out, showing that an attempt had been made to force the door. "Did Mme. de Langrune bolt her door every night?" he asked.

"Yes, always," Dollon answered. "She was very nervous, and if I was the first to come to bid her good morning I always heard her unfasten that bolt when I knocked."

M. de Presles made no reply. He made one more tour of the room, minutely considering the situation of each single article.

"M. Dollon, will you kindly take me where I can have the use of a table and inkstand, and anything else I may need to get on with my preliminary enquiry?"

"Your clerk is waiting for you in the library, sir," the steward replied. "He has everything ready for you there."

"Very well. If it is convenient to you we will join him now."

M. de Presles followed Dollon down to the library on the ground floor, where his enterprising clerk had already established himself. The magistrate took his seat behind a large table and called to the police sergeant.

"I shall ask you to be present during my enquiry, sergeant. The first investigations will devolve upon you, so it will be well for you to hear all the details the witnesses can furnish me with. I suppose you have taken no steps as yet?"

"Beg pardon, sir: I have sent my men out in all directions, with orders to interrogate all tramps and to detain any who do not give a satisfactory account of their time last night."

"Good! By the way, while I think of it, have you sent off the telegram I gave you when I arrived — the telegram to the police head-quarters in Paris, asking for a detective to be sent down?"

"I took it to the telegraph office myself, sir."

His mind made easy on this score, the young magistrate turned to Dollon.

"Will you please take a seat, sir?" he said and, disregarding the disapproving looks of his clerk, who had a particular predilection for all the long circumlocutions and red tape of the law, he pretermitted the usual questions as to name and age and occupation of the witnesses, and began his enquiry by questioning the old steward. "What is the exact plan of the château?" was his first enquiry.

"You know it now, sir, almost as well as I do. The passage from the front door leads to the main staircase, which we went up just now, to the first floor where the bedroom of the Marquise is situated. The first floor contains a series of rooms separated by a corridor. On the right is Mlle. Thérèse's room, and then come guest-chambers which are not occupied now. On the left is the bedroom of the Marquise, followed by her dressing-room on the same side, and after that there is another dressing-room and then the bedroom occupied by M. Charles Rambert."

"Good. And the floor above: how is that arranged?"

"The second floor is exactly like the first floor, sir, except that there are only servants' rooms there. They are smaller, and there are more of them."

"What servants sleep in the house?"

"As a general rule, sir, the two maid-servants, Marie the housemaid and Louise the cook, and also Hervé the butler; but Hervé did not sleep in the château last night. He had asked the mistress's permission to go into the village, and she had given it to him on condition that he did not come back that night."

"What do you mean?" enquired the magistrate, rather surprised.

"The Marquise was rather nervous, sir, and did not like the idea of anyone being able to get into the house at night; so she was always careful to double-lock the front door and the kitchen door herself every night. She went round all the rooms too every night, and made sure that all the iron shutters were properly fastened, and that it was impossible for anyone to get into the house. When Hervé goes out in the evenings he either sleeps in the village and does not return till the following morning, which is what he did to-day, or else he asks the coachman to leave the yard door unlocked, and sleeps in a room above the stables which as a rule is not occupied."

"That is where the other servants sleep, I suppose?"

"Yes, sir. The gardeners, the coachman, and the keepers all live in the out-buildings. With regard to myself, I have a small cottage a little farther away in the park."

M. de Presles sat silent for a few moments, thinking deeply. The only sound in the room was the irritating squeak of the clerk's quill pen, as he industriously wrote down all the steward's replies. At last M. de Presles looked up.

"So, on the night of the crime the only persons sleeping in the château were Mme. de Langrune, her granddaughter Mlle. Thérèse, M. Charles Rambert and the two maids. Is that so?"

"Yes, sir."

"Then it does not seem likely that the crime was committed by anyone living in the château?"

"That is so, sir: — and yet I do not believe that anybody got into the château; only two people had a key of the front door — the Marquise and myself. When I got to the house this morning I found the door open, because Mlle. Thérèse went out early with M. Charles Rambert to meet M. Rambert, senior, at the station, and she opened the door with the keys that the Marquise had given into her care the night before; but she told me herself that when she started to meet the train at five o'clock the door was shut. Mlle. Thérèse had put her keys under her pillow, and my bunch had never left my possession."

"Is it not possible," the magistrate suggested, "that someone may have got in during the day, hidden himself, and have committed the crime when night came? Remember, M. Dollon, the bolt inside Mme. de Langrune's bedroom door has been wrenched away: that means that the murderer made his entrance by that door, and made it by force."

But the steward shook his head.

"No, sir, nobody could have secreted himself in the château during the day; people are always coming to the kitchen, so the back door is under constant supervision; and all yesterday afternoon there were gardeners at work on the lawn in front of the main entrance; if any stranger had presented himself there he would certainly have been seen; and finally, Mme. de Langrune had given orders, which I always attended to myself, to keep the door locked through which one gets down to the cellars. So the murderer could not have hidden in the basement, and where else could he have hidden? Not in the rooms on the ground floor: there was company to dinner last night, and all the rooms were used more or less; the Marquise, or some one of the guests, would certainly have discovered him. So he would have had to be upstairs, either on the first or second floor: that is most unlikely: it would have been very risky; besides, the big house-dog is fastened up at the foot of the staircase during the day, and he would not have let any stranger pass him: either the dog must have known the man, or at all events some meat must have been thrown to him; but there are no traces to show that anything of the sort was done."

The magistrate was much perplexed.

"Then the crime is inexplicable, M. Dollon. You have just told me yourself that there was no one in the château but Mme. de Langrune, the two young people Thérèse and Charles, and the two maids: it certainly is not any one of those who can be the guilty person, for the way in which the crime was committed, and the force of the blows dealt, show that the criminal was a man — a professional murderer in fact. Consequently the guilty person must have got in from outside. Come now, have you no suspicions at all?"

The steward raised his arms and let them fall in utter dejection.

"No," he replied at last, "I do not suspect anybody! I cannot suspect anybody! But, sir, as far as I am concerned, I feel certain that although the murderer was not one of those who occupied the château last night he nevertheless did not come in from outside. It was not possible! The doors were locked and the shutters were fastened."

"Nevertheless," M. de Presles remarked, "inasmuch as someone has committed a murder, it must necessarily be the fact, either that that someone was hidden inside the château when Mme. de Langrune herself locked the front door, or else that he got in during the night. Do you not see yourself, M. Dollon, that one or other of these two hypotheses must be correct?"

The steward hesitated.

"It is a mystery, sir," he declared at last. "I swear to you, sir, that nobody could have got in, and yet it is perfectly clear also that neither M. Charles nor Mlle. Thérèse, nor yet either of the two maids, Marie and Louise, is the murderer."

M. de Presles sat wrapped in thought for a few minutes and then desired the old steward to fetch the two women servants.

"Come back, yourself," he added, as the old man went away; "I may require further particulars from you."

Dollon left the room, and Gigou, the clerk, leant forward towards the magistrate: tact was not the most shining of M. Gigou's qualities.

"When your enquiry is finished, sir — presently — we shall have to pay a visit to the Mayor of Saint-Jaury. That is in accordance with the usual procedure. And then he cannot do less than invite us to stay to dinner!"

IV

"No! I am not Mad!"

The next day but one after the crime, on the Friday, Louise the cook, who was still terribly upset by the dreadful death of the good mistress in whose service she had been for fifteen years, came down to her kitchen early. It was scarcely daybreak, and the good woman was obliged to light a lamp to see by. With her mind anywhere but on her work, she was mechanically getting breakfast for the servants and for the visitors to the château, when a sharp knock on the back door made her jump. She went to open it, and uttered a little scream as she saw the cocked hats of gendarmes silhouetted against the wan light of the early morning.

Between the gendarmes were two miserable-looking specimens of humanity. Louise had only opened the door a few inches when the sergeant, who had known her for many years, took a step forward and gave her a military salute.

"I must ask your hospitality for us and for these two fellows whom we have taken up to-night, prowling about the neighbourhood," he said.

The dismayed Louise broke in.

"Good heavens, sergeant, are you bringing thieves here? Where do you expect me to put them? Surely there's enough trouble in the house as it is!"

The gendarme, Morand, smiled with the disillusioned air of a man who knows very well what trouble is, and the sergeant replied:

"Put them? Why, in your kitchen, of course," and as the servant made a sign of refusal, he added: "I am sorry, but you must; besides, there's nothing for you to be afraid of; the men are handcuffed, and we shall not leave them. We are going to wait here for the magistrate who will examine them."

The gendarmes had pushed their wretched captives in before them, two tramps of the shadiest appearance.

Louise, who had gone mechanically to raise the lid of a kettle beginning to boil over, looked round at his last words.

"The magistrate?" she said: "M. de Presles? Why, he is here now — in the library."

"No?" exclaimed the sergeant, jumping up from the kitchen chair on which he had seated himself.

"He is, I tell you," the old woman insisted; "and the little man who generally goes about with him is here too."

"You mean M. Gigou, his clerk?"

"Very likely," muttered Louise.

"I leave the prisoners with you, Morand," said the sergeant curtly; "don't let them out of your sight. I am going to the magistrate. I have no doubt he will wish to interrogate these fellows at once."

The gendarme came to attention and saluted.

"Trust me, sergeant!"

It looked as if Morand's job was going to be an easy one; the two tramps, huddled up in a corner of the kitchen opposite the stove, showed no disposition to make their escape. The two were utterly different in appearance. One was a tall, strongly built man, with thick hair crowned by a little jockey cap, and was enveloped in a kind of overcoat which might have been black once but which was now of a greenish hue, the result of the inclemency of the weather; he gnawed his heavy moustache in silence and turned sombre, uneasy looks on all, including his companion in misfortune. He wore hobnailed shoes and carried a stout cudgel. He was more like a piece of the human wreckage one sees in the street corners of great cities than a genuine tramp. Instead of a collar, there was a variegated handkerchief round his neck. His name, he had told the sergeant, was François Paul.

The other man, who had been discovered at the back of a farm just as he was about to crawl inside a stack, was a typical country tramp. An old soft felt hat was crammed down on his head, and a shock of rebellious red and grey hair curled up all round it, while a hairy beard entirely concealed all the features of his face. All that could be seen of it was a pair of sparkling eyes incessantly moving in every possible direction. This second man contemplated with interest the place into which the police had conducted him. On his back he bore a heavy sort of wallet in which he stowed articles of the most varied description. Whereas his companion maintained a rigid silence, this man never stopped talking. Nudging his neighbour every now and then he whispered:

"Say, where do you come from? You're not from these parts, are you? I've never seen you before have I? Everybody round here knows me: Bouzille — my name's Bouzille," and turning to the gendarme he said: "Isn't it true, M'sieu Morand, that you and I are old acquaintances? This is the fourth or fifth time you've pinched me, isn't it?"

Bouzille's companion vouchsafed him a glance.

"So it's a habit of yours, is it?" he said in the same low tone; "you often get nabbed?"

"As to 'often,'" the garrulous fellow replied, "that depends on what you mean by the word. In winter time it's not bad business to go back to clink, because of the rotten weather; in the summer one would rather go easy, and then, too, in the summer there isn't so much crime; you can find all you want on the road; country people aren't so particular in the summer, while in the winter it's quite another thing; so they have done me down to-night for mother Chiquard's rabbit, I expect."

The gendarme, who had been listening with no great attention, chimed in.

"So it was you who stole the rabbit, was it, Bouzille?"

"What's the good of your asking me that, M'sieu Morand?" protested Bouzille. "I suppose you would have left me alone if you hadn't been sure of it?"

Bouzille's companion bent his head and whispered very low:

"There has been something worse than that: the job with the lady of this house."

"Oh, that!" said Bouzille with a gesture of complete indifference. But he did not proceed. The sergeant came back to the kitchen and said sternly:

"François Paul, forward: the examining magistrate will hear you now."

The man summoned stepped towards the sergeant, and quietly submitted to being taken by the arm, for his hands were fastened. Bouzille winked knowingly at the gendarme, now his sole remaining confidant, and remarked with satisfaction:

"Good luck! We are getting on to-day! Not too much 'remanded' about it," and as the gendarme, severely keeping his proper distance, made no reply, the incorrigible chatterbox went on merrily: "As a matter of fact it suits me just as well to be committed for trial, since the government give you your board and lodging, and especially since there's a really beautiful prison at Brives now." He leaned familiarly against the gendarme's shoulder. "Ah, M'sieu Morand, you didn't know it — you weren't old enough — why, it was before you joined the force — but the lock-up used to be in an old building just behind the Law Courts: dirty! I should think it was dirty! And damp! Why once, when I did three months there, from January to April, I came out so ill with the rheumatics that I had to go back into the infirmary for another fortnight! Gad!" he went on after a moment's pause during which he snuffed the air around him, "something smells jolly good here!" He unceremoniously addressed the cook who was busy at her work: "Mightn't there perhaps be a bit of a blow out for me, Mme. Louise?" and as she turned round with a somewhat scandalised expression he continued: "you needn't be frightened, lady, you know me very well. Many a time I've come and asked you for any old thing, and you've always given me something. M'sieu Dollon, too: whenever he has an old pair of shoes that are worn out, well, those are mine; and a crust of bread is what nobody ever refuses."

The cook hesitated, touched by the recollections evoked by the poor tramp; she looked at the gendarme for a sign of encouragement. Morand shrugged his shoulders and turned a patronising gaze on Bouzille.

"Give him something, if you like, Mme. Louise. After all, he is well known. And for my own part I don't believe he could have done it."

The tramp interrupted him.

"Ah, M'sieu Morand, if it's a matter of picking up trifles here and there, a wandering rabbit, perhaps, or a fowl that's tired of being lonely, I don't say no; but as for anything else — thank'ee kindly, lady."

Louise had handed Bouzille a huge chunk of bread which he immediately interned in the depths of his enormous bag.

"What do you suppose that other chap can have to tell Mr. Paul Pry? He did not look like a regular! Now when I get before the gentlemen in black, I don't want to contradict them, and so I always say, 'Yes, my lord,' and they are perfectly satisfied; sometimes they laugh and the president of the court says, 'Stand up, Bouzille,' and then he gives me a fortnight, or twenty-one days, or a month, as the case may be."

The sergeant came back, alone, and addressed the gendarme.

"The other man has been discharged," he said. "As for Bouzille, M. de Presles does not think there is any need to interrogate him."

"Am I to be punted out then?" enquired the tramp with some dismay, as he looked uneasily towards the window, against the glass of which rain was lashing.

The sergeant could not restrain a smile.

"Well, no, Bouzille," he said kindly, "we must take you to the lock-up; there's the little matter of the rabbit to be cleared up, you know. Come now, quick march! Take him to Saint-Jaury, Morand!"

The sergeant went back to the library to hold himself at the magistrate's disposal; through the torrential downpour of rain Bouzille and the gendarme wended their way to the village; and left alone in her kitchen, Louise put out her lamp, for despite the shocking weather it was getting lighter now, and communed with herself.

"I've a kind of idea that they would have done better to keep that other man. He was a villainous-looking fellow!"

The sad, depressing day had passed without any notable incident.

Charles Rambert and his father had spent the afternoon with Thérèse and the Baronne de Vibray continuously addressing large black-edged envelopes to the relations and friends of the Marquise de Langrune, whose funeral had been fixed for the next day but one.

A hasty dinner had been served at which the Baronne de Vibray was present. Her grief was distressing to witness. Somewhat futile to outward seeming, this woman had a very kind and tender heart; as a matter of course she had constituted herself the protector and comforter of Thérèse, and she had spent the whole of the previous day with the child at Brives, ransacking the local shops to procure her mourning.

Thérèse was terribly shocked by the dreadful death of her grandmother whom she adored, but she displayed unexpected strength of character and controlled her grief so that she might be able to look after the guests whom she was now entertaining for the first time as mistress of the house. The Baronne de Vibray had failed in her attempt to persuade Thérèse to come with her to Querelles to sleep. Thérèse was determined in her refusal to leave the château and what she termed her "post of duty."

"Marie will stay with me," she assured the kind Baronne, "and I promise you I shall have sufficient courage to go to sleep to-night."

So her friend got into her car alone at nine o'clock and went back to her own house, and Thérèse went up at once to bed with Marie, the faithful servant who, like Louise the cook, had been with her ever since she was born.

After having read all the newspapers, with their minute and often inaccurate account of the tragedy at Beaulieu — for everyone in the château had been besieged the previous day by reporters and representatives of various press agencies — M. Etienne Rambert said to his son simply, but with a marked gravity:

"Let us go upstairs, my son: it is time."

At the door of his room Charles deferentially offered his cheek to his father, but M. Etienne Rambert seemed to hesitate; then, as if taking a sudden resolution, he entered his son's room instead of going on to his own. Charles kept silence and refrained from asking any questions, for he had noticed how lost in sad thought his father had seemed to be since the day before.

Charles Rambert was very tired. He began to undress at once. He had taken off his coat and waistcoat, and was turning towards a looking-glass to undo his tie, when his father came up to him; with an abrupt movement M. Etienne Rambert put both his hands on his son's shoulders and looked him straight in the eyes. Then in a stifled but peremptory tone he said:

"Now confess, unhappy boy! Confess to your father!"

Charles went ghastly white.

"What?" he muttered.

Etienne Rambert kept his eyes fixed upon him.

"It was you who committed the murder!"

The ringing denial that the young man tried to utter was strangled in his throat; he threw out his arms and groped with his hands as if to find something to support him in his faintness; then he pulled himself together.

"Committed the murder? I? You accuse me of having killed the Marquise? It is infamous, hateful, awful!"

"Alas, yes!"

"No, no! Good God, no!"

"Yes!" Etienne Rambert insisted.

The two men faced each other, panting. Charles controlled the emotion which was sweeping over him once more, and looking steadily at his father, said in tones of bitter reproach:

"And it is actually my own father who says that — who suspects me!"

Tears filled the young fellow's eyes and sobs choked him; he grew whiter still, and seemed so near collapse that his father had to support him to a chair, where he remained for several minutes utterly prostrated.

M. Rambert paced up and down the room a few times, then took another chair and sat down in front of his son. Passing a hand across his brow as if to sweep away the horrible nightmare that was haunting him, he spoke again.

"Come now, my boy, my poor boy, let us talk it over quietly. I do not know how it was, but yesterday morning when I saw you at the station I had a presentiment of something: you were haggard, and tired, and your eyes were drawn —— "

"I told you before," Charles answered tonelessly "that I had had a bad night: I was over-excited and did not sleep: I was awake the whole night."

"By Jove, yes!" his father rapped out: "I can believe that! But if you were not asleep, how do you account for your not hearing anything?"

"Thérèse did not hear anything either," said Charles after a moment's reflection.

"Thérèse's room was a long way off," M. Rambert replied, "while there was only a thin wall between yours and that of the Marquise. You must have heard: you did hear! More than that —— , oh, my boy, my unhappy boy!"

Charles was twisting and untwisting his hands, and great drops of cold perspiration beaded his brow.

"You are the only single person who thinks I committed such an awful crime!" he said, half questioningly.

"The only one?" Etienne Rambert muttered. "Perhaps! As yet! But you ought to know that you made a very bad impression indeed upon the friends of the Marquise during the evening before the crime, when President Bonnet was reading the particulars of a murder that had been committed in Paris by — somebody: I forget whom."

"Good heavens!" Charles exclaimed in indignation, "I did not say anything wrong. Do you mean to say that just because I am interested in stories of great criminals like Rocambole and Fantômas —— "

"You created a deplorable impression," his father repeated.

"So they suspect me too, do they?" Charles enquired. "But you can't make accusations like that," he said, warming up: "you've got to have facts, and proofs." He looked at his father for the sympathy and encouragement of affection. "Listen, papa, I know you will believe me when I swear that I am innocent; but do you think other people — —"

M. Etienne Rambert sat with his head between his hands, wrapped in thought; there was a short silence before the unhappy father replied:

"Unfortunately there is evidence against you," he said at last; "and damning evidence, too!" he added with a glance at his son that seemed to pulverise him. "Terrible evidence! Consider, Charles: the magistrates have decided, as a result of their investigations, that no one got into the château on the fatal night; you were the only man who slept there; and none but a man could possibly have committed such a horrible crime, such a monstrous piece of butchery!"

"Someone might have got in from outside," the unhappy lad urged, as if trying to escape from the network in which he was being entangled.

"No one did," Etienne Rambert insisted; "besides, how could you prove it?"

Charles was silent. He stood in the middle of the room, with trembling legs and haggard eyes, seemingly stupefied and incapable of coherent thought, vacantly watching his father. With bent head and shoulders bowed as though beneath a too-heavy load, Etienne Rambert moved towards the dressing-room attached to the bedroom.

"Come here," he said in an almost inaudible voice; "follow me."

He went into the dressing-room, and picking up the towels that were heaped anyhow on the lower rail of the washstand, he selected a very crumpled one and held it out in front of his son.

"Look at that!" he said in a low, curt tone.

And on the towel, thus held in the light, Charles Rambert saw red stains of blood. The lad started, and was about to burst into some protestation, but Etienne Rambert imperiously checked him.

"Do you still deny it? Unhappy, wretched boy, there is the convincing, irrefutable evidence of your guilt! These stains of blood proclaim it. Something always is overlooked! How are you to explain the presence of this blood-stained linen in your room? Can you still deny that it is proof positive of your guilt?"

"But I do deny it, I do deny it! I don't understand! I know nothing about it!" and once more Charles Rambert collapsed into the arm-chair; the unhappy lad was nothing but a human wreck, with no strength to argue or even utter a word.

His father's eyes rested on him, filled with infinite affection and profoundest pity.

"My poor, poor boy!" the unhappy Etienne Rambert murmured, and added, as if speaking only to himself: "I wonder if you are not entirely responsible — if there are circumstances to plead for you!"

"Do you still accuse me, papa? Do you really believe I am the murderer?"

Etienne Rambert shook his head hopelessly.

"Oh, I wish, I wish," he exclaimed, "that for the honour of our name, and for the sake of those who love us, I could prove you had congenital, hereditary tendencies that made you not responsible! Why could not I have watched over your upbringing? Why has fate decreed that I should only see my son three times at most in eighteen years, and come home to find him — a criminal? Oh, if science could but establish the fact that the child of a tainted mother — —"

"Tainted?" Charles exclaimed; "what do you mean?"

"Tainted with a terrible and mysterious disease," Etienne Rambert went on: "a disease before which we are powerless and unarmed — insanity!"

"What?" cried Charles, growing momentarily more distressed and bewildered; "what is that, papa? Are my wits going? My mother insane?" And then he added hopelessly: "My God! You must be right! Often and often I have been amazed by her strange, puzzling looks and behaviour! But I — I have all my proper senses: I know what I am doing!"

"Was it, perhaps, some appalling hallucination," Etienne Rambert suggested: "some moment of irresponsibility?"

But Charles saw what he meant and cut him short.

"No, no, papa! I am not mad! I am not mad! I am not mad!"

In his intense excitement the young fellow never thought of moderating the tone of his voice, but shouted out what was in his mind, shouted it into the silence of the night, heedless of all but this terrible discussion he was having with the father whom he loved. Nor did Etienne Rambert lower his voice: his son's impassioned protest wrung the retort from him:

"Then, Charles, if you are right, your crime is beyond forgiveness! Murderer! Murderer!"

The two men stopped short as a slight sound in the passage caught their attention. A silence fell upon them that they could not break, and they stood dumbfounded, nervous and overwrought.

The door of the room opened very slowly, and a white form appeared against the darkness of the corridor outside.

Robed in a long night-dress, Thérèse stood there, with hair dishevelled, bloodless lips, and eyes dilated with horror; the child was shaking from head to foot; as if every movement hurt her, she painfully raised her arm and pointed to Charles.

"Thérèse!" Etienne Rambert muttered: "Thérèse, you were outside?"

The child's lips moved: she seemed to be making a more than human effort, and a whisper escaped her lips:

"Yes —— "

But she could say no more: her eyes rolled, her whole frame tottered, and then, without sign or cry, she fell rigid and unconscious to the floor.

V
"Arrest Me!"

Twelve or thirteen miles from Souillac the main line from Brives to Cahors, which flanks the slope, describes a rather sharp curve. The journey is a particularly picturesque one, and travellers who make it during the daytime have much that is interesting and agreeable to see; but while they are admiring the country, which marks the transition from the severe region of the Limousin to the more laughing landscapes on the confines of the Midi, the train suddenly plunges into a tunnel which runs for half a mile and more through the heart of the mountain slope. Leaving the tunnel, the line continues along the slope, then gradually descends towards Souillac. Two or three miles from that little station, which is a junction, the line runs alongside the highroad to Salignac, skirts for a brief distance the Corrèze, one of the largest tributaries on the right bank of the Dordogne, and then plunges into the heart of Lot.

Torrential winter rains had seriously affected the railway embankment, particularly near the mouth of the tunnel; a succession of heavy storms in the early part of December had so greatly weakened the ballast that the chief engineers of the Company had been hastily summoned to the scene of the mischief. The experts decided that very important repairs were required close to the Souillac end of the tunnel. It was necessary to put in a complete system of drainage, with underground pipes through which the water that came down from the mountain could escape between the ballast and the side of the rock and so pass underneath the permanent way. The sleepers, too, had been loosened by the bad weather, and some of them had perished so much that the chairs were no longer fast, a matter which was all the more serious because the line described a very sharp curve at that precise spot.

Gangs of first-class navvies had been hurriedly requisitioned, but in spite of the fact that an exceptional rate of wages was paid, a local strike had broken out and for some days all work was stopped. Gradually, however, moderate counsels prevailed and for over a week now, nearly all the men had taken up their tools again. Nevertheless, for a month past, these various circumstances had resulted in all the trains running between Brives and Cahors, being regularly half an hour late. Further, in view of the dangerous state of the line, all engine drivers coming from Brives had received orders to stop their trains two hundred yards from the end of the tunnel, and all drivers coming from Cahors to stop their trains five hundred yards before the entrance to the tunnel, so that should a train appear while any work was going on which rendered it dangerous to pass, it could wait until the work was completed. The order was also issued with the primary object of preventing the workers on the line from being taken by surprise.

Day was just breaking this grey December morning, when the gang of navvies set to work under a foreman, fixing on the down line the new sleepers which had been brought up the day before. Suddenly a shrill whistle was heard, and in the gaping black mouth of the tunnel the light of two lamps became visible; a train bound for Cahors had stopped in accordance with orders, and was calling for permission to pass.

The foreman ranged his men on either side of the down line and walked to a small cabin erected at the mouth of the tunnel, where he pulled the hand-signal so as to show the green light, thereby authorising the train to proceed on its way.

There was a second short, sharp whistle; heavy puffs escaped from the engine, and belching forth a dense volume of black smoke it slowly emerged from the tunnel, followed by a long train of carriages, the windows of which were frosted all over by the cold temperature outside.

A man approached the cabin allotted to the plate-layer in charge of that section of the line in which the tunnel was included.

"I suppose this is the train due at Verrières at 6.55?" he said carelessly.

"Yes," the plate-layer answered, "but it's late, for the clock down there in the valley struck seven several minutes ago."

The train had gone by: the three red lamps fastened at the end of it were already lost in the morning mist.

The man who spoke to the plate-layer was no other than François Paul, the tramp who had been discharged by the magistrate installed at the château of Beaulieu, at precisely the same time the day before, after a brief examination. In spite of the deep wrinkle furrowed in his brow the man seemed to make an effort to appear friendly and to want to carry on the conversation.

"There aren't many people in this morning train," he remarked, "specially in the first-class carriages."

The plate-layer appeared in no wise unwilling to postpone for a few moments his tiring and chilly underground patrol; he put down his pick before answering.

"Well, that's not surprising, is it? People who are rich enough to travel first-class always come by the express which gets to Brives at 2.50 A.M."

"I see," said François Paul; "that's reasonable: and more practical for travellers to Brives or Cahors. But what about the people who want to get out at Gourdon, or Souillac, or Verrières, or any of the small stations where the express doesn't stop?"

"I don't know," said the plate-layer; "but I suppose they have to get out at Brives or Cahors and drive, or else travel by the day trains, which are fast to Brives and slow afterwards."

François Paul did not press the matter. He lit a pipe and breathed upon his benumbed fingers.

"Hard times, these, and no mistake!"

The plate-layer seemed sorry for him.

"I don't suppose you're an independent gentleman, but why don't you try to get taken on here?" he suggested. "They want hands here."

"Oh, do they?"

"That's the fact; this is the foreman coming along now: would you like me to speak to him for you?"

"No hurry," replied François Paul. "'Course, I'm not saying no, but I should like to see what sort of work it is they're doing here: it might not suit me; I shall still have time to get a couple of words with him," and with his eyes on the ground the tramp slowly walked along the embankment away from the plate-layer.

The foreman met and passed him, and came up to the plate-layer at the mouth of the tunnel.

"Well, Michu, how goes it with you? Still got the old complaint?"

"Middling, boss," the worthy fellow answered: "just keeping up, you know. And how's yourself? And the work? When shall you finish? I don't know if you know it, but these trains stopping regularly in my section give me an extra lot of work."

"How's that?" the foreman enquired in surprise.

"The engine drivers take advantage of the stop to empty their ash-pans, and they leave a great heap of mess there in my tunnel, which I'm obliged to clear away. In the ordinary way they dump it somewhere else: where, I don't know, but not in my tunnel, and that's all I care about."

The foreman laughed.

"You're a good 'un, Michu! If I were you I would ask the Company to give me another man or two."

"And do you suppose the Company would?" Michu retorted. "By the way, that poor devil who is going along there, shivering with cold and hunger, was grumbling to me just now, and I advised him to ask you to take him on. What do you think he said? Why, that he would have a look at the work first, and off he went."

"It's a fact, Michu, that it's mighty difficult to come across people who mean business nowadays. It's quite true that I want more hands. But if that chap doesn't ask me to engage him in another minute, I'll kick him out. The embankment is not public property, and I don't trust these rascals who are for ever coming and going among the workmen to see what mischief they can make. I'll go and cast an eye over the bolts and things, for there are all sorts of vagrants about the neighbourhood just now."

"And criminals, too," said old Michu. "I suppose you have heard of the murder up at the château of Beaulieu?"

"Rather! My men are talking of nothing else. But you are right, Michu, I will get a closer look at all strangers, and at your friend in particular."

The foreman stopped abruptly; he had been examining the foot of the embankment, and was standing quite still, watching. The plate-layer followed his glance, and also stood fixed. After a few moments' silence the two men looked at each other and smiled. In the half-light of the valley they had seen the outline of a gendarme; he was on foot and appeared to be looking for somebody, while making no attempt to remain unseen himself.

"Good!" whispered Michu; "that's sergeant Doucet: I know him by his stripes. They say the murder was not committed by anyone belonging to this part of the country; everybody was fond of the Marquise de Langrune."

"Look! Look!" the foreman broke in, pointing to the gendarme who was slowly climbing up the embankment. "It looks as if the sergeant were making for the gentleman who was looking for work just now and hoped he would not find it. The sergeant's got a word for him, eh, what?"

"That might be," said Michu after a moment's further watching. "That chap has a villainous, ugly face. One can tell from the way he's dressed that he don't belong to our parts."

The two men waited with utmost interest to see what was going to happen.

Sergeant Doucet reached the top of the embankment at last and hurried past the navvies, who stopped their work to stare inquisitively after the representative of authority. Fifty yards beyond them, François Paul, wrapped in thought, was walking slowly down towards the station of Verrières. Hearing the sound of steps behind him, he turned. When he saw the sergeant he frowned. He glanced rapidly about him and saw that while he was alone with the gendarme, so that no one could overhear what they said, however loudly they might speak, they were yet in such a position that every sign and movement they made would be perfectly visible to whoever might watch them. And as the gendarme paused a few paces from him and — remarkable fact — seemed to be on the point of bringing his hand to his cap in salute, the mysterious tramp rapped out:

"I thought I said no one was to disturb me, sergeant?"

The sergeant took a pace forward.

"I beg your pardon, Inspector, but I have important news for you."

For this François Paul, whom the sergeant thus respectfully addressed as Inspector, was no other than an officer of the secret police who had been sent down to Beaulieu the day before from head-quarters in Paris.

He was no ordinary officer. As if M. Havard had had an idea that the Langrune affair would prove to be puzzling and complicated, he had singled out the very best of his detectives, the most expert inspector of them all — Juve. It was Juve who for the last forty-eight hours had been prowling about the château of Beaulieu disguised as a tramp, and had had himself arrested with Bouzille that he might prosecute his own investigations without raising the slightest suspicion as to his real identity.

Juve made a face expressive of his vexation at the over-deferential attitude of the sergeant.

"Do pay attention!" he said low. "We are being watched. If I must go back with you, pretend to arrest me. Slip the handcuffs on me!"

"I beg your pardon, Inspector: I don't like to," the gendarme answered.

For all reply, Juve turned his back on him.

"Look here," he said, "I will take a step or two forward as if I meant to run away; then you must put your hand on my shoulder roughly, and I will stumble; when I do, slip the bracelets on."

From the mouth of the tunnel the plate-layer, the foreman and the navvies all followed with their eyes the unintelligible conversation passing between the gendarme and the tramp a hundred yards away. Suddenly they saw the man try to get off and the sergeant seize him almost simultaneously. A few minutes later the individual, with his hands linked together in front of him, was obediently descending the steep slope of the embankment, by the gendarme's side, and then the two men disappeared behind a clump of trees.

"I understand why that chap was not very keen on getting taken on here," said the foreman. "His conscience was none too easy!"

As they walked briskly in the direction of Beaulieu Juve asked the sergeant:

"What has happened at the château, then?"

"They know who the murderer is, Inspector," the sergeant answered. "Little Mlle. Thérèse — —"

"Fantômas, it is Death!"

Hurrying back towards the château with the sergeant, Juve ran into M. de Presles outside the park gate. The magistrate had just arrived from Brives in a motor-car which he had commandeered for his personal use during the last few days.

"Well," said Juve in his quiet, measured tones, "have you heard the news?" And as the magistrate looked at him in surprise he went on: "I gather from your expression that you have not. Well, sir, if you will kindly fill up a warrant we will arrest M. Charles Rambert."

Juve briefly repeated to the magistrate what the sergeant had reported to him, and the sergeant added a few further details. The three men had now reached the foot of the steps before the house and were about to go up when the door of the château was opened and Dollon appeared. He hurried towards them, with unkempt hair and haggard face, and excitedly exclaimed:

"Didn't you meet the Ramberts? Where are they? Where are they?"

The magistrate, who was bewildered by what Juve had told him, was trying to form a coherent idea of the whole sequence of events, but the detective realised the situation at once, and turned to the sergeant.

"The bird has flown," he said. The sergeant threw up his hands in dismay.

Inside the hall Juve and M. de Presles ordered Dollon to give them an exact account of the discovery made by Thérèse in the course of the previous night.

"Well, gentlemen," said the old fellow, who was greatly upset by the discovery of the murderer of the Marquise de Langrune, "when I got to the château early this morning I found the two old servants, Marie and Louise, entirely occupied attending to the young mistress. Marie slept in an adjoining room to hers last night, and was awakened about five o'clock by the poor child's inarticulate cries. Mlle. Thérèse was bathed in perspiration; her face was all drawn and there were dark rings under her eyes; she was sleeping badly and evidently having a dreadful nightmare. She half woke up several times and muttered some unintelligible words to Marie, who thought that it was the result of over-excitement. But about six o'clock, just as I arrived, Mlle. Thérèse really woke up, and bursting into a fit of sobbing and crying, repeated the names of her grandmother and the Ramberts and the Baronne de Vibray. She kept on saying, 'The murderer! the murderer!' and making all sorts of signs of terror, but we were not able to get from her a clear statement of what it was all about. I felt her pulse and found she was very feverish, and Louise prepared a cooling drink, which she persuaded her to take. In about twenty minutes — it was then nearly half-past six — Mlle. Thérèse quietened down, and managed to tell us what she had heard during the night, and the dreadful interview and conversation between M. Rambert and his son which she had seen and overheard."

"What did you do then?" enquired M. de Presles.

"I was dreadfully upset myself, sir, and I sent Jean, the coachman, to Saint-Jaury to fetch the doctor and also to let Sergeant Doucet know. Sergeant Doucet got here first; I told him all I knew, and then I went upstairs with the doctor to see Mlle. Thérèse."

The magistrate turned to the police-sergeant and questioned him.

"Directly M. Dollon told me his story," the sergeant replied, "I thought it my duty to report to M. Juve, who I knew was not far from the château, on his way to Verrières: M. Juve told me last night that he meant to explore that part in the early morning. I left Morand on duty at the entrance to the château, with orders to prevent either of the Ramberts from leaving."

"And Morand did not see them going away?" the magistrate asked.

Juve had already divined what had happened, and replied for the sergeant.

"Morand did not see them go out for the obvious reason that they had left long before — in the middle of the night, directly after their altercation: in a word, before Mlle. Thérèse woke up." He turned to the sergeant. "What has been done since then?"

"Nothing, Inspector."

"Well, sergeant," said Juve. "I imagine his worship will order you to send out your men at once after the runaways." As a matter of courtesy he glanced at the magistrate as if asking for his approval, but he only did so out of politeness, for he took it for granted.

"Of course!" said the magistrate; "please do so at once." The sergeant turned on his heel and left the hall.

"Where is Mlle. Thérèse?" M. de Presles asked Dollon, who was standing nervously apart.

"She is sleeping quietly just now, sir," said the steward, coming forward. "The doctor is with her, and would rather she were not disturbed, if you have no objection."

"Very well," said the magistrate. "Leave us, please," and Dollon also went away.

Juve and M. de Presles looked at one another. The magistrate was the first to break the silence.

"So it is finished?" he remarked. "So this Charles Rambert is the culprit?"

Juve shook his head.

"Charles Rambert? Well, he ought to be the culprit."

"Why that reservation?" enquired the magistrate.

"I say 'ought to be,' for all the circumstances point to that conclusion, and yet in my bones I don't believe he is."

"Surely the presumptions of his guilt, his pseudo-confession, or at least his silence in face of his father's formal accusation, may make us sure he is," said M. de Presles.

"There are some presumptions in favour of his innocence too," Juve replied, but with a slight hesitation.

The magistrate pressed his point.

"Your investigations formally demonstrated the fact that the crime was committed by some person who was inside the house."

"Possibly," said Juve, "but not certainly. The probabilities do not allow us to assert it as a fact."

"Explain yourself."

"Not so fast, sir," Juve replied, and getting up he added: "There is nothing for us to do here, sir; shall we go up to the room Charles Rambert occupied?"

M. de Presles followed the detective, and the two men went into the room, which was as plainly furnished as that of any young girl. The magistrate installed himself comfortably in an easy chair and lighted a cigar, while Juve walked up and down, scrutinising everything with quick, sharp glances, and began to talk:

"I said 'not so fast' just now, sir, and I will tell you why: in my opinion there are two preliminary points in this affair which it is important to clear up: the nature of the crime, and the motive which can have actuated the criminal. Let us take up these two points, and first of all ask ourselves how the murder of the Marquise de Langrune ought to be 'classified' in the technical sense. The first conclusion which must be impressed upon the mind of any observant person who has visited the scene of the crime and examined the corpse of the victim is, that this murder must be placed in the category of crapulous crimes. The murderer seems to have left the implicit mark of his character upon his victim; the very violence of the blows dealt shows that he is a man of the lower orders, a typical criminal, a professional."

"What do you deduce that from?" M. de Presles enquired.

"Simply from the nature of the wound. You saw it, as I did. Mme. de Langrune's throat was almost entirely severed by the blade of some cutting instrument. The breadth and depth of the wound absolutely prove that it was not made with one stroke; the murderer must have gone amok and dealt several blows — have gone on striking even when death had finished his work, or at least was quite inevitable; that shows clearly that the murderer belongs to a class of individuals who feel no repugnance for their horrid work, but who kill without horror, and even without excitement. Again, the nature of the wound shows that the murderer is a strong man; you no doubt know that weak men with feeble muscles strike 'deep' by choice, that is to say with a pointed weapon and aiming at a vital organ, whereas powerful murderers have a predilection for blows dealt 'superficially,' and for broad, ghastly wounds. Besides, that is only following a natural law; a weak man finesses with death, tries to make sure of it at some precise point, penetrating the heart or severing an artery; a brutal man does not care where he hits, but trusts to his own brute strength to achieve his purpose.

"We have next to determine the sort of weapon with which the murder was committed. We have not got it, at any rate up to the present; I have given orders for the drains to be emptied, and the pond to be dragged and the shrubberies to be searched, but, whether our search is crowned with success or not, I am convinced that the instrument was a knife, one of those common knives with a catch lock that apaches always carry. If the murderer had had a weapon whose point was its principal danger, he would have stabbed, and stabbed to the heart, instead of cutting; but he used the edge, the part of a knife that is most habitually used, and he actually cut. When the first wound was made he did not strike anywhere else, but continued working away at the wound and enlarging it. It is a point of capital importance that this murder was committed with a knife, not with a dagger or stiletto, and therefore this is a crapulous crime."

"And what conclusion do you draw from the fact that the crime is a crapulous one?" the magistrate proceeded to enquire.

"Merely that it cannot have been committed by Charles Rambert," Juve answered very gravely. "He is a young man who has been well brought up, he comes of very good stock, and his age makes it most improbable that he can be a professional criminal."

"Obviously, obviously!" murmured the magistrate, not a little embarrassed by the keen logic of the detective.

"And now let us consider the motive or motives of the crime," Juve continued. "Why did the man commit this murder?"

"Doubtless for purposes of robbery," said the magistrate.

"What did he want to steal?" Juve retorted. "As a matter of fact, Mme. de Langrune's diamond rings and watch and purse were all found on her table, in full view of everybody; in the drawers that had been broken open I found other jewels, over twenty pounds in gold and silver, and three bank-notes in a card-case. What is your view, sir, of a crapulous robber who sees valuables like that within his reach, and who does not take them?"

"It is certainly surprising," the magistrate admitted.

"Very surprising; and goes to show that although the crime in itself is a common, sordid one, the criminal may have had higher, or at any rate different, aspirations from those which would lead an ordinary ruffian to commit murder for the sake of robbery. The age and social position and personality of Mme. de Langrune make it very unlikely that she had enemies, or was the object of vengeance, and therefore if she was got rid of, it was very likely that she might be robbed — but robbed of what? Was there something more important than money or jewels to be got? I frankly admit that although I put the question I am at a loss how to answer it."

"Obviously," murmured the magistrate again, still more puzzled by all these logical deductions.

Juve proceeded with the development of his ideas.

"And now suppose we are face to face with a crime committed without any motive, as a result of some morbid impulse, a by no means uncommon occurrence, monomania or temporary insanity?

"In that case, although, in consequence of the crapulous nature of the crime, I had previously dismissed the very serious presumption of guilt attaching to young Rambert, I should be inclined to reconsider my opinion and think it possible that he might be the culprit. We know very little about the young fellow from the physiological point of view; in fact we don't know him at all; but it seems that his family is not altogether normal, and I understand that his mother's mental condition is precarious. If for a moment we regard Charles Rambert as a hysterical subject, we can associate him with the murder of the Marquise de Langrune without thereby destroying our case that the crime is a crapulous one, for a man of only medium physical strength, when suffering from an attack of mental alienation, has his muscular power increased at least tenfold during his paroxysms. Under such influence as that Charles Rambert might have committed murder with all the fierce brutality of a giant!

"But I shall soon be in possession of absolutely accurate knowledge as to the muscular strength of the murderer," Juve proceeded. "Quite lately M. Bertillon invented a marvellous dynamometer which enables us not only to ascertain what kind of lever has been used to force a lock or a piece of furniture, but also to determine the exact strength of the individual who used the tools. I have taken samples of the wood from the broken drawer, and I shall soon have exact information."

"That will be immensely important," M. de Presles agreed. "Even if it does away with our present certainty of Charles Rambert's guilt, we shall be able to find out whether the murder was committed by any other occupant of the house — still assuming that it was committed by some member of the household."

"With regard to that," said Juve, "we can proceed with our method of deduction and elimi-nate from our field of observation everybody who has a good alibi or other defence; it will be so much ground cleared. For my own part I find it impossible to suspect the two old maid-servants, Louise and Marie; the tramps whom we have detained and subsequently released are too simple-minded, elementary people to have been capable of devising the minute precautions which demonstrate the subtle cleverness of the man who murdered the Marquise. Then there is Dollon; but I imagine you will agree with me in thinking that his alibi removes him from suspicion — more especially as the medical evidence proves that the murder was committed during the night, between two and three o'clock."

"Only M. Etienne Rambert is left," the magistrate put in, "and about nine o'clock that evening he left the d'Orsay station in the slow train which reaches Verrières at 6.55 A.M. He spent the whole night in the train, for he certainly arrived by that one. He could not have a better alibi."

"Not possibly," Juve replied. "So we need only trouble ourselves with Charles Rambert," and warming up to the subject the detective proceeded to pile up a crushing indictment against the young man. "The crime was committed so quietly that not the faintest sound was heard; therefore the murderer was in the house; he went to the Marquise's room and announced his arrival by a cautious tap on the door; the Marquise then opened the door to him, and was not surprised to see him, for she knew him quite well; he went into her room with her and — — "

"Oh, come, come!" M. de Presles broke in; "you are romancing now, M. Juve; you forget that the bedroom door was forced, the best proof of that being the bolt, which was found wrenched away and hanging literally at the end of the screws."

"I was expecting you to say that, sir," said Juve with a smile. "But before I reply I should like to show you something rather quaint." He led the way across the passage and went into the bedroom of the Marquise, where order had now been restored; the dead body had been removed to the library, which was transformed into a *chapelle ardente*, and two nuns were watching over it there. "Have a good look at this bolt," he said to M. de Presles. "Is there anything unusual about it?"

"No," said the magistrate.

"Yes, there is," said Juve; "the slide-bolt is out, as when the bolt is fastened, but the socket into which the slide-bolt slips to fasten the door to the wall is intact. If the bolt really had been forced, the socket would have been wrenched away too." Juve next asked M. de Presles to look closely at the screws that were wrenched halfway out of the door. "Do you see anything on those?"

The magistrate pointed to their heads.

"There are tiny scratches on them," he said, rather hesitatingly, for in his inmost heart he knew the detective's real superiority over himself, "and from those I must infer that the screws have not been wrenched out by the pressure exerted on the bolt, but really unscrewed, and therefore — — "

"And therefore," Juve broke in, "this is a mere blind, from which we may certainly draw the conclusion that the murderer wished to make us believe that the door was forced, whereas in reality it was opened to him by the Marquise. Therefore the murderer was personally known to her!"

"The murderer was personally known to her," he repeated. "Now I should like to remind you of young Charles Rambert's equivocal behaviour in the course of the evening that preceded the crime. It struck President Bonnet and shocked the priest. I also recall his hereditary antecedents, his mothers insanity, and finally — — " Juve broke off abruptly and unceremoniously dragged the magistrate out of the room and into Charles Rambert's bedroom. He hurried into the dressing-room adjoining, went down on his knees on the floor, and laid a finger on the middle of the oil-cloth that was laid over the boards. "What do you see there, sir?" he demanded.

The magistrate adjusted his eyeglass and, looking at the place indicated by the detective, saw a little black stain; he wetted his finger, rubbed it on the spot, and then, holding up his hand, observed that the tip of his finger was stained red.

"It is blood," he muttered.

"Yes, blood," said Juve, "and I gather from this that the story of the blood-stained towel which M. Rambert senior found among his son's things, and the sight of which so greatly impressed Mlle. Thérèse, was not an invention on that young lady's part, but really existed; and it forms the most damning evidence possible against the young man. He obviously washed his hands after the crime in the water from the tap over this wash-hand basin here, but one drop of blood falling on the towel and dripping on to the floor has been enough to give him away."

The magistrate nodded.

"It is conclusive," he said. "You have just proved to demonstration, M. Juve, that Charles Rambert is the guilty party. It is beyond argument. It is conclusive — conclusive!"

There were a couple of seconds of silence, and then Juve suddenly said "No!"

"No!" he repeated; "it is quite true that we can adduce perfectly logical arguments to show that the murder was committed by some member of the household and that, therefore, Charles Rambert is the only possible culprit; but we can adduce equally logical arguments to show that the crime was committed by some person who got in from outside: there is nothing to prove that he did not walk into the house through the front door."

"The door was locked," said the magistrate.

"That's nothing," said Juve with a laugh. "Don't forget that there isn't such a thing as a real safety lock nowadays — since all locks can be opened with an outside key. If I had found one of the good old-fashioned catch locks on the door, such as they used to make years ago, I should have said to you: nobody got in, because the only way to get through a door fastened with one of those locks is to break the door down. But here we have a lock that can be opened with a key. Now the key does not exist of which one cannot get an impression, and there is not such a thing as an impression from which one cannot manufacture a false key. The murderer could easily have got into the house with a duplicate key."

The magistrate raised a further objection.

"If the murderer had got in from outside he would inevitably have left some traces round about the château, but there aren't any."

"Yes there are," Juve retorted. "First of all there is this piece of an ordnance map which I found yesterday between the château and the embankment." He took it from his pocket as he spoke. "It is an odd coincidence that this scrap shows the neighbourhood of the château of Beaulieu."

"That doesn't prove anything," said the magistrate. "To find a piece of a map of our district in our district is the most natural thing possible. Now if you were to discover the rest of this map in anybody's possession, then — — "

"You may rest assured that I shall try to do so with the least possible delay," said Juve gently. "But this is not the only argument I have to support my theory. This morning, when I was walking near the embankment, I found some very suspicious footprints. It is true there are any number of footprints near the end of the Verrières tunnel, where the navvies are at work. But at the other end of the tunnel, where there is no occasion for anyone to pass by, I found that the earth of the embankment, which was crisp with the frost, had been disturbed, showing that someone had clambered up the embankment; the tips of his shoes had been driven into the earth, and I could see distinctly where his feet had been placed; but unfortunately the soil there is so dry that the footprints were too faint for me to hope to be able to identify the maker of them. But the fact remains that someone did climb up the embankment, someone who was making for the railway."

The magistrate did not seem to be impressed by Juve's discovery.

"And pray what conclusion do you think ought to be drawn from that?" he enquired.

Juve sat down in an easy chair, threw back his head and closed his eyes as if he were about to indulge in a long soliloquy, and began to express his thoughts aloud.

"Suppose we were to combine the two hypotheses into one; to wit, that the murderer was in the château prior to the accomplishment of the crime and left the château directly it was accomplished. What should you say, sir, of a criminal completing his deed, then hurrying over the couple of miles that separate Beaulieu from the railway, and catching a passing train, and on his way climbing the embankment at the spot where I found the footprints I mentioned."

"I should say," the magistrate replied, "that you can't jump into a moving train as you can into a passing tram, and further, that at night none but express trains run between Brives and Cahors."

"All right," said Juve: "I will merely point out that owing to the work on the line at present, all trains have stopped at the beginning of the tunnel for the last two months. If the murderer had planned to escape in that way he might very well have been aware of this regular stoppage."

The magistrates confidence was a little shaken by these new deductions on the part of the detective, but he submitted yet another objection.

"We have not found any traces round about the château."

"Strictly speaking, no, we have not," Juve admitted; "but it is clear that if the murderer walked on the grass, and he probably did so, he walked on it during the night, that is to say, before the morning dew. Now everybody knows that when the dew rises in the early morning, grass that has been bent down by any passing man or animal, stands up again in its original position, thereby destroying all traces; so if the murderer did walk on the lawn when he was getting away, nobody could tell that he had done so. Nevertheless, on the lawn in front of the window of the room where the murder was committed I have observed, not exactly footprints, but signs that the earth has been disturbed at that spot. I imagine that if I were to jump out of a first floor window on to the soft surface of a lawn, and wanted to efface the marks of my boots, I should smooth the earth and the grass around them in just the same way that the little piece of lawn I speak of seems to have been smoothed."

"I should like to have a look at that," said M. de Presles.

"Well, there's no difficulty about it," Juve replied. "Come along."

The two men hurried down the staircase and out of the house. When they reached the patch of grass which the inspector said had been "made up," they crouched down and scrutinised it closely. Just by the side of the grass, even overhanging it a little, a large rhubarb plant outspread its thick, dentelated leaves almost parallel with the soil. Juve happened to glance casually at the nearest leaf, and uttered an exclamation of surprise and gratification.

"Gad, here's something interesting!" and he drew the magistrate's attention to some little pilules of earth with which the plant was peppered.

"What is that?" enquired M. de Presles.

"Earth," said Juve, who had swept the top of the leaf with the palm of his hand; "ordinary earth, like the rest ten inches below, on the grass."

"Well, what about it?" said the puzzled magistrate.

"Well," said Juve with a smile, "I imagine that ordinary earth, or any kind of earth, has no power to move of its own volition, much less to jump up ten inches into the air and settle on the top of a leaf, even a rhubarb leaf! So I conclude that since this earth did not get here by itself it was brought here. How? That is very simple! Somebody has jumped on to the grass there, M. de Presles; he has removed the marks of his feet by smoothing the earth with his hands; the earth soiled his hands, and he rubbed one against the other quite mechanically; the earth which was on his hands fell off in little balls on to the rhubarb leaf, and remained there for us to discover. And so it is certain — this is one proof more — that even if the murderer did not get in from outside, he did at any rate take to flight after he had committed the crime."

"So it can't be Charles Rambert after all," said the magistrate.

"It 'ought to be' Charles Rambert!" was Juve's baffling reply.

The magistrate waxed irritable.

"My dear sir, your everlasting contradictions end by being rather absurd! You have hardly finished building up one laborious theory before you start knocking it down again. I fail to understand you."

Juve smiled at M. de Presles' sudden irritability, but quickly became grave again.

"I am anxious not to be led away by any preconceived opinion. I put the hypothesis that so and so is guilty, and examine all the arguments in support of that theory; then I submit that the crime was committed by somebody else, and proceed in the same way. My method certainly has the objection that it confronts every argument with a diametrically opposite one, but we are not concerned with establishing any one case in preference to another — it is the truth, and nothing else, that we have to discover."

"And that is tantamount to saying that in spite of the overwhelming circumstantial evidence, and in spite of the fact that he has run away, Charles Rambert is innocent?"

"Charles Rambert is the culprit, sir," Juve replied brightly. "If he were not, whom else could we possibly suspect?"

The detective's placidity and his perpetual self-contradictions exasperated M. de Presles. He held his tongue, and was silently revolving the case in his mind when Juve made yet one more suggestion.

"There is one final hypothesis which I feel obliged to put before you. Do you realise, sir, that this is a typical Fantômas crime?"

M. de Presles shrugged his shoulders as the detective pronounced this half-mythical name.

"Upon my word, M. Juve, I should never have expected you to invoke Fantômas! Why, Fantômas is the too obvious subterfuge, the cheapest device for investing a case with mock honours. Between you and me, you know perfectly well that Fantômas is merely a legal fiction — a lawyers' joke. Fantômas has no existence in fact!"

Juve stopped in his stride. He paused a moment before replying; then spoke in a restrained voice, but with an emphasis on his words that always marked him when he spoke in all seriousness.

"You are wrong to laugh, sir; very wrong. You are a magistrate and I am only a humble detective inspector, but you have three or four years' experience, perhaps less, while I have fifteen years' work behind me. I know that Fantômas does exist, and I do anything but laugh when I suspect his intervention in a case."

M. de Presles could hardly conceal his surprise, and Juve went on:

"No one has ever said of me, sir, that I was a coward. I have looked death in the eyes; I have often hunted and arrested criminals who would not have had the least hesitation in doing away with me. There are whole gangs of rascals who have vowed my death. All manner of horrible revenges threaten me to-day. For all that I have the most complete indifference! But when people talk to me of Fantômas, when I fancy that I can detect the intervention of that genius of crime in any case, then, M. de Presles, I am in a funk! I tell you frankly I am in a funk. I am frightened, because Fantômas is a being against whom it is idle to use ordinary weapons; because he has been able to hide his identity and elude all pursuit for years; because his daring is boundless and his power unmeasurable; because he is everywhere and nowhere at once and, if he has had a hand in this affair, I am not even sure that he is not listening to me now! And finally, M. de Presles, because every one whom I have known to attack Fantômas, my friends, my colleagues, my superior officers, have one and all, one and all, sir, been beaten in the fight! Fantômas does exist, I know, but who is he? A man can brave a danger he can measure, but he trembles when confronted with a peril he suspects but cannot see."

"But this Fantômas is not a devil," the magistrate broke in testily; "he is a man like you and me!"

"You are right, sir, in saying he is a man; but I repeat, the man is a genius! I don't know whether he works alone or whether he is the head of a gang of criminals; I know nothing of his life; I know nothing of his object. In no single case yet has it been possible to determine the exact part he has taken. He seems to possess the extraordinary gift of being able to slay and leave no trace. You don't see him; you divine his presence: you don't hear him; you have a presentiment of him. If Fantômas is mixed up in this present affair, I don't know if we ever shall succeed in clearing it up!"

M. de Presles was impressed in spite of himself by the detective's earnestness.

"But I suppose you are not recommending me to drop the enquiry, are you, Juve?"

The detective forced a laugh that did not ring quite true.

"Come, come, sir," he answered, "I told you just now that I was frightened, but I never said I was a coward. You may be quite sure I shall do my duty, to the very end. When I first began — and that was not yesterday, nor yet the day before — to realise the importance and the power of this Fantômas, I took an oath, sir, that some day I would discover his identity and effect his arrest! Fantômas is an enemy of society, you say? I prefer to regard him first and foremost as my own personal enemy! I have declared war on him, and I am ready to lose my skin in the war if necessary, but by God I'll have his!"

Juve ceased. M. de Presles also was silent. But the magistrate was still sceptical, despite the detective's strange utterance, and presently he could not refrain from making a gentle protest and appeal.

"Do please bring in a verdict against someone, M. Juve, for really I would rather believe that your Fantômas is — a creation of the imagination!"

Juve shrugged his shoulders, seemed to be arriving at a mighty decision, and began:

"You are quite right, sir, to require me to draw some definite conclusion, even if you are not right in denying the existence of Fantômas. So I make the assertion that the murderer is — — "

The sound of hurrying steps behind them made both men turn round. A postman, hot and perspiring, was hurrying to the château; he had a telegram in his hand.

"Does either of you gentlemen know M. Juve?" he asked.

"My name is Juve," said the detective, and he took the telegram and tore the envelope open. He glanced through it and then handed it to the magistrate.

"Please read that, sir," he said.

The telegram was from the Criminal Investigation Department, and ran as follows:

"Return immediately to Paris. Are convinced that extraordinary crime lies behind disappearance of Lord Beltham. Privately, suspect Fantômas' work."

VII

The Criminal Investigation Department

"Does M. Gurn live here, please?"

Mme. Doulenques, the concierge at No. 147 rue Lévert, looked at the enquirer and saw a tall, dark man with a heavy moustache, wearing a soft hat and a tightly buttoned overcoat, the collar of which was turned up to his ears.

"M. Gurn is away, sir," she answered; "he has been away for some little time."

"I know," said the stranger, "but still I want to go up to his rooms if you will kindly go with me."

"You want —— " the concierge began in surprise and doubt. "Oh, I know; of course you are the man from the what's-its-name company, come for his luggage? Wait a bit; what is the name of that company? Something funny — an English name, I fancy."

The woman left the door, which she had been holding just ajar, and went to the back of her lodge; she looked through the pigeon-holes where she kept the tenants' letters ready sorted, and picked out a soiled printed circular addressed to M. Gurn. She was busy putting on her spectacles when the stranger drew near and from over her shoulder got a glimpse of the name for which she was looking. He drew back again noiselessly, and said quietly:

"I have come from the South Steamship Company."

"Yes, that's it," said the concierge, laboriously spelling out the words: "the South — what you said. I can never pronounce those names. Rue d'Hauteville, isn't it?"

"That's it," replied the man in the soft hat in pleasant, measured tones.

"Well, it's very plain that you don't bustle much in your place," the concierge remarked. "I've been expecting you to come for M. Gurn's things for nearly three weeks; he told me you would come a few days after he had gone. However, that's your business."

Mme. Doulenques cast a mechanical glance through the window that looked on to the street, and then surveyed the stranger from top to toe; he seemed to be much too well dressed to be a mere porter.

"But you haven't got any handcart or truck," she exclaimed. "You're not thinking of carrying the trunks on your shoulder, are you? Why, there are at least three or four of them — and heavy!"

The stranger paused before answering, as though he found it necessary to weigh each word.

"As a matter of fact I merely wanted to get an idea of the size of the luggage," he said quietly. "Will you show me the things?"

"If I must, I must," said the concierge with a heavy sigh. "Come up with me: it's the fifth floor," and as she climbed the stairs she grumbled: "It's a pity you didn't come when I was doing my work: I shouldn't have had to climb a hundred stairs a second time then; it counts up at the end of the day, and I'm not so young as I was."

The stranger followed her up the stairs, murmuring monosyllabic sympathy, and regulating his pace by hers. Arrived at the fifth floor, the concierge drew a key from her pocket and opened the door of the flat.

It was a small modest place, but quite prettily decorated. The door on the landing opened into a tiny sort of anteroom, from which one passed into a front room furnished with little but a round table and a few arm-chairs. Beyond this was a bedroom, almost filled by the large bed, which was the first thing one saw on entering, and on the right there was yet another room, probably a little office. Both the first room, which was a kind of general living room, and the bedroom had wide windows overlooking gardens as far as one could see. An advantage of the flat was that it had nothing opposite, so that the occupant could move about with the windows open if he liked, and yet have nothing to fear from the inquisitiveness of neighbours.

The rooms had been shut up for several days, since the tenant had gone away indeed, and there was a stuffy smell about them, mingled with a strong smell of chemicals.

"I must air the place," the concierge muttered, "or else M. Gurn won't be pleased when he comes back. He always says he is too hot and can't breathe in Paris."

"So he does not live here regularly?" said the stranger, scanning the place curiously as he spoke.

"Oh, no, sir," the concierge answered. "M. Gurn is a kind of commercial traveller and is often away, sometimes for a month or six weeks together," and the gossiping woman was beginning a long and incoherent story when the stranger interrupted her, pointing to a silver-framed photograph of a young woman he had noticed on the mantelpiece.

"Is that Mme. Gurn?"

"M. Gurn is a bachelor," Mme. Doulenques replied. "I can't fancy him married, with his roaming kind of life."

"Just a little friend of his, eh?" said the man in the soft hat, with a wink and a meaning smile.

"Oh, no," said the concierge, shaking her head. "That photograph is not a bit like her."

"So you know her, then?"

"I do and I don't. That's to say, when M. Gurn is in Paris, he often has visits from a lady in the afternoon: a very fashionable lady, I can tell you, not the sort that one often sees in this quarter. Why, the woman who comes is a society lady, I am sure: she always has her veil down and passes by my lodge ever so fast, and never has any conversation with me; free with her money, too: it's very seldom she does not give me something when she comes."

The stranger seemed to find the concierge's communications very interesting, but they did not interrupt his mental inventory of the room.

"In other words, your tenant does not keep too sharp an eye on his money?" he suggested.

"No, indeed: the rent is always paid in advance, and sometimes M. Gurn even pays two terms in advance because he says he never can tell if his business won't be keeping him away when the rent falls due."

Just then a deep voice called up the staircase:

"Concierge: M. Gurn: have you any one of that name in the house?"

"Come up to the fifth floor," the concierge called back to the man. "I am in his rooms now," and she went back into the flat. "Here's somebody else for M. Gurn," she exclaimed.

"Does he have many visitors?" the stranger enquired.

"Hardly any, sir: that's why I'm so surprised."

Two men appeared; their blue blouses and metal-peaked caps proclaimed them to be porters. The concierge turned to the man in the soft hat.

"I suppose these are your men, come to fetch the trunks?"

The stranger made a slight grimace, seemed to hesitate and finally made up his mind to remain silent.

Rather surprised to see that the three men did not seem to be acquainted with each other, the concierge was about to ask what it meant, when one of the porters addressed her curtly:

"We've come from the South Steamship Company for four boxes from M. Gurn's place. Are those the ones?" and taking no notice of the visitor in the room, the man pointed to two large trunks and two small boxes which were placed in a corner of the room.

"But aren't you three all together?" enquired Mme. Doulenques, visibly uneasy.

The stranger still remained silent, but the first porter replied at once.

"No; we have nothing to do with the gentleman. Get on to it, mate! We've no time to waste!"

Anticipating their action, the concierge got instinctively between the porters and the luggage: so too did the man in the soft hat.

"Pardon," said he politely but peremptorily. "Please take nothing away."

One of the porters drew a crumpled and dirty memorandum book from his pocket and turned over the pages, wetting his thumb every time. He looked at it attentively and then spoke.

"There's no mistake: this is where we were told to come," and again he signed to his mate. "Let's get on with it!"

The concierge was puzzled. She looked first at the mysterious stranger, who was as quiet and silent as ever, and then at the porters, who were beginning to be irritated by these incomprehensible complications.

Mme. Doulenques' mistrust waxed greater, and she sincerely regretted being alone on the fifth floor with these strangers, for the other occupants of this floor had gone off to their daily work long ago. Suddenly she escaped from the room, and called shrilly down the stairs:

"Madame Aurore! Madame Aurore!"

The man in the soft hat rushed after her, seized her gently but firmly by the arm, and led her back into the room.

"I beg you, madame, make no noise: do not call out!" he said in a low tone. "Everything will be all right. I only ask you not to create a disturbance."

But the concierge was thoroughly alarmed by the really odd behaviour of all these men, and again screamed at the top of her voice:

"Help! Police!"

The first porter was exasperated.

"It's unfortunate to be taken for thieves," he said with a shrug of his shoulders. "Look here, Auguste, just run down to the corner of the street and bring back a gendarme. The gentleman can explain to the concierge in his presence, and then we shall be at liberty to get on with our job."

Auguste hastened to obey, and several tense moments passed, during which not a single word was exchanged between the three people who were left together.

Then heavy steps were heard, and Auguste reappeared with a gendarme. The latter came swaggering into the room with a would-be majestic air, and solemnly and pompously enquired:

"Now then, what's all this about?"

At sight of the officer every countenance cleared. The concierge ceased to tremble; the porter lost his air of suspicion. Both were beginning to explain to the representative of authority, when the man in the soft hat waved them aside, stepped up to the guardian of the peace and looking him straight in the eyes, said:

"Criminal Investigation Department! Inspector Juve!"

The gendarme, who was quite unprepared for this announcement, stepped back a pace and raised his eyes towards the man who addressed him: then suddenly raised his hand to his *képi* and came to attention.

"Beg pardon, Inspector, I didn't recognise you! M. Juve! And you have been in this division a long time too!" He turned angrily to the foremost porter. "Step forward, please, and let's have no nonsense!"

Juve, who had thus disclosed his identity as a detective, smiled, seeing that the gendarme assumed that the South Steamship Company's porter was a thief.

"That's all right," he said. "Leave the man alone. He's done no harm."

"Then who am I to arrest?" the puzzled gendarme asked.

The concierge broke in to explain: she had been much impressed by the style and title of the stranger.

"If the gentleman had told me where he came from I would certainly never have allowed anyone to go for a gendarme."

Inspector Juve smiled.

"If I had told you who I was just now, madame, when you were, quite naturally, so upset, you would not have believed me. You would have continued to call out. Now, I am particularly anxious to avoid any scandal or noise at the present moment. I rely on your discretion." He turned to the two porters, who were dumb with amazement and could make nothing of the affair. "As for you, my good fellows, I must ask you to leave your other work and go back at once to your office in the rue d'Hauteville and tell your manager — what is his name?"

"M. Wooland," one of the men replied.

"Good: tell M. Wooland that I want to see him here at the earliest possible moment; and tell him to bring with him all the papers he has that refer to M. Gurn. And not a word to anyone about all this, please, especially in this neighbourhood. Take my message to your manager, and that's all."

The porters had left hurriedly for the rue d'Hauteville and a quarter of an hour went by. The detective had requested the concierge to ask the Madame Aurore to whom she had previously appealed so loudly for help, to take her place temporarily in the lodge. Juve kept Mme. Doulenques upstairs with him partly to get information from her, and partly to prevent her from gossiping downstairs.

While he was opening drawers and ransacking furniture, and plunging his hand into presses and cupboards, Juve asked the concierge to describe this tenant of hers, M. Gurn, in whom he appeared to be so deeply interested.

"He is a rather fair man," the concierge told him, "medium height, stout build, and clean shaven like an Englishman; there is nothing particular about him: he is like lots of other people."

This very vague description was hardly satisfactory. The detective told the policeman to unscrew the lock on a locked trunk, and gave him a small screw-driver which he had found in the kitchen. Then he turned again to Mme. Doulenques who was standing stiffly against the wall, severely silent.

"You told me that M. Gurn had a lady friend. When used he to see her?"

"Pretty often, when he was in Paris; and always in the afternoon. Sometimes they were together till six or seven o'clock, and once or twice the lady did not come down before half-past seven."

"Used they to leave the house together?"

"No, sir."

"Did the lady ever stay the night here?"

"Never, sir."

"Yes: evidently a married woman," murmured the detective as if speaking to himself.

Mme. Doulenques made a vague gesture to show her ignorance on the point.

"I can't tell you anything about that, sir."

"Very well," said the detective; "kindly pass me that coat behind you."

The concierge obediently took down a coat from a hook and handed it to Juve who searched it quickly, looked it all over and then found a label sewn on the inside of the collar: it bore the one word *Pretoria*.

"Good!" said he, in an undertone; "I thought as much."

Then he looked at the buttons; these were stamped on the under side with the name *Smith*.

The gendarme understood what the detective was about, and he too examined the clothes in the first trunk which he had just opened.

"There is nothing to show where these things came from, sir," he remarked. "The name of the maker is not on them."

"That's all right," said Juve. "Open the other trunk."

While the gendarme was busy forcing this second lock Juve went for a moment into the kitchen and came back holding a rather heavy copper mallet with an iron handle, which he had found there. He was looking at this mallet with some curiosity, balancing and weighing it in his hands, when a sudden exclamation of fright from the gendarme drew his eyes to the trunk, the lid of which had just been thrown back. Juve did not lose all his professional impassivity, but even he leaped forward like a flash, swept the gendarme to one side, and dropped on his knees beside the open box. A horrid spectacle met his eyes. For the trunk contained a corpse!

The moment Mme. Doulenques caught sight of the ghastly thing, she fell back into a chair half fainting, and there she remained, unable to move, with her body hunched forward, and haggard eyes fixed upon the corpse, of which she caught occasional glimpses as the movements of Juve and the gendarme every now and then left the shocking thing within the trunk exposed to her view.

Yet there was nothing especially gruesome or repellent about the corpse. It was the body of a man of about fifty years of age, with a pronounced brick-red complexion, and a lofty brow, the height of which was increased by premature baldness. Long, fair moustaches drooped from the upper lip almost to the top of the chest. The unfortunate creature was doubled up in the trunk, with knees bent and head forced down by the weight of the lid. The body was dressed with a certain fastidiousness, and it was obviously that of a man of fashion and distinction; there was no wound to be seen. The calm, quiet face suggested that the victim had been taken by surprise while in the full vigour of life and killed suddenly, and had not been subjected to the anguish of a fight for life or to any slow agony.

Juve half turned to the concierge.

"When did you see M. Gurn last? Exactly, please: it is important."

Mme. Doulenques babbled something unintelligible and then, as the detective pressed her, made an effort to collect her scattered wits.

"Three weeks ago at least, sir: yes, three weeks exactly; no one has been here since, I will swear."

Juve made a sign to the gendarme, who understood, and felt the body carefully.

"Quite stiff, and hard, sir," he said; "yet there is no smell from it. Perhaps the cold — — "

Juve shook his head.

"Even severe cold could not preserve a body in that condition for three weeks, and it's not cold now, but there is this:" and he showed his subordinate a small yellowish stain just at the opening of the collar, close to the Adam's apple, which, in spite of the comparative thinness of the body, was very much developed.

Juve took the corpse under the arm-pits and raised it gently, wishing to examine it closely, but anxious, also, not to alter its position. On the nape of the neck was a large stain of blood, like a black wen and as big as a five-shilling piece, just above the last vertebra of the spinal column.

"That's the explanation," the detective murmured, and carefully replacing the body he continued his investigation. With quick, clever hands he searched the coat pockets and found the watch in its proper place. Another pocket was full of money, chiefly small change, with a few louis. But Juve looked in vain for the pocket-book which the man had doubtless been in the habit of carrying about with him: the pocket-book probably containing some means of identification.

The inspector merely grunted, got up, began pacing the room, and questioned the concierge.

"Did M. Gurn have a motor-car?"

"No, sir," she replied, looking surprised. "Why do you ask?"

"Oh, for no particular reason," said the inspector with affected indifference, but at the same time he was contemplating a large nickel pump that lay on a what-not, a syringe holding perhaps half a pint, like those that chauffeurs use. He looked at it steadfastly for several minutes. His next question was addressed to the gendarme who was still on his knees by the trunk.

"We have found one yellow stain on the neck; you will very likely find some more. Have a look at the wrists and the calves of the legs and the stomach. But do it carefully, so as not to disturb the body." While the gendarme began to obey his chief's order, carefully undoing the clothing on the corpse, Juve looked at the concierge again.

"Who did the work of this flat?"

"I did, sir."

Juve pointed to the velvet curtain that screened the door between the little anteroom and the room in which they were.

"How did you come to leave that curtain unhooked at the top, without putting it to rights?"

Mme. Doulenques looked at it.

"It's the first time I've seen it like that," she said apologetically; "the curtain could not have been unhooked when I did the room last without my noticing it. Anyhow, it hasn't been like that long. I ought to say that as M. Gurn was seldom here I didn't do the place out thoroughly very often."

"When did you do it out last?"

"Quite a month ago."

"That is to say M. Gurn went away a week after you last cleaned the place up?"

"Yes, sir."

Juve changed the subject, and pointed to the corpse.

"Tell me, madame, did you know that person?"

The concierge fought down her nervousness and for the first time looked at the unfortunate victim with a steady gaze.

"I have never seen him before," she said, with a little shudder.

"And so, when that gentleman came up here, you did not notice him?" said the inspector gently.

"No, I did not notice him," she declared, and then went on as if answering some question which occurred to her own mind. "And I wonder I didn't, for people very seldom enquired for M. Gurn; of course when the lady was with him M. Gurn was not at home to anybody. This — this dead man must have come straight up himself."

Juve nodded, and was about to continue his questioning when the bell rang.

"Open the door," said Juve to the concierge, and he followed her to the entrance of the flat, partly fearing to find some intruder there, partly hoping to see some unexpected person whose arrival might throw a little light upon the situation.

At the opened door Juve saw a young man of about twenty-five, an obvious Englishman with clear eyes and close-cropped hair. With an accent that further made his British origin unmistakable, the visitor introduced himself:

"I am Mr. Wooland, manager of the Paris branch of the South Steamship Company. It seems that I am wanted at M. Gurn's flat on the fifth floor of this house, by desire of the police."

Juve came forward.

"I am much obliged to you for putting yourself to this inconvenience, sir: allow me to introduce myself: M. Juve, an Inspector from the Criminal Investigation Department. Please come in."

Solemn and impassive, Mr. Wooland entered the room; a side glance suddenly showed him the open trunk and the dead body, but not a muscle of his face moved. Mr. Wooland came of a good stock, and had all that admirable self-possession which is the strength of the powerful Anglo-Saxon race. He looked at the inspector in somewhat haughty silence, waiting for him to begin.

"Will you kindly let me know, sir, the instructions your firm had with regard to the forwarding of the baggage which you sent for to this flat of M. Gurn's this morning?"

"Four days ago, Inspector," said the young man, "on the 14th of December to be precise, the London mail brought us a letter in which Lord Beltham, who had been a client of ours for several years, instructed us to collect, on the 17th of December, that is, to-day, four articles marked H. W. K., 1, 2, 3 and 4, from M. Gurn's apartments, 147 rue Lévert. He informed us that the concierge had orders to allow us to take them away."

"To what address were you to despatch them?"

"Our client instructed us to forward the trunks by the first steamer to Johannesburg, where he would send for them; we were to send two invoices with the goods as usual; the third invoice was to be sent to London, Box 63, Charing Cross Post Office."

Juve made a note of Box 63, Charing Cross in his pocket-book.

"Addressed to what name or initials?"

"Simply Beltham."

"Good. There are no other documents relating to the matter?"

"No, I have nothing else," said Mr. Wooland.

The young fellow relapsed into his usual impassive silence. Juve watched him for a minute or two and then said:

"You must have heard the various rumours current in Paris three weeks ago, sir, about Lord Beltham. He was a very well-known personage in society. Suddenly he disappeared; his wife left nothing undone to give the matter the widest publicity. Were you not rather surprised when you received a letter from Lord Beltham four days ago?"

Mr. Wooland was not disconcerted by the rather embarrassing question.

"Of course I had heard of Lord Beltham's disappearance, but it was not for me to form any official opinion about it. I am a business man, sir, not a detective. Lord Beltham might have disappeared voluntarily or the reverse: I was not asked to say which. When I got his letter I simply decided to carry out the orders it contained. I should do the same again in similar circumstances."

"Are you satisfied that the order was sent by Lord Beltham?"

"I have already told you, sir, that Lord Beltham had been a client of ours for several years; we have had many similar dealings with him. This last order which we received from him appeared to be entirely above suspicion: identical in form and in terms with the previous letters we had had from him." He took a letter out of his pocket-book, and handed it to Juve. "Here is the order, sir; if you think proper you can compare it with similar documents filed in our office in the rue d'Hauteville"; and as Juve was silent, Mr. Wooland, with the utmost dignity, enquired: "Is there any further occasion for me to remain here?"

"Thank you, sir, no," Juve replied. Mr. Wooland made an almost imperceptible bow and was on the point of withdrawing when the detective stayed him once more. "M. Wooland, did you know Lord Beltham?"

"No, sir: Lord Beltham always sent us his orders by letter; once or twice he has spoken to us over the telephone, but he never came to our office, and I have never been to his house."

"Thank you very much," said Juve, and with a bow Mr. Wooland withdrew.

With meticulous care Juve replaced every article which he had moved during his investigations. He carefully shut the lid of the trunk, thus hiding the unhappy corpse from the curious eyes of the gendarme and the still terrified Mme. Doulenques. Then he leisurely buttoned his overcoat and spoke to the gendarme.

"Stay here until I send a man to relieve you; I am going to your superintendent now." At the door he called the concierge. "Will you kindly go down before me, madame? Return to your lodge, and please do not say a word about what has happened to anyone whatever."

"You can trust me, sir," the worthy creature murmured, and Juve walked slowly away from the house with head bowed in thought.

There could be no doubt about it: the body in the trunk was that of Lord Beltham! Juve knew the Englishman quite well. But who was the murderer?

"Everything points to Gurn," Juve thought, "and yet would an ordinary murderer have dared to commit such a crime as this? Am I letting my imagination run away with me again? I don't know: but it seems to me that about this murder, committed in the very middle of Paris, in a crowded house where yet nobody heard or suspected anything, there is an audacity, a certainty of impunity, and above all a multiplicity of precautions, that are typical of the Fantômas manner!" He clenched his fists and an evil smile curled his lips as he repeated, like a threat, the name of that terrible and most mysterious criminal, of whose hellish influence he seemed to be conscious yet once again. "Fantômas! Fantômas! Did Fantômas really commit this murder? And if he did, shall I ever succeed in throwing light upon this new mystery, and learning the secret of that tragic room?"

VIII
A Dreadful Confession

While Juve was devoting his marvellous skill and incomparable daring to the elucidation of the new case with which the Criminal Investigation Department had entrusted him in Paris, things were marching at Beaulieu, where the whole machinery of the law was being set in motion for the discovery and arrest of Charles Rambert.

With a mighty clatter and racket Bouzille came down the slope and stopped before old mother Chiquard's cottage. He arrived in his own equipage, and an extraordinary one it was!

Bouzille was mounted upon a tricycle of prehistoric design, with two large wheels behind and a small steering wheel in front, and a rusty handle-bar from which all the plating was worn off. The solid rubber tyres which once had adorned the machine had worn out long ago, and were now replaced by twine twisted round the felloes of the wheels; this was for ever fraying away and the wheels were fringed with a veritable lace-work of string. Bouzille must have picked up this impossible machine for an old song at some local market, unless perhaps some charitable person gave it to him simply to get rid of it. He styled this tricycle his "engine," and it was by no means the whole of his equipage. Attached to the tricycle by a stout rope was a kind of wicker perambulator on four wheels, which he called his "sleeping-car," because he stored away in it all the bits of rag he picked up on his journeys, and also his very primitive bedding and the little piece of waterproof canvas under which he often slept in the open air. Behind the sleeping-car was a third vehicle, the restaurant-car, consisting of an old soap box mounted on four solid wooden wheels, which were fastened to the axles by huge conical bolts; in this he kept his provisions; lumps of bread and fat, bottles and vegetables, all mixed up in agreeable confusion. Bouzille made quite long journeys in this train of his, and was well known throughout the south-west of France. Often did the astonished population see him bent over his tricycle, with his pack on his back, pedalling with extraordinary rapidity down the hills, while the carriages behind him bumped and jumped over the inequalities in the surface of the road until it seemed impossible that they could retain their equilibrium.

Old mother Chiquard had recognised the cause of the racket. The healthy life of the country had kept the old woman strong and active in spite of the eighty-three years that had passed over her head, and now she came to her door, armed with a broom, and hailed the tramp in angry, threatening tones.

"So it's you, is it, you thief, you robber of the poor! It's shocking, the way you spend your time in evil doing! What do you want now, pray?"

Slowly and sheepishly and with head bowed, Bouzille approached mother Chiquard, nervously looking out for a whack over the head with the broom the old lady held.

"Don't be cross," he pleaded when he could get in a word; "I want to come to an arrangement with you, mother Chiquard, if it can be done."

"That's all according," said the old woman, eyeing the tramp with great mistrust; "I haven't much faith in arrangements with you: rascals like you always manage to do honest folk."

Mother Chiquard turned back into her cottage; it was no weather for her to stop out of doors, for a strong north wind was blowing, and that was bad for her rheumatism. Bouzille deliberately followed her inside and closed the door carefully behind him. Without ceremony he walked up to the hearth, where a scanty wood fire was burning, and put down his pack so as to be able to rub his hands more freely.

"Miserable weather, mother Chiquard!"

The obstinate old lady stuck to her one idea.

"If it isn't miserable to steal my rabbit, this is the finest weather that ever I saw!"

"You make a lot of fuss about a trifle," the tramp protested, "especially since you will be a lot the better by the arrangement I'm going to suggest."

The notion calmed mother Chiquard a little, and she sat down on a form, while Bouzille took a seat upon the table.

"What do you mean?" the old woman enquired.

"Well," said Bouzille, "I suppose your rabbit would have fetched a couple of shillings in the market; I've brought you two fowls that are worth quite eighteen-pence each, and if you will give me some dinner at twelve o'clock I will put in a good morning's work for you."

Mother Chiquard looked at the clock upon the wall; it was eight o'clock. The tramp's proposal represented four hours' work, which was not to be despised; but before striking the bargain she insisted on seeing the fowls. These were extracted from the pack; tied together by the feet, and half suffocated, the unfortunate creatures were not much to look at, but they would be cheap, which was worth considering.

"Where did you get these fowls?" mother Chiquard asked, more as a matter of form than anything else, for she was pretty sure they had not been honestly come by.

Bouzille put his finger to his lip.

"Hush!" he murmured gently; "that's a secret between me and the poultry. Well, is it a go?" and he held out his hand to the old lady.

She hesitated a moment and then made up her mind.

"It's a go," she said, putting her horny fingers into the man's hard palm. "You shall chop me some wood first, and then go down to the river for the rushes I have put in to soak; they must be well swollen by this time."

Bouzille was glad to have made it up with mother Chiquard, and pleased at the prospect of a good dinner at midday; he opened the cottage door, and leisurely arranged a few logs within range of the axe with which he was going to split them; mother Chiquard began to throw down some grain to the skinny and famished fowls that fluttered round her.

"I thought you were in prison, Bouzille," she said, "over stealing my rabbit, and also over that affair at the château of Beaulieu."

"Oh, those are two quite different stories," Bouzille replied. "You mustn't mix them up together on any account. As for the château job, every tramp in the district has been run in: I was copped by M'sieu Morand the morning after the murder; he took me into the kitchen of the château and Mme. Louise gave me something to eat. There was another chap there with me, a man named François Paul who doesn't belong to these parts; between you and me, I thought he was an evil-looking customer who might easily have been the murderer, but it doesn't do to say that sort of thing, and I'm glad I held my tongue because they let him go. I heard no more about it, and five days later I went back to Brives to attend the funeral of the Marquise de Langrune. That was a ceremony if you like! The church all lighted up, and all the nobility from the neighbourhood present. I didn't lose my time, for I knew all the gentlemen and ladies and took the best part of sixteen shillings, and the blind beggar who sits on the steps of the church called me all the names he could put his tongue to!"

The tramp's story interested mother Chiquard mightily, but her former idea still dominated her mind.

"So they didn't punish you for stealing my rabbit?"

"Well, they did and they didn't," said Bouzille, scratching his head. "M'sieu Morand, who is an old friend of mine, took me to the lock-up at Saint-Jaury, and I was to have gone next morning to the court at Brives, where I know the sentence for stealing domestic animals is three weeks. That would have suited me all right just now, for the prison at Brives is quite new and very comfortable, but that same night Sergeant Doucet shoved another man into the clink with, me at Saint-Jaury, a raving lunatic who started smashing everything up, and tried to tear my eyes out. Naturally, I gave him as good as I got, and the infernal row we made brought in the sergeant. I told him the chap wanted to throttle me, and he was nonplussed, for he couldn't do anything with the man, who was fairly mad, and couldn't leave me alone there with him. So at last the sergeant took me to one side and told me to hook it and not let him see me again. So there it is."

While he was chattering like this Bouzille had finished the job set him by mother Chiquard, who meanwhile had peeled some potatoes and poured the soup on the bread. He wiped his brow, and seeing the brimming pot, gave a meaning wink and licked his tongue.

"I'll make the fire up, mother Chiquard; I'm getting jolly hungry."

"So you ought to be, at half-past eleven," the old woman replied. "Yes, we'll have dinner, and you can get the rushes out afterwards."

Mother Chiquard was the proud free-holder of a little cottage that was separated from the bank of the Dordogne by the high road between Martel and Montvalent. Round the cottage she had a small orchard, and opposite, through a gap in the trees, was a view of the yellow waters of the Dordogne and the chain of hills that stood up on the far side of the river. Living here summer and winter, with her rabbits and her fowls, mother Chiquard earned a little money by making baskets; but she was crippled with rheumatism, and was miserable every time she had to go down to the river to pull out the bundles of rushes that she put there to soak; the work meant not merely an hour's paddling in mud up to the knees, but also a fortnight's acute agony and at least a shilling for medicine. So whoever wanted to make a friend of the old woman only had to volunteer to get the rushes out for her.

As he ate, Bouzille told mother Chiquard of his plans for the coming spring.

"Yes," he said, "since I'm not doing any time this winter I'm going to undertake a long journey." He stopped munching for a second and paused for greater effect. "I am going to Paris, mother Chiquard!" Then, seeing that the old lady was utterly dumbfounded by the announcement, he leant his elbows on the table and looked at her over his empty plate. "I've always had one great desire — to see the Eiffel Tower: that idea has been running in my head for the last fifteen years. Well, now I'm going to gratify the wish. I hear you can get a room in Paris for twopence-halfpenny a night, and I can manage that."

"How long will it take you to get there?" enquired the old woman, immensely impressed by Bouzille's venturesome plan.

"That depends," said the tramp. "I must allow quite three months with my train. Of course if I got run in on the way for stealing, or as a rogue and vagabond, I couldn't say how long it would take."

The meal was over, and the old woman was quietly washing up her few plates and dishes, when Bouzille, who had gone down to the river to fetch the rushes, suddenly called shrilly to mother Chiquard.

"Mother Chiquard! Mother Chiquard! Come and look! Just fancy, I've earned twenty-five francs!"

The summons was so urgent, and the news so amazing, that the old lady left her house and hurried across the road to the river bank. She saw the tramp up to his waist in the water, trying, with a long stick, to drag out of the current a large object which was not identifiable at a first glance. To all her enquiries Bouzille answered with the same delighted cry, "I have earned twenty-five francs," too intent on bringing his fishing job to a successful issue even to turn round. A few minutes later he emerged dripping from the water, towing a large bundle to the safety of the bank. Mother Chiquard drew nearer, greatly interested, and then recoiled with a shriek of horror.

Bouzille had fished out a corpse!

It was a ghastly sight: the body of a very young man, almost a boy, with long, slender limbs; the face was so horribly swollen and torn as to be shapeless. One leg was almost entirely torn from the trunk. Through rents in the clothing strips of flesh were trailing, blue and discoloured by their long immersion in the water. On the shoulders and back of the neck were bruises and stains of blood. Bouzille, who was quite unaffected by the ghastliness of the object and still kept up his gay chant "I have fished up a body, I've earned twenty-five francs," observed that there were large splinters of wood, rotten from long immersion, sticking in some of the wounds. He stood up and addressed mother Chiquard who, white as a sheet, was watching him in silence.

"I see what it is: he must have got caught in some mill wheel: that's what has cut him up like that."

Mother Chiquard shook her head uneasily.

"Suppose it was a murder! That would be an ugly business!"

"It's no good my looking at him any more," said Bouzille. "I don't recognise him; he's not from the country."

"That's sure," the old woman agreed. "He's dressed like a gentleman."

The two looked at each other in silence. Bouzille was not nearly so complacent as he had been a few minutes before. The reward of twenty-five francs prompted him to go at once to inform the police; the idea of a crime, suggested by the worthy woman, disturbed him greatly, and all the more because he thought it was well founded. Another murder in the neighbourhood would certainly vex the authorities, and put the police in a bad temper. Bouzille knew from experience that the first thing people do after a tragedy is to arrest all the tramps, and that if the police are at all crotchety they always contrive to get the tramps sentenced for something else. He had had a momentary inclination to establish his winter quarters in prison, but since then he had formed the plan of going to Paris, and liberty appealed to him more. He reached a sudden decision.

"I'll punt him back into the water!"

But mother Chiquard stayed him, just as he was putting his idea into execution.

"You mustn't: suppose somebody has seen us already? It would land us in no end of trouble!"

Half an hour later, convinced that it was his melancholy duty, Bouzille left two-thirds of his train in mother Chiquard's custody, got astride his prehistoric tricycle and slowly pedalled off towards Saint-Jaury.

New Year's Day is a melancholy and a tedious one for everybody whose public or private relations do not make it an exceptionally interesting one. There is the alteration in the date, for one thing, which is provocative of thought, and there is the enforced idleness for another, coming upon energetic folk like a temporary paralysis and leaving them nothing but meditation wherewith to employ themselves.

Juve, comfortably installed in his own private study, was realising this just as evening was falling on this first of January. He was a confirmed bachelor, and for several years had lived in a little flat on the fifth floor of an old house in the rue Bonaparte. He had not gone out to-day, but though he was resting he was not idle. For a whole month past he had been wholly engrossed in his attempt to solve the mystery surrounding the two cases on which he was engaged, the Beltham case, and the Langrune case, and his mind was leisurely revolving round them now as he sat in his warm room before a blazing wood fire, and watched the blue smoke curl up in rings towards the ceiling. The two cases were very dissimilar, and yet his detective instinct persuaded him that although they differed in details their conception and execution emanated not only from one single brain but also from one hand. He was convinced that he was dealing with a mysterious and dangerous individual, and that while he himself was out in the open he was fighting a concealed and invisible adversary; he strove to give form and substance to the adversary, and the name of Fantômas came into his mind. Fantômas! What might Fantômas be doing now, and, if he had a real existence, as the detective most firmly believed, how was he spending New Year's Day?

A sharp ring at the bell startled him from his chair, and not giving his man-servant time to answer it, he went himself to the door and took from a messenger a telegram which he hastily tore open and read:

"Have found in the Dordogne drowned body of young man, face unrecognisable, from description possibly Charles Rambert. Please consider situation and wire course you will take."

The telegram had been handed in at Brives and was signed by M. de Presles.

"Something fresh at last," the detective muttered. "Drowned in the Dordogne, and face unrecognisable! I wonder if it really is Charles Rambert?"

Since M. Etienne Rambert and his son had disappeared so unaccountably, the detective naturally had formulated mentally several hypotheses, but he had arrived at no conclusion which really satisfied his judgment. But though their flight had not surprised him greatly, he had been rather surprised that the police had not been able to find any trace of them, for rightly or wrongly Juve credited them with a good deal of cleverness and power. So it was by no means unreasonable to accept the death of the fugitives as explanation of the failure of the police to find them. However, this was a fresh development of the case, and he was about to draft a reply to M. de Presles when once more the bell rang sharply.

This time Juve did not move, but listened while his man spoke to the visitor. It was an absolute rule of Juve's never to receive visitors at his flat. If anyone wanted to see him on business, he was to be found almost every day in his office at head-quarters about eleven in the morning; to a few people he was willing to give appointments at a quiet and discreet little café in the boulevard Saint-Michel; but he invited no one to his own rooms except one or two of his own relations from the country, and even they had to be provided with a password before they could obtain admission. So now, to all the entreaties of the caller, Juve's servant stolidly replied with the assurance that his master would see no one; yet the visitor's insistence was so great that at last the servant was prevailed upon to bring in his card, albeit with some fear as to the consequences for himself. But to his extreme relief and surprise, Juve, when he had read the name engraved upon the card, said sharply:

"Bring him in here at once!"

And in another couple of seconds M. Etienne Rambert was in the room!

The old gentleman who had fled so mysteriously a few days before, taking with him the son over whom so dread a charge was hanging, bowed deferentially to the detective, with the pitiful mien of one who is crushed beneath the burden of misfortune. His features were drawn, his face bore the stamp of deepest grief, and in his hand he held an evening paper, which in his agitation he had crumpled almost into a ball.

"Tell me, sir, if it is true," he said in low trembling tones. "I have just read that."

Juve pointed to a chair, took the paper mechanically, and smoothing it out, read, below a large head-line, "Is this a sequel to the Beaulieu Crime?" a story similar to that he had just gathered from M. de Presles' telegram.

Juve contemplated M. Etienne Rambert in silence for a few minutes, and then, without replying directly to his visitor's first question, asked him a question in that quiet voice of his, the wonderful indifferent tonelessness of which concealed the least clue to his inmost thoughts.

"Why do you come to me, sir?"

"To find out, sir," the old man answered.

"To find out what?"

"If that poor drowned corpse is — my son's: is my poor Charles!"

"It is rather you who can tell me, sir," said Juve, impassive as ever.

There was a pause. Despite his emotion, M. Rambert seemed to be thinking deeply. Suddenly he appeared to make an important decision, and raising his eyes to the detective he spoke very slowly:

"Have pity, sir, on a broken-hearted father. Listen to me: I have a dreadful confession to make!"

Juve drew his chair close to M. Etienne Rambert.

"I am listening," he said gently, and M. Etienne Rambert began his "dreadful confession."

IX

All for Honour

Society had mustered in force at the Cahors Law Courts, where the Assizes were about to be held. Hooting motor-cars and antiquated coaches drawn by pursy horses were arriving every minute, bringing gentry from the great houses in the neighbourhood, squireens and well-to-do country people, prosperous farmers and jolly wine-growers, all of them determined not to miss "the trial" that was causing such immense excitement because the principal figure in it was well known as a friend of one of the oldest families in those parts; and because he was not merely a witness, nor even the victim, but actually the defendant in the case, although he had been admitted to bail in the interval by order of the court.

Compared with those of large towns, this court room at Cahors was small, but it was filled by a considerable and most select crowd. Quiet greetings and low-toned conversation were freely exchanged, but there was an air of melancholy about every person present, and it was obvious that they were drawn there by no mere curiosity or desire for horrid details, but by legitimate interest in the development of great drama.

One of the leading heroines in the case was pointed out with particular sympathy.

"That's Thérèse Auvernois, over there in the first row! The President of the Court gave her that seat; the officer who took the card of admission over to Querelles told me so."

"That's where Mme. de Vibray lives, isn't it?"

"Yes: she is sitting next to Thérèse now: that pretty woman in grey. Since Mme. de Lan-grune's death she has kept the child with her, thinking, very rightly, that it would be too painful for her to be at Beaulieu. The family council have appointed President Bonnet temporary guardian of Thérèse. He is that tall, thin man over there, talking to the steward, Dollon."

The Baronne de Vibray turned affectionately to Thérèse, who was looking dreadfully pale in her long mourning veil.

"Are you sure this won't tire you too much, dear? Shall we go outside for a little while?"

"Oh, no, please do not worry about me," Thérèse replied. "Indeed I shall be all right."

President Bonnet sat by the two ladies. He had been engaged solemnly exchanging bows with everyone in the court room whom he considered it flattering to himself to know; now he took part in the conversation, and displayed his special knowledge by explaining the constitution of the court and pointing out where the clerk sat, and where the public prosecutor sat, and where the jury sat, all at great length and much to the interest of the people near him: with, however, one exception; a man dressed entirely in black, with his head half buried in the huge collar of a travelling ulster, and dark glasses over his eyes, appeared to be vastly bored by the old magistrate's disquisition. Juve — for it was he — knew too much about legal procedure to require explanations from President Bonnet.

Suddenly a thrill ran through the room and conversation stopped abruptly. M. Etienne Rambert had just walked down the gangway in the court to the seat reserved for him, just in front of the witness box and close to a kind of rostrum in which Maître Dareuil, an old member of the Cahors Bar, immediately took his place. M. Etienne Rambert was very pale, but it was obvious that he was by no means overwhelmed by the fatality overhanging him. He was, indeed, a fine figure as he took his seat and mechanically passed his hand through his long white curls, flinging them back and raising his head almost as if in defiance of the inquisitive crowd that was gazing at him.

Almost immediately after he had taken his seat a door was thrown open and the jury filed in, and then a black-gowned usher came forward and shrilly called for silence.

"Stand up, gentlemen! Hats off, please! Gentlemen, the Court!"

With solemn, measured steps, and heads bent as if absorbed in profoundest meditation, the judges slowly proceeded to their seats. The president formally declared the court open, whereupon the clerk rose immediately to read the indictment.

The Clerk of the Court at Cahors was a most excellent man, but modesty was his distinguishing characteristic and his chief desire appeared to be to shun responsibility, figure as little prominently as possible, and even escape observation altogether. Assizes were not often held at Cahors, and he had had few occasions to read an indictment as tragic as this present one, with the result that he lacked confidence now. He read in a toneless, monotonous voice, so nervously and softly that nobody in the body of the court could hear a word he said, and even the jury were obliged to lean their elbows on the desk before them and make an ear trumpet of their hands to find out what it was all about.

Etienne Rambert, however, was only a few feet from the clerk; he did not miss a word, and it was evident from his nervous movements every now and then that some passages in the indictment hit him very hard indeed, and even lessened his general confidence.

When the clerk had finished Etienne Rambert sat still, with his forehead resting in his hands, as if crushed by the weight of the memories the indictment had evoked. Then the sharp, thin voice of the President of the Court snapped the chain of his thoughts.

"Stand up, sir!"

And pale as death Etienne Rambert rose and folded his arms across his breast. In firm, yet somehow muffled tones, he answered the preliminary formal questions. His name was Hervé Paul Etienne Rambert; his age, fifty-nine; his occupation, a merchant, owning and working rubber plantations in South America. Then followed the formal enquiry whether he had heard and understood the indictment which had just been read.

"I followed it all, sir," he replied, with a little gesture expressive of his sense of the gravity of the facts detailed and the weight of the evidence adduced, which won general sympathy for him. "I followed it all, but I protest against some of the allegations, and I protest with my whole energy against the suggestion that I have failed in my duty as a man of honour and as a father!"

The President of the Court checked him irritably.

"Excuse me, I do not intend to permit you to extend the pleadings indefinitely. I shall examine you on the various points of the indictment, and you may protest as much as you please." The unfeeling rudeness provoked no comment from the defendant, and the President proceeded. "Well, you have heard the indictment. It charges you first with having aided and abetted the escape of your son, whom an enquiry held in another place had implicated in the murder of the Marquise de Langrune; and it charges you secondly with having killed your son, whose body has been recovered from the Dordogne, in order that you might escape the penalty of public obloquy."

At this brutal statement of the case Etienne Rambert made a proud gesture of indignation.

"Sir," he exclaimed, "there are different ways of putting things. I do not deny the purport of the indictment, but I object to the summary of it that you present. No one has ever dared to contend that I killed my son in order to escape public obloquy, as you have just insinuated. I am entirely indifferent to the worlds opinion. What the indictment is intended to allege, the only thing it can allege, is that I wrought justice upon a criminal who ought to have filled me with horror but whom, nevertheless, I ought not to have handed over to the public executioner."

This time it was the judge's turn to be astonished. He was so accustomed to the cheap triumphs that judges look to win in court that he had expected to make mincemeat of this poor, broken old man whom the law had delivered to his tender mercy. But he discovered that the old man had fine courage and replied with spirit to his malevolent remarks.

"We will discuss your right to take the law into your own hands presently," he said, "but that is not the question now: there are other points which it would be well for you to explain to the jury. Why, in the first place, did you obstinately decline to speak to the examining magistrate?"

"I had no answer to make to the examining magistrate," Etienne Rambert answered slowly, as if he were weighing his words, "because in my opinion he had no questions to put to me! I do not admit that I am charged with anything contrary to the Code, or that any such charge can be formulated against me. The indictment charges me with having killed my son because I believed him to be guilty of the murder of Mme. de Langrune and would not hand him over to the gallows. I have never confessed to that murder, sir, and nothing will ever make me do so. And that is why I would not reply to the examining magistrate, because I would not admit that there was anything before the court concerning myself: because, since the dreadful tragedy in my private life was exposed to public opinion, I desired that I should be judged by public opinion, which, sir, is not represented by you who are a professional judge, but by the jury here who will shortly say whether I am really a criminal wretch: by the jury, many of whom are fathers themselves and, when they think of their own sons, will wonder what appalling visions must have passed through my mind when I was forced to believe that my boy, my own son, had committed a cowardly murder! What sort of tragedy will they think that must have been for a man like me, with sixty years of honour and of honourable life behind him?"

The outburst ended on a sob, and the whole court was moved with sympathy, women wiping their eyes, men coughing, and even the jury striving hard to conceal the emotion that stirred them.

The judge glared round the court, and after a pause addressed the defendant again with sarcastic phrases.

"So that is why you stood mute during the enquiry, was it, sir? Odd! very odd! I admire the interpretation you place upon your duty as an honourable man. It is — quaint!"

Etienne Rambert interrupted the sneering speech.

"I am quite sure, sir, that there are plenty of people here who will understand and endorse what I did."

The declaration was so pointedly personal that the judge took it up.

"And I am quite sure that people of principle will understand me when I have shown them your conduct as it really was. You have a predilection for heroics; it will not be without interest to bring things to the point. Your attitude throughout this affair has been this: — it is not for me to anticipate the issue of the enquiry which will be held some day into the murder of Mme. de Langrune, but I must recall the fact that the moment you believed your son was the murderer, the moment you discovered the blood-stained towel which furnished the circumstantial evidence of his guilt, you — the man of honour, mind you, — never thought of handing over the culprit to the police who were actually in the precincts of the château, but only thought of securing his escape, and helping him to get away! You even accompanied him in his flight, and so became in a sense his accomplice. I suppose you do not deny that?"

Etienne Rambert shook with emotion and answered in ringing tones.

"If you are of opinion, sir, that that was an act of complicity on my part, I will not only not deny it, I will proclaim it from the housetops! I became the accomplice of a murderer by inducing him to run away, did I? You forget, sir, that at the moment when I first believed my son was the culprit — I was not his accomplice then, I suppose? — there was a bond between him and me already that I could not possibly break: he was my son! Sir, the duty of a father — and I attach the very loftiest meaning to the word 'duty' — can never entail his giving up his son!"

A fresh murmur of sympathy through the court annoyed the judge, who shrugged his shoulders.

"Let us leave empty rhetoric alone," he said. "You have plenty of fine phrases with which to defend your action; that, indeed, is your concern, as the jury will doubtless appreciate; but I think it will be more advantageous to clear up the facts a little — not more advantageous to you, perhaps, but that is what I am here to do. So will you please tell me whether your son confessed to having murdered Mme. de Langrune, either during that night when you persuaded him to run away, or afterwards? Yes or no, please."

"I can't answer, sir. My son was mad! I will not believe my son was a criminal! There was absolutely no motive to prompt him to the deed, and his mother is in an asylum! That is the whole explanation of the crime! If he committed murder, it was in a fit of temporary insanity! He is dead; I refuse to cover his memory with the stain of infamy!"

"In other words, according to you Charles Rambert did confess, but you don't want to say so."

"I do not say he did confess."

"You leave it to be inferred."

Etienne Rambert made no reply, and the judge passed on to another point.

"What exactly did you do after you left the château?"

"What anyone does, I suppose, when he runs away. We wandered miserably about, going through fields and woods, I accusing him and he defending himself. We avoided the villages, scarcely venturing even in the early morning to go and buy food, and walked quickly, wishing to get as far away as possible. We spent the most frightful time it is possible to conceive."

"How long was all this?"

"I was with my son for four days, sir."

"So it was on the fourth day that you killed him?"

"Have pity, sir! I did not kill my son. It was a murderer that I had with me, a murderer for whom the police were hunting and for whom the guillotine was waiting!"

"A murderer, if you prefer it so," said the judge, entirely heedless of the unhappy man's protests. "But you had no right to assume the functions of executioner. Come, you admit you did kill him?"

"I do not admit it."

"Do you deny that you killed him?"

"I did what my duty told me to do!"

"Still the same story!" said the judge, angrily drumming his fingers on the desk. "You refuse to answer. But even in your own interests you must have the courage to adopt some definite theory. Well, would you have been glad if your son had taken his own life?"

"May I entreat you to remember that my son is dead!" Etienne Rambert said once more. "I can only remember the one fact that he was my son. I can't say that I desired his death. I don't even know now if he was guilty. Whatever horror I may feel for a crime, I can only remember now that Charles was not in his right mind, and that he was the son of my loins!"

Again a tremor of emotion passed through the court, and again the judge made an angry gesture ordering silence.

"So you decline to answer any of the principal points of the indictment? The jury will no doubt appreciate the reason. Well, can you let us know any of the advice you gave your son? If you did not desire him to take his own life, and if you had no intention of killing him, what did you want?"

"Oblivion," said Etienne Rambert, more calmly this time. "It was not for me to give my son up, and I could only desire for him oblivion, and if that was impossible, then death. I implored him to think of the life that was before him, and the future of shame, and I urged him to disappear for ever."

"Ah, you admit you did recommend him to commit suicide?"

"I mean I wanted him to go abroad."

The president feigned to be occupied with his notes, purposely giving time for the importance of the last admission he had wrung from Etienne Rambert to sink into the minds of the jury. Then, without raising his head, he asked abruptly:

"You were very surprised to hear of his death?"

"No," said Rambert dully.

"How did you part from each other?"

"The last night we slept out of doors, under a stack; we were both worn out and heart-sick; I prayed God of His mercy to have pity on us. It was by the bank of the Dordogne. Next morning when I woke up I was alone. He — my son — had disappeared. I know no more."

The judge quelled the emotion in the court by a threatening glance, and sprang a question on the defendant which was like a trap to catch him lying.

"If at that time you knew no more, how was it that a few days later you called on Inspector Juve and asked him at once what was known about the dead body of your son? The body had only been recovered within the previous hour or two, and had not been absolutely identified;

the newspapers, at any rate, only suggested the identity, with the utmost reserve. But you, sir, had no doubt on the subject! You knew that the corpse was that of your son! Why? How?"

It was one of the strongest points that could be made in support of the theory that Etienne Rambert had murdered his son, and the defendant immediately saw the difficulty he would have in giving an adequate answer without compromising himself. He turned to the jury, as though he had more hope in them than in the court.

"Gentlemen," he cried, "this is torture! I can bear no more! I cannot answer any more. You know quite enough to form your judgment of me! Form it now! Say if I failed in my duty as a man of honour and a father! I, at least, can answer no more questions!" and he sank back in his place like a beaten man, crushed by the distress evoked by all these painful memories.

The judge nodded to the jury with the grim complacency of a man who has run down his game.

"This refusal to answer my questions is in itself tantamount to a confession," he said acidly. "Well, we will proceed to call the witnesses. I should like to say that the most interesting witness would undoubtedly be Bouzille, the tramp who recovered the body of Charles Rambert; but unfortunately that individual has no fixed abode and it has not been possible to serve him with a subpoena."

A number of witnesses succeeded one another in the box, without, however, throwing any fresh light upon the matter; they were peasants who had met the two Ramberts when they were flying from the château, village bakers who had sold them bread, and lockkeepers who had seen, but been unable to recover, the floating corpse. The people in the court began to weary of the proceedings, the more so as it was confidently rumoured that Etienne Rambert had proudly declined to call any witnesses on his behalf, and even to allow his counsel to make any rhetorical appeal to the jury. It might be imprudent, but there was something fine in his defiance.

There was, however, one more thrill of interest for the public. The judge had explained that he deemed it unnecessary to call the detective Juve, inasmuch as all the information he had to give was already detailed in the long indictment, but as Mme. de Langrune's granddaughter was present in court, he would exercise his discretion and request her to answer one or two questions. And, much taken aback by this unexpected publicity, Thérèse Auvernois followed the usher to the witness-box.

"Mademoiselle Thérèse Auvernois, I need hardly ask if you recognise M. Rambert: but do you identify him as the person whose conversation with young Charles Rambert you overheard on that fatal night at the château of Beaulieu?"

"Yes, sir, that is M. Etienne Rambert," she replied in low tones, and with a long and tender look of pity at the defendant.

"Will you please tell us anything you know that has any bearing upon the charge brought against the defendant, the charge of having killed his son?"

Thérèse made a visible effort to restrain her distress.

"I can only say one thing, sir: that M. Rambert was talking to his son in tones of such terrible distress that I knew his heart was broken by the tragedy. I have heard so much from my dear grandmother about M. Etienne Rambert that I can only remember that she always declared him to be a man of the very highest principle, and I can only tell him here how dreadfully sorry I am for him, and that everybody pities him as much as I do."

The judge had expected that Thérèse would be a witness hostile to the defendant, whereas anything she was going to say would obviously be much to his advantage. He cut her short.

"That is enough, mademoiselle. Thank you," and while Thérèse was going back to her seat, wiping away the tears that would come to her eyes despite her bravest efforts to keep her self-control in the presence of so many strangers, the judge announced that there were no other witnesses to be heard, and called upon the Public Prosecutor to address the court.

That personage rose at once and made a harangue that was eloquent enough, no doubt, but introduced no new features into the case. He relied upon his law rather than his facts: rapidly recapitulated the defendant's contradictions and pitifully weak arguments, if arguments they could be called: claimed that the facts had been proved despite the defendant's steady refusal to answer questions: and insisted on the point that the defendant had no right whatever to take the law into his own hands, and either kill his son or aid and abet in his flight. He concluded by asking for a verdict of guilty, and a sentence of penal servitude for life.

To him succeeded counsel for the defendant, whose speech was brevity itself. He declined to make any appeal *ad misericordiam*, but simply asked the jury to decide whether the defendant had not acted as any high-principled father would act when he discovered that his son had committed a crime during a fit of insanity. He asked only for an impartial decision on the facts, from men of high principle, and he sat down conscious of having focussed the issue on the proper point and secured the sympathy of the public.

The judges withdrew to their room, the jury retired to consider their verdict, and Etienne Rambert was removed between two warders. Juve had not stirred during the whole trial, or displayed the least sign of approval or disapproval at any of the questions and answers exchanged. He sat now unobtrusively listening to the conversation that passed near him, relative to the issue of the case.

President Bonnet opined that Etienne Rambert had blundered in refusing to put up any defence: he had shown contempt of court, which was always unwise, and the court would show him no mercy. Dollon was of another opinion: according to him Etienne Rambert was a sport of fate, deserving pity rather than severity, and the court would be very lenient. Another man declared that Etienne Rambert had been in an impasse: however fondly he loved his son he could not but hope that he might commit suicide: if a friend committed an offence against the laws of honour, the only thing to do was to put a pistol into his hand. And so on: the only point on which all were unanimous was their sympathy with the defendant.

But a bell rang sharply; grave and impassive, the jury returned, the judges filed once more into their seats, Etienne Rambert was led back into court by the warders. In tense silence the foreman of the jury spoke:

"In the presence of God and of man, and upon my honour and my conscience I declare that the answer of the jury is 'no' to all the questions put, and that is the answer of them all."

It was acquittal!

There was no applause, but yet it seemed as if the words that set the defendant free had relieved every bosom of an overwhelming dread; the air seemed easier to breathe; and there was no one there but seemed physically better and also happier, for hearing a verdict which gave sanction for the general pity they had felt for the unhappy defendant, a man of honour and a most unhappy father!

By their verdict the jury had implicitly applauded and commiserated Etienne Rambert; but he still sat in the dock, broken and prostrated by terrible distress, sobbing unreservedly and making no effort to restrain his immeasurable grief.

X
Princess Sonia's Bath

Four months had passed since Etienne Rambert had been acquitted at the Cahors Assizes, and the world was beginning to forget the Beaulieu tragedy as it had already almost forgotten the mysterious murder of Lord Beltham. Juve alone did not allow his daily occupation to put the two cases out of his mind. True, he had ceased to make any direct enquiries, and gave no sign that he still had any interest in those crimes; but the detective knew very well that in both of them he had to contend with no ordinary murderer and he was content to remain in the shadow, waiting and watching, in seeming inactivity, for some slip which should betray the person or persons who had perpetrated two of the most puzzling murders that he had ever had to deal with.

It was the end of June, and Paris was beginning to empty. But the spring had been late and cold that year, and although it was within a couple of days of July society had lingered on in the capital; luxuriously appointed carriages still swept along the Champs Elysées when the audiences poured out of theatres and concert rooms, and fashionably attired people still thronged the broad pavements and gathered before the brilliantly lighted cafés on the Rond-Point; even at that late hour the Champs Elysées were as animated as in the busiest hours of the day.

At the Royal Palace Hotel the greatest animation prevailed. The entire staff was hurrying about the vast entrance halls and the palatial rooms on the ground floor; for it was the hour when the guests of the Royal Palace Hotel were returning from their evening's amusements, and the spacious vestibules of the immense hotel were crowded with men in evening dress, young fellows in dinner jackets, and women in low-cut gowns.

A young and fashionable woman got out of a perfectly appointed victoria, and M. Louis, the manager of the staff, came forward and bowed low, as he only did to clients of the very highest distinction. The lady responded with a gracious smile, and the manager called a servant.

"The lift for Mme. la Princesse Sonia Danidoff," and the next moment the beautiful vision, who had created quite a sensation merely in passing through the hall, had disappeared within the lift and was borne up to her apartments.

Princess Sonia was one of the most important clients that the Royal Palace Hotel possessed. She belonged to one of the greatest families in the world, being, by her marriage with Prince Danidoff, cousin to the Emperor of Russia and, so, connected with many royal personages. Still barely thirty years of age, she was not pretty but remarkably lovely, with wonderful blue eyes which formed a strange and most bewitching contrast to the heavy masses of black hair that framed her face. A woman of immense wealth, and typically a woman of the world, the Princess spent six months of the year in Paris, where she was a well-known and much-liked figure in the most exclusive circles; she was clever and cultivated, a first-rate musician, and her reputation was spotless, although it was very seldom that she was accompanied by her husband, whose duties as Grand Chamberlain to the Tsar kept him almost continuously in Russia. When in Paris she occupied a suite of four rooms on the third floor of the Royal Palace Hotel, a suite identical in plan and in luxury with that reserved for sovereigns who came there incognito.

The Princess passed through her drawing-room, a vast, round room, with a superb view over the Arc de Triomphe, and went into her bedroom where she switched on the electric light.

"Nadine," she called, in her grave, melodious voice, and a young girl, almost a child, sprang from a low divan hidden in a corner. "Nadine, take off my cloak and unfasten my hair. Then you can leave me: it is late, and I am tired."

The little maid obeyed, helped her mistress to put on a silken dressing gown, and loosened the masses of her hair. The Princess passed a hand across her brow, as if to brush away a headache.

"Before you go, get a bath ready for me; I think that would rest me."

Ten minutes later Nadine crept back like a shadow, and found the Princess standing dreamily on the balcony, inhaling deep breaths of the pure night air. The child kissed the tips of her mistress's fingers. "Your bath is quite ready," she said, and then withdrew.

A few more minutes passed, and Princess Sonia, half undressed, was just going into her dressing-room when suddenly she turned and went back to the middle of the bedroom which she had been on the point of leaving.

"Nadine," she called, "are you still there?" No answer came. "I must have been dreaming," the Princess murmured, "but I thought I heard someone moving about."

Sonia Danidoff was not unduly nervous, but like most people who live much alone and in large hotels, she was wont to be careful, and wished to make sure that no suspicious person had made his way into her rooms. She made a rapid survey of her bedroom, glanced into the brilliantly lighted drawing-room, and then moved to her bed and saw that the electric bell board, which enabled her to summon any of her own or of the hotel's servants, was in perfect order. Then, satisfied, she went into her dressing-room, quickly slipped off the rest of her clothes, and plunged into the perfumed water in her bath.

She thrilled with pleasure as her limbs, so tired after a long evening, relaxed in the warm water. On a table close to the bath she had placed a volume of old Muscovite folk tales, and she was glancing through these by the shaded light from a lamp above her, when a fresh sound made her start. She sat up quickly in the water and looked around her. There was nothing there. Then a little shiver shook her and she sank down again in the warm bath with a laugh at her own nervousness. And she was just beginning to read once more, when suddenly a strange voice, with a ring of malice in it, sounded in her ear. Someone was looking over her shoulder, and reading aloud the words she had just begun!

Before Sonia Danidoff had time to utter a cry or make a movement, a strong hand was over her lips, and another gripped her wrist, preventing her from reaching the button of the electric bell that was fixed among the taps. The Princess was almost fainting. She was expecting some horrible shock, expecting to feel some horrible weapon that would take her life, when the pressure on her lips and the grip upon her wrist gradually relaxed; and at the same moment, the mysterious individual who had thus taken her by surprise, moved round the bath and stood in front of her.

He was a man of about forty years of age, and extremely well dressed. A perfectly cut dinner jacket proved that the strange visitor was no unclean dweller in the Paris slums: no apache such as the Princess had read terrifying descriptions of in luridly illustrated newspapers. The hands which had held her motionless, and which now restored her liberty of movement to her, were white and well manicured and adorned with a few plain rings. The man's face was a distinguished one, and he wore a very fine black beard; slight baldness added to the height of a forehead naturally large. But what struck the Princess most, although she had little heart to observe the man very closely, was the abnormal size of his head and the number of wrinkles that ran right across his temples, following the line of the eyebrows.

In silence and with trembling lips Sonia Danidoff made an instinctive effort again to reach the electric bell, but with a quick movement the man caught her shoulder and prevented her from doing so. There was a cryptic smile upon the stranger's lips, and with a furious blush Sonia Danidoff dived back again into the milky water in the bath.

The man still stood in perfect silence, and at length the Princess mastered her emotion and spoke to him.

"Who are you? What do you want? Go at once or I will call for help."

"Above all things, do not call out, or you are a dead woman!" said the stranger harshly. Then he gave a little ironical shrug of his shoulders. "As for ringing — that would not be easy: you would have to leave the water to do so! And, besides, I object."

"If it is money, or rings you want," said the Princess between clenched teeth, "take them! But go!"

The Princess had laid several rings and bracelets on the table by her side, and the man glanced at them now, but without paying much attention to what the Princess said.

"Those trinkets are not bad," he said, "but your signet ring is much finer," and he calmly took the Princess's hand in his and examined the ring that she had kept on her third finger. "Don't be frightened," he added as he felt her hand trembling. "Let us have a chat, if you don't mind! There is nothing especially tempting about jewels apart from their personality," he said after a little pause, "apart, I mean, from the person who habitually wears them. But the bracelet on a wrist, or the necklace round a neck, or the ring upon a finger is another matter!"

Princess Sonia was as pale as death and utterly at a loss to understand what this extraordinary visitor was driving at. She held up her ring finger, and made a frightened little apology.

"I cannot take this ring off: it fits too tight."

The man laughed grimly.

"That does not matter in the least, Princess. Anyone who wanted to get a ring like that could do it quite simply." He felt negligently in his waistcoat pocket and produced a miniature razor, which he opened. He flashed the blade before the terrified eyes of the Princess. "With a sharp blade like this a skilful man could cut off the finger that had such a splendid jewel on it, in a couple of seconds," and then, seeing that the Princess, in fresh panic, was on the very point of screaming, quick as a flash he laid the palm of his hand over her lips, while still speaking in gentle tones to her. "Please do not be so terrified; I suppose you take me for some common hotel thief, or highway robber, but, Princess, can you really believe that I am anything of the kind?"

The man's tone was so earnest, and there was so deferent a look in his eyes, that the Princess recovered some of her courage.

"But I do not know who you are," she said half questioningly.

"So much the better," the man replied; "there is still time to make one another's acquaintance. I know who you are, and that is the main thing. You do not know me, Princess? Well, I assure you that on very many an occasion I have mingled with the blessed company of your adorers!"

The Princess's anger rose steadily with her courage.

"Sir," she said, "I do not know if you are joking, or if you are talking seriously, but your behaviour is extraordinary, hateful, abominable — — "

"It is merely original, Princess, and it pleases me to reflect that if I had been content to be presented to you in the ordinary way, in one or other of the many drawing-rooms we both frequent, you would certainly have taken much less notice of me than you have taken to-night; from the persistence of your gaze I can see that from this day onwards, not a single feature of my face will be unfamiliar to you, and I am convinced that, whatever happens, you will remember it for a very long time."

Princess Sonia tried to force a smile. She had recovered her self-possession, and was wondering what kind of man she had to deal with. If she was still not quite persuaded that this was not a vulgar thief, and if she had but little faith in his professions of admiration of herself, she was considerably exercised by the idea that she was alone with a lunatic. The man seemed to read her thoughts for he, too, smiled a little.

"I am glad to see, Princess, that you have a little more confidence now: we shall be able to arrange things ever so much better. You are certainly much more calm, much less uneasy now. Oh, yes, you are!" he added, checking her protest. "Why, it is quite five minutes since you last tried to ring for help. We are getting on. Besides, I somehow can't picture the Princess Sonia Danidoff, wife of the Grand Chamberlain and cousin of His Majesty the Emperor of All the Russias, allowing herself to be surprised alone with a man whom she did not know. If she were to ring, and someone came, how would the Princess account for the gentleman to whom she had accorded an audience in the most delightful, but certainly the most private of all her apartments?"

"But tell me," pleaded the unhappy woman, "how did you get in here?"

"That is not the question," the stranger replied. "The problem actually before us is, how am I to get out? For, of course, Princess, I shall not be so indelicate as to prolong my visit unduly, too happy only if you will permit me to repeat it on some other evening soon." He turned his head, and plunging his hand into the bath in the most natural manner possible, took out the thermometer which was floating on the perfumed water. "Thirty degrees, centigrade, Princess! Your bath is getting cold: you must get out!"

In her blank astonishment Princess Sonia did not know whether to laugh or cry. Was she alone with a monster who, after having played with her as a cat plays with a mouse, would suddenly turn and kill her? Or was this merely some irresponsible lunatic, whom chance alone had enabled to get into her rooms? Whatever the fact might be, the man's last words had made her aware that her bath really was getting cold. A shiver shook her whole frame, and yet —— —

"Oh, go, please go!" she implored him.

He shook his head, an ironical smile in his eyes.

"For pity's sake," she entreated him again, "have mercy on a woman — a good woman!"

The man appeared to be considering.

"It is very embarrassing," he murmured, "and yet we must decide upon something soon, for I am most anxious you should not take a chill. Oh, it is very simple, Princess: of course you know the arrangement of everything here so well that you could find your dressing-gown at once, by merely feeling your way? We will put out the light, and then you will be able to get out of the bath in the dark without the least fear." He was on the very point of turning off the switch of the lamp, when he stopped abruptly and came back to the bath. "I was forgetting that exasperating bell," he said. "A movement is so very easily made: suppose you were to ring, by mere inadvertence, and regret it afterwards?" Putting his idea into action, the man made a quick cut with his razor and severed the two electric wires several feet above the ground. "That is excellent," he said. "By the way, I don't know where these other two wires go that run along the wall, but it is best to be on the safe side. Suppose there were another bell?" He lifted his razor once more and was trying to sever the electric wires when the steel blade cut the insulator and an alarming flash of light resulted. The man leaped into the air, and dropped his razor. "Good Lord!" he growled, "I suppose that will make you happy, madame: I have burnt my hand most horribly! These must be wires for the light! But no matter: I have still got one sound hand, and that will be enough for me to secure the darkness that you want. And anyhow, you can press the button of your bell as much as you like: it won't ring. So I am sure of a few more minutes in your company."

Sudden darkness fell upon the room. Sonia Danidoff hesitated for a moment and then half rose in the bath. All her pride as a great lady was in revolt. If she must defend her honour and her life, she was ready to do so, and despair would give her strength; but in any event she would be better out of the water, and on her feet, prepared. The darkness was complete, both in the bathroom and in the adjacent bedroom, and the silence was absolute. Standing up in the bath, Sonia Danidoff swept her arms round in a circle to feel for any obstacle. Her touch met nothing. She drew out one foot, and then the other, sprang towards the chair on which she had left her dressing-gown, slipped into it with feverish haste, slid her feet into her slippers, stood motionless for just a second and then, with sudden decision, moved to the switch by the door and turned on the light.

The man had gone from the bathroom, but taking two steps towards her bedroom Sonia Danidoff saw him smiling at her from the far end of that room.

"Sir," she said, "this — pleasantry — has lasted long enough. You must go. You shall, you shall!"

"Shall?" the stranger echoed. "That is a word that is not often used to me. But you are forgiven for not knowing that, Princess. I forgot for the moment that I have not been presented to you. But what is in your mind now?"

Between them was a little escritoire, on the top of which was lying the tiny inlaid revolver that Sonia Danidoff always carried when she went out at night. Could she but get that into her hands it would be a potent argument to induce this stranger to obey her. The Princess also knew that in the drawer of that escritoire which she could actually see half open, she had placed, only a few minutes before going in to her bath, a pocket-book filled with bank-notes for a hundred and twenty thousand francs, money she had withdrawn from the strong-room of the hotel that very morning in order to meet some bills next day. She looked at the drawer and wondered if the pocket-book was still there, or if this mysterious admirer of hers was only a vulgar hotel thief after all. The man had followed her eyes to the revolver.

"That is an unusual knick-knack to find in a lady's room, Princess," and he sprang in front of her as she was taking a step towards the escritoire, and took possession of the revolver. "Do not be alarmed," he added, noticing her little gesture of terror. "I would not do you an injury for anything in the world. I shall be delighted to give this back to you in a minute, but first let me render it harmless." He deftly slipped the six cartridges out of the barrel and then handed the now useless weapon to the Princess with a gallant little bow. "Do not laugh at my excess of caution: but accidents happen so easily!"

It was in vain that the Princess tried to get near her escritoire to ascertain if the drawer had been tampered with: the man kept between her and it all the time, still smiling, still polite, but watching every movement that she made. Suddenly he took his watch from his pocket.

"Two o'clock! Already! Princess, you will be vexed with me for having abused your hospitality to such an extent. I must go!" He appeared not to notice the sigh of relief that broke from her, but went on in a melodramatic tone. "I shall take my departure, not through the window like a lover, nor up the chimney like a thief, nor yet through a secret door behind the arras like a brigand of romance, but like a gentleman who has come to pay his tribute of homage and respect to the most enchanting woman in the world — through the door!" He made a movement as if to go, and came back. "And what do you think of doing now, Princess? Perhaps you will be angry with me? Possibly some unpleasant discovery, made after my departure, will raise some animosity in your breast against me? You might even ring, directly my back is turned, and alarm the staff, merely to embarrass me in my exit, and without paying any attention to the subsequent possible scandal. That is a complicated arrangement of bells and telephones beside your bed! It would be a pity to spoil such a pretty thing, and besides, I hate doing unnecessary damage!" The Princess's eyes turned once more to the drawer: it was practically certain that her money was not there now! But the man broke in again upon her thoughts. "What can I be thinking of? Just fancy my not having presented myself to you even yet! But as a matter of fact I do not want to tell you my name out loud: it is a romantic one, utterly out of keeping with the typically modern environment in which we are now. Ah, if we were only on the steep side of some mountain with the moon like a great lamp above us, or by the shore of some wild ocean, there would be some fascination in the proclamation of my identity in the silence of the night, or in the midst of lightning and thunder as the hurricane swept the seas! But here — in a third-floor suite of the Royal Palace Hotel, surrounded by telephones and electric light, and standing by a window overlooking the Champs Elysées — it would be a positive anachronism!" He took a card out of his pocket and drew near the little escritoire. "Allow me, Princess, to slip my card into this drawer, left open on purpose, it would seem," and while the Princess uttered an exclamation she could not repress, he suited the action to the word. "And now, Princess," he went on, compelling her to retreat before him right to the door of the anteroom opening on to the corridor, "you are too well bred, I am sure, not to wish to conduct your visitor to the door of your suite." His tone altered abruptly, and in a deep imperious voice that made the Princess quake he ordered her: "And now, not a word, not a cry, not a movement until I am outside, or I will kill you!"

Clenching her fists, and summoning all her strength to prevent herself from swooning, Sonia Danidoff led the man to the anteroom door. Slowly she unlocked the door and held it open, and the man stepped quietly through. The next second he was gone!

Leaping back into her bedroom Sonia Danidoff set every bell a-ringing; with great presence of mind she telephoned down to the hall porter: "Don't let anybody go out! I have been robbed!" and she pressed hard upon the special button that set the great alarm bell clanging. Footsteps and voices resounded in the corridor: the Princess knew that help was coming and ran to open her door. The night watchman, and the manager of the third floor came running up and waiters appeared in numbers at the end of the corridor.

"Stop him! Stop him!" the Princess shouted. "He has only just gone out: a man in a dinner jacket, with a great black beard!"

A lad came hurrying out of the lift.

"Where are you going? What is the matter?" enquired the hall porter, whose lodge was at the far end of the hall, next to the courtyard of the hotel, the door into which he had just closed.

"I don't know," he answered. "There is a thief in the hotel! They are calling from the other side."

"It's not in your set, then? By the way, what floor are you on?"

"The second."

"All right," said the hall porter, "it's the third floor that they are calling from. Go up and see what is wrong."

The lad turned on his heel, and disregarding the notice forbidding servants to use the passenger lift, hurried back into it and upstairs again. He was a stoutly built fellow, with a smooth face and red hair. On the third floor he stopped, immediately opposite Sonia Danidoff's suite. The Princess was standing at her door, taking no notice of the watchman Muller's efforts to soothe her excitement, and mechanically twisting between her fingers the blank visiting card which her strange visitor had left in place of her pocket-book and the hundred and twenty thousand francs. There was no name whatever on the card.

"Well," said Muller, to the red-headed lad, "where do you come from?"

"I'm the new man on the second floor," the fellow answered. "The hall porter sent me up to find out what was the matter."

"Matter!" said Muller. "Somebody has robbed the Princess. Here, send someone for the police at once."

"I'll run, sir," and as the lift, instead of being sent down, had carelessly been sent up to the top floor, the young fellow ran down the staircase at full speed.

Through the telephone, Muller was just ordering the hall porter to send for the police, when the second-floor servant rushed up and caught him by the arm, dragging him away from the instrument.

"Open the door for the Lord's sake! I'm off to the police station," and the hall porter made haste to facilitate his departure.

On the top floor cries of astonishment re-echoed. The servants had been alarmed by the uproar and, surprised to see the lift stop and nobody get out of it, they opened the door and found a heap of clothing, a false beard, and a wig. Two housemaids and a valet gazed in amazement at these extraordinary properties, and never thought of informing the manager, M. Louis. Meantime, however, that gentleman had hurried through the mazes of the hotel, and had just reached the third floor when he was stopped by the Baronne Van den Rosen, one of the hotel's oldest patronesses.

"M. Louis!" she exclaimed, bursting into sobs. "I have just been robbed of my diamond necklace. I left it in a jewel-case on my table before going down to dinner. When I heard the noise just now, I got up and looked through my jewel-case, and the necklace is not there."

M. Louis was too dazed to reply. Muller ran up to him.

"Princess Sonia Danidoff's pocket-book has been stolen," he announced; "but I have had the hotel doors shut and we shall be sure to catch the thief."

The Princess came near to explain matters, but at that moment the servants came down from upstairs, bringing with them the make-up articles which they had found in the lift. They laid these on the ground without a word and M. Louis was staring at them when Muller had a sudden inspiration.

"M. Louis, what is the new man on the second floor like?"

Just at that instant a servant appeared at the end of the corridor, a middle-aged man with white whiskers and a bald head.

"There he is, coming towards us," M. Louis replied. "His name is Arnold."

"Good God!" cried Muller; "and the red-headed fellow: the carroty chap?" M. Louis shook his head, not understanding, and Muller tore himself away and rushed down to the hall porter. "Has he gone out? Has anyone gone out?"

"No one," said the porter, "except, of course, the servant from the second floor, whom you sent for the police."

"The carroty chap?" Muller enquired.

"Yes, the carroty chap."

Princess Sonia Danidoff lay back in an easy chair, receiving the anxious attentions of Nadine, her Circassian maid. M. Louis was holding salts to her nostrils. The Princess still held in her hands the card left by the mysterious stranger who had just robbed her so cleverly of a hundred and twenty thousand francs. As she slowly came to herself the Princess gazed at the card as if fascinated, and this time her haggard eyes grew wide with astonishment. For upon the card, which hitherto had appeared immaculately white, marks and letters were gradually becoming visible, and the Princess read:

"Fan — tô — mas!"

XI
Magistrate and Detective

M. Fuselier was standing in his office in the law courts at Paris, meditatively smoothing the nap of his silk hat. His mind was busy with the enquiries he had been prosecuting during the day, and although he had no reason to be dissatisfied with his day's work he had no clear idea as to what his next steps ought to be.

Three discreet taps on the door broke in upon his thoughts.

"Come in," he said, and then stepped forward with a hearty welcome as he recognised his visitor. "Juve, by all that is wonderful! What good wind has blown you here? I haven't seen you for ages. Busy?"

"Frightfully."

"Well, it's a fact that there's no dearth of sensational crime just now. The calendar is terribly heavy."

Juve had ensconced himself in a huge easy chair in a corner of the room.

"Yes," he said, "you are quite right. But unfortunately the calendar won't be a brilliant one for the police. There may be lots of cases, but there are not lots that they have worked out to a finish."

"You've got nothing to grumble at," M. Fuselier smiled. "You have been in enough cases lately that were worked out to a finish. Your reputation isn't in any danger of diminishing."

"I don't know what you mean," Juve said deprecatingly. "If you refer to the Beltham and Langrune cases, you must admit that your congratulations are not deserved. I have achieved no definite result in either of those affairs."

M. Fuselier also dropped into a comfortable chair. He lighted a cigarette.

"You have found out nothing fresh about that mysterious murder of Lord Beltham?"

"Nothing. I'm done. It is an insoluble mystery to me."

"You seem to be very sorry for yourself, but really you needn't be, Juve. You cleared up the Beltham case, and you solved the Langrune case, although you try to make out you didn't. And allow me to inform you, those two successes count, my friend."

"You are very kind, but you are rather misinformed. Unfortunately I have not cleared up the Beltham case at all."

"You found the missing peer."

"Well, yes, but —— "

"That was an amazing achievement. By the way, Juve, what led you to go to the rue Lévert to search Gurn's trunks?"

"That was very simple. You remember what an excitement there was when Lord Beltham disappeared? Well, when I was called in I saw at once that all ideas of accident or suicide might be dismissed, and that consequently the disappearance was due to crime. Once convinced of that, I very naturally suspected every single person who had ever had relations with Lord Beltham, for there was no single individual for me to suspect. Then I found out that the ex-Ambassador had been in continuous association with an Englishman named Gurn whom he had known in the South African war, and who led a very queer sort of life. That of course took me to Gurn's place, if for nothing else than to pick up information. And — well, that's all about it. It was just by going to Gurn's place to pump him, rather than anything else, that I found the noble lord's remains locked away in the trunk."

"Your modesty is delightful, Juve," said M. Fuselier with an approving nod. "You present things as if they were all matters of course, whereas really you are proving your extraordinary instinct. If you had arrived only twenty-four hours later the corpse would have been packed off to the Transvaal, and only the Lord knows if after that the extraordinary mystery ever would have been cleared up."

"Luck," Juve protested: "pure luck!"

"And were your other remarkable discoveries luck too?" enquired M. Fuselier with a smile. "There was your discovery that sulphate of zinc had been injected into the body to prevent it from smelling offensively."

"That was only a matter of using my eyes," Juve protested.

"All right," said the magistrate, "we will admit that you did not display any remarkable acumen in the Beltham case, if you would rather have it so. That does not alter the fact that you have solved the Langrune case."

"Solved it!"

M. Fuselier flicked the ash off his cigarette, and leant forward towards the detective.

"Of course you know that I know you were at the Cahors Assizes, Juve? What was your impression of the whole affair — of the verdict, and of Etienne Rambert's guilt or innocence?"

Juve got up and began to walk up and down the room, followed by the magistrate's eyes. He seemed to be hesitating as to whether he would answer at all, but finally he stopped abruptly and faced his friend.

"If I were talking to anybody but you, M. Fuselier, I would either not answer at all, or I would give an answer that was no answer! But as it is —— , well, in my opinion, the Langrune case is only just beginning, and nothing certain is known at all."

"According to that, Charles Rambert is innocent?"

"I don't say that."

"What then? I suppose you don't think the father was the murderer?"

"The hypothesis is not absurd! But there! What is the real truth of the whole affair? That is what I am wondering all the time. That murder is never out of my head; it interests me more and more every day. Oh, yes, I've got lots of ideas, but they are all utterly vague and improbable: sometimes my imagination seems to be running away with me."

He stopped, and M. Fuselier wagged a mocking finger at him.

"Juve," he said, "I charge you formally with attempting to implicate Fantômas in the murder of the Marquise de Langrune!"

The detective replied in the same tone of raillery.

"Guilty, my lord!"

"Good lord, man!" the magistrate exclaimed, "Fantômas is a perfect obsession with you," and as Juve acquiesced with a laugh the magistrate dropped his bantering tone. "Shall I tell you something, Juve? I too am beginning to have an obsession for that fantastic miscreant! And what I want to know is why you have not come to me before to ask me about that sensational robbery at the Royal Palace Hotel?"

"The robbery from Princess Sonia Danidoff?"

"Yes: the Fantômas robbery!"

"Fantômas, eh?" Juve protested. "That remains to be seen."

"Why, man," M. Fuselier retorted, "you have heard that detail about the card the man left, haven't you? — the visiting card that was blank when the Princess found it, and on which the name of Fantômas afterwards became visible?"

"There's no Fantômas about that, in my opinion."

"Why not?"

"Well, it isn't one of Fantômas' little ways to leave clear traces behind him. One might as well picture him committing robbery or murder in a cap with a neat little band round it: 'Fantômas and Co.' He might even add 'Discretion and Dispatch!' No, it's most unlikely."

"You don't think Fantômas capable of throwing down his glove to the police in the shape of some such material proof of his identity?"

"I always base my arguments on the balance of probabilities," Juve replied. "What emerges from this Royal Palace story is that some common hotel thief conceived the ingenious idea of casting suspicion on Fantômas: it was just a trick to mislead the police: at least, that is my opinion."

But M. Fuselier declined to be convinced.

"No, you are wrong, Juve: it was no common hotel thief who stole Mme. Van den Rosen's necklace and Princess Sonia's hundred and twenty thousand francs; the prize was big enough to appeal to Fantômas: and the amazing audacity of the crime is suggestive too. Just think what coolness the man must have had to be able to paralyse the Princess's power of resistance when she tried to call for help: and also to get clear away in spite of the hosts of servants in the hotel and all the precautions taken!"

"Tell me all about the robbery, M. Fuselier," said Juve.

The magistrate sat down at his desk and took up the notes he had made in the course of his official enquiry that day. He told Juve everything he had been able to elicit.

"The most amazing thing to me," he said in conclusion, "is the way the fellow, when he had once got out of Princess Sonia's room, contrived to get into the lift, shed his evening dress, get into livery, and make his first attempt to escape. When the hall porter stopped him he did not lose his head, but got into the lift again, sent that flying up to the top of the hotel with the clothes that would have betrayed him, calmly presented himself before Muller, the night watchman, and contrived to be told to go for the police, ran down the stairs again, and took advantage of the night watchman's telephoning to the hall porter to get the latter to open the door for him, and so marched off as easily as you please. A man who kept his nerve like that and could make such amazing use of every circumstance, who was so quick and daring, and who was capable of carrying through such a difficult comedy in the middle of the general uproar, richly deserves to be taken for Fantômas!"

Juve sat in deep consideration of the whole story.

"That isn't what interests me most," he said at last. "His escape from the hotel might have been effected by any clever thief. What I think more remarkable is the means he took to prevent the Princess from screaming when he was just leaving her rooms: that really was masterly. Instead of trying to get her as far away as possible and shut her up in her bedroom, to take her with him to the very door opening on to the corridor, where the faintest cry might have involved the worst possible consequences, and to be sure that the terror he had inspired would prevent her from uttering that cry, to be able to assume that the victim was so overwrought that she would make no effort at all and could do nothing — that is really very good indeed: quite admirable psychology! Fine work!"

"So you see there are some unusual features in the case," said M. Fuselier complacently: "this, for instance: why do you suppose the fellow stayed such a long time with the Princess and went through all that comedy business in the bathroom? Don't forget that she came in late, and it is extremely probable that he might have finished his job before she returned."

Juve passed his hand through his hair, a characteristic trick when his mind was working.

"I can imagine only one answer to that question, M. Fuselier. But you have inspected the scene of the crime: tell me first, where do you think the rascal was hidden?"

"Oh, I can answer that definitely. The Princess's suite of rooms ends in the bathroom, you know, and the chief things there are the famous bath, some cupboards, and a shower bath: the shower bath is one of those large model Norchers with lateral as well as vertical sprays, and a waterproof curtain hanging from rings at the top right down to the tub at the bottom. There were footmarks on the enamel of the tub, so it is clear that the thief hid there, behind the curtain, until the Princess got into her bath."

"And I suppose the shower bath is in the corner of the room near the window?" Juve went on. "And the window was partly open, or had been until the maid went in to prepare her mistress's bath? It's quite interesting! The man had just succeeded in stealing the necklace from Mme. Van den Rosen, whose rooms are next to Princess Sonia's: for some reason or other he had not been able to escape through the corridor, and so he naturally made up his mind to get into the Princess's suite, which he did by the simple process of stepping over the railing on the balcony and walking in through the open window of the dressing-room."

"And then Nadine came in, and he had to hide?"

"No, no!" said Juve, "you are getting on too fast. If that had been so, there would have been no need for all the bath business; besides, the Princess was robbed, too, you know. That was not just chance, it was planned; and so if the thief hid in the shower bath he did so on purpose to wait for the Princess."

"But he did not want her!" Fuselier retorted: "very much the reverse. If he was in the room before anybody else, all he had to do was, take the pocket-book and go!"

"Not a bit of it!" said Juve. "This robbery took place at the end of the month, when the Princess would have big monthly bills to meet, as the thief must have known. He must have found out that she had withdrawn her portfolio and money from the custody of the hotel. But he must have been ignorant of where she had placed the portfolio; and he waited for her to ask her — and she told him!"

"That's a pretty tall yarn!" M. Fuselier protested. "What on earth do you base it all upon? The Princess would never have shown the man the drawer where the money was taken from!"

"Yes, she did!" said Juve. "Look here: this is what happened: the fellow wanted to steal this pocket-book, and did not know where it was. He hid in the shower bath and waited, either for the Princess to go to bed or take a bath, either of which would place her at his mercy. When the lady was in the bath he appeared, threatened her, until she was terrified, and then bucked her up a bit again and hit on the dodge of putting out the electric light — not out of respect for her wounded feelings, but simply in order to get a chance to search through her clothes and make sure that the pocket-book was not there. I am convinced that if he had found it then he would have bolted at once. But he didn't find it. So he went to the end of the next room and waited for the Princess to come to him there, which is precisely what she did. He did not know where the money was, so he watched every movement of her eyes and saw them go automatically towards the drawer and stay there; then he slipped his card into the drawer, abstracted the pocket-book, and took his leave, driving his impudence and skill to the length of making her see him to the door!"

"Upon my word, Juve, you are a wonder," M. Fuselier said admiringly. "I've spent the entire day cross-examining everybody in the hotel, and came to no definite conclusion; and you, who have not seen anything or anybody connected with it, sit in that chair and in five minutes clear up the entire mystery. What a pity you won't believe that Fantômas had a finger in this pie! What a pity you won't take up the search!"

Juve paid no heed to the compliments to his skill. He took out his watch and looked at the time.

"I must go," he said; "it's quite time I was at my own work. Well, we may not have been wasting our time, M. Fuselier. I admit I had not paid much attention to the Royal Palace Hotel robbery. You have really interested me in it. I won't make any promises, but I think I shall very likely come again in a day or two for another talk with you about the case. It really interests me now. And when once I'm quit of one or two pressing jobs, I don't say I shan't ask leave to go thoroughly into it with you."

XII
A Knock-out Blow

The staff of the Royal Palace Hotel were just finishing dinner, and the greatest animation prevailed in the vast white-tiled servants' hall. The tone of the conversation varied at different tables, for the servants jealously observed a strict order of precedence among themselves, but the present topic was the same at all, the recent sensational robbery from Mme. Van den Rosen and the Princess Sonia Danidoff. At one table, smaller than the rest, a party of upper servants sat, under-managers or heads of departments: M. Louis was here, the general manager, M. Muller the superintendent of the second floor, M. Ludovic chief valet, M. Maurice head footman, M. Naud chief cashier, and last but not least Mlle. Jeanne the young lady cashier whose special duty it was to take charge of all the moneys and valuables deposited in the custody of the hotel by guests who wished to relieve themselves of the responsibility of keeping these in their own rooms. This small and select company was increased to-night by the addition of M. Henri Verbier, a man of about forty years of age, who had left the branch hotel at Cairo belonging to the same Company to join the staff at the Royal Palace Hotel in Paris.

"I am afraid, M. Verbier, you will form a very bad opinion of our establishment," said M. Muller to him. "It is really a pity that you should have left the Cairo branch and come here just when these robberies have put the Royal Palace under a cloud."

Henri Verbier smiled.

"You need not be afraid of my attaching too much importance to that," he said. "I've been in hotel life for fifteen years now, in one capacity or another, and, as you may suppose, I've known similar cases before, so they don't surprise me much. But one thing does surprise me, M. Muller, and that is that no clue has yet been found. I suppose the Board have done everything that can be done to trace the culprit? The reputation of the hotel is at stake."

"I should think they have looked for him!" said M. Louis, with a pathetic shrug of his shoulders. "Why, they even upbraided me for having had the door opened for the thief! Luckily I had a good friend in Muller, who admitted that he had been completely imposed upon and that he had given the order for the fellow, whom he supposed to be the second-floor waiter, to be allowed to go out. I knew nothing about it."

"And how was I to guess that the man was an impostor?" Muller protested.

"All the same," Henri Verbier retorted, "it is uncommonly annoying for everybody when things like that happen."

"So long as one has not committed any breach of orders, and so can't be made a scapegoat of, one mustn't grumble," M. Muller said. "Louis and I did exactly what our duty required and no one can say anything to us. The magistrate acknowledged that a week ago."

"He does not suspect anybody?" Henri Verbier asked.

"No: nobody," Muller answered.

M. Louis smiled.

"Yes, he did suspect somebody, Verbier," he said, "and that was your charming neighbour Mlle. Jeanne there."

Verbier turned towards the young cashier.

"What? The magistrate tried to make out that you were implicated in it?"

The girl had only spoken a few words during the whole of dinner, although Henri Verbier had made several gallant attempts to draw her into the general conversation. Now she laughingly protested.

"M. Louis only says that to tease me."

But M. Louis stuck to his guns.

"Not a bit of it, Mademoiselle Jeanne: I said it because it is the truth. The magistrate was on to you: I tell you he was! Why, M. Verbier, he cross-examined her for more than half an hour after the general confrontation, while he finished with Muller and me in less than ten minutes."

"Gad, M. Louis, a magistrate is a man, isn't he?" said Henri Verbier gallantly. "The magistrate may have enjoyed talking to Mlle. Jeanne more than he did to you, if I may suggest it without seeming rude."

There was a general laugh at this sally on the part of the new superintendent, and then M. Louis continued:

"Well, if he wanted to make up to her he went a funny way to work, for he made her angry."

"Did he really?" said Henri Verbier, turning again to the girl. "Why did the magistrate cross-examine you so much?"

The young cashier shrugged her shoulders.

"We have thrashed it out so often, M. Verbier! But I will tell you the whole story: during the morning of the day when the robbery was committed I had returned to Princess Sonia Danidoff the pocket-book containing a hundred and twenty thousand francs which she had given into my custody a few days before; I could not refuse to give it to her when she asked for it, could I? How was I to know that it would be stolen from her the same evening? Customers deposit their valuables with me and I hand them a receipt: they give me back the receipt when they demand their valuables, and all I have to do is comply with their request, without asking questions. Isn't that so?"

"But that was not what puzzled the magistrate I suppose," said Henri Verbier. "You are the custodian of all valuables, and you only complied strictly with your orders."

"Yes," M. Muller broke in, "but Mlle. Jeanne has only told you part of the story. Just fancy: only a few minutes before the robbery Mme. Van den Rosen had asked Mlle. Jeanne to take charge of her diamond necklace, and Mlle. Jeanne had refused!"

"That really was bad luck for you," said Henri Verbier to the girl with a laugh, "and I quite understand that the magistrate thought it rather odd."

"They are unkind!" she protested. "From the way they put it, M. Verbier, you really might think that I refused to take charge of Mme. Van den Rosen's jewellery in order to make things easy for the thief, which is as much as to say that I was his accomplice."

"That is precisely what the magistrate did think," M. Louis interpolated.

The girl took no notice of the interruption, but went on with her explanation to Henri Verbier.

"What happened was this: the rule is that I am at the disposal of customers, to take charge of deposits or to return them to the owners, until nine P.M., and until nine P.M. only. After that, my time is up, and all I have to do is lock my safe and go: I am free until nine o'clock next morning. You know that it does not do to take liberties in a position like mine. So when, on the day of the robbery, Mme. Van den Rosen came with her diamond necklace at half-past nine, I was perfectly within my rights in refusing to accept the deposit."

"That's right enough," said M. Muller, who, having finished his dessert, was now sipping coffee into which he had tipped sugar until it was as thick as syrup: "but you were disobliging, my dear young lady, and that was what struck the magistrate; for really it would not have been much trouble to register the new deposit and take charge of Mme. Van den Rosen's necklace for her."

"No, it wouldn't," the girl replied; "but when there is a rule it seems to me that it ought to be obeyed. My time is up at nine o'clock, and I am forbidden to accept any deposits after nine o'clock: and that's why I refused that lady's. I was perfectly right; and I should do the same again, if the same thing happened."

Henri Verbier was manifestly anxious to conciliate the young cashier. He expressed his approval of her conduct now.

"I quite agree with you, it never does to put interpretations upon orders. It was your duty to close your safe at nine o'clock, and you did close it then, and no one can say anything to you. But, joking apart, what did the magistrate want?"

The girl shrugged her shoulders with a gesture of indifference.

"You see I was right just now: M. Louis is only trying to tease me by saying that the magistrate cross-examined me severely. As a matter of fact I was simply asked what I have just told you, and when I gave all this explanation, no fault at all was found with me." As she spoke, Mlle. Jeanne folded her napkin carefully, pushed back her chair and shook hands with her two neighbours at table. "Good night," she said. "I am going up to bed."

Mlle. Jeanne had hardly left the room before Henri Verbier also rose from the table and prepared to follow her example.

M. Louis gave M. Muller a friendly dig in his comfortable paunch.

"A pound to a penny," he said, "that friend Verbier means to make up to Mlle. Jeanne. Well, I wish him luck! But that young lady is not very easy to tame!"

"You didn't succeed," M. Muller replied unkindly, "but it doesn't follow that nobody else will!"

M. Louis was not deceived: Henri Verbier evidently did think his neighbour at table a very charming young woman.

Mlle. Jeanne had hardly reached her room on the fifth floor of the hotel, and flung open her window to gaze over the magnificent panorama spread out below her and inhale the still night air, when a gentle tap fell upon the door and, complying with her summons to come in, Henri Verbier entered the room.

"My room is next to yours," he said, "and as I saw you were standing dreaming at your window I thought perhaps you would condescend to smoke an Egyptian cigarette. I have brought some back from Cairo: it is very mild tobacco — real ladies' tobacco."

The girl laughed and took a dainty cigarette from the case that Henri Verbier offered her.

"It's very kind of you to think of me," she said. "I don't make a habit of smoking, but I let myself be tempted sometimes."

"If I have been kind, you can show your gratitude very easily," Henri Verbier replied: "by allowing me to stay here a few minutes and smoke a cigarette with you."

"By all means," said Mlle. Jeanne. "I love to spend a little time at my window at night, to get the air before going to bed. You will prevent me from getting tired of my own company, and can tell me all about Cairo."

"I'm afraid I know very little about Cairo," Henri Verbier replied; "you see I spent almost the whole of my time in the hotel. But as you seem so kind and so friendly disposed I wish you would tell me things."

"But I am a very ignorant young woman."

"You are a woman, and that's enough. Listen: I am a new-comer here, and I am quite aware that my arrival, and my position, will make me some enemies. Now, whom ought I to be on my guard against? Who is there, among the staff, of whom I ought to be careful as doubtful associates? I ask with all the more concern because I will tell you frankly that I had no personal introduction to the Board: I have not got the same chance that you have."

"How do you know I had any introduction?" the girl enquired.

"Gad, I'm sure of it," Henri Verbier answered: he was leaning his elbows on the window-sill and gradually drawing closer to the young cashier. "I don't suppose that an important position like the one you hold, requiring absolute integrity and competence, is given without fullest investigation. Your work is not tiring, but that does not mean it would be entrusted to anybody."

"You are quite right, M. Verbier: I did have an introduction to the Board: and I had first-rate testimonials too."

"Have you been in business long? Two years — three years?"

"Yes," Mlle. Jeanne replied, purposely refraining from being explicit.

"I only asked because I fancy I have seen you before somewhere. I recognise your eyes!" Henri Verbier smiled, and looked meaningly at the girl. "Mlle. Jeanne, on summer nights like this, when you are looking at a lovely view like this, don't you have a funny sort of feeling?"

"No. What do you mean?"

"Oh, I don't know. But you see, I'm a sentimental chap unfortunately, and I really suffer a lot from always living in lonely isolation, without any affection: there are times when I feel as if love were an absolute necessity."

The cashier looked at him ironically.

"That's all foolishness. Love is only stupid, and ought to be guarded against as the worst possible mistake. Love always means misery for working people like us."

"It is you who are foolish," Henri Verbier protested gently, "or else you are mischievous. No: love is not stupid for working people like us; on the contrary, it is the only means we have of attaining perfect happiness. Lovers are rich!"

"In wealth that lets them die of hunger," she scoffed.

"No, no," he answered: "no. Look here: all to-day you and I have been working hard, earning our living; well, suppose you were not laughing at me but we were really lovers, would not this be the time to enjoy the living we have earned?" and as the girl did not reply, Henri Verbier, who like an experienced wooer had been drawing closer to her all the time, until now his shoulder was touching hers, took her hand. "Would not this be sweet?" he said. "I should take your little fingers into mine — like this; I should look at them so tenderly, and raise them to my lips — — "

But the girl wrested herself away.

"Let me go! I won't have it! Do you understand?" And then, to mitigate the sharpness of her rebuke, and also to change the conversation, she said: "It is beginning to turn cold. I will put a cloak over my shoulders," and she moved away from the window to unhook a cloak from a peg on the wall.

Henri Verbier watched her without moving.

"How unkind you are!" he said reproachfully, disregarding the angry gleam in her eyes. "Can it really be wrong to enjoy a kiss, on a lovely night like this? If you are cold, Mademoiselle Jeanne, there is a better way of getting warm than by putting a wrap over one's shoulders: and that is by resting in someone else's arms."

He put out his arms as he spoke, ready to catch the girl as she came across the room, and was on the very point of taking her into his arms as he had suggested, when she broke from his grasp with a sudden turn and, furious with rage, dealt him a tremendous blow right on the temple. With a stifled groan, Henri Verbier dropped unconscious to the floor.

Mlle. Jeanne stared at him for a moment, as if dumbfounded. Then with quite amazing rapidity the young cashier sprang to the window and hurriedly closed it. She took down her hat from a hook on the wall, and put it on with a single gesture, opened a drawer and took out a little bag, and then, after listening for a minute to make sure that there was nobody in the passage outside her room, she opened her door, went out, rapidly turned the key behind her and ran down the stairs.

Two minutes later Mlle. Jeanne smilingly passed the porter on duty and wished him good night.

"Bye-bye," she said. "I'm going out to get a little fresh air!"

Slowly, as if emerging from some extraordinary dream, Henri Verbier began to recover from his brief unconsciousness: he could not understand at first what had happened to him, why he was lying on the floor, why his head ached so much, or why his blood-shot eyes saw everything through a mist. He gradually struggled into a sitting posture and looked around the room.

"Nobody here!" he muttered. Then as if the sound of his own voice had brought him back to life, he got up and hurried to the door and shook it furiously. "Locked!" he growled angrily. "And I can call till I'm black in the face! No one has come upstairs yet. I'm trapped!" He turned towards the window, with some idea of calling for help, but as he passed the mirror over the mantelpiece he caught sight of his own reflection and saw the bruise on his forehead, with a tiny stream of blood beginning to trickle from a cut in the skin. He went close to the glass and looked at himself in dismay. "Juve though I am," he murmured, "I've let myself be knocked out by a woman!" And then Juve, for Juve it was, cleverly disguised, uttered a sudden oath, clenching his fists and grinding his teeth in rage. "Confound it all, I'll take my oath that blow was never dealt by any woman!"

XIII

Thérèse's Future

M. Etienne Rambert was in the smoking-room of the house which he had purchased a few months previously in the Place Pereire, rue Eugène-Flachat, smoking and chatting with his old friend Barbey, who also was his banker. The two had been discussing investments, and the wealthy merchant had displayed considerable indifference to the banker's recommendation of various gilt-edged securities.

"To tell you the truth, my dear fellow," he said at length, "these things interest me very little; I've got used to big enterprises — am almost what you would call a plunger. Of course you know that nothing is so risky as the development of rubber plantations. No doubt the industry has prospered amazingly since the boom in motor-cars began, but you must remember that I went into it when no one could possibly foresee the immense market that the new means of locomotion would open for our produce. That's enough to prove to you that I'm no coward when it's a question of risking money." The banker nodded: his friend certainly did display a quite extraordinary energy and will-power for a man of his age. "As a matter of fact," M. Rambert went on, "any business of which I am not actually a director, interests me only slightly. You know I am not boasting when I say that my fortune is large enough to justify me in incurring a certain amount of financial risk without having to fear any serious modification of my social position if the ventures should happen to turn out ill. I've got the sporting instinct."

"It's a fine one," M. Barbey said with some enthusiasm. "And I don't mind telling you that if I were not your banker, and so had a certain responsibility in your case, I should not hesitate to put a scheme before you that has been running in my head for a year or two now."

"A scheme of your own, Barbey?" said M. Rambert. "How is it you have never told me about it? I should have thought we were close enough friends for that."

The hint of reproach in the words pricked the banker, and also encouraged him to proceed.

"It's rather a delicate matter, and you will understand my hesitation when I tell you — for I'll burn my boats now — that it isn't any ordinary speculation, such as I am in the habit of recommending to my customers. It is a speculation in which I am interested personally: in short, I want to increase the capital of my Bank, and convert my House into a really large concern."

"Oh-ho!" said M. Etienne Rambert, half to himself. "Well, you are quite right, Barbey. But if you want to suggest that I shall help to finance it, you had better put all the cards on the table and let me know exactly what the position is; I need not say that if nothing comes of it, I shall regard any information you give me as absolutely confidential."

The two men plunged into the subject, and for a good half-hour discussed it in all its bearings, making endless calculations and contemplating all contingencies. At last M. Rambert threw down his pen and looked up.

"I'm accustomed to the American method of hustle, Barbey. In principle I like your proposition quite well; but I won't be one of your financial partners; if the thing goes through I'll be the only one, or not one at all. I know what is in your mind," he went on with a smile, as he noticed the banker's surprise; "you know what my fortune is, or rather you think you do, and you are wondering where I shall get the million sterling, or thereabouts, that you want. Well, make your mind easy about that; if I talk like this, it's because I've got it." The banker's bow was very deferent, and M. Rambert continued: "Yes, the last year or two have been good, even very good, for me. I've made some lucky speculations and my capital has further been increased by some lotteries which have turned out right quite lately. Well!" he broke off with a sigh, "I suppose one can't always be unlucky in everything, though money can't cure, or even touch, the wounds in one's heart."

The banker made no answer: he shrank from waking, by untimely words, the sad memories which were hardly dormant yet in the old man's mind. But M. Rambert soon reverted to his business tone.

"I'm quite disposed to be interested in a financial venture like yours, Barbey. But you must understand that you will have a good deal more than a sleeping partner in me. Will that suit you? I should not ask you to abdicate your authority, but I tell you frankly I should follow all the operations of your house very closely indeed."

"There shall be no secrets from you, my dear friend, my dear partner, if I may call you that," said M. Barbey, rising: "quite the contrary!"

The banker looked towards the mantelpiece, as if expecting to see a clock there; M. Rambert understood the instinctive action and drew out his watch.

"Twenty minutes to eleven, Barbey: late hours for you. So off with you." He cut short the banker's half-hearted apologies for not prolonging the evening. "I am turning you out quite unceremoniously, my dear chap, and besides, as you know, I'm not lonely to-night as I generally am. I have a young and very charming companion, for whom I have the greatest possible affection, and I am going to join her."

M. Etienne Rambert conducted his friend to the hall door, heard the sound of his motor-car die away in the distance, and then walked across the hall and, instead of going back to the smoking-room, turned into the adjoining drawing-room. He paused for a moment in the doorway, tenderly contemplating the charming spectacle that met his eyes.

The shaded light from an electric lamp fell upon the bent head, oval face and delicate features of Thérèse Auvernois, who was intent upon a book. The girl was emerging from childhood into young womanhood now, and sorrow had heightened her natural distinction by giving her a stamp of gravity that was new. Her figure showed slight and supple, delicate and graceful, and her long, tapered fingers turned over the pages of the book with slow and regular movement. Thérèse looked round towards Etienne Rambert when she heard him coming in, and laying down her book she came forward to meet him, moving with a very graceful, easy carriage.

"I am sure I am keeping you up most dreadfully late, dear M. Rambert," she said apologetically, "but what am I to do? I must wait for the Baronne de Vibray, and the dear thing is so often late!"

The tragedy at the château of Beaulieu had had one effect in knitting all the friends of the Marquise de Langrune in closer bonds of friendship. Prior to that event Etienne Rambert had scarcely known the Baronne de Vibray; now the two were intimate friends. The Baronne had not desisted from her first generous effort until she had persuaded the family council to appoint her guardian of the orphaned Thérèse Auvernois. At first she had installed the child at Querelles, and remained there with her, leading the quietest possible life, partly out of respect for Thérèse's grief, and partly because she herself was also much upset by the distressing tragedy. She had even enjoyed the rest, and her new interest in playing mother, or rather elder sister, to Thérèse. But as the weeks went by and time accomplished its healing work, Paris called to the Baronne once more, and yielding to the solicitations of her many friends she brought her new ward to the capital and settled in a little flat in the rue Boissy-d'Anglais. At first she protested that she would go out nowhere, or at most pay only absolutely necessary visits, but by degrees she accepted first one and then many invitations, though always deploring the necessity of leaving Thérèse for several hours at a time.

Happily there was always Etienne Rambert, who was also staying in Paris just now. It had gradually become the custom of the Baronne de Vibray, when she was dining out, to entrust Thérèse to Etienne Rambert's care, and the young girl and the old man got on together perfectly. Their hearts had met across the awful chasm that fate had tried to cut between them.

To Thérèse's last words now Etienne Rambert replied:

"You need not apologise for staying late, dear; you know how glad I am to see you. I wish the house were yours."

The girl glanced round the room that had grown so familiar to her, and with a sudden rush of feeling slipped her arm around the old man's neck and laid her fair head on his shoulder.

"I should so love to stay here with you, M. Rambert!"

The old man looked oddly at her for a moment, repressing the words that he might perhaps have wished to say, and then gently released himself from her affectionate clasp and led her to a sofa, on which he sat down by her side.

"That is one of the things that we must not allow ourselves to think about, my dear," he said. "I should have rejoiced to receive you in my home, and your presence, and the brightness of your dear fair face would have given a charm to my lonely fireside; but unfortunately those are vain dreams. We have to reckon with the world, and the world would not approve of a young girl like you living in the home of a lonely man."

"Why not?" Thérèse enquired in surprise. "Why, you might be my father."

Etienne Rambert winced at the word.

"Ah!" he said, "you must not forget, Thérèse, that I am not your father, but — his: the father of him who — — " but Thérèse's soft hand laid upon his lips prevented him from finishing what he would have said.

To change the conversation Thérèse feigned concern about her own future.

"When we left Querelles," she said, "President Bonnet told me that you would tell me something about my affairs. I gather that my fortune is not a very brilliant one."

It was indeed the fact that after the murder of the Marquise the unpleasant discovery had been made that her fortune was by no means so considerable as had generally been supposed. The estate was mortgaged, and President Bonnet and Etienne Rambert had had long and anxious debates as to whether it might not be well for Thérèse to renounce her inheritance to Beaulieu, so doubtful did it seem whether the assets would exceed the liabilities.

Etienne Rambert made a vague, but significant gesture when he heard the girl raise the point now, but Thérèse had all the carelessness of youth.

"Oh, I shall not be down-hearted," she exclaimed. "My poor grannie always gave me an example of energy and hard work; I've got plenty of pluck, and I will work too. Suppose I turn governess?"

M. Rambert looked at her thoughtfully.

"My dear child, I know how brave and earnest you are, and that gives me confidence. I have thought about your future a great deal already. Some day, of course, some nice and wealthy young fellow will come along and marry you — — Oh, yes, he will: you'll see. But in the meantime it will be necessary for you to have some occupation. I am wondering whether it will not be necessary to let, or even to sell Beaulieu. And, on the other hand, you can't always stay with the Baronne de Vibray."

"No, I realise that," said Thérèse, who, with the native tact that was one of her best qualities, had quickly seen that it would not be long before she would become a difficulty in the way of the independence of the kind Baronne. "That is what troubles me most."

"Your birth and your upbringing have been such that you would certainly suffer much in taking up the difficult and delicate, and sometimes painful, position of governess in a family; and, without wishing to be offensive, I must remind you that you need to have studied very hard to be a governess nowadays, and I am not aware that you are exactly a blue-stocking. But I have an idea, and this is it: for a great many years now I have been on the very friendliest terms with a lady who belongs to the very best English society: Lady Beltham; you may perhaps have heard me speak of her." Thérèse opened wide eyes of astonishment, and Rambert went on: "A few months ago Lady Beltham lost her husband in strange circumstances, and since then she has been good enough to give me more of her confidence than previously. She is immensely rich, and very charitable, and I have frequently been asked by her to look after some of her many financial interests. Now I have often noticed that she has with her several young English ladies who live with her, not as companions, but, shall I say, secretaries? Do you understand the difference? She treats them like friends or relatives, and they all belong to the very best social class, some of them indeed being daughters of English peers. If Lady Beltham, to whom I could speak about it, would admit you into her little company, I am sure you would be in a most delightful *milieu*, and Lady Beltham, whom, I know, you would please, would almost certainly interest herself in your future. She knows what unhappiness is as well as you do, my dear," he added, bending fondly over the girl, "and she would understand you."

"Dear M. Rambert!" murmured Thérèse, much moved: "do that; speak to Lady Beltham about me; I should be so glad!"

Thérèse did not finish all she would have said. A loud ring at the front door bell broke in upon her words, and Etienne Rambert rose and walked across the room.

"That must be the good Baronne de Vibray come for you," he said.

XIV
Mademoiselle Jeanne

After she had so roughly disposed of the enterprising Henri Verbier, whose most unseemly advances had so greatly scandalised her, Mlle. Jeanne took to her heels, directly she was out of sight of the Royal Palace Hotel, and ran like one possessed. She stood for a moment in the brilliantly lighted, traffic-crowded Avenue Wagram, shaking with excitement and with palpitating heart, and then mechanically hailed a passing cab and told the driver to take her towards the Bois. There she gave another heedless order to go to the boulevard Saint-Denis, but as the cab approached the place de l'Etoile she realised that she was once more near the Royal Palace Hotel, and stopping the driver by the tram lines she dismissed him and got into a tram that was going to the station of Auteuil. It was just half-past eleven when she reached the station.

"When is the next train for Saint-Lazaire?" she asked.

She learned that one was starting almost at once, and hurriedly taking a second-class ticket she jumped into a ladies' carriage and went as far as Courcelles. There she alighted, went out of the station, looked around her for a minute or two to get her bearings, and then walked slowly towards the rue Eugène-Flachat. She hesitated a second, and then walked firmly towards a particular house, and rang the bell.

"A lady to see you, sir," the footman said to M. Rambert.

"Bring her in here at once," said M. Rambert, supposing that the man had kept the Baronne de Vibray waiting in the anteroom.

The drawing-room door was opened a little way, and someone came in and stepped quickly into the shadow by the door. Thérèse, who had risen to hurry towards the visitor, stopped short when she perceived that it was a stranger and not her guardian. Noticing her action, M. Etienne Rambert turned and looked at the person who had entered.

It was a lady.

"To what am I indebted —— " he began with a bow; and then, having approached the visitor, he broke off short. "Good heavens ——!"

The bell rang a second time, and on this occasion the Baronne de Vibray hurried into the room, a radiant incarnation of gaiety.

"I am most dreadfully late!" she exclaimed, and was hurrying towards M. Etienne Rambert with outstretched hands, full of some amusing story she had to tell him, when she too caught sight of the strange lady standing stiffly in the corner of the room, with downcast eyes.

Etienne Rambert repressed his first emotion, smiled to the Baronne, and then went towards the mysterious lady.

"Madame," he said, not a muscle of his face moving, "may I trouble you to come into my study?"

"Who is that lady, M. Rambert?" said Thérèse when presently M. Rambert came back into the drawing-room. "And how white you are!"

M. Rambert forced a smile.

"I am rather tired, dear. I have had a great deal to do these last few days."

The Baronne de Vibray was full of instant apologies.

"It is all my fault," she exclaimed. "I am dreadfully sorry to have kept you up so late," and in a few minutes more the Baronne's car was speeding towards the rue Boissy-d'Anglais.

M. Rambert hurried back to his study, shut and locked the door behind him, and almost sprang towards the unknown lady, his fists clenched, his eyes starting out of his head.

"Charles!" he exclaimed.

"Papa!" the girl replied, and sank upon a sofa.

There was silence. Etienne Rambert seemed utterly dumbfounded.

"I won't, I won't remain disguised as a woman any longer. I've done with it. I cannot bear it!" the strange creature murmured.

"You must!" said Rambert harshly, imperiously. "I insist!"

The pseudo Mlle. Jeanne slowly took off the heavy wig that concealed her real features, and tore away the corsage that compressed her bosom, revealing the strong and muscular frame of a young man.

"No, I will not," replied the strange individual, to whom M. Rambert had not hesitated to give the name of Charles. "I would rather anything else happened."

"You have got to expiate," Etienne Rambert said with the same harshness.

"The expiation is too great," the young fellow answered. "The torture is unendurable."

"Charles," said M. Rambert very gravely, "do you forget that legally, civilly, you are dead?"

"I would a thousand times rather be really dead!" the unhappy lad exclaimed.

"Alas!" his father murmured, speaking very fast, "I thought your mind was more unhinged than it really is. I saved your life, regardless of all risk, because I thought you were insane, and now I know you are a criminal! Oh, yes, I know things, I know your life!"

"Father," said Charles Rambert with so stern and determined an expression that Etienne Rambert felt a moment's fear. "I want to know first of all how you managed to save my life and make out that I was dead. Was that just chance, or was it planned deliberately?"

Confronted with this new firmness of his son's, Etienne Rambert dropped his peremptory tone; his shoulders drooped in distress.

"Can one anticipate things like that?" he said. "When we parted, my heart bled to think that you, my son, must fall into the hands of justice, and that your feet must tread the path that led to the scaffold or, at least, to the galleys; I wondered how I could save you; then chance, chance, mark you, brought that poor drowned body in my way: I saw the fortunate coincidence of a faint resemblance, and resolved to pass it off for you; I got those woman's clothes which you exchanged for yours, buried the dead man's clothes and put yours on the corpse. Do you know, Charles, that I have suffered too? Do you know what agony and torture I, as a man of honour, have endured? Have you not heard the story of my appearance at the Assizes and of my humiliation in court?"

"You did all that!" Charles Rambert murmured. "Strange chance, indeed!" Then his tone changed and he sobbed. "Oh, my poor father, what an awful fatality it all is!" Suddenly he sprang to his feet. "But I committed no crime, papa! I never killed the Marquise de Langrune! Oh, do believe me! Why, you have just this minute said that you know I am not mad!"

Etienne Rambert looked at his son with distress.

"Not mad, my poor boy? Yet perhaps you were mad — then?" Then he stopped abruptly. "Don't let us go over all that again! I forbid it absolutely." He leaned back on his writing-table, folded his arms and asked sternly: "Have you come here only to tell me that?"

The curt question seemed to affect the lad strangely. All his former audacity dropped from him. Nervously he stammered:

"I can't remain a woman any longer!"

"Why not?" snapped Etienne Rambert.

"I can't."

The two men looked at each other in silence, as if trying to read one another's thoughts. Then Etienne Rambert seemed to see the inner meaning of the words his son had just said.

"I see!" he answered slowly. "I understand.... The Royal Palace Hotel, where Mlle. Jeanne held a trusted post, has just been the scene of a daring robbery. Obviously, if anyone could prove that Charles Rambert and the new cashier were one and the same person — — "

But the young fellow understood the insinuation and burst out:

"I did not commit that robbery!"

"You did!" Etienne Rambert insisted: "you did. I read the newspaper accounts of the robbery, read them with all the agony that only a father like me with a son like you could feel. The detectives and the magistrates were at a loss to find the key to the mystery, but I saw clearly and at once what the solution of the mystery was. And I knew and understood because I knew it was — you!"

"I did not commit the robbery," Charles Rambert shouted. "Do you mean to begin all your horrible insinuations again, as you did at Beaulieu?" he demanded in almost threatening tones. "What evil spirit obsesses you? Why will you insist that your unhappy son is a criminal? I had nothing to do with those robberies at the hotel; I swear I had not, father!"

M. Rambert shrugged his shoulders and clasped his hands.

"What have I done," he muttered, "to have so heavy a cross laid on me?" He turned again to his son. "Your defence is childish. What is the use of mere denials? Words don't mean anything without proofs to support them." The lad was silent, seeming to think it useless to attempt to convince a father who appeared so certain of his guilt, and also crushed by the thought of all that had happened at the hotel. His father betrayed some uneasiness at a new thought that had come into his mind. "I told you not to come to me again except as a last resource, when punishment was actually overtaking you, or when you had proved your innocence: why are you here now? Has something happened that I do not know about? What has happened? What else have you done? Speak!"

Charles Rambert answered in a toneless voice, as if hypnotised:

"There has been a detective in the hotel for the last few days. He called himself Henri Verbier, and was disguised, but I knew him, for I had seen him too lately, and in circumstances too deeply impressed upon my mind for me to be able to forget him, although I only saw him then for a few minutes."

"What do you mean?" said the elder man uneasily.

"I mean that Juve was at the Royal Palace Hotel."

"Juve?" exclaimed Etienne Rambert. "And then — go on!"

"Juve, disguised as Henri Verbier, subjected me to a kind of examination, and I don't know what conclusion he came to. Then, this evening, barely two hours ago, he came up to my room and had a long talk, and while he was trying to get some information from me about a matter that I know nothing about — for I swear, papa, that I had nothing whatever to do with the robbery — he came up to me and took hold of me as a man does when he wants to make up to a woman. And I lost my head! I felt that in another minute all would be up with me — that he would establish my identity, which he perhaps suspected already — and I thought of all you had done to save my life by representing that I was dead, and — — "

Charles paused for breath. His father's fists were clenched and his face contracted.

"Go on!" he said, "go on, but speak lower!"

"As Juve came close," Charles went on, "I dealt him a terrific blow on the forehead, and he fell like a stone. And I got away!"

"Is he dead?" Etienne Rambert whispered.

"I don't know."

For ten minutes Charles Rambert remained alone in the study, where his father had left him, thinking deeply. Then the door opened and Etienne Rambert came back carrying a bundle of clothes.

"There you are," he said to his son: "here are some man's clothes. Put them on, and go!"

The young man hastily took off his woman's garments and dressed himself in silence, while his father walked up and down the room, plunged in deepest thought. Twice he asked: "Are you quite sure it was Juve?" and twice his son replied "Quite sure." And once again Etienne Rambert asked, in tones that betrayed his keen anxiety: "Did you kill him?" and Charles Rambert shrugged his shoulders and replied: "I told you before, I do not know."

And now Charles Rambert stood upon the threshold of the house, about to leave his father without a word of farewell or parting embrace. M. Etienne Rambert stayed him, holding out a pocket-book, filled full with bank-notes.

"There: take that," he said, "and go!"

XV
The Mad Woman's Plot

When Dr. Biron built his famous private asylum in the very heart of Passy, intended, according to his prospectus, to provide a retreat for people suffering from nervous breakdown or from overwork or over-excitement, and to offer hospital treatment to the insane, in order to secure a kind of official sanction for his institution, he took the wise precaution to proclaim from the housetops that he would enlist the services of ex-medical officers of the hospitals. The idea was a shrewd and a successful one, and his establishment throve.

Perret and Sembadel were having breakfast, and also were grumbling.

"I shouldn't curse the meanness of the management quite so much if they didn't put us on to all the jobs," said Sembadel. "Hang it all, man, we are both qualified, and when we undertook to assist Dr. Biron we did so, I presume, in order to top off our theoretical training with some practical clinical experience."

"Who's stopping you?" Perret enquired.

"How can we find the time, when besides all our actual work with the patients, we have to do all this administrative work, writing to people to say how the patients are, and all that? That ought to be done by clerks, not by us."

"Isn't one job as good as another?" Perret retorted. "Besides, we are the only people who know how the patients really are, so it's common sense that we should have to write to their friends."

"They might let us have a secretary, anyhow," Sembadel growled.

Perret saw that his friend was in a bad temper, so did not try to carry on the argument.

"Say," he said, "you ought to make a special note of that case of No. 25, for your thesis. She was in your ward for about six months, wasn't she?"

"No. 25?" said Sembadel. "Yes, I know: a woman named Rambert; age about forty; hallucination that people are persecuting her; anæmic, with alternate crises of excitement and melancholia, punctuated by fits of passion; treatment: rest, nourishment, anodynes."

"You evidently remember the case distinctly."

"She interested me; she has marvellous eyes. Well, what about her?"

"Why, when she was moved into my pavilion the diagnosis was bad and the prognosis very bad: she was supposed to be incurable. Just go and see her now: her brain is restored: she's a new woman." He came to the table and picked up some notepaper. "I wrote to her husband a day or two ago and told him he might expect to hear that his wife had recovered, but I imagine my letter miscarried, for I've had no answer. I have a good mind to write to him again and ask for permission to send her to the convalescent home. The mischief of it is that this Etienne Rambert may want to remove her altogether, and that would mean one paying patient less, which would put our worthy director in a bad temper for a month."

He turned to his correspondence, and for some minutes the silence in the room was only broken by the scratching of pens on paper. Then an attendant came in, bringing a quantity of letters. Perret picked them up and began to sort them out.

"None for you," he said to Sembadel. "Not one of those little mauve envelopes which you look for every day and which decide what your temper will be. I must look out for storms."

"Shan't even have time to grouse to-day," Sembadel growled again. "You forget that Swelding pays us an official visit to-day."

"The Danish professor? Is it this morning that he is coming?"

"So it seems."

"Who is the fellow?"

"Just one of those foreign savants who haven't succeeded in becoming famous at home and so go abroad to worry other people under a pretext of investigations. That's why he wants to come here. Wrote some beastly little pamphlet on the ideontology of the hyper-imaginative. Never heard of it myself."

The conversation dropped, and presently the two men went off to their wards to see their patients, and warn the attendants to have everything in apple-pie order for the official inspection.

Meantime, in the great drawing-room, elaborate courtesies were being exchanged between Dr. Biron and Professor Swelding.

Dr. Biron was a man of about forty, with a high-coloured face and an active, vigorous frame. He gesticulated freely and spoke in an unctuous, fawning tone.

"I am delighted at the great compliment you pay me by coming here, sir," he said. "When I started this institution five years ago I certainly did not dare to hope that it would so soon win sufficient reputation to entitle it to the honour of inspection by men so eminent in the scientific world as yourself."

The professor listened with a courteous smile but evinced no hurry in replying.

Professor Swelding was certainly a remarkable figure. He might have been sixty, but he bore very lightly the weight of the years that laid their snows upon his thick and curly but startlingly white hair. It was this hair that attracted attention first; it was of extraordinary thickness and was joined on to a heavy moustache and a long and massive beard. He was like a man who might have taken a vow never to cut his hair. It covered his ears and grew low upon his forehead, so that hardly a vestige of the face could be seen, while, further, all the expression of the eyes was concealed behind large blue spectacles. The professor was enveloped in a heavy cloak, in spite of the bright sunshine; evidently he was one of those men from the cold North who do not know what real warmth is and have no idea of what it means to be too thickly clothed. He spoke French correctly, but with a slight accent and a slow enunciation that betrayed a foreign origin.

"I was really anxious, sir, to observe for myself the measures you have taken which have set your institution in the forefront of establishments of the kind," he replied. "I have read with the very greatest interest your various communications to the transactions of learned societies. It is a great advantage for a practitioner like myself to be able to profit by the experience of a savant of your high standing."

A few further compliments were exchanged and then Dr. Biron suggested a visit to the various wards, and led his guest out into the grounds of the institution.

If Dr. Biron did not possess that theoretical knowledge of insanity which has made French alienists famous throughout the world, he was certainly a first-rate organiser. His sanatorium was a model one. It was situated in one of the wealthiest, quietest and airiest quarters of Paris, and stood in a vast enclosure behind high walls; within this enclosure a number of small pavilions were built, all attractive in design, and communicating by broad flights of steps with a beautiful garden studded with trees and shrubs, but further subdivided into a series of little gardens separated from one another by white latticed palings.

"You see, Professor, I rely entirely on the isolation principle. A single block would have involved a deleterious collocation of various types of insanity, so I built this series of small pavilions, where my patients can be segregated according to their type of alienation. The system has great therapeutic advantages, and I am sure it is the explanation of my high percentage of cures."

Professor Swelding nodded approval.

"We apply the system of segregation in Denmark," he said, "but we have never carried it so far as to divide the general grounds. I see that each of your pavilions has its own private garden."

"I regard that as indispensable," Dr. Biron declared. He led his visitor to one of the little gardens, where a man of about fifty was walking about between two attendants. "This man is a megalomaniac," he said: "he believes that he is the Almighty."

"What is your treatment here?" Professor Swelding enquired. "I am aware that the books prescribe isolation, but that is not sufficient by itself."

"I nurse the brain by nursing the body," Dr. Biron replied. "I build up my patient's system by careful attention to hygiene, diet, and rest, and I pretend to ignore his mental alienation. There is always a spark of sound sense in a diseased brain. This man imagines he is the Almighty, but when he is hungry he has to ask for something to eat, and then we pretend to wonder why he has any need to eat if he is the Almighty; he has to concoct some explanation, and very gradually his reasoning power is restored. A man ceases to be insane the moment he begins to comprehend that he is insane."

The Professor followed the doctor, casting curious eyes at the various patients who were walking in their gardens.

"Have you many cures?"

"That is a difficult question to answer," said Dr. Biron. "The statistics are so very different in the different categories of insanity."

"Of course," said Professor Swelding; "but take some particular type of dementia, say, hallucination of persecution. What percentage of cures can you show there?"

"Twenty per cent absolute recoveries, and forty per cent definite improvements," the doctor replied promptly, and as the Professor evinced unmistakable astonishment at so high a percentage, Dr. Biron took him familiarly by the arm and drew him along. "I will show you a patient who actually is to be sent home in a day or two. I believe that she is completely cured, or on the very point of being completely cured."

A woman of about forty was sitting in one of the gardens by the side of an attendant, quietly sewing. Dr. Biron paused to draw his visitor's particular attention to her.

"That lady belongs to one of the best of our great merchant families. She is Mme. Alice Rambert, wife of Etienne Rambert, the rubber merchant. She has been under my care for nearly ten months. When she came here she was in the last stage of debility and anæmia and suffered from the most characteristic hallucination of all: she thought that assassins were all round her. I have built up her physical system, and now I have cured her mind. At the present moment that lady is not mad at all, in the proper sense of the term."

"She never shows any symptoms of reverting to her morbid condition?" Professor Swelding enquired with interest.

"Never."

"And would not, even if violently upset?"

"I do not think so."

"May I talk to her?"

"Certainly," and Dr. Biron led the visitor towards the seat on which the patient was sitting. "Madame Rambert," he said, "may I present Professor Swelding to you? He has heard that you are here and would like to pay his respects."

Mme. Rambert put down her needlework and rose and looked at the Danish professor.

"I am delighted to make the gentleman's acquaintance," she said, "but I should like to know how he was aware of my existence, my dear doctor."

"I regret that I cannot claim to know you, madame," said Professor Swelding, replying for Dr. Biron, "but I know that in addressing you I shall be speaking to the inmate of this institution who will testify most warmly to the scientific skill and the devotion of Dr. Biron."

"At all events," Mme. Rambert replied coldly, "he carries his kindness to the extent of wishing his patients never to be dull, since he brings unexpected visitors to see them."

The phrase was an implicit reproach of Dr. Biron's too ready inclination to exhibit his patients as so many rare and curious wild animals, and it stung him all the more because he was convinced that Mme. Rambert was perfectly sane. He pretended not to hear what she said, giving some order to the attendant, Berthe, who was standing respectfully by.

"I understand, madame," Professor Swelding replied gently. "You object to my visit as an intrusion?"

Mme. Rambert had picked up her work and already was sewing again, but suddenly she sprang up, so abruptly that the professor recoiled, and exclaimed sharply:

"Who called me? Who called me? Who — — "

The Professor was attempting to speak when the patient interrupted him.

"Oh!" she cried, "Alice! Alice! His voice — his voice! Go away! You frighten me! Who spoke? Go away! Oh, help! help!" and she fled screaming towards the far end of the garden, with the attendant and Dr. Biron running after her. With all the cleverness of the insane she managed to elude them, and continued to scream. "Oh, I recognised him! Do go away, I implore you! Go! Murder! Murder!"

The attendant tried to reassure the doctor.

"Don't be frightened, sir. She is not dangerous. I expect the visit from that gentleman has upset her."

The poor demented creature had taken refuge behind a clump of shrubs, and was standing there with eyes dilated with anguish fixed on the Professor and hand pointing to him, trembling in every limb.

"Fantômas!" she cried: "Fantômas! There — I know him! Oh, help!"

The scene was horribly distressing, and Dr. Biron put an end to it by ordering the attendant to take Mme. Rambert to her room and induce her to rest, and to send at once for M. Perret. Then he turned to Professor Swelding.

"I am greatly distressed by this incident, Professor. It proves that the cure of this poor creature is by no means so assured as I had believed. But there are other cases which will not shake your faith in my judgment like this, I hope. Shall we go on?"

Professor Swelding tried to comfort the doctor.

"The brain is a pathetically frail thing," he said. "You could not have a more striking case to prove it: that poor lady, whom you believed to be cured, suddenly having a typical crisis of her form of insanity provoked by — what? Neither you nor I look particularly like assassins, do we?" And he followed Dr. Biron, who was much discomfited, to be shown other matters of interest.

"Better now, madame? Are you going to be good?"

Mme. Rambert was reclining on a sofa in her room, watching her attendant, Berthe, moving about and tidying up the slight disorder caused by her recent ministrations. The patient made a little gesture of despair.

"Poor Berthe!" she said. "If you only knew how unhappy I am, and how sorry for having given way to that panic just now!"

"Oh, that was nothing," said the attendant. "The doctor won't attach any importance to that."

"Yes, he will," said the patient with a weary smile. "I think he will attach importance to it, and in any case it will delay my discharge from this place."

"Not a bit of it, madame. Why, you know they have written to your home to say you are cured?"

Mme. Rambert did not reply for a minute or two. Then she said:

"Tell me, Berthe, what do you understand by the word 'cured'?"

The attendant was rather nonplussed.

"Why, it means that you are better: that you are quite well."

Her patient smiled bitterly.

"It is true that my health is better now, and that my stay here has done me good. But that is not what I was talking about. What is your opinion about my madness?"

"You mustn't think about that," the attendant remonstrated. "You are no more mad than I am."

"Oh, I know the worst symptom of madness is to declare you are not mad," Mme. Rambert answered sadly; "so I will be careful not to say it, Berthe. But, apart from this last panic, the reason for which I cannot tell you, have you ever known me do, or heard me say, anything that was utterly devoid of reason, in all the time that I have been in your charge?"

Struck by the remark, the attendant, in spite of herself, was obliged to confess:

"No, I never have — that is — —"

"That is," Mme. Rambert finished for her, "I have sometimes protested to you that I was the victim of an abominable persecution, and that there was a tragic mystery in my life: in short, that if I was shut up here, it was because someone wanted me to be shut up. Come now, Berthe, has it never occurred to you that perhaps I was telling the truth?"

The attendant had been shaken for a minute by the calm self-possession of her patient; now she resumed her professional manner.

"Don't worry any more, Mme. Rambert, for you know as well as I do that Dr. Biron acknowledges that you are cured now. You are going to leave the place and resume your ordinary life."

"Ah, Berthe," said Mme. Rambert, twisting and untwisting her hands, "if you only knew! Why, if I leave this sanatorium, or rather if the doctor sends me back to my family, I shall certainly be put in some other sanatorium before two days are past! No, it isn't merely an idea that I have got into my head," she went on as the attendant protested. "Listen: during the whole ten months that I have been here, I have never once protested that I was not insane. I was quite glad to be in this place! For I felt safe here. But now I am not sure of that. I must go, but I must not go merely to return to my husband! I must be free, free to go to those who will help me to escape from the horrible trap in which I have spent the last few years of my life!"

Mme. Rambert's earnest tone convinced the attendant in spite of her own instinct.

"Yes?" she said enquiringly.

"I suppose you know that I am rich, Berthe?" Mme. Rambert went on. "I have always been generous to you, and higher fees are paid for me here than are paid for any other patient. Would you like to make sure of your future for ever, and quite easily? I have heard you talk about getting married. Shall I give you a dot? You might lose your situation here, but if you trust me I will make it up to you a hundredfold, if you will help me to escape from this place! And it cannot be too soon! I have not a minute to lose!"

Berthe tried to get away from her patient, but Mme. Rambert held her back, almost by force.

"Tell me your price," she said. "How much do you want? A thousand pounds? Two thousand pounds?" and as the attendant, bewildered by the mere suggestion of such fabulous sums, was silent, Mme. Rambert slipped a diamond ring off her finger and held it out to the young woman. "Take that as proof of my sincerity," she said. "If anybody asks me about it I will say that I have lost it. And from now, Berthe, begin to prepare a way for me to escape! The very night that I am free I swear you shall be a rich woman!"

Berthe got up, swaying, hardly knowing if she was awake or dreaming.

"A rich woman!" she murmured. "A rich woman!" and over the girl's face there suddenly crept a horrible expression of cupidity and desire.

XVI
Among the Market Porters

"Boulevard Rochechouart," said Berthe, the young asylum nurse, to the conductor as she sprang into the tram just as it was starting.

It was a September afternoon, one of the last fine days of the now fast-dying summer, and the girl had just got her fortnightly leave for forty-eight hours. She had gone off duty at noon, and now had until noon on the next day but one to resume her own personality and shake off the anxieties that beset all those who are charged with the constant care of the insane, the most distressing kind of patients that exists. As a general rule Berthe spent her fortnightly holidays with her old grand-parents in their cottage outside Paris, but on this occasion she had elected to remain in the city, influenced thereto by the long conversation she had had with the patient confided to her particular care, No. 25, Mme. Rambert. Since that first talk with her, on the day of Professor Swelding's visit to the asylum, she had had others, and Berthe had now elaborated a plan to enable the supposed lunatic to escape, and had decided to spend her short holiday in bringing the plan to a point.

At the boulevard Rochechouart Berthe got out of the tram, looked around to get her bearings in the somewhat unfamiliar neighbourhood, and then turned into the rue Clignancourt and stood on the left-hand side of the street, looking at the shops. The third one was a wine shop, only the first of many in the street.

Berthe pushed the door of this establishment a little way open and looked at the rather rowdy company gathered round the zinc counter, all with flushed faces and all talking loudly. She did not venture inside, but in a clear voice asked, "Is M. Geoffroy here?" No definite answer was forthcoming, but the men turned round, hearing her enquiry, and seeing her pretty figure began to nudge one another and jest and laugh coarsely. "Come in, missy," said one of them, but already Berthe had quickly closed the door and lightly gone on her way.

A few yards further on there was another bar, and into this, also, Berthe peeped and once more asked, "Is M. Geoffroy here?" adding by way of further explanation, "Hogshead Geoffroy, I mean." This time a roar of laughter followed, and the girl fled, flushed with indignation.

Yet she did not desist from her strange search, and at last, at the sixth shop, her question was answered by a deep bass voice from the far end of a smoke-clouded den. "Hogshead Geoffroy? Here!" and heaving a sigh of relief Berthe went inside the shop.

When you want to see M. "Hogshead" Geoffroy, your procedure is simplicity itself. As he has no known address, all you have to do is to start at the bottom of the rue Clignancourt on the left-hand side, look into every wineshop, and ask, in tones loud enough to be heard above the clatter of conversation, whether Hogshead Geoffroy is there, and it will be mighty bad luck if, at one or other of the bars, you do not hear the answer, "Hogshead Geoffroy? Here," followed immediately by that gentleman's order to the *patronne*: "Half a pint, please: the gentleman will pay!" It is a safe order; the *patronne* knows from past experience that she can serve the half-pint without anxiety: Hogshead Geoffroy rapidly drains it, and then holds out a huge and hairy hand to the visitor and enquires, "Well, what is it?"

If, as often happens, the Hogshead finds himself confronted by a stranger, he feels no surprise; he knows his own popularity, and is a modest soul, so he calls his visitor by his Christian name at once, taps him amicably on the shoulder, and calls him "old boy," and invites him to stand a drink. The Hogshead is an artist in his line; he hires himself out to public halls to announce in his powerful voice, reinforced by a trumpet, the various items on the programme or the results of performances achieved. He also harangues the crowd on behalf of showmen, or hurls threats at too excited demonstrators at public demonstrations. Between whiles he rolls hogsheads down into cellars, or bottles wine, and even drinks it when he is among friends who have money to pay withal.

At sight of Berthe, Hogshead Geoffroy so far departed from custom as not to give an order to the *patronne* at the bar; instead, he rose and went towards the girl and unceremoniously embraced her.

"Ah-ha, little sister, there you are! Why, I was just that moment thinking of you!" He drew her to the back of the shop, towards a bunch of sturdy, square-shouldered fellows drinking there, to whom he introduced her. "Now then, mates, try to behave yourselves; I'm bringing a charming young lady to see you, my sister Berthe, little Bob — Bobinette, as we called her when we lived with the old folks." The girl blushed, a little uneasy at finding herself in such a mixed company, but Hogshead Geoffroy put every one at ease; he put his great hand under Berthe's chin and tilted her head back. "Don't you think she is pretty, this little sister of mine? She's the very spit of her brother!" There was a general roar of laughter. The contrast between the two figures was so great that it seemed impossible there could be any relationship between them: the graceful, slender, tiny *Parisienne* looking tinier still beside the huge colossus of a man six feet high, with the chest of a bull and the shoulders of an athlete. "We don't seem to be built on quite the same lines," M. Geoffroy admitted, "but all the same there is a family likeness!"

The men made room for the girl, and after she had yielded to the general insistence and accepted a glass of white wine, Geoffroy bent forward and spoke in a lower tone.

"Well, what do you want with me?"

"I want to talk to you about something which will interest you, I'm sure," Berthe answered.

"Anything to be got out of it?" was the giant's next enquiry.

Berthe smiled.

"I expect so, or I wouldn't have troubled you."

"Whenever there's any money to be picked up the Hogshead's always on," he replied: "especially just now when things aren't any too bright, though I may tell you I think there's going to be an alteration in that respect."

"Have you got a situation?" Berthe asked in some surprise.

Hogshead Geoffroy laid a finger on his lip.

"It's still a secret," he said, "but there's no harm in talking it over, for everybody here knows all about it," and at interminable length, and with many a pause for libations, he explained that he was a candidate for an appointment as Market Porter. He had been cramming for a fortnight past, in order to emerge triumphantly from the examination to which candidates were always subjected, and that very morning he had sat in the Hôtel de Ville wrestling with nothing less than a problem in arithmetic. In proof, he produced from his pocket a crumpled, greasy and wine-stained sheet of paper scrawled all over with childish writing and figures, and showed it to his sister, immensely proud of the effect he was producing on her. "A problem," he repeated. "See here: two taps fill a tank at the rate of twenty litres a minute, and a third tap empties it at the rate of fifteen hundred litres an hour. How long will it take for the tank to get full?"

A friend of Geoffroy's broke in: it was Mealy Benoît, his most formidable competitor for the appointment.

"And how long will it take for you to get full?" he asked with a great laugh.

Hogshead Geoffroy banged his fist on the table.

"This is a serious conversation," he said, and turned again to his sister, who wanted to know if he had succeeded in finding the answer to the problem. "Maybe," he replied. "I worked by rule of thumb, for, as you know, arithmetic and all those devil's funniments aren't in my line. To sit for an hour, writing at a table in the great hall of the Hôtel de Ville — not much! It made me sweat more than carrying four hundredweight!"

But the company was preparing to make a move. Time was getting on, and at six o'clock the second part of the examination, the physical test, was to be held in the Fish Market. Mealy Benoît had paid his score already, and Hogshead Geoffroy's deferent escort of friends was getting restless. Berthe won fresh favour in her brother's eyes by paying for their refreshments with a ten franc piece and leaving the change to be placed to his credit, and then with him she left the wineshop.

The annual competition for an appointment as Market Porter is held at the end of September. It is a great event. There are generally many candidates, but only two or three, and sometimes less, of the best are picked. The posts are few and good, for the number of porters is limited. The examination is in two parts: one purely intellectual, consisting of some simple problem and a little dictation, the other physical, in which the candidates have to carry a sack of meal weighing three hundredweight a distance of two hundred yards in the shortest time.

At six o'clock punctually the market women were all in their places along the pavement by their respective stalls. The hall was decorated with flags; the salesmen and regular shopmen were provided with chairs, and their assistants were behind them, with the sweepers and criers; at the back stood three or four rows of the general public, all eager to witness the impressive display.

The two-hundred-yard course was carefully cleared, every obstacle having been scrupulously swept off the asphalte, especially pieces of orange-peel, lettuce leaves and bits of rotten veg-etable matter, which might have caused a competitor to slip when trying to break the record for carrying the sack. A high official of the Hôtel de Ville and three of the senior Market Porters formed the jury, and there were also two officials of the Cyclists' Union, expert in the use of stop watches, armed with tested chronometers and deputed to take the exact time of each performance.

The crowd of onlookers was as odd, and eclectic, and keen, as can possibly be imagined. Berthe, who knew that false modesty is quite out of place in popular gatherings, mingled freely in the general conversation. Among other picturesque types she had noticed one particularly extraordinary individual who, although he was in the last row of all, overtopped the rest by quite half of his body, being perched on an antiquated tricycle, which provoked the hilarity of the mob.

"What ho, Bouzille!" somebody called out, for the man was a well-known and popular figure, and everybody knew his name. "Is that Methuselah's tricycle that you have pinched?" and to some of the sallies the fellow replied with a smile that was almost lost in his matted beard, and to others with a jest uttered in the purest dialect of Auvergne.

Someone spoke softly in Berthe's ear and she turned and saw a sturdy fellow of about twenty-five, wearing a blue blouse, a red handkerchief round his neck, and a drover's cap; he was a well-built, powerful man, and in spite of his humble dress, had an intelligent face and an al-most distinguished manner. Berthe responded amiably, and a few commonplace remarks were exchanged between the two.

"In case you care to know, my name's Julot," said the man.

And Berthe replied frankly, but without otherwise compromising herself.

"And I am Bob, or Bobinette, whichever you like. I am Hogshead Geoffroy's sister," she added with a little touch of pride.

A murmur ran round the crowd. Mealy Benoît was going through his trial. The great fellow came along with rapid, rhythmical step, with supple limbs and chest hunched forward. Surely balanced on his broad shoulders and the nape of his neck was an enormous sack of meal, ac-curately weighed to scale three hundredweight. Without the least hesitation or slackening of pace, he covered the two hundred yards, reaching the goal perfectly fresh and fit; he stood for a moment or two in front of the judges, displaying the mighty muscles of his naked chest, over which the perspiration was running, and evincing genuine delight in not freeing himself from his heavy burden at the earliest possible moment. The applause was enthusiastic and immediate, but silence quickly fell again and all eyes turned towards the starting-post. It was Hogshead Geoffroy's turn.

The giant was really a splendid sight. Instead of walking as his rival had done, he began to step like a gymnast, and the crowd yelled their delight. It seemed that he must beat his rival's time easily, but all at once the great sack on his shoulders was seen to shake, and Geoffroy almost stopped, uttering a heavy groan before he got going again. The crowd looked on in surprise: where he had just set his feet there was a wet mark upon the asphalte: Geoffroy had slipped on a piece of orange-peel. But he managed to restore the equilibrium of the sack, and, taught caution by the risk he had just run, he finished the course with measured steps.

Two hours later the result of the competition was announced. Hogshead Geoffroy and Mealy Benoît were bracketed equal, having taken exactly the same time to cover the course; upon the result of the written examination would depend the final issue, and the matter was all the more important because this year there was but one vacancy for a Market Porter.

Berthe, or Bobinette, was vehemently discussing with her neighbours the mishap that had befallen Geoffroy during his trial. A man dressed in a shabby black overcoat buttoned up to the chin, and wearing a kind of jockey cap on his greasy hair, was watching her intently, seeming to agree with all she said while really interested in something else. Berthe, who was very intent upon the matter in hand, did not notice this individual's manner; it was Julot, her faithful squire for the last two hours, who got her away.

"Come," he said, taking her by the sleeve, "you know your brother is waiting for you," and as she yielded to his insistence he whispered in her ear, "That chap's a dirty-looking rascal: I don't think much of him!"

"He certainly is uncommonly ugly," the girl admitted, and then like the trained nurse that she was, she added, "and did you notice his complexion? The man must be ill: he is absolutely green!"

XVII
At the Saint-Anthony's Pig

"Pay for a drink, and I'll listen to you," said Hogshead Geoffroy to his sister.

After numerous visits to the many bars and drinking saloons that surround the markets, they had finally gone for a late supper into the Saint-Anthony's Pig, the most popular tavern in the neighbourhood, Geoffroy having reconciled himself to waiting for the result of the examination, which would not be announced until the following day.

A new and original attraction had been stationed outside the Saint-Anthony's Pig for the last few days. After the formal enquiries succeeding his discovery of the drowned body in the river, Bouzille had come to Paris to see the Eiffel Tower. He had met with but a week's delay in his itinerary, having been locked up for that time at Orleans for some trifling misdemeanour.

On entering the capital, Bouzille's extraordinary equipage had caused quite a sensation, and as the worthy fellow, with utter disregard of the heavy traffic in the city, had careered about in it through the most crowded streets, he had very soon been run in and taken to the nearest lock-up. His train had been confiscated for forty-eight hours, but as there was nothing really to be objected against the tramp, he had merely been requested to make himself scarce, and not to do it again.

Bouzille did not quite know what to make of it all. But while he was towing his two carriages behind his tricycle towards the Champ-de-Mars, from which point he would at last be able to contemplate the Eiffel Tower, he had fallen in with the editor of the *Auto*, to whom, in exchange for a bottle of wine at the next café, he had ingenuously confided his story. A sensational article about the globe-trotting tramp appeared in the next number of that famous sporting journal, and Bouzille woke to find himself famous. The next thing that happened was that François Bonbonne, the proprietor of the Saint-Anthony's Pig, shrewdly foreseeing that this original character with his remarkable equipage would furnish a singular attraction, engaged him to station himself outside the establishment from eleven to three every night, in return for his board and lodging and a salary of five francs a day.

It need not be said that Bouzille had closed with the offer. But getting tired of cooling his heels on the doorstep, he had gradually taken to leaving his train on the pavement and himself going down into the basement hall, where he generously returned his five francs every night to the proprietor, in exchange for potations to that amount.

In the basement of the Saint-Anthony's Pig the atmosphere was steadily getting cloudier, and the noise louder. The time was about a quarter to two. The "swells," and the young men about town who went to have a bowl of onion soup at the popular café because that was the latest correct thing to do, had withdrawn. The few pale and shabby dancers had given their show, and in another ten minutes, when the wealthy customers had departed, the supper room would resume its natural appearance and everybody would be at home. François Bonbonne had just escorted the last toffs up the narrow corkscrew staircase that led from the basement to the ground-floor, and now he stood, his stout person entirely filling the only exit, unctuously suggesting that perhaps somebody would like to give an order for a hot wine salad.

Berthe was sitting in a corner beside her brother, whom the warmth of the room and his numerous potations had rendered drowsy, and thinking it an opportune moment to tell him of her scheme, before he became talkative or quarrelsome, she began to explain.

"There's nothing much to do, but I want a strong man like you."

"Any barrels to roll anywhere?" he enquired in a thick voice.

Berthe shook her head, her glance meanwhile resting mechanically on a small young man with a budding beard and a pale face, who had just taken a seat opposite her and was timidly ordering a portion of sauerkraut.

"I want some bars removed from a window; they are iron bars set in stone, but the stone is worn and the bars are very rusty, and anybody with a little strength could wrench them out."

"And that's all?" Geoffroy enquired suspiciously.

"Yes, that's all."

"Then I shall be very glad to help you: I suppose it will be worth something, won't it?" He broke off short, noticing that a man sitting close by seemed to be listening attentively to the conversation. Berthe followed his eyes, and then turned with a smile to her brother.

"That's all right; don't mind; I know that man," and in proof of the statement she held out a friendly hand to the individual who seemed to be spying upon them. "Good evening again, M. Julot: how are you, since I saw you just now? I did not notice you were here."

Julot shook hands with her and without evincing any further interest in her, went on with the conversation he was having with his own companion, a clean-shaven fellow.

"Go on, Billy Tom," he said in low tones. "Tell me what has happened."

"Well, there has been the devil to pay at the Royal Palace, owing to that — — accident, you know; of course I was not mixed up in it in any way: I'm only interpreter, and I stick to my own job. But three weeks after the affair, Muller was suddenly kicked out, owing to the door having been opened for the chap who worked the robbery."

"Muller, Muller?" said Julot, seeming to be searching his memory. "Who is Muller?"

"Why, the watchman on the second floor."

"Oh, ah, yes; and who turned him out?"

"I think his name is Juve."

"Oh — ho!" Julot muttered to himself. "I thought as much!"

There was a noise at the entrance of the hall, and down the corkscrew staircase came two people who, judging by the greeting they received, were very popular: Ernestine, a well-known figure, and Mealy Benoît, who was very drunk.

Benoît lurched from one table to another, leaning on every head and pair of shoulders that came his way, and reached an empty seat on a lounge into which he crushed, half squashing the pale young man with the budding beard. The lad made no protest, seeming to be afraid of his neighbour's bulk, but merely wriggled sideways and tried to give the new-comer all the room he wanted. Benoît did not seem even to notice the humble little fellow, but Ernestine took pity on him and assured him that she would look after him.

"All right, sonny," she said, "Mealy won't squash you; and if he tries any of his games on you, Ernestine will look after you." She took his head between her two hands and kissed his forehead affectionately, ignoring Mealy Benoît's angry protests. "He's a dear little chap: I like him," she said to the company at large. "What's your name, deary?"

The boy blushed to the tips of his ears.

"Paul," he murmured.

But François Bonbonne the proprietor, with his usual keen eye to business, arrived just then and set down before Mealy Benoît the famous hot wine salad of which he had spoken before. Behind Bonbonne came Bouzille, who had left his turn-out on the pavement and come down into the supper room to eat and drink his five francs, and more if credit could be got.

Benoît caught sight of Hogshead Geoffroy and immediately offered to clink glasses with him; he pushed a glass towards him, inviting him to dip it with the rest into the steaming bowl; but Geoffroy was warming up under the influence of alcohol, and broke into a sudden flame of wrath at sight of Mealy Benoît. If Benoît should be given the first place, it would be a rank injustice, he reflected, for he, Geoffroy, was most certainly the stronger man. And besides, the sturdy Hogshead was beginning to wonder whether his rival might not have devised an odious plot against him and put the famous piece of orange-peel upon the track, but for which Geoffroy would have won hands down. So Geoffroy, very drunk, offered Benoît, who was no whit more sober, the gross affront of refusing to clink glasses with him!

"Why, it's you!" exclaimed Bouzille, in ringing tones of such glad surprise that everybody turned round to see whom he was addressing. Julot and Berthe looked with the rest.

"Why, it's the green man of just now," said the asylum nurse to her companion, and he assented, moodily enough.

"Yes, it's him right enough."

Bouzille took no notice of the attention he had provoked, and did not seem to notice that the green man appeared to be anything but pleased at having been recognised.

"I've seen you before, I know," he went on; "where have I met you?"

The green man did not answer; he affected to be engrossed in a most serious conversation with the friend he had brought with him into the supper room, a shabby individual who carried a guitar. But Bouzille was not to be put off, and suddenly he exclaimed, with perfect indifference to what his neighbours might think:

"I know: you are the tramp who was arrested with me down there in Lot! The day of that murder — you know — the murder of the Marquise de Langrune!"

Bouzille in his excitement had caught the green man by the sleeve, but the green man impatiently shook him off, growling angrily.

"Well, and what about it?"

For some minutes now Hogshead Geoffroy and Mealy Benoît had been exchanging threatening glances. Geoffroy had given voice to his suspicions, and kind friends had not failed to report his words to Benoît. Inflamed with drink as they were, the two men were bound to come to blows before long, and a dull murmur ran through the room heralding the approaching altercation. Berthe, anxious on her brother's behalf, and a little frightened on her own, did all she could to induce Geoffroy to come away, but even though she promised to pay for any number of drinks elsewhere, he refused to budge from the bench where he was sitting hunched up in a corner.

When at length he got rid of Bouzille and his exasperating garrulity, the green man resumed his conversation with his friend with the guitar.

"It's rather odd that he hasn't a trace of accent," the latter remarked.

"Oh, it's nothing for a fellow like Gurn to speak French like a Frenchman," said the green man in a low tone; then he stopped nervously. Ernestine was walking about among the company, chatting to one and another and getting drinks, and he fancied that she was listening to what he said.

But another duologue rose audible in another part of the room.

"If the gentleman would like to show his strength there's someone ready to take him on."

Hogshead Geoffroy had thrown down his glove!

Silence fell upon the room. It was Mealy Benoît's turn to answer. At that precise moment, however, Benoît was draining the salad bowl. He slowly swallowed the last of the red liquid — one can't do two things at once — laid the bowl down, empty, on the table, and in thundering, dignified tones demanded another, wiped his lips on the back of his sleeve, and turned his huge head towards the corner where Geoffroy was hunched up, saying, "Will the gentleman kindly repeat his last remark?"

Ernestine moved furtively to Julot's side, and affecting to be interested only in the argument going on between Geoffroy and Benoît, said without looking at him:

"The pale man, with the greenish complexion, said to the man with the guitar, 'It's he, all right, because of the burn in the palm of his hand.'"

Julot choked back an oath, and instinctively clenched his fist, but Ernestine already had moved on and was huskily chaffing the young man with the budding beard. Julot sat with sombre face and angry eyes, only replying in curt monosyllables to the occasional remarks of his next neighbour, Billy Tom. Marie, the waitress, was passing near him and he signed to her to stop.

"Say, Marie," he said, nodding towards the window that was behind him, "what does that window open on to?"

The girl thought for a moment.

"On to the cellar," she said; "this hall is in the basement."

"And the cellar," Julot went on; "how do you get out of that?"

"You can't," the servant answered; "there's no door; you have to come through here."

Momentarily becoming more uneasy, Julot scrutinised the long tunnel of a room at the extreme end of which he was sitting; there was only one means of egress, up the narrow corkscrew staircase leading to the ground-floor, and at the very foot of that staircase was the table occupied by the green man and the man with the guitar.

A plate aimed by Hogshead Geoffroy at Mealy Benoît crashed against the opposite wall. Everyone jumped to his feet, the women screaming, the men swearing. The two market porters stood confronting one another, Hogshead Geoffroy brandishing a chair, Benoît trying to wrench the marble top from a table to serve as a weapon. The mêlée became general, plates smashing on the floor, and dinner things flying towards the ceiling.

Suddenly a shot rang out, but quickly though it had been fired, the green man and the man with the guitar had seen who fired it. For the last few minutes, indeed, these two mysterious individuals had never taken their eyes off Julot.

Julot, whom Berthe had supposed from his appearance to be an honest cattle-drover, was undoubtedly a wonderful shot. Having observed that the room was lighted by a single chandelier composed of three electric lamps, and that the current was supplied by only two wires running along the cornice, Julot had taken aim at the wires and cut them clean in two with a single shot!

Immediately following upon the shot, the room was plunged into absolute darkness. A perfectly incredible uproar ensued, men and women struggling together and shouting and trampling one another down, and crockery and dinner things crashing down from the side-boards and tables on to the floor.

Above the din a sudden hoarse cry of pain rang out, "Help!" and simultaneously Berthe, who was lost among the mob, heard a muttered exclamation in her ear and felt two hands groping all over her body as if trying to identify her. The young nurse was the only woman in the room wearing a hat. Half swooning with terror, she felt herself picked up and thrust upon a bench, and then someone whispered in a vinous voice: "You are not to help no. 25, the Rambert woman, to escape."

Berthe was so utterly astonished that she overcame her fright sufficiently to stammer out a question:

"But what — but who — — ?"

Lower still, but yet more peremptorily, the voice became audible again.

"Fantômas forbids you to do it! And if you disobey, you die!"

The nurse dropped back upon the bench half fainting with fright, and the row in the supper room grew worse. Three men were fighting now, the green man being at grips with two at once. The green man did not seem to feel the blows rained on him, but with a strength that was far beyond the ordinary he gripped hold of an arm and slid his hands along the sleeve, never letting go of the arm, until he reached the wrist, when wrenching open the clenched fist he slipped his fingers on to the palm of the hand. A little exclamation of triumph escaped him, and simultaneously the owner of the hand uttered an exclamation of pain, for the green man's fingers had touched a still raw wound upon the hollow of the palm.

But at that instant his leg was caught between two powerful knees, and the slightest pressure more would have broken it. The green man was forced to let go the hand he held; he fell to the ground with his adversary upon him, and for a moment thought that he was lost. But at the same moment his adversary let go of him in turn, having been taken by surprise by yet a third combatant who joined in the fray and separated the first two, devoting himself to a furious assault upon the man whom the green man had tried to capture. The green man passed a rapid hand over the individual who had just rescued him from the fierce assault, and was conscious of a shock of surprise as he identified the young man with the budding beard; thereupon he collared him firmly by the neck and did not let him go.

In the crush the combatants had been forced towards the staircase, and at this narrow entrance into the hall bodies were being trampled underfoot and piercing screams rent the air. François Bonbonne had not made the least attempt to interfere. He knew exactly the proper procedure when trouble of this sort broke out, and he had gone to the corner of the street and sent the constable on duty there to the nearest police station for help. Directly the first gendarmes arrived, François Bonbonne led them behind the counter in the shop and showed them the fire hose; with the skill acquired by long practice, they rapidly unrolled the pipe, introduced it into the narrow mouth of the staircase, turned on the tap, and proceeded to drench everybody in the supper room below.

The unexpected sousing pulled the combatants up short, separated all the champions, and drove the howling and shrieking mob back to the far end of the room. The operation lasted for a good five minutes, and when the gendarmes considered that the customers of the Saint-Anthony's Pig were sufficiently quieted down, the sergeant threw the light of a lantern, which the proprietor obligingly had ready for him, over the supper room, and peremptorily ordered the company to come up, one by one.

Seeing that resistance would be futile, the company obeyed. As they slowly emerged at the top of the corkscrew staircase, meek and subdued, the gendarmes at the top arrested them, slipped handcuffs on them, and sent them off in couples to the station. When the sergeant assumed that every one had come out, he went down into the supper room, just to make sure that nobody was still hiding there. But the room was not quite empty. One unfortunate man was lying on the floor, bathed in his own blood. It was the man with the guitar, and a knife had been driven through his breast!

The couple consisting of the green man and the young man with the budding beard, of whom his companion had never once let go since identifying him during the fight in the supper room, were taken to the station. The clerk, who was taking down the names of the prisoners, with difficulty repressed an exclamation of surprise when the green man produced an identification card, and whispered a few words in his ear.

"Release that gentleman at once," said the clerk. "With regard to the other —— "

"With regard to the other," the green man broke in, "kindly release him too. I want to keep him with me."

The clerk bowed in consent, and both men were immediately released from their handcuffs. The young man stared in astonishment at the individual who a minute before had been his companion in bonds, and was about to thank him, but the other grasped him firmly by the wrist, as though to warn him of the impossibility of flight, and led him out of the police station. In the street they met the sergeant with a gendarme bringing in the unfortunate man with the guitar, who was just breathing, and in whom the officials had recognised a detective-inspector. Without letting go of the youth, the green man bent forward to the sergeant and had a brief but animated conversation with him.

"Yes, sir, that's all," the sergeant said respectfully; "I haven't anyone else."

The green man stamped his foot in wrath.

"Good Lord! Gurn has got away!"

Towards the rue Montmartre the green man rapidly dragged his companion, who was trembling in every limb, and utterly at a loss to guess what the future held in store for him. Suddenly the green man halted, just under the light of a street lamp outside the church of Saint-Eustache. He stood squarely in front of his prisoner and looked him full in the eyes.

"I am Juve," he said, "the detective!" and as the young man stared at him in silent dismay, Juve went on, emphasising each of his words, and with a sardonic smile flickering over his face. "And you, Mademoiselle Jeanne — you are Charles Rambert!"

XVIII
A Prisoner and a Witness

Juve had spoken in a tone of command that brooked no reply. His keen eyes seemed to pierce through Paul and read his inmost soul. The winking light of the street lamp shed a wan halo round the lad, who obviously wanted to move away from its radius, but Juve held him fast.

"Come now, answer! You are Charles Rambert, and you were Mademoiselle Jeanne?"

"I don't understand," Paul declared.

"Really!" sneered Juve. He hailed a passing cab. "Get in," he ordered briefly, and pushing the lad in before him he gave an address to the driver, entered the cab and shut the door. Juve sat there rubbing his hands as if well pleased with his night's work. For several minutes he remained silent, and then turned to his companion.

"You think it is clever to deny it," he remarked, "but do you imagine it isn't obvious to anyone that you are Charles Rambert, and that you were disguised as Mademoiselle Jeanne?"

"But you are wrong," Paul insisted. "Charles Rambert is dead."

"So you know that, do you? Then you admit that you know whom I am talking about?"

The lad coloured and began to tremble. Juve looked out of the window, pretending not to notice him, and smiled gently. Then he went on in a friendly tone. "But you know it's stupid to deny what can't be denied. Besides, you should remember that if I know you are Charles Rambert I must know something else as well; and therefore — — "

"Well, yes," Paul acknowledged, "I *am* Charles Rambert, and I was disguised as Mademoiselle Jeanne. How did you know it? Why were you at the Saint-Anthony's Pig? Had you come to arrest me? And where are you taking me now — to prison?"

Juve shrugged his shoulders.

"You want to know too much, my boy. Besides, you ought to know Paris, and so ought to be able to guess where I told the driver to go, merely by looking at the streets we are passing through."

"That is exactly what frightens me," Charles Rambert replied. "We are on the quays, near the Law Courts."

"And the Police Station, my son. Quite so. Now it's quite useless to make a scene: you will gain nothing by attempting to get away. You are in the hands of justice, or rather in my hands, which is not quite the same thing, so come quietly. That is really good advice!"

A few minutes later the cab stopped at the Tour Pointue which has such melancholy associations for so many criminals. Juve alighted and made his companion alight as well, paid the driver, and walked up the staircase to the first floor of the building. It was daylight now, and the men were coming on duty; all of them saluted Juve as he walked along with his trembling captive. The detective went down one long passage, turned into another, and opened a door.

"Go in there," he ordered curtly.

Charles Rambert obeyed, and found himself in a small room the nature of which he recognised immediately from the furniture it contained. It was the measuring room of the anthropometric service. So what he feared was about to happen: Juve was going to lock him up!

But the detective called out in a loud tone: "Hector, please!" and one of the men who remained on duty in the department, in case they were required by any of the detective inspectors to find the records of any previously convicted criminal, came hurrying in.

"Ah, M. Juve, and with a bag too! So early! You think he has been here before?"

"No," said Juve in a dry tone that put a stop to further indiscreet questions. "I don't want you to look up my companion's record, but to take his measurements, and very carefully too."

The man was somewhat surprised at the order, for it was not usual to be asked to do such work at so very early an hour. He was rather irritable too at being disturbed from the rest he was enjoying, and it was very curtly that he spoke to Charles Rambert.

"Come here, please: the standard first: take off your boots."

Charles Rambert obeyed and stood under the standard of measurement, and then, as the assistant ordered him, he submitted to having his fingers smeared with ink so that his finger prints might be taken, to being photographed, full face and in profile, and finally to having the width of his head, from ear to ear, measured with a special pair of caliper compasses.

Hector was surprised by his docility.

"I must say your friend is not very talkative, M. Juve. What has he been up to?" and as the detective merely shrugged his shoulders and did not reply, he went on: "That's done, sir. We will develop the negatives and take the prints, and recopy the measurements, and the record shall be classified in the register in a couple of hours."

Charles Rambert grew momentarily more scared. He felt that he was definitely arrested now. But Juve left the arm-chair in which he had been resting, and coming up to him laid his hand upon his shoulder, speaking the while with a certain gentleness.

"Come: there are some other points as to which I wish to examine you." He led him from the anthropometric room along a dark corridor, and presently taking a key from his pocket, opened a door and pushed the lad in before him. "Go in there," he said. "This is where we make the dynamometer tests."

A layman looking round the room might almost have supposed that it was merely some carpenter's shop. Pieces of wood, of various shapes and sizes and sorts, were arranged along the wall or laid upon the floor; in glass cases were whole heaps of strips of metal, five or six inches long, and of varying thickness.

Juve closed the door carefully behind him.

"For pity's sake, M. Juve, tell me what you are going to do with me," Charles Rambert implored.

The detective smiled.

"Well, there you ask a question which I can't answer off-hand. What am I going to do with you, eh? That still depends upon a good many things."

As he spoke Juve tossed his hat aside and, looking at a rather high kind of little table, proceeded to remove from it a grey cloth which protected it from dust, and drew it into the middle of the room. This article was composed of a metal body screwed on to a strong tripod, with a lower tray that moved backwards and forwards, and two lateral buttresses with a steel cross-piece firmly bolted on to them above. Upon this framework were two dynamometers worked by an ingenious piece of mechanism. Juve looked at Charles Rambert and explained.

"This is Dr. Bertillon's effraction dynamometer. I am going to make use of it to find out at once whether you are or are not deserving of some little interest. I don't want to tell you more just at present." Juve slipped into a specially prepared notch a thin strip of wood, which he had selected with particular care from one of the heaps of material arranged along the wall. From a chest he took a tool which Charles Rambert, who had had some intimate experience of late with the light-fingered community, immediately recognised as a jemmy. "Take hold of that," said Juve, and as Charles took it in his hand he added: "Now put the jemmy into this groove, and press with all your force. If you can move that needle to a point which I know, and which it is difficult but not impossible to reach, you may congratulate yourself on being in luck."

Stimulated by this encouragement from the detective, Charles Rambert exerted all his force upon the lever, only afraid that he might not be strong enough. Juve stopped him very soon.

"That's all right," he said, and substituting a strip of sheet-iron for the strip of wood, he handed another tool to the lad. "Now try again."

A few seconds later Juve took a magnifying lens, and closely examined both the strip of metal and the strip of wood. He gave a little satisfied click with his tongue, and seemed to be very pleased.

"Charles Rambert," he remarked, "I think we are going to do a very good morning's work. Dr. Bertillon's new apparatus is an uncommonly useful invention."

The detective might have gone on with his congratulatory monologue had not an attendant come into the room at that moment.

"Ah, there you are, M. Juve: I have been looking for you everywhere. There is someone asking for you who says he knows you will receive him. I told him this was not the proper time, but he was so insistent that I promised to bring you his card. Besides, he says you have given him an appointment."

Juve took the card and glanced at it.

"That's all right," he said. "Take the gentleman into the parlour and tell him I will be with him in a minute." The attendant went out and Juve looked at Charles Rambert with a smile. "You are played out," he said; "before we do anything else common humanity requires that you should get some rest. Come, follow me; I will take you to a room where you can throw yourself on a sofa and get a sleep for a good hour at least while I go and see this visitor." He led the lad into a small waiting-room, and as Charles Rambert obediently stretched himself upon the sofa, Juve looked at the pale and nervous and completely silent boy, and said with even greater gentleness: "There, go to sleep; sleep quietly, and presently —— "

Juve left the room, and called a man to whom he gave an order in a low tone.

"Stay with that gentleman, please. He is a friend of mine, but a friend, you understand, who must not leave this place. I am going to see some one, but I will come up again presently," and Juve hurried downstairs to the parlour.

The visitor rose as the door opened, and Juve made a formal bow.

"M. Gervais Aventin?" he said.

"M. Gervais Aventin," that gentleman replied. "And you are Detective-Inspector Juve?"

"I am, sir," the detective answered, and pointing his visitor to a chair he took a seat himself at a small table littered with official documents.

"Sir," Juve began, "I ventured to send you that pressing invitation to come to Paris to-day, because from enquiries I had made about you, I was sure that you were a man with a sense of duty, who would not resent being put to inconvenience when it was a question of co-operating in a work of justice and of truth."

The visitor, a man of perhaps thirty, of somewhat fashionable appearance and careful though quiet dress, manifested much surprise.

"Enquiries about me, sir? And pray, why? I must confess that I was very much astonished when I received your letter informing me that the famous Detective-Inspector Juve wished to see me, and at first I suspected some practical joke. On consideration I decided to obey your summons without further pressing, but I did not imagine that you would have made any enquiries about me. How do you know me, may I ask?"

Juve smiled.

"Is it the fact," he enquired, instead of replying directly, for like the good detective that he was, intensely keen on his work, he enjoyed mystifying people with whom he conversed, "is it the fact that your name is Gervais Aventin? A civil engineer? The possessor of considerable private means? About to be married? And that lately you made a short journey to Limoges?"

The young man nodded and smiled.

"Your information is perfectly correct in every particular. But I do not yet understand what crime of mine can have subjected me to these enquiries on your part."

Juve smiled again.

"I wondered, sir, why you vouchsafed no answer to the local enquiries which have been made at my instance, to the advertisements which I have had inserted in the papers, in which I discreetly made it known that the police wanted to get into communication with all the passengers who travelled first class, in the slow train from Paris to Luchon, on the night of the 23rd of December last."

This time the young man looked anxious.

"Great Scott!" he exclaimed, "are you in the employment of my future father-in-law?"

Juve burst into a roar of laughter.

"First acknowledge that you did travel by that train on that night: that you got into it at Vierzon, where you live and where you are going to be married; and that you were going to

Limoges to see a lady — and that you did not want your fiancée's family to know anything about it."

Gervais Aventin pulled himself together.

"I had no idea that the official police undertook espionage of that sort," he said rather drily. "But it is true, sir, that I went to Limoges — my last post before I was appointed to Vierzon — to take a final farewell to a lady. But since you are so accurately informed about all this, since you even know what train I went by, a train I deliberately chose because in little places like Vierzon so much notice is taken of people who travel by the express, you must also know — —"

Juve checked him with a wave of the hand.

"A truce to jesting," he said; "excuse me, sir, I was only amusing myself by observing once more how quickly decent people, who have a little peccadillo on their conscience, are disturbed when they think they have been found out. Your love affairs do not matter to me, sir; I don't want to know if you have a lady friend, or not. The information I want from you is of a very different nature. Tell me simply this: in what circumstances did you make that journey? What carriage did you get into? Who travelled with you in that carriage? I am asking you because, sir, I have every reason to believe that you travelled that night with a murderer who committed a crime of particular atrocity, and I think you may be able to give me some interesting information."

The young man, who had been looking grave, smiled once more.

"I would rather have that than an enquiry into my defunct love affairs. Well, sir, I got into the train at Vierzon, into a first-class carriage — —"

"What kind of carriage?"

"One of the old-fashioned corridor carriages; that is to say, not a corridor communicating with the other carriages, but a single carriage with four compartments, two in the middle opening on to the corridor, and two at the ends communicating with the corridor by a small door."

"I know," said Juve; "the lavatory is in the centre, and the end compartments are like the ordinary noncorridor compartments, except that they have only seven seats, and also have the little door communicating with the narrow passage down one side of the carriage."

"That's it. I got into the smoking compartment at the end."

"Don't go too quick," said Juve. "Tell me whom you saw in the various compartments. Let us go even farther back. You were on the platform, waiting for the train; it came in; what happened then?"

"You want to be very precise," Gervais Aventin remarked. "Well, when the train pulled up I looked for the first-class carriage; it was a few yards away from me, and the corridor was alongside the platform. I got into the corridor and wanted to choose my compartment. I remember clearly that I went first to the rear compartment, the last one in the carriage. I could not get into that, for the door opening into it from the corridor was locked."

"That is correct," Juve nodded. "I know from the guard that that compartment was empty. What did you do then?"

"I turned back and, passing the ladies' compartment and the lavatory, decided to take my seat in the one next it communicating with the corridor. But luck was against me: a pane of glass was broken and it was bitterly cold there; so I had to fall back on the only compartment left, the smoking one towards the front of the train."

"Were there many of you there?"

"I thought at first that I was going to have a fellow-traveller, for there was some luggage and a rug arranged on the seat. But the passenger must have been in the lavatory, for I didn't see him. I lay down on the other seat and went to sleep. When I got out of the train at Limoges, my fellow-traveller must have been in the lavatory again, for I remember quite distinctly that he was not on the opposite seat. I thought at the time how easy it would have been for me to steal his luggage and walk off with his valise: nobody would have seen me."

Juve had listened intently to every word of the story. He asked for one further detail with a certain anxiety in his tone.

"Tell me, sir, when you woke up did you have any impression that the baggage arranged on the seat opposite yours had been disturbed at all? Might the traveller, whom you did not see, have come in for a sleep while you yourself were asleep?"

Gervais Aventin made a little gesture of uncertainty.

"I can't answer in the affirmative, M. Juve. I did not notice that; and, besides, when I got into the compartment, the shade was pulled down over the lamp, and the curtains were drawn across the windows. I hardly saw how the things were arranged. And then, when I got out at Limoges I was in a hurry, and only thought about finding my ticket and jumping on to the platform. But I do not think the other fellow did take his place while I was asleep. I did not hear a sound, and yet I did not sleep at all heavily."

"So you travelled in a first-class compartment in the slow train from Paris to Luchon on the night of the 23rd of December, and in that compartment there was the luggage of a traveller whom you did not see — who may not have been there?"

"Yes," said Gervais Aventin, and, as the detective sat silent for a moment, he enquired: "Is my information too vague to be of any use to you?"

Juve was wondering inwardly why the dickens Etienne Rambert was not in that compartment when, according to the depositions of the guard, he must have been there; but he said nothing of this. Instead, he said:

"Your information is most valuable, sir. You have told me everything I wanted to know."

Gervais Aventin displayed still more surprise.

"Well," he said, "by way of return, M. Juve, tell me something which puzzles me. How did you know I travelled by that train that night?"

The detective drew out his pocket-book, and from an inner pocket produced a first-class ticket, which he held out to the engineer.

"That is very simple," he replied. "Here is your ticket. I wanted to know exactly who everyone was who travelled in that first-class compartment, so I sent for all the first-class tickets which were given up by passengers who left the train at the different stations. That's how I got yours: it had been issued at Vierzon, the station where you got in, so I interrogated the clerk at the booking-office who gave me a description of you; then I sent down an inspector to Vierzon to make discreet enquiries, and he got me all the information I required. All I had to do then was to write and ask you to come here to-day; and the regrettable story of your broken relations with the lady was an ample guarantee to me that you would be punctual at the appointment!"

Whistling a quick-step, sure sign with him of a light heart, Juve opened the door of the little room where he had left Charles Rambert, and looked at the sleeping lad.

"It's a fine thing to be young," he remarked to the man he had left on guard; "that boy plunges into the wildest adventures and shaves the scaffold by an inch, and yet after one late night he sleeps as peacefully as any chancellor of the Legion of Honour!" He shook the lad with a friendly hand. "Get up, lazy-bones! It's ten o'clock: high time for me to carry you off."

"Where to?" the unhappy boy asked, rubbing his eyes.

"There's no doubt about inquisitiveness being your besetting sin," Juve replied cryptically. "Well, we've got a quarter of an hour's drive in front of us. But you're not going to prison; I'm going to take you home with me!"

Juve had taken off his collar and tie and put on an old jacket, had set a great bowl of bread and milk in front of Charles Rambert, and was leisurely enjoying his own breakfast.

"I didn't want to answer any questions just now," he said, "because I hate talking in cabs where I have to sit by a man's side, and can't see him or hear half he says. But now that we are snug and comfortable here, I've no right to keep you waiting any longer, and I'll give you a bit of good news."

"Snug" and "comfortable" were the right words with which to describe Juve's private abode. The detective had attained an honourable and lucrative position in his profession, and, exposed as he was in the course of his work to all manner of dangers and privations, had compensated himself by making an entirely satisfactory, if not luxurious, nest where he could rest after his labours.

When he had finished his breakfast he lighted a big cigar and sank into an easy chair, crossing his hands behind his head. He turned a steady gaze upon Charles Rambert, who was still completely puzzled, and half frightened by this sudden amiability, and did not know whether he was a prisoner or not.

"I will give you a bit of good news; that is, that you are innocent of the Langrune affair when you were Charles Rambert, and innocent also of the Danidoff affair, when you were Mademoiselle Jeanne. I need not say anything about the scrap last night, in which you played a still more distinguished part."

"Why tell me that?" asked Charles Rambert nervously. "Of course I know I did not rob Princess Sonia Danidoff; but how did you recognise me last night, and how did you find out that I was Mademoiselle Jeanne?"

Juve smiled, and shook back a lock of hair that was falling over his eyes.

"Listen, my boy: do you suppose that thundering blow you dealt the excellent Henri Verbier when he was making love to Mademoiselle Jeanne, could fail to make me determined to find out who that young lady was who had the strength of a man?"

The allusion made Charles Rambert most uneasy.

"But that does not explain how you recognised me in Paul to-night. I recognised you in Henri Verbier at the hotel, but I had no idea that it was you last night."

"That's nothing," said Juve with a shake of the head. "And you may understand once for all that when I have once looked anybody square in the face, he needs to be an uncommonly clever fellow to escape me afterwards by means of any disguise. You don't know how to make up, but I do; and that's why I took you in and you did not take me in."

"What makes you believe I did not rob Princess Sonia Danidoff?" Charles Rambert asked after a pause. "I am quite aware that everything points to my having been the thief."

"Not quite everything," Juve answered gently. "There are one or two things you don't know, and I'll tell you one of them. The Princess was robbed by the same man who robbed Mme. Van den Rosen, wasn't she? Well, Mme. Van den Rosen was the victim of a burglary: some of the furniture in her room was broken into, and the tests I made this morning with the dynamometer proved to me that you are not strong enough to have caused those fractures."

"Not strong enough?" Charles Rambert ejaculated.

"No. I told you at the time that your innocence would be proved if you were strong enough, but I said that to prevent you from playing tricks and not putting out all your strength. As a matter of fact it was your comparative weakness that saved you. The dynamometer tests and the figures I obtained just now prove absolutely that you are innocent of the Van den Rosen robbery and, consequently, of the robbery from Sonia Danidoff."

Again the lad reflected for a minute or two.

"But you didn't know who I was when you came to the hotel, did you? And therefore had no suspicion that I was Charles Rambert? That's true, isn't it? How did you find out? I was supposed to be dead."

"That was a child's job," Juve replied. "I got the anthropometric records of the body that had been buried as yours, and I planned to get symmetrical photographs of you in your character of Mademoiselle Jeanne, as I did of you to-day at head-quarters. My first job was to lay hands upon Mademoiselle Jeanne, and I very soon found her, as I expected, turned into a man again, and living in the most disreputable company. I made any number of enquiries, and when I went to the Saint-Anthony's Pig last evening I knew that it was some unknown person who had been buried in your stead; that Paul was Mademoiselle Jeanne; and that Mademoiselle Jeanne was Charles Rambert. It was my intention to arrest you, and to ascertain definitely by means of the dynamometer that you were innocent of the Langrune and the Danidoff crimes."

"What you tell me about the dynamometer explains how you know I am not the man who committed the robbery at the hotel, but what clears me in your eyes of the Langrune murder?"

"Bless my soul!" Juve retorted, "you are arguing as if you wanted to prove you were guilty. Well, my boy, it's the same story as the other. The man who murdered the Marquise de Langrune smashed things, and the dynamometer has proved that you are not strong enough to have been the man."

"And suppose I had been mad at the time," Charles Rambert said, his hesitation and his tone betraying his anxiety about the answer, "could I have been strong enough then? Might I have committed these crimes without knowing anything about it?"

But Juve shook his head.

"I know: you are referring to your mother, and are haunted by an idea that through some hereditary taint you might be a somnambulist and have done these things in your sleep. Come, Charles Rambert, finish your breakfast and put all that out of your head. To begin with, you would not have been strong enough, even then; and in the next place there is nothing at present to show that you are mad, nor even that your poor mother — — But I need not go on: I've got some rather odd notions on that subject."

"Then, M. Juve — —"

"Drop the 'monsieur'; call me 'Juve.'"

"Then, if you know that I am innocent, you can go and tell my father? I have nothing to fear? I can reappear in my own name?"

Juve looked at the lad with an ironical smile.

"How you go ahead!" he exclaimed. "Please understand that although I do believe you are innocent, I am almost certainly the only person who does. And unfortunately I have not yet got any evidence that would be sufficiently convincing and certain to put the persuasion of your guilt out of your father's head, or anybody else's. This is not the time for you to reappear: it would simply mean that you would be arrested by some detective who knows less than I do, and thrown into prison as you confidently expected to be this morning."

"Then what is to become of me?"

"What do you think of doing yourself?"

"Going to see my father."

"No, no," Juve protested once more. "I tell you not to go. It would be stupid and utterly useless. Wait a few days, a few weeks if need be. When I have put my hand on Fantômas' shoulder, I will be the very first to take you to your father, and proclaim your innocence."

"Why wait until Fantômas is arrested?" Charles Rambert asked, the mere sound of the name seeming to wake all his former enthusiasm on the subject of that famous criminal.

"Because if you are innocent of the charge brought against you, it is extremely likely that Fantômas is the guilty party. When he is laid by the heels you will be able to protest your innocence without any fear."

Charles Rambert sat silent for some minutes, musing on the odd chance of destiny which required him to make his own return to normal life contingent on the arrest of a mysterious criminal, who was merely suspected, and had never been seen nor discovered.

"What do you advise me to do?" he asked presently.

The detective got up and began to pace the room.

"Well," he began, "the first fact is that I am interested in you, and the next is, that while I was having that rough-and-tumble last night with that scoundrel in the supper-room, I thought for a minute or two that it was all up with me: your chipping in saved my life. On the other hand I may be said to have saved your life now by ascertaining your innocence and preventing your arrest. So we are quits in a way. But you began the delicate attentions, and I have only paid you back, so it's up to me to start a new series and not turn you out into the street where you would inevitably get into fresh trouble. So this is what I propose: change your name and go and take a room somewhere; get into proper clothes and then come back to me, and I'll give you a letter to a friend of mine who is on one of the big evening papers. You are well educated, and I know you are energetic. You are keen on everything connected with the police, and you'll get on splendidly as a reporter. You will be able to earn an honest and respectable name that way. Would you like to try that idea?"

"It's awfully good of you," Charles Rambert said gratefully. "I should love to be able to earn my living by work so much to my taste."

Juve cut his thanks short, and held out some bank-notes.

"There's some money; now clear out; it's high time we both got a little sleep. Get busy settling into rooms, and in a fortnight I shall expect you to be editor of *La Capitale*."

"Under what name shall you introduce me to your friend?" Charles Rambert asked, after a little nervous pause.

"H'm!" said Juve with a smile: "it will have to be an alias of course."

"Yes; and as it will be the name I shall write under it ought to be an easy one to remember."

"Something arresting, like Fantômas!" said Juve chaffingly, amused by the curious child-ishness of this lad, who could take keen interest in such a trifle when he was in so critical a situation. "Choose something not too common for the first name; and something short for the other. Why not keep the first syllable of Fantômas? Oh, I've got it — Fandor; what about Jérôme Fandor?"

Charles Rambert murmured it over.

"Jérôme Fandor! Yes, you are right, it sounds well."

Juve pushed him out of the door.

"Well, Jérôme Fandor, leave me to my slumbers, and go and rig yourself out, and get ready for the new life that I'm going to open up for you!"

Bewildered by the amazing adventures of which he had just been the central figure, Charles Rambert, or Jérôme Fandor, walked down Juve's staircase wondering. "Why should he take so much trouble about me? What interest or what motive can he have? And how on earth does he find out such a wonderful lot of things?"

XX
A Cup of Tea

After the tragic death of her husband, Lady Beltham — whose previous life had inclined to the austere — withdrew into almost complete retirement. The world of gaiety and fashion knew her no more. But in the world where poverty and suffering reign, in hospital wards and squalid streets, a tall and beautiful woman might often be seen, robed all in black, with distinguished bearing and eyes serene and grave, distributing alms and consolation as she moved. It was Lady Beltham, kind, good and very pitiful, bent on the work of charity to which she had vowed her days.

Yet she had not allowed herself to be crushed by sorrow; after the tragedy which left her a widow, she had assumed the effective control of her husband's property, and, helped by faithful friends, had carried on his interests and administered his estates, spreading a halo of kindness all around her.

To help her in the heavy correspondence entailed by all these affairs, she found three secretaries none too many. On M. Etienne Rambert's recommendation, Thérèse Auvernois was now one of these, and the young girl was perfectly happy in her new surroundings; time was helping her to forget the tragedy which had taken her grandmother from her at Beaulieu, and she enjoyed the company of the well-born, well-bred English gentlewomen.

Lady Beltham was reclining on a sofa in the great hall of her house at Neuilly. It was a spacious room, furnished half as a lounge and half as an office, and Lady Beltham liked to receive people there. A large glass-enclosed balcony commanded a view over the garden and the boulevard Richard Wallace beyond, with the Bois de Boulogne beyond that again. A few minutes before, a footman had brought in a table and set out tea-things, and Lady Beltham was reading while Thérèse and the two young English girls were chattering among themselves.

The telephone bell rang and Thérèse answered it.

"Hullo? Yes ...yes: you want to know if you may call this evening? The Reverend — oh, yes: you have just come from Scotland? Hold on a minute." She turned to Lady Beltham. "It is Mr. William Hope, and he wants to know if you will see him to-night. He has just come from your place in Scotland."

"The dear man!" exclaimed Lady Beltham; "of course he may come," and as Thérèse turned lightly to convey her permission to the clergyman waiting at the other end of the line, she caught a smile on the face of one of the other girls. "What is the joke, Lisbeth?" she enquired.

The girl laughed brightly.

"I think the worthy parson must have smelt the tea and toast, and wants to make up for the wretched dinner he got in the train."

"You are incorrigible," Lady Beltham replied. "Mr. Hope is above such material matters."

"Indeed he isn't, Lady Beltham," the girl persisted. "Why, only the other day he told Thérèse that all food deserved respect and esteem directly a blessing had been asked upon it, and that a badly cooked steak was a kind of sacrilege."

"A badly cooked pheasant," Thérèse corrected her.

"You are both wicked little slanderers," Lady Beltham protested gently, "and don't know the blessing a good appetite is. You do, Susannah, don't you?"

Susannah, a pretty Irish girl, looked up from a letter she was reading, and blushed.

"Oh, Lady Beltham, I've been ever so much less hungry since Harry's ship sailed."

"I don't quite see the connection," Lady Beltham answered. "Love is good nourishment for the soul, but not for the body. However, a good appetite is nothing to be ashamed of, and you ought to keep your roses for your future husband, and qualify in every way to be an excellent mother of a family."

"With lots and lots of children," Lisbeth went on wickedly: "seven or eight daughters at the very least, all of whom will marry nice young clergymen when their time comes and —— "

She stopped speaking and the light chatter died away as a footman entered and announced the Reverend William Hope, who followed him immediately into the room, an elderly man with a full, clean-shaven face and a comfortable portliness of figure.

Lady Beltham offered him a cordial hand.

"I am delighted you are back," she said. "Will you have a cup of tea with us?"

The parson made a general bow to the girls gathered about the table.

"I got a wretched dinner in the train," he began, but Lisbeth interrupted him.

"Don't you think this tea smells delicious?" she asked.

The parson put out his hand to take the cup she offered to him, and bowed and smiled.

"Precisely what I was going to observe, Miss Lisbeth."

Thérèse and Susannah turned away to hide their amusement, and Lady Beltham adroitly changed the subject. She moved towards her writing-table.

"Mr. Hope must have much to tell me, girls, and it is getting late. I must get to business. Did you have a good journey?"

"Quite as good as usual, Lady Beltham. The people at Scotwell Hill are very plucky and good, but it will be a hard winter; there is snow on the hills already."

"Have the women and children had all their woollen things?"

"Oh, yes: twelve hundred garments have been distributed according to a list drawn up by the under-steward; here it is," and he handed a paper to Lady Beltham, who passed it on to Susannah.

"I will ask you to check the list," she said to the girl, and turned again to the clergyman. "The under-steward is a good fellow, but he is a rabid politician; he may have omitted some families that are openly radical; but I think charity should be given equally to all, for poverty makes no political distinctions."

"That is the right Christian view," the clergyman said approvingly.

"And what about the sanatorium at Glasgow?" Lady Beltham went on.

"It is very nearly finished," the good man answered. "I have got your lawyers to cut down the contractor's accounts by something like fifteen per cent, which means a saving of nearly three hundred pounds."

"Excellent," said Lady Beltham, and she turned to Thérèse. "You must add that three hundred pounds to the funds of the Scotwell Hill coal charity," she said. "They will want all of it if the winter is going to be a hard one," and Thérèse made a note of the instruction, full of admiration for Lady Beltham's simple generosity.

But Mr. Hope was fidgeting on his chair. He seized an opportunity when Lady Beltham, busy making notes, had turned her deep and steady eyes away from him, to say in a low tone:

"Have I your permission just to mention — poor Lord Beltham?"

Lady Beltham started, and her face betrayed an emotion which she bravely controlled. Hearing the name pronounced, the three girls withdrew to the far end of the room, where they began to talk among themselves. Lady Beltham signified her assent, and Mr. Hope began.

"You know, dear friend, this has been my first visit to Scotland since Lord Beltham's death. I found your tenants still grievously upset by the tragedy that occurred nearly a year ago. They have got by heart all the newspaper accounts of the mysterious circumstances attending Lord Beltham's death, but those are not enough to satisfy the sympathetic curiosity of these excellent people, and I was obliged to tell them over and over again in full detail — all we knew."

"I hope no scandal has gathered round his name," said Lady Beltham quickly.

"You need have no fear of that," the clergyman replied in the same low tone. "The rumour that got about when the crime was first discovered, that Lord Beltham had been surprised in an intrigue and killed in revenge, has not won acceptance. Local opinion agrees that he was decoyed into a trap and killed by the man Gurn, who meant to rob him, but who was either surprised or thought he was going to be, and fled before he had time to take the money or the jewels from the body of his victim. They know that the murderer has never been caught, but they also know that there is a price on his head, and they all hope the police — — Oh, forgive me for recalling all these painful memories!"

While he had been speaking, Lady Beltham's face had expressed almost every shade of emotion and distress; it seemed to be drawn with pain at his concluding words. But she made an effort to control herself, and spoke resignedly.

"It cannot be helped, dear Mr. Hope. Go on."

But the clergyman changed the topic.

"Oh, I was quite forgetting," he said more brightly. "The under-steward has turned out the two Tillys, quite on his own authority: you must remember them, two brothers, blacksmiths, who drank a great deal and paid very little, and created so much scandal in the place."

"I object to the under-steward doing any such thing without referring to me first," Lady Beltham exclaimed warmly. "Man's duty is to persuade and forgive, not to judge and punish. Kindness breeds kindness, and it is pity that wins amendment. Why should a subordinate, my under-steward, presume to do what I would not permit myself to do?"

She had sprung to her feet and was pacing excitedly about the room; she had wholly dropped the impassive mask she habitually wore, concealing her real personality.

The three girls watched her in silence.

The door opened anew, and Silbertown came in, the major-domo of Lady Beltham's establishment at Neuilly. He brought the evening letters, and the girls speedily took all the envelopes and newspapers from the tray and began to sort and open them, while the major-domo entered into conversation with his mistress, and the Rev. William Hope seized the opportunity to say good night, and take his leave.

Many of the letters were merely appeals to help in money or in kind, but one long letter Lisbeth handed to Lady Beltham. She glanced at the signature.

"Ah, here is news of M. Etienne Rambert," she exclaimed, and as Thérèse instinctively drew near, knowing that she, too, might hear something of what her old friend had written, Lady Beltham put the letter into her hand. "You read it, my dear, and then you can tell me presently what he has to say."

Thérèse read the letter eagerly. M. Etienne Rambert had left Paris a week before, upon a long and important journey. The energetic old fellow was to make a trip in Germany first, and then go from Hamburg to England, where he had some business to attend to on behalf of Lady Beltham, with whom he was on more confidential terms than ever. Then he meant to sail from Southampton and spend the winter in Colombia, where he had important interests of his own to look after.

While Thérèse was reading, Lady Beltham continued her conversation with her major-domo.

"I am glad you had the park gate seen to this afternoon," she said. "You know how nervous I am. My childhood in Scotland was very lonely, and ever since then I have had a vague terror of solitude and darkness."

The major-domo reassured her: he had no lack of self-confidence.

"There is nothing for your ladyship to be afraid of; the house is perfectly safe, and carefully guarded. Walter, the porter, is a first-rate watch-dog and always sleeps with one eye open. And I, too — — "

"Yes, I know, Silbertown," the young widow replied; "and when I give myself time to think I am not nervous. Thank you; you can leave me now."

She turned to the three girls.

"I am tired, dears; we won't stay up any later."

Lisbeth and Susannah kissed her affectionately and went away. Thérèse lingered a moment, to bring a book, a Bible, and place it on a table close to Lady Beltham's chair. Lady Beltham laid a hand upon her head as if in blessing, and said gently:

"Good night; God bless you, dear child!"

XXI
Lord Beltham's Murderer

It was on the point of midnight, and absolute stillness reigned throughout the house.

But Lady Beltham had not gone to bed. Although she had remained in the great hall where she did her work, she had been unable to settle down to any occupation. She had read a little, and begun a letter, got up and sat down; and finally, beginning to feel chilly, she had drawn an easy chair up to the hearth, where a log was just burning out, and stretching out her slippers to the warmth had fallen into a waking dream.

A sound caught her ear and she sat upright. At first she thought it was some trick of the imagination, but in another minute the noise grew louder; there was the hurrying of feet and voices, muffled at first but rapidly becoming louder, and at last a regular uproar, doors banging, glass breaking, and shouts from all parts of the house. Lady Beltham jumped up, nervous and trembling; she was just going to the window when she heard a shot and stopped dead where she stood. Then she rushed out into the vestibule.

"Help!" she screamed. "What on earth is the matter?" and remembering the girls for whom she had assumed responsibility, she called out anxiously for them. "Lisbeth! Thérèse! Susannah! Come to me!"

Doors upstairs were flung open, and with their hair streaming over their night-dresses Thérèse and Susannah rushed downstairs and crouched down by her side, stifling moans of terror.

"Lisbeth? Where is Lisbeth?" Lady Beltham asked sharply.

At the same moment she appeared, her face distorted with fright.

"Oh, Lady Beltham, it's dreadful! There's a man, a burglar in the garden! And Walter is throttling him! They are fighting dreadfully! They'll kill one another!"

Silbertown, the major-domo, came rushing in just then. Seeing the three girls in their night-dresses he made as if to draw back, but Lady Beltham called him in and demanded explanations.

"We had just finished our rounds," he answered breathlessly, "when we caught sight of a man hiding in the shadows, a thief probably. When we shouted to him he ran away, but we ran after him and seized him; he resisted and there was a fight. But we have got him and the police will take him away in a few minutes."

Lady Beltham listened, with jaw set and hands clenched.

"A thief?" she said, controlling her emotion. "How do you know he is a thief?"

"Well," stammered the major-domo, "he is very poorly dressed, and besides, what was he doing in the garden?"

Lady Beltham was recovering her calm.

"What excuse did he give for being there?" she asked coldly.

"We didn't give him time to invent one," said the major-domo. "We collared him almost as soon as we saw him. And you know, madame, how tremendously powerful Walter is: Walter gave him all he deserved!" and the major-domo clenched his fists and made an expressive exhibition of the porter's reception of the stranger.

Lisbeth was still overcome by what she had seen.

"Oh, the blood!" she muttered hysterically; "it was streaming!"

Lady Beltham spoke angrily to the major-domo.

"I hate brutality: is the man seriously hurt? I hope not. You ought to have questioned him before assaulting him. No one in my house has a right to use violence. 'Whoso smites with the sword shall perish by the sword'!"

The major-domo heard her in silent astonishment: it was not at all what he expected to be told, in view of all the circumstances.

Lady Beltham went on more gently:

"I suppose I shall have to apologise to this man for your wrong and thoughtless behaviour."

"Apologise?" exclaimed Silbertown in amazement. "Surely your ladyship will not do that?"

"One must not shrink from humiliation when one has been in the wrong," said Lady Beltham, in the pulpit manner she affected. "Tell Walter to come to me."

A few minutes later the porter, a muscular giant of a man, came into the room and made a clumsy bow.

"How was it possible for anyone to get into the house at this time of night?" his mistress enquired coldly.

Walter dropped his eyes and twisted his cap nervously.

"I hope your ladyship will forgive me. I caught the fellow, and as he was struggling I hit him. Then two of the footmen came, and they are looking after him in the kitchen."

"Has he given any explanation of his presence here since you assaulted him — at which I am very angry?" said Lady Beltham.

"He hasn't said anything; at least ——"

"Well?"

"I don't like to tell you."

"Please do like!" said Lady Beltham irritably.

"Well," Walter replied, overcoming his nervousness with an effort, "he says your ladyship is well known for your charity to everybody, and — he wants to see you."

There was a moment's pause.

"I will see him," said Lady Beltham at last, in a half-stifled voice.

"Will your ladyship allow me to point out the danger of doing any such thing?" Silbertown exclaimed. "Very likely the man is a lunatic! Or it may be a trick: Lord Beltham was murdered, and perhaps ——"

Lady Beltham looked intently at the major-domo, seemingly trying to read his thoughts. Then she answered slowly:

"I will see him. I will be more pitiful than you," and as the major-domo and the porter made a gesture of futile protest, she added peremptorily: "I have given my orders: kindly obey."

When the two men had reluctantly left the room, Lady Beltham turned to the three girls.

"You had better leave me, darlings," she said, kindly but firmly. "Run away: excitement is bad for you. Go back to bed. No, I assure you I shall be in no danger whatever," and for a few minutes she was left alone.

"Speak," said Lady Beltham in a toneless voice.

The major-domo and the porter had led in, and placed before her, a man with unkempt hair and ragged beard; he was dressed entirely in black, and his face was tired and haggard. Lady Beltham, ghastly pale, was leaning for support against the back of an arm-chair. The man did not raise his eyes to her.

"I will not speak unless we are alone," he answered dully.

"Alone?" said Lady Beltham, fighting down her emotion. "Then it is something serious you have to tell me?"

"If you know anything of people in misfortune, Madame," the man answered gently, "you know that they do not like to humiliate themselves before — before those who cannot understand," and he nodded towards the major-domo and the porter.

"I do know something of misfortune," Lady Beltham replied, in firmer tones; "and I will hear you alone." She looked at her two servants. "Leave us, please."

The major-domo started.

"Leave you alone with him? It's madness!" and as Lady Beltham merely looked at him in haughty surprise, he began to withdraw in confusion, but still protesting. "It's — it's ——Your ladyship has no idea what this fellow wants: do please ——"

But Lady Beltham curtly cut him short.

"That is enough!"

A heavy velvet curtain fell over the closing door, and in the room, that was dimly lighted by a small electric lamp, Lady Beltham was alone with the strange individual to whom she had so readily, so oddly, consented to accord a private interview. She followed her servants to the door and locked it after them. Then with a sudden movement she sprang towards the man, who was standing motionless in the middle of the room following her with his eyes, and flung herself into his arms.

"Oh, Gurn, my darling, my darling!" she cried. "I love you! I love you, darling!" She looked up at him and saw blood upon his forehead. "Good God! The brutes have hurt you! What pain you must be in! Give me your eyes, your lips!" With kisses from her own lips she stanched the blood that was trickling down his cheeks, and with her fingers she smoothed his hair. "I am so happy!" she murmured, and broke off again. "But you are mad! Why, why come here like this, and let yourself be caught and tortured so?"

Moodily Gurn answered, returning kiss for kiss.

"Time has been so long without you! And this evening I was prowling round and saw a light. I thought that every one would be asleep — except you, of course. And so I came straight to you, over walls, and gates — drawn to you like a moth to a candle: and that is all!"

With shining eyes and heaving breast Lady Beltham clung to her lover.

"I love you so! How brave you are! Yes, I am wholly, only yours. But this is madness! You might be arrested and given up to no one knows what horror, without my knowing!"

Gurn seemed to be hypnotised by the fierce and passionate love of this great lady.

"I never gave that a thought," he murmured. "I only thought of you!"

Silence fell upon these tragic lovers as they stood reading love in one another's eyes, and recalling memories common to both, utterly unlike as they were to outward seeming, yet linked by the strongest bond of all, the bond of love.

"What happy hours we lived together out there!" Lady Beltham whispered. Her thoughts had wandered to the far Transvaal and the battle-field where first she had set eyes on Gurn, the sergeant of artillery with powder-blackened face; and then to the homeward voyage on the mighty steamer that bore them across the blue sea, towards the dull white cliffs of England.

Gurn's thoughts followed hers.

"Out there! Yes; and then on the vast ocean, on the ship homeward bound! The quiet and peace of it all! And our meetings every day: our long, long talks, and longer silences — in the clear starlight of those tropical skies! We were learning to know each other —— "

"We were learning to love each other," she said. "And then — London, and Paris, and all the fever of life threatening our love. But that is the strongest thing in the world: and — do you remember? Oh, the ecstasy of it all! But, do you remember too what you did for me — through me — thirteen months ago?"

She had risen, and with white lips and haggard eyes held Gurn's hands within her own in an even tighter grip. Emotion choked her further utterance.

"Yes, I remember," Gurn went on slowly: "it was in our little room in the rue Lévert, and I was on my knees beside you when the door opened quietly, and there stood Lord Beltham, mad with rage and jealousy!"

"I don't know what happened then," Lady Beltham whispered in a hopeless undertone, drooping her head again.

"I do," muttered Gurn. "His eyes sought you, and a pistol was pointed at your heart! He would have fired, but I sprang and struck him down! And then I strangled him!"

Lady Beltham's eyes were fixed on the man's hands, that she still held between her own.

"And I saw the muscles in these hands swell up beneath the skin as they tightened on his throat!"

"I killed him!" groaned the man.

But Lady Beltham, swept by a surge of passion, sprang up and sought his lips.

"Oh, Gurn!" she sobbed — "my darling!"

"Listen," said Gurn harshly, after a pause of anxious silence. "I had to see you to-night, for who knows if to-morrow —— " Lady Beltham shrank at the words, but Gurn went on unheeding. "The police are after me. Of course I have made myself almost unrecognisable, but twice just lately I have been very nearly caught."

"Do you think the police have any accurate idea of what happened?" Lady Beltham asked abruptly.

"No," said Gurn after a moment's hesitation. "They think I killed him with the mallet. They have not found out that I had to strangle him. As far as I know, they found no marks of my hands on his throat. At all events, they could not have been clear, for his collar — you understand." The man spoke of his crime without the least sign of remorse or repugnance now; his only dread was lest he should be caught. "But, none the less, they have identified me. That detective Juve is very clever."

"We did not have enough presence of mind," Lady Beltham said despairingly. "We ought to have led them to suspect someone else: have made them think that it was, say, Fantômas."

"Not that!" said Gurn nervously; "don't talk about Fantômas! We did all we could. But the main thing now is that I should escape them. I had better get away, — across the Channel, — across the Atlantic, — anywhere. But — would you come too?"

Lady Beltham did not hesitate. She flung her arms around the neck of the man who had murdered her own husband, and yielded to a paroxysm of wild passion.

"You know that I am yours, wherever you may go. Shall it be to-morrow? We can meet — you know where — and arrange everything for your flight."

"My flight?" said Gurn, with reproachful emphasis on the pronoun.

"For our flight," she replied, and Gurn smiled again.

"Then that is settled," he said. "I have seen you, and I am happy! Good-bye."

He made a step towards the door, but Lady Beltham stayed him gently.

"Wait," she said. "Walter shall let you out of the house. Do not say anything: I will explain; I will invent some story to satisfy the servants as to your coming here, and also to justify your being allowed to go."

They clung to one another in a parting caress. Lady Beltham tore herself away.

"Till to-morrow!" she whispered.

She stole to the door and unlocked it noiselessly, then crossed the room and rang the bell placed near the fireplace. Resuming her impassive mask, and the haughty air and attitude of cold indifference that were in such utter contrast to her real character, she waited, while Gurn stood upright and still in the middle of the room.

Walter, the porter, came in.

"Take that man to the door, and let no harm be done to him," said Lady Beltham proudly and authoritatively. "He is free."

Without a word, or sign, or glance, Gurn went out of the room, and Walter followed behind him to obey his mistress's command.

Once more alone in the great hall, Lady Beltham waited nervously to hear the sound of the park gate closing behind Gurn. She did not dare go on to the balcony to follow her departing lover with her eyes. So, shaken by her recent emotions, she stood waiting and listening, in an agony to know that he was safe. Then, of a sudden, the noise that she had heard an hour before broke on her ears again: the noise of hurrying feet and broken shouts, and words, vague at first but rapidly growing clearer. She crouched forward listening, filled with a horrible fear, her hand laid upon her scarcely beating heart.

"There he is: hold him!" some one shouted. "That's him all right! Look out, constable!"

"This way, Inspector! Yes, it's him, it's Gurn! Ah, would you!"

Paler than death, Lady Beltham cowered down upon a sofa.

"Good God! Good God!" she moaned. "What are they doing to him!"

The uproar in the garden decreased, then voices sounded in the corridor, Silbertown's exclamations rising above the frightened cries of the three young girls.

"Gurn! Arrested! The man who murdered Lord Beltham!" Lisbeth called out in anxious terror.

"But Lady Beltham? Dear God, perhaps he has murdered her too!"

The door was flung open and the girls rushed in. Lady Beltham by a tremendous effort of will had risen to her feet, and was standing by the end of the sofa.

"Lady Beltham! Alive! Yes, yes!" and Thérèse and Lisbeth and Susannah rushed sobbing to her, and smothered her with caresses.

But the agonised woman motioned them away. With hard eyes and set mouth she moved towards the window, straining her ears to listen. From the park outside Gurn's voice rang distinctly; the lover wished to let his mistress know what had happened, and to take a last farewell.

"I am caught, I am caught! Yes, I am Gurn, and I am caught!"

The fatal words were still ringing in Lady Beltham's ears when the major-domo, Silbertown, came bursting into the room, with radiant face and shining eyes and smiling lips, and hurried to his mistress.

"I thought as much!" he exclaimed excitedly. "It was the villain all right. I recognised him from the description, in spite of his beard. I informed the police! As a matter of fact they have been watching for the last two days. Just fancy, your ladyship, a detective was shadowing Gurn — and when he was going out of the house I gave him the signal!"

Lady Beltham stared at the major-domo in mute horror.

"Yes?" she muttered, on the point of swooning.

"I pointed him out to the police, and it's thanks to me, your ladyship, that Gurn, the murderer, has been arrested at last!"

For just another moment Lady Beltham stared at the man who gave her these appalling tidings, seemed to strive to utter something, then fell prone to the floor, unconscious.

The major-domo and the girls sprang to her side to lavish attentions upon her.

At that moment the door was pushed a little way open, and the figure of Juve appeared.

"May I come in?" said he.

XXII
The Scrap of Paper

It was three o'clock when Juve arrived at the rue Lévert, and he found the concierge of number 147 just finishing her coffee.

Amazed at the results achieved by the detective, the details of which she had learned from the sensational articles in the daily paper she most affected, Mme. Doulenques had conceived a most respectful admiration for the Inspector of the Criminal Investigation Department.

"That man," she constantly declared to Madame Aurore, "it isn't eyes he has in his head, it's telescopes, magnifying glasses! He sees everything in a minute — even when it isn't there!"

She gave him an admiring "good afternoon, Inspector," as he came into her lodge, and going to a board on which numbers of keys were hanging, took one down and handed it to him.

"So there's something fresh to-day?" she said. "I've just seen in the paper that M. Gurn has been arrested. So it was my lodger who did it? What a dreadful man! Whoever would have thought it? It turns my blood cold to think of him!"

Juve was never a man for general conversation, and he was still less interested in the garrulity of this loquacious creature. He took the key and cut short her remarks by walking to the door.

"Yes, Gurn has been arrested," he said shortly; "but he has made no confession, so nothing is known for certain yet. Please go on with your work exactly as though I were not in the house, Mme. Doulenques."

It was his usual phrase, and a constant disappointment to the concierge, who would have asked nothing better than to go upstairs with the detective and watch him at his wonderful work.

Juve went up the five floors to the flat formerly occupied by Gurn, reflecting somewhat moodily. Of course Gurn's arrest was a success, and it was satisfactory to have the scoundrel under lock and key, but in point of fact Juve had learned nothing new in consequence of the arrest, and he was obsessed with the idea that this murder of Lord Beltham was an altogether exceptional crime. He did not yet know why Gurn had killed Lord Beltham, and he did not even know exactly who Gurn himself was; all he could declare was that the murder had been planned and carried out with marvellous audacity and skill, and that was not enough.

Juve let himself into the flat and closed the door carefully behind him. The rooms were in disorder, the result of the searches effected by the police. The rent had not been paid for some time, and as no friend or relation had come forward to assume control of Gurn's interests, the furniture and ornaments of the little flat were to be sold by auction.

The detective walked through the rooms, then flung himself into an arm-chair. He did not know precisely why he had come. He had searched the place a dozen times already since his discovery of the corpse within the trunk, and had found nothing more, no tell-tale marks or fresh detail, to assist in the elucidation of the mystery. He would have given very much to be able to identify Gurn with some other of the many criminals who had passed through his hands, and still more to be able to identify him with that one most mysterious criminal whose fearful deeds had shocked the world so greatly. Somehow the particular way in which this murder was committed, the very audacity of it, led him to think, to "sense," almost to swear that — —

Juve got up. It was little in accord with his active temperament to sit still. Once more he went all round the flat.

"The kitchen? Let me see: I have been through everything? The stove? The cupboards? The saucepans? Why, I went so far as to make sure that there was no poison in them, though it seemed a wild idea. The anteroom? Nothing there: the umbrella stand was empty, and the one interesting thing I did see, the torn curtain, has been described and photographed officially." He went back into the dining-room. "I've searched all the furniture: and I went through all the parcels Gurn had done up before he left, and would, no doubt, have come back for at his leisure, had it not been for my discovery of the body, and the unfortunate publicity the newspapers gave to that fact." In one corner of the room was a heap of old newspapers, crumpled and torn, and thrown down in disorder. Juve kicked them aside. "I've looked through all that, even read the agony columns, but there was nothing there." He went into the bedroom and contemplated the bed, that the concierge had stripped, the chairs set one on top of another in a corner, and the wardrobe that stood empty, its former contents scattered on the floor by the police during their search. There, too, nothing was to be found.

Against the wall, near the fireplace, was a little escritoire with a cupboard above it, containing a few battered books.

"My men have been all through that," Juve muttered; "it's most unlikely that they missed anything, but perhaps I had better see."

He sat down before it and began methodically to sort the scattered papers; with quick, trained glance he scanned each document, putting one after another aside with a grimace expressive of disappointment. Almost the last document he picked up was a long sheet of parchment, and as he unfolded it an exclamation escaped his lips. It was an official notice of Gurn's promotion to the rank of sergeant when fighting under Lord Beltham in the South African War. Juve read it through — he knew English well — and laid it down with a gesture of discouragement.

"It is extraordinary," he muttered. "That seems to be perfectly authentic; it is authentic, and it proves that this fellow was a decent fellow and a brave soldier once; that is a fine record of service." He drummed his fingers on the desk and spoke aloud. "Is Gurn really Gurn, then, and have I been mistaken from start to finish in the little romance I have been weaving round him? How am I to find the key to the mystery? How am I to prove the truth of what I feel to be so very close to me, but which eludes me every time, just as I seem to be about to grasp it?"

He went on with his search, and then, looking at the bookcase, took the volumes out and, holding each by its two covers, shook it to make sure that no papers were hidden among the leaves. But all in vain. He did the same with a large railway time-table and several shipping calendars.

"The odd thing is," he thought, "that all these time-tables go to prove that Gurn really was the commercial traveller he professed to be. It's exactly things such as these one would expect to find in the possession of a man who travelled much, and always had to be referring to the dates of sailing to distant parts of the world."

In the bookcase was a box, made to represent a bound book, and containing a collection of ordnance maps. Juve took them out to make sure that no loose papers were included among them, and one by one unfolded every map.

Then a sharp exclamation burst from his lips.

"Good Lord! Now there — — "

In his surprise he sprang up so abruptly that he pushed back his chair, and overturned it. His excitement was so great that his hands were shaking as he carefully spread out upon the desk one of the ordnance maps he had taken from the case.

"It's the map of the centre district all right: the map which shows Cahors, and Brives, and Saint-Jaury and — Beaulieu! And the missing piece — it is the missing piece that would give that precise district!"

Juve stared at the map with hypnotised gaze; for a piece had been cut out of it, cut out with a penknife neatly and carefully, and that piece must have shown the exact district where the château stood which had been occupied by the Marquise de Langrune.

"Oh, if I could only prove it: prove that the piece missing from this map, this map belonging to Gurn, is really and truly the piece I found near Verrières Station just after the murder of the Marquise de Langrune — what a triumph that would be! What a damning proof! What astounding consequences this discovery of mine might have!"

Juve made a careful note of the number of the map, quickly and nervously, folded it up again, and prepared to leave the flat.

He had made but a step or two towards the door when a sharp ring at the bell made him jump.

"The deuce!" he exclaimed softly; "who can be coming to ring Gurn up when everybody in Paris knows he has been arrested?" and he felt mechanically in his pocket to make sure that his revolver was there. Then he smiled. "What a fool I am! Of course it is only Mme. Doulenques, wondering why I am staying here so long."

He strode to the door, flung it wide open, and then recoiled in astonishment.

"You?" he exclaimed, surveying the caller from top to toe. "You? Charles Rambert! Or, I should say, Jérôme Fandor! Now what the deuce does this mean?"

XXIII
The Wreck of the "Lancaster"

Jérôme Fandor entered the room without a word. Juve closed the door behind him. The boy was very pale and manifestly much upset.

"What is the matter?" said Juve.

"Something terrible has happened," the boy answered. "I have just heard awful news: my poor father is dead!"

"What?" Juve exclaimed sharply. "M. Etienne Rambert dead?"

Jérôme Fandor put a newspaper into the detective's hand. "Read that," he said, and pointed to an article on the front page with a huge head-line: *"Wreck of the 'Lancaster': 150 Lives Lost."* There were tears in his eyes, and he had such obvious difficulty in restraining his grief, that Juve saw that to read the article would be the speediest way to find out what had occurred.

The Red Star liner *Lancaster*, plying between Caracas and Southampton, had gone down with all hands the night before, just off the Isle of Wight, and at the moment of going to press only one person was known to have been saved. There was a good sea running, but it was by no means rough, and the vessel was still within sight of the lighthouse and making for the open sea at full speed, when the lighthousemen suddenly saw her literally blown into the air and then disappear beneath the waves. The alarm was given immediately and boats of all kinds put off to the scene of the disaster, but though a great deal of wreckage was still floating about, only one man of the crew was seen, clinging to a spar; he was picked up by the *Campbell* and taken to hospital, where he was interviewed by *The Times*, without, however, being able to throw any light upon what was an almost unprecedented catastrophe in the history of the sea. All he could say was that the liner had just got up full speed and was making a perfectly normal beginning of her trip, when suddenly a tremendous explosion occurred. He himself was engaged at the moment fastening the tarpaulins over the baggage hold, and he was confident that the explosion occurred among the cargo. But he could give absolutely no more information: the entire ship seemed to be riven asunder, and he was thrown into the sea, stunned, and knew no more until he recovered consciousness and found himself aboard the *Campbell*.

"It's quite incomprehensible," Juve muttered; "surely there can't have been any powder aboard? No explosives are carried on these great liners; they only take passengers and the mails." He scanned the list of passengers. "Etienne Rambert's name is given among the first-class passengers, right enough," he said. "Well, it's odd!"

Jérôme Fandor heaved a profound sigh.

"It is a fatality which I shall never get over," he said. "When you told me the other day that you knew I was innocent, I ought to have gone to see my father, in spite of what you said. I am sure he would have believed me and come to see you; then you could have convinced him, and I should not have this horrible grief of remembering that he had died without learning that his son was not a bad man, but was quite deserving of his affection."

Jérôme Fandor was making a brave struggle to maintain his self-control, and Juve looked at him without concealing the real sympathy he felt for him in his grief. He put his hand kindly on his shoulder.

"Listen, my dear boy; odd as you may think it, you can take my word for it that there is no need for you to despair; there is nothing to prove that your father is dead; he may not have been on board."

The boy looked up in surprise.

"What do you mean, Juve?"

"I don't want to say anything, my boy, except that you would be very wrong to give way to distress at present. If you have any confidence in me, you may believe me when I say that. There is nothing yet to prove that you have had this loss: and, besides, you still have your mother, who is perfectly sure to get quite well: do you understand? — *perfectly sure!*" He changed the subject abruptly. "There is one thing I should like to know: what the dickens brought you here?"

"You were the first person I thought of in my trouble," Fandor replied. "Directly I read about the disaster in that paper I came to tell you at once."

"Yes, I quite understand that," Juve answered. "What I do not understand is how you guessed that you would find me here, in Gurn's flat."

The question seemed to perturb the boy.

"It — it was quite by chance," he stammered.

"That is the kind of explanation one offers to fools," Juve retorted. "By what chance did you see me come into this house? What the deuce were you doing in the rue Lévert?" The lad showed some inclination to make for the door, but Juve stayed him peremptorily. "Answer my question, please: how did you know I was here?"

Driven into a corner, the boy blurted out the truth:

"I had followed you."

"Followed me?" Juve exclaimed. "Where from?"

"From your rooms."

"You mean, and you may as well own up to it at once, that you were shadowing me."

"Well, yes, M. Juve, it is true," Fandor confessed, all in one breath. "I was shadowing you: I do every day!"

Juve was dumbfounded.

"Every day? And I never saw you! Gad, you are jolly clever! And may I enquire why you have been exercising this supervision over me?"

Jérôme Fandor hung his head.

"Forgive me," he faltered; "I have been very stupid. I thought you — I thought you were — Fantômas!"

The idea tickled the detective so much that he dropped back into a chair to laugh at his ease.

"'Pon my word," he said, "you have an imagination! And what made you suppose that I was Fantômas?"

"M. Juve," Fandor said earnestly, "I made a vow that I would find out the truth, and discover the scoundrel who has made such awful havoc of my life. But I did not know where to begin. From all you have said I realised that Fantômas was a most extraordinarily clever man; I did not know anyone who could be cleverer than you; and so I watched you! It was merely logical!"

Far from being angry, Juve was rather flattered.

"I am amazed by what you have just told me, my boy," he said with a smile. "In the first place your reasoning is not at all bad. Of course it is obvious that I cannot suspect myself of being Fantômas, but I quite admit that if I were in your place I might make the supposition, wild as it may seem. And, in the next place, you have shadowed me without my becoming aware of the fact, and that is very good indeed: a proof that you are uncommonly smart." He looked at the lad attentively for a few moments, and then went on more gravely: "Are you satisfied now that your hypothesis was wrong? Or do you still suspect me?"

"No, I don't suspect you now," Fandor declared; "not since I saw you come into this house; Fantômas certainly would not have come to search Gurn's rooms because — — "

He stopped, and Juve, who was looking at him keenly, did not make him finish what he was saying.

"Shall I tell you something?" he said at last. "If you continue to display as much thought and initiative in the career you have chosen as you have just displayed, you will very soon be the first newspaper detective of the day!" He jumped up and led the boy off. "Come along: I've got to go to the Law Courts at once."

"You've found out something fresh?"

"I'm going to ask them to call an interesting witness in the Gurn affair."

Rain had been falling heavily all the morning and afternoon, but within the last few minutes it had almost stopped. Dollon, the steward, put his hand out of the window and found that only a few drops were falling now from the heavy grey sky.

He was an invaluable servant, and a few months after the death of the Marquise de Langrune, the Baronne de Vibray had gladly offered him a situation, and a cottage on her estate at Querelles.

He walked across the room, and called his son.

"Jacques, would you like to come with me? I am going down to the river to see that the sluices have been opened properly. The banks are anything but sound, and these rains will flood us out one of these days."

The steward and his son went down the garden towards the stream which formed one boundary of Mme. de Vibray's park.

"Look, father," Jacques exclaimed, "the postman is calling us."

The postman, a crusty but good-hearted fellow, came hurrying up to the steward.

"You do make me run, M. Dollon," he complained. "I went to your house this morning to take you a letter, but you weren't there."

"You might have left it with anybody."

"Excuse me!" the man retorted; "it's against the regulations: I've got an official letter for you, and I can only give it to you yourself," and he held out an envelope which Dollon tore open.

"Magistrates' office?" he said enquiringly, as he glanced at the heading of the notepaper. "Who can be writing to me from the Law Courts?" He read the letter aloud:

"Sir: As time does not permit of a regular summons being sent to you by an usher of the court, I beg you to be so good as to come to Paris immediately, the day after to-morrow if possible, and attend at my office, where your depositions are absolutely required to conclude a case in which you are interested. Please bring, without exception, all the papers and documents entrusted to you by the Clerk of Assizes at Cahors, at the conclusion of the Langrune enquiry."

"It is signed Germain Fuselier," Dollon remarked. "I've often seen his name in the papers. He is a very well-known magistrate, and is employed in many criminal cases." He read the letter through once more, and turned to the postman. "Will you take a glass of wine, Muller?"

"That's a thing I never say 'no' to."

"Well, go into the house with Jacques, and while he is attending to you I will write a reply telegram which you can take to the office for me."

While the man was quenching his thirst Dollon wrote his reply:

"Will leave Verrières to-morrow evening by 7.20 train, arriving Paris 5 A.M. Wire appointment at your office to me at Hôtel Francs-Bourgeois, 152 rue du Bac."

He read the message over, signed it "Dollon" and considered.

"I wonder what they can want me for? Oh, if only they have found out something about the Langrune affair, how glad I shall be!"

XXIV
Under Lock and Key

After the preliminary examination as to his identity and so on, Gurn had been transferred to the Santé prison. At first the prisoner seemed to have terrible difficulty in accustoming himself to the rigours of confinement; he suffered from alternate paroxysms of rage and despair, but by sheer strength of character he fought these down. As a prisoner on remand he was entitled to the privilege of a separate cell, also during the first forty-eight hours he had been able to have his meals sent in from outside. Since then, however, his money had given out, and he was obliged to content himself with the ordinary prison dietary. But Gurn was not fastidious; this man whom Lady Beltham had singled out, or accepted, as her lover had often given proofs of an education and an intelligence above the average, yet now he appeared quite at ease in the atmosphere of a prison.

Gurn was walking quickly and alone round the exercise yard, when a breathless voice sounded in his ear.

"'Gad, Gurn, you know how to march! I was going to join you for a bit, but I could not keep up with you."

Gurn turned and saw old Siegenthal, the warder in charge of his division, in whose custody he was particularly placed.

"My word!" the old fellow panted, "anybody could tell you had been in the infantry. Well, so have I; though that wasn't yesterday, nor yet the day before; but we never marched as fast as you do. We made a fine march once though — at Saint-Privat."

Out of pity for the decent old fellow Gurn slackened his pace. He had heard the story of the battle of Saint-Privat a dozen times already, but he was quite willing to let Siegenthal tell it again. The warder, however, wandered to another point.

"By the way, I heard you were promoted sergeant out in the Transvaal: is that so?" and as Gurn nodded assent, he went on: "I never rose above the rank of corporal, but at any rate I have always led an honest life." A sudden compassion for his prisoner seized the old man, and he laid a kindly hand on Gurn's shoulder. "Is it really possible that an old soldier like you, who seem to be such a steady, serious, kind of man, can have committed such a crime?"

Gurn dropped his eyes and did not reply.

"I suppose there was a woman at the bottom of it?" Siegenthal said tentatively. "You acted on impulse, in a fit of jealousy, eh?"

"No," Gurn answered with sudden bluntness, "I may as well own up that I did it in anger, because I wanted money — for the sake of robbery."

"I'm sorry," said the old warder simply. "You must have been desperately hard up."

"No I wasn't."

Siegenthal stared at his prisoner. The man must be utterly callous to talk like that, he thought. Then a clock struck and the warder gave a curt order.

"Time, Gurn! We must go back," and he conducted the unresisting prisoner up the three flights of stairs that led to the division in which his cell was. "By the way," he remarked as they went, "I forgot to tell you that you and I have got to part."

"Oh?" said Gurn. "Am I to be transferred to another prison?"

"No, it's I who am going. Just fancy, I have been appointed head warder at Poissy; I go on leave to-night, and take up my new post in a week." Both halted before the door of cell number 127. "In with you," said Siegenthal, and when Gurn had obeyed he turned to go. Then he wheeled round again quickly, and put out his hand hurriedly, as if half afraid of being seen. "Put it there, Gurn," he said; "no doubt you are a murderer and, as you have confessed yourself, a thief; but I can't forget that if you had kept straight, you were the sergeant and I should have had to obey you. I'm sorry for you!" Gurn was touched and murmured a word of thanks. "That's all right, that's all right," Siegenthal muttered, not attempting to hide his emotion; "let us hope that everything will turn out well," and he left Gurn alone in the cell to his meditations.

Twice, Gurn reflected, relying on the sympathy which he knew he had evoked in the old warder's heart despite the number of criminals who had passed through his hands, he had been on the point of broaching a serious and delicate matter to him; but he had not actually spoken, being deterred by some undefinable scruple, as well as half suspecting that his application would be made in vain. And now he was glad he had been so cautious, for even if the warder had been amenable, his approaching removal to another prison would have prevented the idea from coming to fruition.

A sing-song voice echoed in the corridor.

"Number 127, you are wanted in the barristers' room. Get ready," and the next minute the door of the cell was thrown open, and a cheery-looking warder, with a strong Gascon accent, appeared. Gurn had noticed him before: he was the second warder in this division, a man named Nibet, and no doubt he would be promoted to Siegenthal's place when the chief warder left. Nibet looked curiously at Gurn, a certain sympathy in his quick brown eyes. "Ready, Gurn?"

Gurn growled an answer and pulled on his coat again. His counsel was Maître Barberoux, one of the foremost criminal barristers of the day; Gurn had thought it prudent to retain him for his defence, more especially as it would cost him nothing personally. But he had no particular desire to talk to him now; he had already told him everything he intended to tell him, and he had no intention of allowing the case to be boomed as a sensation; quite the reverse indeed: in his opinion, the flatter the case fell, the better it would be for his interests, though no doubt Maître Barberoux would not be of the same way of thinking.

But he said nothing, and merely walked in front of Nibet along the corridor towards the barristers' room, the way to which he was already familiar with. On the way they passed some masons who were at work in the prison, and these men stopped to watch him pass, but contrary to Gurn's apprehensions they did not seem to recognise him. He hoped it meant that the murder was already ceasing to be a nine days' wonder for the public at large.

Nibet pushed Gurn into the barristers' room, saying respectfully to the person in it already, "You only have to ring, sir, when you have finished," and then withdrew, leaving Gurn in presence, not of his counsel as he had expected, but of that personage's assistant, a young licentiate in law named Roger de Seras, who was also a most incredible dandy.

Roger de Seras greeted Gurn with an engaging smile and advanced as if to shake hands with him, but suddenly wondering whether that action might not suggest undue familiarity, he raised his hand to his own head instead and scratched it; the young fellow was still younger in his business, and did not rightly know whether it was etiquette for a barrister, or even a barrister's junior, to shake hands with a prisoner who was implicated in a notorious murder.

Gurn felt inclined to laugh, and on the whole was glad that it was the junior whom he had to see; the futile verbosity of this very young licentiate might possibly be amusing.

Maître Roger de Seras began with civil apologies.

"You will excuse me if I only stay for a few minutes, but I am most frightfully busy; besides, two ladies are waiting for me outside in my carriage: I may say confidentially that they are actresses, old friends of mine, and, just fancy, they are most frightfully anxious to see you! That's what it means to be famous, M. Gurn; eh, what?" Gurn nodded, not feeling unduly flattered. Roger de Seras continued. "Just to please them I have made any number of applications to the governor of the prison, but there was nothing doing, my dear chap; that beast of a magistrate, Fuselier, insists on your being kept in absolute seclusion. But none the less, I've got some news for you. I know heaps: why, my friends at the Law Courts call me 'the peripatetic paragraph!' Not bad, eh, what?" Gurn smiled and Roger de Seras was encouraged. "It's given me no end of a boom, my leader acting for you, and my being able to come and see you whenever I like! Everybody asks me how you are, and what you are like, and what you say, and what you think. You can congratulate yourself on having caused a sensation in Paris."

Gurn began to be irritated by all this chatter.

"I must confess I'm not the least interested in what people are saying about me. Is there anything new in my case?"

"Absolutely nothing that I am aware of," Roger de Seras replied serenely, without stopping to think whether there was or not. "I say — Lady Beltham — —"

"Yes?" said Gurn.

"Well, I know her very well, you know: I go out a frightful lot and I have often met her: a charming woman, Lady Beltham!"

Gurn really did not know how to treat the idiot. Never one to suffer fools gladly, he grew irritable and would almost certainly have said something that would have put the garrulous young bungler in his place, had not the latter suddenly remembered something, just as he was on the point of getting up to go.

"Oh, by the way," he said with a laugh, "I was nearly forgetting the most important thing of all. Just fancy, that beast Juve, the marvellous detective whom the newspapers rave about, went to your place yesterday afternoon to make another official search!"

"Alone?" enquired Gurn, much interested.

"Quite alone. Now what do you suppose he found; the place has been ransacked dozens of times, you know; of course I mean something sensational in the way of a find. I bet you a thousand — —"

"I never bet," Gurn snapped. "Tell me at once what it was."

The young fellow was proud of having caught the attention of his leader's notorious client, if only for a moment; he paused and wagged his head, weighing each word to give them greater emphasis.

"He found an ordnance map in your bookcase, my dear chap — an ordnance map with a bit torn out of it."

"Oh! And what then?" said Gurn, a frown upon his face.

The young barrister did not notice the expression on the murderer's countenance.

"Well, then it appears that Juve thought it was very important. Between you and me, my opinion is that Juve tries to be frightfully clever and succeeds in looking a fool. How, I ask you, can the discovery of that map affect your case or influence the decision of the jury? By the way, there is no need for you to worry about the result; I have had a frightful lot of experience in criminal cases, and so be assured you are all right: extenuating circumstances, you know. But — oh, yes, there is one thing more I wanted to tell you. A fresh witness is going to be called at the examination; let me see, what's his name? Dollon: that's it: the steward, Dollon."

"I don't understand," said Gurn; his head was bent and his eyes cast down.

A glimmer of light dawned in the young licentiate's brain.

"Wait, there is some connection," he said. "The steward, Dollon, is in the employment of a lady who calls herself the Baronne de Vibray. And the Baronne de Vibray is guardian to the young lady who was staying with Lady Beltham the day, or rather the night, when you — you — well, you know. And that young lady, Mlle. Thérèse Auvernois, was placed with Lady Beltham by M. Etienne Rambert. And M. Etienne Rambert is the father of the young man who murdered the Marquise de Langrune last year. I tell you all these things without attempting to draw any deductions from them, for, for my own part, I haven't the least idea why the steward, Dollon, has been summoned in our case at all."

"Nor have I," said Gurn, and the frown on his brow was deeper.

Roger de Seras hunted all round the little room for his gloves and found them in his pocket.

"Well, my dear chap, I must leave you. We have been chatting for a whole half-hour, and those ladies are still waiting for me. What on earth will they say to me?"

He was about to ring for the warder when Gurn abruptly stayed him.

"Tell me," he said with a sudden air of interest, "when is that man coming — what's his name? Dollon?"

The young barrister was on the point of saying he did not know, when a brilliant recollection came into his mind.

"'Gad, how frightfully stupid I am! Why, I have a copy of the telegram he sent the magistrate in my portfolio here now." He opened the portfolio and picked out a sheet of blue paper. "Here it is."

Gurn took it from him and read:

"Will leave Verrières to-morrow evening by 7.20 train, arriving Paris 5 A.M...."

Gurn appeared to be sufficiently edified: at all events he paid no attention to the rest of the message. Lord Beltham's murderer handed the document back to the barrister without a word.

A few minutes later Maître Roger de Seras had rejoined his lady friends, and the prisoner was once more in his cell.

XXV
An Unexpected Accomplice

Gurn was walking nervously up and down in his cell after this interview, when the door was pushed open and the cheery face of the warder Nibet looked in.

"Evening, Gurn," he said; "it's six o'clock, and the restaurant-keeper opposite wants to know if he is to send your dinner in to you."

"No," Gurn growled. "I'll have the prison ordinary."

"Oh — ho!" said the warder; "funds low, eh? Of course, it's not for you to despise our dietary, but still, Government beans — — " He came further into the cell, ignoring Gurn's impatient preference for his room to his company, and said in a low tone: "There, take that," and thrust a bank-note into the hand of the dumbfounded prisoner. "And if you want any more, they will be forthcoming," he added. He made a sign to Gurn to say nothing, and went to the door. "I'll be back in a few minutes: I'll just go and order a decent dinner for you."

Gurn felt as if a tremendous weight had been lifted from him; the cell seemed larger, the prison walls less high; he had an intuition that Lady Beltham was not deserting him. He had never doubted the sincerity of her feelings for him, but he quite realised how a woman in her delicate position might feel embarrassed in trying to intervene in favour of any prisoner, and much more so in the case of the one whom the entire world believed to be the single-handed murderer of her husband. But now Lady Beltham had intervened. She had succeeded in communicating with him through the medium of this warder. And almost certainly she would do much more yet.

The door opened again, and the warder entered, carrying a long rush basket containing several dishes and a bottle of wine.

"Well, Gurn, that's a more agreeable sort of dinner, eh?"

"Gad, I wanted it after all," said the murderer with a smile. "It was a good idea of yours, M. Nibet, to insist on my getting my dinner sent in from outside."

Nibet winked; he appreciated his prisoner's tact; obviously he was not one to make untimely allusions to the warder's breach of discipline in conveying money to him so simply, but so very irregularly.

As he ate Gurn chatted with Nibet.

"I suppose it is you who will get Siegenthal's place?"

"Yes," said Nibet, sipping the wine Gurn had offered him. "I have asked for the berth no end of times, but it never came; I was always told to wait because the place was not free, and another berth must be found first for Siegenthal, who was my senior. But the old beast would never make any application. However, three days ago, I was sent for to the Ministry, and one of the staff told me that some one in the Embassy, or the Government, or somewhere, was taking an interest in me, and they asked me a lot of questions and I told them all about it. And then, all of a sudden, Siegenthal was promoted to Poissy and I was given his billet here."

Gurn nodded: he saw light.

"And what about the money?"

"That's stranger still, but I understood all the same. A lady met me in the street the other night and spoke to me by name. We had a chat there on the pavement, for the street was empty, and she shoved some bank-notes in my hand — not just one or two, but a great bunch — — , and she told me that she was interested in me — in you — — , and that if things turned out as she wished there were plenty more bank-notes where those came from."

While the warder was talking Gurn watched him carefully. The murderer was an experienced reader of character in faces, and he speedily realised that his lady's choice had fallen on an excellent object. Thick lips, a narrow forehead, and prominent cheek-bones suggested a material nature that would hesitate at nothing which would satisfy his carnal appetites, so Gurn decided that further circumlocution was so much waste of time, and that he might safely come to the point. He laid his hand familiarly on the warder's shoulder.

"I'm getting sick of being here," he remarked.

"I dare say," the warder answered uneasily; "but you must be guided by reason; time is going on, and things arrange themselves."

"They do when you help them," Gurn said peremptorily; "and you and I are going to help them."

"That remains to be seen," said the warder.

"Of course, everything has got to be paid for," Gurn went on. "One can't expect a warder to risk his situation merely to help a prisoner to escape." He smiled as the warder made an exclamation of nervous warning. "Don't be frightened, Nibet. We're not going to play any fool games, but let us talk seriously. Of course you have another appointment with the worthy lady who gave you that money?"

"I am to meet her to-night at eleven, in the boulevard Arago," Nibet said, after a moment's hesitation.

"Good," said Gurn. "Well, you are to tell her that I must have ten thousand francs."

"What?" exclaimed the man, in utter astonishment, but his eyes shone with greed.

"Ten thousand francs," Gurn repeated calmly, "and by to-morrow morning. Fifteen hundred of those are for you; I will go away to-morrow evening."

There was a tense silence; the warder seemed doubtful, and Gurn turned the whole of his will power upon him to persuade him.

"Suppose they suspect me?" said Nibet.

"Idiot!" Gurn retorted; "all you will do will be to make a slip in your duty: I don't want you to be an accomplice. Listen: there will be another five thousand francs for you, and if things turn out awkwardly for you, all you will have to do will be to go across to England, and live there comfortably for the rest of your days."

The warder was obviously almost ready to comply.

"Who will guarantee me?" he asked.

"The lady, I tell you — the lady of the boulevard Arago. Here, give her this," and he tore a leaf out of his pocket-book and, scribbling a few words on it, handed it to Nibet.

"Well," said the warder hesitatingly: "I don't say 'no.'"

"You've got to say 'yes,'" Gurn retorted.

The two looked steadily in each other's eyes; then the warder blenched.

"Yes," he said.

Nibet was going away, and was already almost in the corridor when Gurn calmly called him back.

"You will evolve a plan, and I will start to-morrow. Don't forget to bring me a time-table; the Orleans Company time-table will do."

The murderer was not disappointed in his expectations. The next morning Nibet appeared with a mysterious face and eager eyes. He took a small bundle from underneath his jersey and gave it to Gurn.

"Hide that in your bed," he said, and Gurn obeyed.

The morning passed without further developments; numerous warders came and went in the corridor, attending to the prisoners, and Gurn could get no private talk with Nibet, who contrived, however, to come into his cell several times on various pretexts and assure him with a nod or a word that all was going well. But presently, when walking in the exercise yard, the two men were able to have a conversation.

Nibet manifested an intelligence of which his outer appearance gave no indication; but it seems to be an established fact that the inventive faculties, even of men of inferior mental quality, are sharpened when they are engaged in mischief.

"For the last three weeks," he said, "about a score of masons have been working in the prison, repairing the roof and doing up some of the cells. Cell number 129, the one next yours, is empty, and there are no bars on the window; the masons go through that cell and that window to get on to the roof. They knock off work soon after six o'clock. The gate-keeper knows them all, but he does not always look closely at their faces when they go by, and you might perhaps be able to go out with them.

"In the bundle that I gave you there is a pair of workman's trousers, and a waistcoat and a felt hat; put those on. At about a quarter to six, the men who went up on to the roof through the cell, come down by way of the skylights to the staircase that leads to the clerk's office, pass the office, where they are asked no questions, cross the two yards and go out by the main gate. I will open the door of your cell a few minutes before six, and you must go into the empty cell next yours, slip up on to the roof and take care to hide behind the chimney stacks until the men have done work. Let them go down in front of you, and follow behind with a pick or a shovel on your shoulder, and when you are passing the clerk, or anywhere where you might be observed, mind you let the men go a yard or two in front of you. When the gate is just being shut after the last workman, call out quietly, but as naturally as you can, 'Hold on, M. Morin; mind you don't lock me in; I'm not one of your lodgers; let me out after my mates.' Make some joke of that sort, and when you are once outside the gate, by George, my boy, you'll have to vamoose!"

Gurn listened attentively to the warder's instructions. Lady Beltham must, indeed, have been generous and have made the man perfectly easy on the score of his own future.

"In one of the pockets of the clothes," Nibet went on, "I have put ten hundred-franc notes; you asked for more, but I could not raise it: we can settle that some other time."

Gurn made no comment.

"When will my escape be discovered?" he asked.

"I am on night duty," the warder answered. "Arrange your clothes on your bed to make it look as if you were in bed, and then they will think I might have been deceived. I go off duty at five; the next round is at eight. My mate will open the door of the cage, and by that time you will be miles away."

Gurn nodded comprehension. Time did not permit of longer conversation. The bell had rung some minutes ago, proclaiming that the exercise time was over. The two men hurried upstairs to cell number 127 on the third floor, and the prisoner was locked in alone, while Nibet went about his duty as usual.

XXVI
A Mysterious Crime

Arriving in good time at the little station at Verrières, where he was about to take a train to Paris to keep his appointment at the Law Courts, the old steward Dollon gave his parting instructions to his two children, who had come to see him off.

"I must, of course, call upon Mme. de Vibray," he said, "and I don't yet know what time M. Fuselier wants to see me at his office. Anyhow, if I don't come back to-morrow, I will the next day, without fail. Well, little ones, I'm just off now, so say good-bye and get home as fast as you can. It looks to me as if there was going to be a storm, and I should like to know that you were safe at home."

With heavy creaking of iron wheels, and hoarse blowing off of steam from the engine, the Paris train drew into the station. The steward gave a final kiss to his little son and daughter and got into a second-class carriage.

In a neighbouring village a clock had just struck three.

The storm had been raging since early in the evening, but now it seemed informed with a fresh fury: the rain was lashing down more fiercely, and the wind was blowing harder still, making the slender poplars along the railway line bow and bend before the squalls and assume the most fantastic shapes, but vaguely shown against the night. The night was inky black. The keenest eye could make out nothing at all distinctly, even at the distance of a few yards: the darkness was so dense as to seem absolutely solid.

Nevertheless, along the railway embankment, a man was making his way with steady step, seeming not a whit disturbed by the tragic horror of the storm.

He was a man of about thirty, rather well dressed in a large waterproof coat, the collar of which, turned up to his ears, hid the lower part of his face, and a big felt hat with brim turned down protecting him fairly well from the worst of the weather. The man fought his way against the wind, which drove into his overcoat with such force that sometimes it almost stopped his progress, and he trod the stony track without paying heed to the sorry plight into which it would most surely put the thin boots he was wearing.

"Awful weather!" he growled: "I don't remember such a shocking night for years: wind, rain, every conceivable thing! But I mustn't grumble, for the total absence of moon will be uncommonly useful for my purpose." A flash of lightning streaked the horizon, and the man stopped and looked quickly about him. "I can't be far from the place," he thought, and again went on his way. Presently he heaved a sigh of relief. "Here I am at last."

At this spot the line was completely enclosed between two high slopes, or ran at the bottom of a deep cutting.

"It's better here," the man said to himself; "the wind passes well above my head, and the cutting gives good shelter." He stopped and carefully deposited on the ground a rather bulky bundle he had been carrying under his arm; then he began to pace up and down, stamping his feet in an effort to keep warm. "It has just struck three," he muttered. "From the time-table I can't expect anything for another ten minutes. Well, better too soon than too late!" He contemplated the bundle which he had laid down a few minutes before. "It's heavier than I thought, and deucedly in the way. But it was absolutely necessary to bring it. And down here in this cutting, there is nothing for me to be anxious about: the grass is thick, so I can run, and the line is so straight that I shall see the lights of the train a long way off." A thin smile curled his lips. "Who would have thought, when I was in America, that I should ever find it so useful to have learnt how to jump a train?"

A dull sound in the distance caught his ear. In a second he had sprung to his bundle, picked it up, and, choosing a spot on the ballast, crouched down listening. At the place where he stood the line ran up a steep acclivity. It was from the lower end of this that the noise he had heard proceeded, and now was growing louder, almost deafening. It was the heavy, regular puffing of a powerful engine coming up a steep gradient, under full steam.

"No mistake: my star is with me!" the man muttered, and as the train approached he stretched his muscles and, taking a firmer grip of his bundle, he bent forward in the stooping attitude that runners take when about to start off in a race.

With a heavy roar, and enveloped in clouds of steam, the train came up to where he was, travelling slowly because of the steep gradient, certainly less than twenty miles an hour. The moment the engine had passed him, the man started off, lithe as a cat, and ran at the top of his speed. The train, of course, gained upon him; the tender, luggage vans, and third-class carriages passed him, and a second-class carriage was just coming up with him. The pace alone would have deprived almost anyone else of power of thought, but this man was evidently a first-rate athlete, for the moment he caught sight of the second-class carriage he took his decision. With a tremendous effort he caught hold of the hand-rail and sprang upon the footboard, where, with extraordinary skill, he contrived to remain.

Reaching the summit of the slope, the train gathered speed, and with an even louder roar began its headlong journey through the darkness and the storm, which seemed to increase in intensity with every passing minute.

For a few seconds the man hung on where he was. Then, when he had regained his breath, he got on to the upper step and listened at the door of the corridor at which he found himself. "No one there," he muttered. "Besides, everyone will be asleep," and, chancing everything, he rose up, opened the door, and stepped into the second-class carriage with a grunt of relief.

Making no attempt to conceal himself, he walked boldly into the lavatory and washed his face that was blackened with the smoke from outside, and then, in the most leisurely, natural way possible, he came out of the lavatory and walked along the corridor, soliloquising aloud, manifestly not minding whether he were overheard.

"It's positively maddening! No one can sleep, with travelling companions like that!"

As he spoke he went along the corridor, rapidly glancing into every compartment. In one, three men were asleep, obviously unaware that anyone was surveying them from outside. The door of the compartment was ajar, and the stranger noiselessly stepped within. The fourth corner was unoccupied, and here the man took his seat, laying his bundle down beside him, and feigning sleep. He waited, motionless, for a good quarter of an hour, until he was quite satisfied that his companions were really sleeping soundly, then he slid his hand into the bundle by his side, seemed to be doing something inside it, then withdrew his hand noiselessly, stepped out of the compartment, and carefully closed the door.

In the corridor he drew a sigh of relieved satisfaction, and took a cigar from his pocket. "Everything is going splendidly," he said to himself. "I was cursing this awful storm just now, but it is wonderfully useful to me. On such a night as this no one would dream of opening the windows." He strolled up and down, holding on to the hand-rail with one hand to maintain himself against the rocking of the train, and every now and then taking out his watch with the other to see the time. "I haven't any too much time," he muttered. "I shall have to be quick, or my friend will miss his train!" He smiled, as if amused at the idea, and then, holding his cigar away from him so as not to inhale the smoke, he drew several deep breaths. "There is a faint smell," he said, "but you would have to be told of it to detect it. The devil of it is that it so often causes nightmare; that would be awful!" He suspended his patrol and listened again. There was no sound to be heard from within the compartments except the snoring of a few travellers and the monotonous, rhythmical noise of the wheels passing over the joints of the rails. "Come: I've waited twenty minutes; it would be risky to wait longer; let's get to work!"

He stepped briskly back into the compartment, and furtively glancing into the corridor to make sure that no one was there, he went across to the opposite window and opened it wide. He put his head out into the air for a minute or two, and then turned to examine his travelling companions. All three were still sound asleep.

The man gave vent to a dry chuckle. He drew his bundle towards him, felt until he found something within it, and flung it back on to the seat. Then he walked up to the man opposite him, slipped his hand inside his coat and abstracted a pocket-book and began to examine the papers it contained. "Ah!" he exclaimed suddenly; "that was what I was afraid of!" and taking one of the papers he put it inside his own pocket-book, chose one from his own and put it into the other man's pocket-book, and then, having effected this exchange, replaced the man's property and chuckled again. "You do sleep!"

And indeed, although the pick-pocket took no particular precaution, the man continued to sleep soundly, as did the other two men in the compartment.

The thief looked once more at his watch.

"Time!"

He leaned out of the open window and slipped back the safety catch. Then he opened the door quite wide, took the sleeping traveller by the shoulders and picked him up from the seat, and with all his strength sent him rolling out on to the line!

The next moment he seized from the rack the light articles that evidently belonged to his victim, and threw them out after him.

When he had finished his ghastly work he rubbed his hands in satisfaction. "Good!" he said, and closing the door again, but leaving the window down, he left the compartment, not troubling to pick up his belongings, and walked along the corridors to another second-class compartment, towards the front of the train, in which he calmly installed himself.

"Luck has been with me," he muttered as he stretched himself out on the seat. "Everything has gone off well; no one has seen me, and those two fools who might have upset my plans will wake up quite naturally when they begin to feel the cold; and they will attribute the headache they will probably feel to their tiring journey."

A train, travelling in the opposite direction, suddenly roared past the window and made him jump. He started up, and smiled.

"'Gad! I said my friend would miss his train, but he'll catch it in another five minutes! In another five minutes, luggage and body and the entire caboodle will be mincemeat!" and as if completely reassured by the idea he chuckled again. "Nothing could have gone better: I can have a rest, and in an hour's time I shall be at Juvisy, where, thanks to my forethought, I shall be able to whitewash myself — literally." One thing, however, still seemed to worry him: he did not know exactly where on the line he had thrown his unhappy victim, but he had an idea that the train had run through a small station shortly afterwards; if that was so, the body might be found sooner than he would have liked. He tried to dismiss the notion from his mind, but he caught sight of the telegraph posts speeding past the windows, and he shook his fist at them malignantly. "That is the only thing that can harm me now," he muttered.

"Juvisy! Juvisy! Wait here two minutes!"

It was barely half-past six, and the porters hurried along the train, calling out the name of the station, and rousing sleepy travellers from their dreams. A man jumped nimbly out of a second-class carriage and walked towards the exit from the station, holding out his ticket. "Season," he said, and passed out rapidly.

"Good idea, that season ticket," he said to himself; "much less dangerous than an ordinary ticket which the police could have traced."

He walked briskly towards the subway, crossed the main road, and took a side turning that led down towards the Seine. Taking no notice of the mud, the man went into a field and hid himself in a little thicket on the river bank. He looked carefully all around him to make sure that he was unobserved, then took off his overcoat, jacket and trousers, and drawing a bundle from one of the pockets of his large waterproof, proceeded to dress himself anew. As soon as he was dressed, he spread the waterproof out on the ground, folded up in it the clothes and hat he had previously been wearing, added a number of heavy stones, and tied the whole bundle up with a piece of string. He swung it once or twice at the full length of his arm, and sent it hurtling right into the middle of the river, where it sank at once.

A few minutes later a bricklayer in his working clothes presented himself at the Juvisy booking office.

"A workman's ticket to Paris, please, missus," he said, and having got it, the man went on to the departure platform. "It would have been risky to use my own ticket," he muttered. "This return ticket will put them off the scent," and with a smile he waited for the train that would take him to Paris.

The slow train from Luchon was drawing near its Paris terminus and the travellers were all making hasty toilettes and tidying themselves up after their long night journey. Just, however, as it was approaching the goods station it slowed down and stopped. The passengers, surprised, put their heads out of the windows, to ascertain the reason for the unexpected delay, hazarding various conjectures but unanimous in their vituperation of the company.

Three men were walking slowly along the line, looking carefully at every door. Two were porters, and they were manifesting the most respectful attention to everything the third man said: he was a grave individual, very correctly attired.

"Look there, sir," one of the porters exclaimed; "there is a door where the safety catch has either been undone or not fastened; that is the only one on the train."

"That is so," said the gentleman, and grasping the handle he opened the door of the compartment and got in. Two travellers were busy strapping up their bags, and they turned round in simultaneous surprise.

"You will pardon me, gentlemen, when you know who I am," said the intruder, and throwing open his coat he showed his tricolour scarf. "I have to make enquiry relative to a dead body that has been found on the line near Brétigny; it probably fell from this train, and perhaps from this compartment, for I have just observed that the safety catch is not fastened. Where did you get into the train?"

The two passengers looked at one another in astonishment.

"What a dreadful thing!" one of them exclaimed. "Why, sir, to-night, while my friend here and I were asleep, one of our fellow-travellers did disappear. I made a remark about it, but this gentleman very reasonably pointed out that he must have got out at some station while we were asleep."

The official was keenly interested.

"What was this passenger like?"

"Quite easily recognised, sir; a man of about sixty, rather stout, and wearing whiskers."

"That tallies with the description. Might he have been a butler or a steward?"

"That is exactly what he looked like."

"Then that must be the man whose body has been found upon the line. But I do not know whether it is to be regarded as a case of suicide or of murder, for some hand baggage has been picked up as well: a suicide would not have thrown his luggage out, and a thief would not have wanted to get rid of it."

The passenger who had not yet spoken, broke in.

"You are wrong, sir; at any rate all his luggage was not thrown on to the line," and he pointed to the bundle left upon the seat. "I thought that belonged to the gentleman here, but he has just told me it isn't his."

The official rapidly unfastened the straps and started back.

"Hullo! A bottle of liquid carbonic acid! Now what does that mean?" He looked at it. "Did this bundle belong to the man who disappeared?"

The two passengers shook their heads.

"I don't think so," one of them said; "I should certainly have noticed that Scotch rug; but I did not see it."

"Then there was a fourth passenger in this compartment?" the official enquired.

"No, we travelled alone," said one of the men, but the other dissented.

"It is very odd, and I am not sure about it, but I really am wondering whether someone did not get into our compartment last night while we were asleep. I have a vague impression that someone did, but I can't be sure."

"Do try to remember, sir," the official urged him; "it is of the very highest importance."

But the passenger shook his shoulders doubtfully.

"No, I really can't say anything definite; and, besides, I have a shocking headache."

The official was silent for a minute or two.

"In my opinion, gentlemen, you have been uncommonly lucky to escape murder yourselves. I do not quite understand yet how the murder was done, but I incline to think it proves almost incredible daring. However —— " He stopped and put his head out of the window. "You can send the train on now," he called to a porter, and resumed: "However, I must ask you to accompany me to the stationmaster's office and give me your names and addresses, and to help me afterwards in the conduct of the legal investigation."

The two travellers looked at one another in distressed surprise.

"It is really appalling," said one of them; "you're not safe anywhere nowadays."

"You really aren't," the other agreed. "Such a number of awful murders and crimes are being perpetrated every day that you would think not one, but a dozen Fantômas were at work!"

XXVII
Three Surprising Incidents

Nibet went off duty at five in the morning, and returned to his own home to go to bed. As a general rule he slept like a top, after a night on duty, but on this occasion he could not close an eye, being far too uneasy about the consequences of his co-operation in Gurn's escape.

A few minutes before six in the evening he had taken advantage of no warders being about to slip Gurn from cell number 127 into number 129, whence he could make his way to the roof. At six, when he actually came on duty, Nibet opened the peephole in the door of number 127, as he did in all the others, and saw that Gurn had made an admirable dummy figure in the bed: it was so good that it even deceived a head warder who made a single rapid inspection of all the cells when Nibet was on one of his several rounds during the night. Obviously Gurn must have got clear away from the prison, for if he had been caught it would certainly have become generally known.

These reflections somewhat comforted the restless man, but he knew that the most difficult part of his task was still before him: the difficulty of simulating astonishment and distress when he should get back to the prison presently and be told by his fellow-warders of the prisoner's escape, and the difficulty of answering in a natural manner to the close interrogation to which he would be subjected by the governor and the police, and possibly even M. Fuselier, who would be in a fine rage when he learned that his captive had escaped him. Nibet meant to pretend ignorance and even stupidity. He would far rather be called a fool, than found out to be a knave and an accomplice.

About half-past eleven Nibet got up; Gurn's escape must certainly be known at the prison by this time. The warder on duty would have gone to the cell about seven to wake the prisoner, and though nothing might have been detected then, the cell would infallibly have been found to be empty at eight o'clock, when the morning broth was taken round. And then —— —

As he walked from his home round to the prison, Nibet met the gang of masons coming out for dinner; he crossed the street towards them, hoping to hear some news, but they passed by him in silence, one or two of them giving a careless nod or word of greeting; at first Nibet took their silence for a bad sign, thinking they might have been warned to give him no alarm, but he reflected that if Gurn's escape were discovered, as it surely must be, the authorities would probably prefer not to let the matter become widely known.

As he reached the porter's lodge his heart beat violently. What would old Morin have to tell him? But old Morin was very busy trying to make his kitchen fire burn properly instead of sending all the smoke pouring out into the room; the old man's slovenly figure was just visible in a clearing in the smoke, and he returned Nibet's salutation with nothing more than a silent salute.

"That's funny!" thought Nibet, and he passed through the main courtyard towards the clerks' offices at the end. Through the windows he could see the staff, a few bending over their work, most of them reading newspapers, none of them obviously interested in anything special. Next he presented himself before the warders' turnkey, and again he was allowed to pass on without a word.

By this time Gurn's accomplice was in a state of such nervous tension that he could hardly restrain himself from catching hold of one or other of the warders whom he saw at their work, and asking them questions. How could the escape of so important a prisoner as the man who had murdered Lord Beltham create so little excitement as this? Nibet longed to rush up the flights of stairs to number 127 and interrogate the warder who had gone on duty after himself, and whom he was now about to relieve in turn. He must surely know all about it. But it would not do to create suspicion, and Nibet had sufficient self-control left to go upstairs at his usual leisurely pace. Outwardly calm and steady, he reached his post just as the clock was striking twelve; he was ever punctuality itself, and he was due on duty at noon.

"Well, Colas," he said to his colleague, "here I am; you can go now."

"Good!" said the warder. "I'll be off at once. I'm on again at six to-night," and he moved away.

"Everything all right?" Nibet enquired, in a tone he tried to make as casual as possible, but that trembled a little nevertheless.

"Quite," said Colas, perfectly naturally, and he went away.

Nibet could contain himself no longer, and the next second he threw caution to the winds: rushing to Gurn's cell he flung the door open.

Gurn was there, sitting on the foot of his bed with his legs crossed and a note-book on his knees, making notes with the quietest attention: he scarcely appeared to notice Nibet's violent invasion.

"Oh! So you are there?" stammered the astonished warder.

Gurn raised his head and looked at the warder with a cryptic gaze.

"Yes, I'm here."

All manner of notions crowded through Nibet's brain, but he could find words for none of them. Had the plot been discovered before Gurn had had time to get away, or had a trap been laid for himself through the medium of one of the prisoners to test his own incorruptibility? Nibet went white, and leaned against the wall for support. At last Gurn spoke again, reassuring him with a smile.

"Don't look so miserable," he said. "I am here. That is a matter of absolutely no importance. We will suppose that nothing passed between us yesterday, and — that's an end to it."

"So you haven't gone, you didn't go?" said Nibet again.

"No," Gurn replied; "since you are so interested, all I need say is that I was afraid to risk it at the last minute."

Nibet had cast a keen and experienced eye all over the cell; under the washstand he saw the little bundle of clothes which he had brought the prisoner the previous day. He rightly opined that the first thing to do was to remove these dangerous articles, whose presence in Gurn's cell would appear very suspicious if they happened to be discovered. He took the bundle and was hurriedly stowing it away under his own clothes, when he uttered an exclamation of surprise; the things were wet, and he knew from his own experience that the rain had never ceased throughout the whole of the night.

"Gurn," he said reproachfully, "you are up to some trick! These things are soaked. You must have gone out last night, or these things would not be like this."

Gurn smiled sympathetically at the warder.

"Not so bad!" he remarked; "that's pretty good reasoning for a mere gaoler." And as Nibet was about to press the matter, Gurn anticipated his questions, and made frank confession. "Well, yes, I did try to get out, — got as far as the clerk's office last evening, but at the last minute I funked it, and went back on to the roof. But when I got into number 129 again I found I could not get back into my own cell, for, as you know, 129 was locked outside; so to avoid detection I returned to the roof and spent the night there; at daybreak I took advantage of the little disturbance caused by the workmen coming in, and slipped down from the roof just as they were going up. As soon as I found myself on this floor I ran along this corridor and slipped into my cell. When your friend Colas brought me my broth he did not notice that my cell was unlocked, — and there you are!"

The explanation was not altogether convincing, but Nibet listened to it and pondered the situation. On the whole, it was much better that things should be as they were, but the warder was wondering how the great lady, who paid so mighty well, might take the matter. She most certainly had not promised so large a sum of money, nor paid the good round sum of ten thousand francs down in advance, merely in order that Gurn might have a little walk upon the tiles. What was to be done with regard to that personage? With much ingenuousness Nibet confided his anxiety to the prisoner, who laughed.

"It's not all over yet," he declared. "Indeed, it is only just beginning. What if we only wanted to test you, and prove your quality? Make your mind easy, Nibet. If Gurn is in prison at the present moment it is because he has his own reasons for being there. But who is able to predict the future?"

It was time for Gurn to go to the exercise yard, and Nibet, reassuming the uncompromising attitude that all warders ought to maintain when in custody of prisoners, led the murderer down to the courtyard.

In his office at the Law Courts, M. Fuselier was having a private interview with Juve, and listening with much interest to what the clever detective inspector was saying to him.

"I tell you again, sir, I attach great importance to the finding of this ordnance map in Gurn's rooms."

"Yes?" said M. Fuselier, with a touch of scepticism.

"And I will tell you why," Juve went on. "About a year ago, when I was engaged on the case of the murder of the Marquise de Langrune at her château of Beaulieu, down in Lot, I found a small piece of a map showing the district in which I was at the time. I took it to M. de Presles, the magistrate who was conducting the enquiry. He attached no importance to it, and I myself could not see at the time that it gave us any new evidence."

"Quite so," said M. Fuselier. "There is nothing particularly remarkable in finding a map, or a piece of a map, showing a district, in the district itself."

"Those are M. de Presles' very words to me," said Juve with a smile. "And I will give you the same answer I gave him, namely, that if some day we could find the other portion of the map which completed the first piece we found, and could identify the owner of the two portions, there would then be a formal basis on which to proceed to base an argument."

"Proceed to base it," M. Fuselier suggested.

"That's very easy," said Juve. "The fragment of map numbered 1, found at Beaulieu, belongs to X. I do not know who X is; but in Paris, in Gurn's rooms, I find the fragment of map numbered 2, which belongs to Gurn. If it turns out, as I expect, that the two fragments of map, when placed together, form a single and complete whole, I shall conclude logically that X, who was the owner of fragment number 1, is the same as the owner of fragment number 2, to wit, Gurn."

"How are you going to find out?" enquired M. Fuselier.

"It is in order to find it out that we have sent for Dollon," Juve replied. "He was steward to the late Marquise de Langrune, and has all the circumstantial evidence relating to that case. If he has still got the fragment of map, it will be simplicity itself to prove what I have suggested, and perhaps to make the identification I suggest."

"Yes," said M. Fuselier, "but if you do succeed, will it be of really great importance in your opinion? Will you be able to infer from that one fact that Gurn and the man who murdered the Marquise de Langrune are one and the same person? Is not that going rather far? Especially as, if I remember rightly, it was proved that the murderer in that case was the son of a M. Rambert, and this young Rambert committed suicide after the crime?"

Juve evaded the issue.

"Well, we shall see," was all he said.

The magistrate's clerk came into the room and unceremoniously interrupted the conversation.

"It has gone two, sir," he said. "There are some prisoners to examine, and a whole lot of witnesses," and he placed two bulky bundles of papers before the magistrate and waited for a sign to call the various persons, free or otherwise, whom the magistrate had to see.

The first bundle caught Juve's attention. It was endorsed "Royal Palace Hotel Case."

"Anything new about the robbery from Mme. Van den Rosen and Princess Sonia Danidoff?" he enquired, and as the magistrate shook his head, he added, "Are you going to examine Muller now?"

"Yes," said the magistrate; "at once."

"And after that you are to examine Gurn, aren't you, in connection with the Beltham case?"

"Quite so."

"I wish you would oblige me by confronting the two men here, in my presence."

M. Fuselier looked up in surprise: he could not see what connection there could be between the two utterly dissimilar cases. What object could Juve have in wanting the man who had murdered Lord Beltham to be confronted with the unimportant little hotel servant who had really been arrested rather as a concession to public opinion than because he was actually deemed capable of burglary or attempted burglary? Might not Juve, with his known mania for associating all crimes with each other, be going just a little too far in the present instance?

"You have got some idea in the back of your head?" said M. Fuselier.

"I've got a — a scar in the palm of my hand," Juve answered with a smile, and as the magistrate confessed that he failed to understand, Juve enlightened him. "We know that the man who did that robbery at the Royal Palace Hotel burned his hand badly when he was cutting the electric wires in the Princess's bathroom. Well, a few weeks ago, while I was on the look out for someone with a scar from such a wound, I was told of a man who was prowling about the slums. I had the fellow followed up, and the very night the hunt began I was going to arrest him, when, a good deal to my surprise, I discovered that he was no other than Gurn. He escaped me that time, but when he was caught later on I found that he has an unmistakable scar inside the palm of his right hand; it is fading now, for the burn was only superficial, but it is there. Now do you see my idea?"

"Yes, I do," the magistrate exclaimed, "and I am all the more glad to hear of it, since I am to have both the men here now. Shall I have Muller in first?"

Juve assented....

"So you still refuse to confess?" said the magistrate at last. "You still maintain that your — extraordinary — order to let the red-haired waiter out, was given in good faith?"

"Yes, yes, yes, sir," the night watchman answered. "That very evening a new servant had joined the staff. I had not even set eyes on him. When I saw this — stranger — — , I took him to be the servant who had been engaged the day before, and I told them to open the door for him. That is the real truth."

"And that is all?"

"That is positively all."

"We are only charging you with complicity," the magistrate went on, "for the man who touched the electric wires burned his hand; that is a strong point in your favour. And you also say that if the thief were put before you, you could recognise him?"

"Yes," said the man confidently.

"Good!" said M. Fuselier, and he signed to his clerk to call in another personage.

The clerk understood, and Gurn was brought in between two municipal guards, and was followed by the young licentiate in law, Maître Roger de Seras, who represented his leader at most of these preliminary examinations. As Gurn came in, with the light from the window falling full on his face, M. Fuselier gave a curt order.

"Muller, turn round and look at this man!"

Muller obeyed, and surveyed with some bewilderment, and without the least comprehension, the bold head and the well-built, muscular frame of Lord Beltham's murderer. Gurn did not flinch.

"Do you recognise that man?" the magistrate demanded.

Muller ransacked his brains and looked again at Gurn, then shook his head.

"No, sir."

"Gurn, open your right hand," the magistrate ordered. "Show it," and he turned again to Muller. "The man before you seems to have been burned in the palm of the hand, as that scar shows. Can you not remember having seen that man at the Royal Palace Hotel?"

Muller looked steadily at Gurn.

"On my honour, sir, although it would be to my interest to recognise him, I am bound to acknowledge that I really and truly don't."

M. Fuselier had a brief conversation aside with Juve, and then, the detective appearing to agree with him, turned once more to the night watchman.

"Muller," he said, "the court is pleased with your frankness. You will be set free provisionally, but you are to hold yourself at the disposal of the court of enquiry," and he signed to the municipal guards to lead the gratefully protesting man away.

Meanwhile Gurn's case appeared to him to be becoming much more serious, and much more interesting. He had the prisoner placed in front of him, while Juve, who had withdrawn into a dark corner of the room, never took his eyes off the murderer.

"Gurn," he began, "can you give me an account of your time during the second half of December of last year?"

Gurn was unprepared for the point-blank question, and made a gesture of doubt. M. Fuselier, probably anticipating a sensation, was just on the point of ordering Dollon to be called, when he was interrupted by a discreet tap on the door. His clerk went to answer it, and saw a gendarme standing at the door. At almost the first words he said, the clerk uttered an exclamation and wheeled round to the magistrate.

"Oh, M. Fuselier, listen! They have just told me —— "

But the gendarme had come in. He saluted the magistrate and handed him a letter which M. Fuselier hastily tore open and read.

"To M. Germain Fuselier, Examining Magistrate,
The Law Courts, Paris.

"The special commissioner at Brétigny station has the honour to report that this morning at 8 A.M. the police informed him of the discovery on the railway line, five kilomètres from Brétigny on the Orléans side, of the dead body of a man who must either have fallen accidentally or been thrown intentionally from a train bound for Paris. The body had been mutilated by a train travelling in the other direction, but papers found on the person of the deceased, and in particular a summons found in his pocket, show that his name was Dollon, and that he was on his way to Paris to wait upon you.

"The special commissioner at Brétigny station has, quite late, been informed of the following facts: passengers who left the train on its arrival at the Austerlitz terminus at 5 A.M. were examined by the special commissioner at that station, and subsequently allowed to go. Possibly you have already been informed. We have, however, thought it our duty, after having searched the body, to report this identification to you, and have therefore requisitioned an officer of the police at Brétigny to convey to you the information contained in this communication."

M. Fuselier had turned pale as he read this letter. He handed it to Juve. With feverish haste the famous detective read it through and wheeled round to the gendarme.

"Tell me, do you know what has been done? Do you know if this man's papers, all his papers, were found and have been preserved?"

The man shook his head in ignorance. Juve clasped the magistrate's hand. "I'm off to Brétigny this instant," he said in a low tone.

Throughout this incident Maître Roger de Seras had remained in a state of blank incomprehension.

Gurn's face was more expressionless and impenetrable than ever.

XXVIII

The Court of Assize

"Call Lady Beltham!"

It was a perfect May day, and everyone who could pretend, on any conceivable ground, to belong to "Paris" had schemed and intrigued to obtain admission to a trial over which public opinion had been excited for months: the trial of Gurn for the murder of Lord Beltham, ex-Ambassador and foremost man of fashion, whose murder, two years before, had caused a great sensation.

The preliminary formalities of the trial had furnished nothing to tickle the palates of the sensation-loving crowd. The indictment had been almost inaudible, and, besides, it contained nothing that had not already been made public by the Press. Nor had the examination of the prisoner been any more interesting; Gurn sat, strangely impassive, in the dock between two municipal guards, and hardly listened to his counsel, the eminent Maître Barberoux, who was assisted by a galaxy of juniors, including young Roger de Seras. Moreover, Gurn had frankly confessed his guilt almost immediately after his arrest. There was not much for him to add to what he had said before, although the President of the Court pressed him as to some points which were still not satisfactorily clear with respect to his own identity, and the motives which had prompted him to commit his crime, and, subsequently, to pay that most risky visit to Lady Beltham, at the close of which Juve had effected his arrest.

But Lady Beltham's evidence promised to be much more interesting. Rumour had been busy for a long time with the great lady and her feelings, and odd stories were being whispered. She was said to be beautiful, wealthy and charitable; people said, under their breath, that she must know a good deal about the murder of her spouse, and when she made her appearance in the box a sudden hush fell upon the crowded court. She was, indeed, a most appealing figure, robed in long black weeds, young, graceful, and very pale, so sympathetic a figure that scandal was forgotten in the general tense desire to hear her answers to the President of the Court.

Following the usher to the witness-box, she took off her gloves as desired, and, in a voice that trembled slightly but was beautifully modulated, repeated the words of the oath, with her right hand raised the while. Noticing her agitation, the President mitigated somewhat the harshness of the tone in which he generally spoke to witnesses.

"Pray compose yourself, madame. I am sorry to be obliged to subject you to this examination, but the interests of Justice require it. Come now: you are Lady Beltham, widow of the late Lord Beltham, of English nationality, residing in Paris, at your own house in Neuilly?"

"Yes."

"Will you kindly turn round, madame, and tell me if you know the prisoner in the dock?"

Lady Beltham obeyed mechanically; she glanced at Gurn, who paled a little, and answered the President.

"Yes, I know the prisoner; his name is Gurn."

"Very good, madame. Can you tell me first of all how you came to be acquainted with him?"

"When my husband was in South Africa, at the time of the Boer War, Gurn was a sergeant in the regular army. It was then that I first met him."

"Did you know him well at that time?"

Lady Beltham seemed to be unable to prevent herself from casting long glances at the prisoner; she appeared to be almost hypnotised and frightened by his close proximity.

"I saw very little of Gurn in the Transvaal," she answered. "It was just by chance that I learned his name, but of course the difference between his own rank and my husband's position made the relations that I could have with a mere sergeant very limited indeed."

"Yes, Gurn was a sergeant," the President said. "And after the war, madame, did you see the prisoner again?"

"Yes, immediately after the war; my husband and I went to England by the same boat on which Gurn went home."

"Did you see much of him on board?"

"No; we were first-class passengers, and he, I believe, went second. It was just by accident that my husband caught sight of him soon after the boat sailed."

The President paused and made a note.

"Were those all the relations your husband had with the prisoner?"

"They are at any rate all the relations I had with him," Lady Beltham replied in tones of some distress; "but I know that my husband employed Gurn on several occasions, to help him in various affairs and matters of business."

"Thank you," said the President; "we will return to that point presently. Meanwhile there is one question I should like to ask you. If you had met the prisoner in the street a few months ago, should you have recognised him? Was his face still distinct in your memory, or had it become blurred and vague?"

Lady Beltham hesitated, then answered confidently.

"I am sure I should not have recognised him; and some proof of this is, that just before his arrest was effected I was conversing with the prisoner for several minutes, without having the faintest idea that the poor man with whom I imagined I had to do was no other than the man Gurn for whom the police were looking."

The President nodded, and Maître Barberoux leaned forward and spoke eagerly to his client in the dock. But the President continued immediately.

"You must forgive me, madame, for putting a question that may seem rather brutal, and also for reminding you of your oath to tell us the entire truth. Did you love your husband?"

Lady Beltham quivered and was silent for a moment, as though endeavouring to frame a right answer.

"Lord Beltham was much older than myself — — ," she began, and then, perceiving the meaning implicit in her words, she added: "I had the very highest esteem for him, and a very real affection."

A cynical smile curled the lip of the President, and he glanced at the jury as though asking them to pay still closer attention.

"Do you know why I put that question to you?" he asked, and as Lady Beltham confessed her ignorance he went on: "It has been suggested, madame, by a rumour which is very generally current in the newspapers and among people generally, that the prisoner may possibly have been greatly enamoured of you: that perhaps — well, is there any truth in this?"

As he spoke the President bent forward, and his eyes seemed to pierce right through Lady Beltham.

"It is a wicked calumny," she protested, turning very pale.

Throughout the proceedings Gurn had been sitting in an attitude of absolute indifference, almost of scorn; but now he rose to his feet and uttered a defiant protest.

"Sir," he said to the President of the Court, "I desire to say publicly here that I have the most profound and unalterable respect for Lady Beltham. Anyone who has given currency to the malignant rumour you refer to, is a liar. I have confessed that I killed Lord Beltham, and I do not retract that confession, but I never made any attempt upon his honour, and no word, nor look, nor deed has ever passed between Lady Beltham and myself, that might not have passed before Lord Beltham's own eyes."

The President looked sharply at the prisoner.

"Then tell me what your motive was in murdering your victim."

"I have told you already! Lady Beltham is not to be implicated in my deed in any way! I had constant business dealings with Lord Beltham; I asked him, over the telephone, to come to my place one day. He came. We had an animated discussion; he got warm and I answered angrily; then I lost control of myself and in a moment of madness I killed him! I am profoundly sorry for my crime and stoop to crave pardon for it; but I cannot tolerate the suggestion that the murder I committed was in the remotest way due to sentimental relations with a lady who is, I repeat, entitled to the very highest respect from the whole world."

A murmur of sympathy ran through the court at this chivalrous declaration, by which the jury, who had not missed a word, seemed to be entirely convinced. But the President was trained to track truth in detail, and he turned again to Lady Beltham who still stood in the witness-box, very pale, and swaying with distress.

"You must forgive me if I attach no importance to a mere assertion, madame. The existence of some relations between yourself and the prisoner, which delicacy would prompt him to conceal, and honour would compel you to deny, would alter the whole aspect of this case." He turned to the usher. "Recall Mme. Doulenques, please."

Mme. Doulenques considered it a tremendous honour to be called as witness in a trial with which the press was ringing, and was particularly excited because she had just been requested to pose for her photograph by a representative of her own favourite paper. She followed the usher to where Lady Beltham stood.

"You told us just now, Mme. Doulenques," the President said suavely, "that your lodger, Gurn, often received visits from a lady friend. You also said that if this lady were placed before you, you would certainly recognise her. Now will you kindly look at the lady in the box: is this the same person?"

Mme. Doulenques, crimson with excitement, and nervously twisting in her hands a huge pair of white gloves which she had bought for this occasion, looked curiously at Lady Beltham.

"Upon my word I can't be sure that this is the lady," she said after quite a long pause.

"But you were so certain of your facts just now," the President smiled encouragingly.

"But I can't see the lady very well, with all those veils on," Mme. Doulenques protested.

Lady Beltham did not wait for the request which the President would inevitably have made, but haughtily put back her veil.

"Do you recognise me now?" she said coldly.

The scorn in her tone upset Mme. Doulenques. She looked again at Lady Beltham and turned instinctively as if to ask enlightenment from Gurn, whose face, however, was expressionless, and then replied:

"It's just what I told you before, your worship: I can't be sure; I couldn't swear to it."

"But you think she is?"

"You know, your worship," Mme. Doulenques protested, "I took an oath just now to tell the truth, and nothing but the truth; so I don't want to tell any stories; well, this lady might be the same lady, and again she mightn't be."

"In other words, you cannot give a definite answer."

"That's it," said the concierge. "I don't know; I can't swear. This lady is like the other lady — there's a sort of family likeness between them — — , but at the moment I do not exactly recognise her; it's much too serious!"

Mme. Doulenques would willingly have continued to give evidence for ever and a day, but the President cut her short.

"Very well; thank you," he said, and dismissed her with the usher, turning again meanwhile to Lady Beltham.

"Will you kindly tell me now what your personal opinion is as to the relative culpability of the prisoner? Of course you understand that he has confessed to the crime, and your answer will bear chiefly on the motive that may have actuated him."

Lady Beltham appeared to have recovered some of her confidence.

"I cannot say anything definite, can only express a very vague feeling about the matter. I know my husband was quick-tempered, very quick-tempered, and even violent; and his peremptory temper predisposed him to positive convictions. He maintained what he considered his rights at all times and against all comers; if, as the prisoner says, there was a heated discussion, I should not be surprised if my husband did make use of arguments that might have provoked anger."

The President gently gave a clearer turn to the phrase she used.

"So, in your opinion, the prisoner's version of the story is quite permissible? You admit that Lord Beltham and his murderer may have had a heated discussion, as a consequence of which Gurn committed this crime? That is your honest belief?"

"Yes," Lady Beltham answered, trying to control her voice; "I believe that that may be what took place. And then, it is the only way in which I can find the least excuse for the crime this man Gurn committed."

The President picked up the word, in astonishment.

"Do you want to find excuses for him, madame?"

Lady Beltham stood erect, and looked at the President.

"It is written that to pardon is the first duty of good Christians. It is true that I have mourned my husband, but the punishment of his murderer will not dry my tears; I ought to forgive him, bow beneath the burden that is laid upon my soul: and I do forgive him!"

Ghastly pale, Gurn was staring at Lady Beltham from the dock; and this time his emotion was so visible that all the jury noticed it. The President held a brief colloquy with his colleagues, asked the prisoner's counsel whether he desired to put any questions to the witness, and, receiving a reply in the negative, dismissed Lady Beltham with a word of thanks, and announced that the Court would adjourn.

Immediately a hum of conversation broke out in the warm and sunny court; barristers in their robes moved from group to group, criticising, explaining, prophesying; and in their seats the world of beauty and fashion bowed and smiled and gossiped.

"She's uncommonly pretty, this Lady Beltham," one young lawyer said, "and she's got a way of answering questions without compromising herself, and yet without throwing blame on the prisoner, that is uncommonly clever."

"You are all alike, you men," said a pretty, perfectly dressed woman in mocking tones; "if a woman is young, and hasn't got a hump on her back, and has a charming voice, your sympathies are with her at once! Oh, yes, they are! Now shall I tell you what your Lady Beltham really is? Well, she is nothing more nor less than a barnstormer! She knew well enough how to get on the soft side of the judge, who was quite ridiculously amiable to her, and to capture the sympathy of the Court. I think it was outrageous to declare that she had married a man who was too old for her, and to say that she felt nothing but esteem for him!"

"There's an admission!" the young barrister laughed. *"Vive l'amour,* eh? And *mariages de convenance* are played out, eh?"

On another bench a little further away, a clean-shaven man with a highly intelligent face was talking animatedly.

"Bosh! Your Lady Beltham is anything you like: what do I care for Lady Beltham? I shall never play women's parts, shall I? She does not stand for anything. But Gurn, now! There's a type, if you like! What an interesting, characteristic face! He has the head of the assassin of genius, with perfect mastery of self, implacable, cruel, malignant, a Torquemada of a man!"

"Your enthusiasm is running away with you," someone laughed.

"I don't care! It is so seldom one comes across figures in a city that really are figures, entities. That man is not an assassin: he is The Assassin — the Type!"

Two ladies, sitting close to this enthusiast, had been listening keenly to this diatribe.

"Do you know who that is?" one whispered to the other. "That is Valgrand, the actor," and they turned their lorgnettes on the actor who was waxing more animated every moment.

A bell rang, and, heralded by the usher proclaiming silence, the judges returned to the bench and the jury to their box. The President cast an eagle eye over the court, compelling silence, and then resumed the proceedings.

"Next witness: call M. Juve!"

XXIX

Verdict and Sentence

Once more a wave of sensation ran through the court. There was not a single person present who had not heard of Juve and his wonderful exploits, or who did not regard him as a kind of hero. All leaned forward to watch him as he followed the usher to the witness-box, wholly unaffected in manner and not seeking to make any capital out of his popularity. Indeed, he seemed rather to be uneasy, almost nervous, as one of the oldest pressmen present remarked audibly.

He took the oath, and the President of the Court addressed him in friendly tones.

"You are quite familiar with procedure, M. Juve. Which would you prefer: that I should interrogate you, or that I should leave you to tell your story in your own way? You know how important it is; for it is you who are, so to speak, the originator of the trial to-day, inasmuch as it was your great detective skill that brought about the arrest of the criminal, after it had also discovered his crime."

"Since you are so kind, sir," Juve answered, "I will make my statement first, and then be ready to answer any questions that may be put to me by yourself, or by counsel for the defence."

Juve turned to the dock and fixed his piercing eyes on the impassive face of Gurn, who met it unflinchingly. Juve shrugged his shoulders slightly, and, turning half round to the jury, began his statement. He did not propose, he said, to recite the story of his enquiries, which had resulted in the arrest of Gurn, for this had been set forth fully in the indictment, and the jury had also seen his depositions at the original examination: he had nothing to add to, or to subtract from, his previous evidence. He merely asked for the jury's particular attention; for, although he was adducing nothing new in the case actually before them, he had some unexpected disclosures to make about the prisoner's personal culpability. The first point which he desired to emphasise was that human intelligence should hesitate before no improbability, however improbable, provided that some explanation was humanly conceivable, and no definite material object rendered the improbability an impossibility. His whole statement would be based on the principle that the probable is incontestable and true, until proof of the contrary has been established.

"Gentlemen," he went on, "hitherto the police have remained impotent, and justice has been disarmed, in presence of a number of serious cases of crime, committed recently and still unsolved. Let me recall these cases to your memory: they were the murder of the Marquise de Langrune at her château of Beaulieu; the robberies from Mme. Van den Rosen and the Princess Sonia Danidoff; the murder of Dollon, the former steward of the Marquise de Langrune, when on his way from the neighbourhood of Saint-Jaury to Paris in obedience to a summons sent him by M. Germain Fuselier; and, lastly, the murder of Lord Beltham, prior to the cases just enumerated, for which the prisoner in the dock is at this moment standing his trial. Gentlemen, I have to say that all these cases, the Beltham, Langrune and Dollon murders, and the Rosen-Danidoff burglaries, are absolutely and indisputably to be attributed to one and the same individual, to that man standing there — Gurn!"

Having made this extraordinary assertion, Juve again turned round towards the prisoner. That mysterious person appeared to be keenly interested in what the detective said, but it would have been difficult to say whether he was merely surprised, or not rather perturbed and excited as well. Juve hushed, with a wave of his hand, the murmur that ran round the court, and resumed his address.

"My assertion that Gurn is the sole person responsible for all these crimes has surprised you, gentlemen, but I have proofs which must, I think, convince you. I will not go into the details of each of those cases, for the newspapers have made you quite familiar with them, but I will be as brief and as lucid as I can.

"My first point, gentlemen, is this: the murderer of the Marquise de Langrune and the man who robbed Mme. Van den Rosen and Princess Sonia Danidoff are one and the same person.

"That is shown beyond dispute by tests made in the two cases with a Bertillon dynamometer, an instrument of the nicest exactitude, which proved that the same individual operated in both cases; that is one point made good. And next, the man who robbed Mme. Van den Rosen and Princess Sonia is Gurn. That is proved to equal demonstration by the fact that the burglar burned his hand while engaged upon his crime, and that Gurn has a scar on his hand which betrays him as the criminal; the scar is faint now perhaps, but I can testify that it was very obvious at the time of a disturbance which occurred at a low café named the Saint-Anthony's Pig, where, accompanied by detective Lemaroy, who is still in hospital for treatment for injuries received on that occasion, I attempted, and failed, to arrest this man Gurn.

"Thus, gentlemen, I prove that the Langrune and Danidoff cases are the work of but one man, and that man, Gurn.

"I come to another point. As you know, the murder of the Marquise de Langrune was attended by some strange circumstances. At the inquest it was proved that the murderer most probably got into the house from outside, opening the front door with a skeleton key, and that he obtained admission into the bedroom of the Marquise, not by burglarious means — I lay insistence upon that — but by the simple means of her having opened the door to him, which she did on the strength of his name, and, finally, that if robbery was the motive of the crime, the nature of the robbery remained a mystery.

"Now I have ascertained, gentlemen, and — if, as I shall ask you presently, you decide to have an adjournment and a supplementary investigation — I shall be able to prove two important facts. The first is that the Marquise had in her possession a lottery ticket which had just won a large first prize; this ticket had been sent to her by M. Etienne Rambert. This ticket was not found at the time, but it was subsequently traced to a person, who for the moment has utterly disappeared, who declared that it was given to him by M. Etienne Rambert. And it is further noteworthy that M. Etienne Rambert seemed to be in greater funds from that time. The second fact I have ascertained is that, although M. Etienne Rambert pretended to get into a first-class carriage of a slow train at the gare d'Orsay, he most certainly was not in that train between Vierzon and Limoges: I can, if you wish, call a witness who inspected all the compartments of that carriage, and can prove that he was not there.

"The probable, almost certain, inference is that M. Etienne Rambert got into that slow train at the gare d'Orsay for the definite purpose of establishing an alibi, and then got out of it on the other side, and entered an express that was going in the same direction, and in front of the slow train.

"You may remember that it was shown that all trains stopped at the mouth of the Verrières tunnel, near Beaulieu, and that it was possible for a man to get out of the express, commit the crime and then return — I would remind you of the footprints found on the embankment — and get into the slow train which followed the express at an interval of three hours and a half, and get out of that train at Verrières station. The passenger who did that, was the criminal, and it was M. Etienne Rambert.

"As I have already proved that it was Gurn who murdered the Marquise de Langrune, it seems to follow necessarily that M. Etienne Rambert must be Gurn!"

Juve paused to make sure that the jury had followed his deductions and taken all his points. He proceeded, in the most tense hush.

"We have just identified Gurn with Rambert and proved that Rambert-Gurn is guilty of the Beltham and Langrune murders, and the robbery from Mme. Van den Rosen and Princess Sonia Danidoff. There remains the murder of the steward, Dollon.

"Gentlemen, when Gurn was arrested on the single charge of the murder of Lord Beltham, you will readily believe that his one fear was that all these other crimes, for which I have just shown him to be responsible, might be brought up against him. I was just then on the very point of finding out the truth, but I had not yet done so. A single link was missing in the chain which would connect Gurn with Rambert, and identify the murderer of Lord Beltham as the author of the other crimes. That link was some common clue, or, better still, some object belonging to the murderer of Lord Beltham, which had been forgotten and left on the scene of the Langrune murder.

"That object I found. It was a fragment of a map, picked up in a field near the château of Beaulieu, in the path which Etienne Rambert must have followed from the railway line; it was a fragment cut out of a large ordnance map, and the rest of the map I found in Gurn's rooms, thereby identifying Gurn with Rambert.

"Gentlemen, the fragment of map which was picked up in the field was left in the custody of the steward Dollon. That unfortunate man was summoned to Paris by M. Germain Fuselier. There was only one person who had any interest in preventing Dollon from coming, and that person was Gurn, or it would be better to say Rambert-Gurn; and you know that Dollon was killed before he reached M. Germain Fuselier. Is it necessary to declare that it was Gurn, Rambert-Gurn, who killed him?"

Juve said the last words in tones of such earnest and solemn denunciation that the truth of them seemed beyond all doubt. And yet he read incredulous surprise in the attitude of the jury. From the body of the court, too, a murmur rose that was not sympathetic. Juve realised that the sheer audacity of his theory must come as a shock, and he knew how difficult it would be to convince anyone who had not followed every detail of the case as he himself had done.

"Gentlemen," he said, "I know that my assertions about the multiple crimes of this man Gurn must fill you with amazement. That does not dismay me. There is one other name which I must mention, perhaps to silence your objections, perhaps to show the vast importance I attach to the deductions which I have just been privileged to detail to you. This is the last thing I have to say:

"The man who has been capable of assuming in turn the guise of Gurn, and of Etienne Rambert, and of the man of fashion at the Royal Palace Hotel: who has had the genius to devise and to accomplish such terrible crimes in incredible circumstances, and to combine audacity with skill, and a conception of evil with a pretence of respectability; who has been able to play the Proteus eluding all the efforts of the police; — this man, I say, ought not to be called Gurn! He is, and can be, no other than Fantômas!"

The detective suddenly broke off from his long statement, and the syllables of the melodramatic name seemed to echo through the court, and, taken up by all those present, to swell again into a dread murmur.

"Fantômas! He is Fantômas!"

For a space of minutes judges and jury seemed to be absorbed in their own reflections; and then the President of the Court made an abrupt gesture of violent dissent.

"M. Juve, you have just enunciated such astounding facts, and elaborated such an appalling indictment against this man Gurn, that I have no doubt the Public Prosecutor will ask for a supplementary examination, which this Court will be happy to grant, if he considers your arguments worth consideration. But are they? I will submit three objections." Juve bowed coldly. "First of all, M. Juve, do you believe that a man could assume disguise with the cleverness that you have just represented? M. Etienne Rambert is a man of sixty; Gurn is thirty-five. M. Rambert is an elderly man, slow of movement, and the man who robbed Princess Sonia Danidoff was a nimble, very active man."

"I have anticipated that objection, sir," Juve said with a smile, "by saying that Gurn is Fantômas! Nothing is impossible for Fantômas!"

"Suppose that is true," said the President with a wave of his hand, "but what have you to say to this: you charge Etienne Rambert with the murder of Mme. de Langrune; but do you not know that Etienne Rambert's son, Charles Rambert, who, according to the generally received, and most plausible, opinion was the real murderer of the Marquise, committed suicide from remorse? If Etienne Rambert was the guilty party, Charles Rambert would not have taken his own life."

Juve's voice shook a little.

"You would be quite right, sir, if again it were not necessary to add that Etienne Rambert is Gurn — that is to say, Fantômas! Is it not a possible hypothesis that Fantômas might have affected the mind of that lad: have suggested to him that it was he who committed the crime in a period of somnambulism: and at last have urged him to suicide? Do you not know the power of suggestion?"

"Suppose that also is true," said the President with another vague wave of his hand. "I will only put two incontestable facts before you. You accuse Etienne Rambert of being Gurn, and Etienne Rambert was lost in the wreck of the *Lancaster*; you also accuse Gurn of having murdered Dollon, and at the time that murder was committed Gurn was in solitary confinement in the Santé prison."

This time the detective made a sign as if of defeat.

"If I have waited until to-day to make the statement you have just listened to, it was obviously because hitherto I have had no absolute proofs, but merely groups of certainties. I spoke to-day, because I could keep silent no longer; if I am still without some explanations in detail, I am sure I shall have them some day. Everything comes to light sooner or later. And as to the two facts you have just put before me, I would reply that there is no proof that M. Rambert was lost in the wreck of the *Lancaster*: it has not been legally established that he ever was on board that ship. Of course, I know his name was in the list of passengers, but a child could have contrived a device of that sort. Besides, all the circumstances attending that disaster are still an utter mystery. My belief is that a Fantômas would be perfectly capable of causing an explosion on a ship and blowing up a hundred and fifty people, if thereby he could dispose of one of his identities, especially such a terribly compromising identity as that of Etienne Rambert."

The President dismissed the theory with a word.

"Pure romance!" he said. "And what about the murder of Dollon? I should like, further, to remind you that the fragment of map which, according to you, was the real reason for this man's death, was found on his body, and does not correspond in the least with the hole cut in the map you found in Gurn's rooms."

"As for that," Juve said with a smile, "the explanation is obvious. If Gurn, whom I charge with the murder of Dollon, had been content merely to abstract the real fragment, he would so to speak have set his signature to the crime. But he was much too clever for that: he was subtle enough to abstract the compromising fragment and substitute another fragment for it — the one found on the body."

"Perhaps," said the President; "that is possible, but I repeat, Gurn was in prison at the time."

"True! True!" said Juve, throwing up his hands. "I am prepared to swear that it was Gurn who did the murder, but I cannot yet explain how he did it, since he was in solitary confinement in the Santé."

Silence fell upon the court; Juve refrained from saying anything more, but a sarcastic smile curled his lip.

"Have you anything else to say?" the President asked after a pause.

"Nothing: except that anything is possible to Fantômas."

The President turned to the prisoner.

"Gurn, have you anything to say, any confession to make? The jury will listen to you."

Gurn rose to his feet.

"I do not understand a word of what the detective has just been saying," he said.

The President looked at Juve again.

"You suggest that there shall be a supplementary investigation?"

"Yes."

"Mr. Solicitor-General, have you any application to make on that subject?" the President asked the Public Prosecutor.

"No," said the functionary. "The witness's allegations are altogether too vague."

"Very well. The Court will deliberate forthwith."

The judges gathered round the President of the Court, and held a short discussion. Then they returned to their places and the President announced their decision. It was that after consideration of the statement of the witness Juve, their opinion was that it rested merely upon hypotheses, and their decision was that there was no occasion for a supplementary enquiry.

And the President immediately called upon the Public Prosecutor to address the Court.

Neither in the lengthy address of that functionary, nor in the ensuing address of Maître Barberoux on behalf of the defendant, was the slightest allusion made to the fresh facts adduced by the detective. The theories he put forward were so unexpected and so utterly astonishing that nobody paid the least attention to them! Then the sitting was suspended while the jury considered their verdict. The judges retired and guards removed the prisoner, and Juve, who had accepted the dismissal of his application for a further enquiry with perfect equanimity, went up to the press-box and spoke to a young journalist sitting there.

"Shall we go out for a quarter of an hour, Fandor?" and when they were presently in the corridor, he smote the young fellow in a friendly way on the shoulder and enquired: "Well, my boy, what do you say to all that?"

Jérôme Fandor seemed to be overwhelmed.

"You accuse my father? You really accuse Etienne Rambert of being Gurn? Surely I am dreaming!"

"My dear young idiot," Juve growled, "do pray understand one thing: I am not accusing your father, your real father, but only the man who represented himself to be your father! Just think: if my contention is right — that the Etienne Rambert who killed the Marquise is Gurn — it is perfectly obvious that Gurn is not your father, for he is only thirty-five years of age! He has merely represented himself to be your father."

"Then who is my real father?"

"I don't know anything about that," said the detective. "That's a matter we will look into one of these fine days! You take it from me that we are only just at the beginning of all these things."

"But the Court has refused a supplementary enquiry."

"'Gad!" said Juve, "I quite expected it would! I have not got the proofs to satisfy the legal mind; and then, too, I had to hold my tongue about the most interesting fact that I knew."

"What was that?"

"Why, that you are not dead, Charles Rambert! I had to conceal that fact, my boy, for the melancholy reason that I am a poor man and depend on my job. If I had let out that I had known for a long time that Charles Rambert was alive when he was supposed to be dead, and that I had known him first as Jeanne and then as Paul, and yet had said nothing about it, I should have been dismissed from the service as sure as eggs are eggs — and it is equally certain that you would have been arrested; which is precisely what I do not wish to happen!"

In tense silence the foreman of the jury rose.

"In the presence of God and man, and upon my honour and my conscience, I declare that the answer of a majority of the jury is 'yes' to all the questions submitted to them."

Then he sat down: he had made no mention of extenuating circumstances.

The words of the fatal verdict fell like a knell in the silent Court of Assize, and many a face went white.

"Have you anything to say before sentence is passed?"

"Nothing," Gurn replied.

In rapid tones the President read the formal pronouncement of the Court. It seemed horribly long and unintelligible, but presently the President's voice became slower as it reached the fatal words: there was a second's pause, and then he reached the point:

" — the sentence on the prisoner Gurn is death."

And almost simultaneously he gave the order:

"Guards, take the condemned away!"

Juve, who had returned to court with Fandor, spoke to the young journalist.

"'Gad!" he exclaimed, "I know what pluck is. That man is a truly remarkable man: he never turned a hair!"

XXX
An Assignation

The final curtain had fallen upon the first performance of the new drama at the Grand Treteau.

The night had been one long triumph for Valgrand, and although it was very late the Baronne de Vibray, who plumed herself on being the great tragedian's dearest friend, had made her way behind the scenes to lavish praise and congratulations on him, and have a little triumph of her own in presenting her friends to the hero of the hour. In vain had Charlot, the old dresser, tried to prevent her invasion of his master's dressing-room. He was not proof against her perseverance, and ere long she had swept into the room with the proud smile of a general entering a conquered town. The Comte de Baral, a tall young man with a single eyeglass, followed close in her wake.

"Will you please announce us," he said to the dresser.

Charlot hesitated a moment in surprise, then broke into voluble explanations.

"M. Valgrand is not here yet. What, didn't you know? Why, at the end of the performance the Minister of Public Instruction sent for him to congratulate him! That's a tremendous honour, and it's the second time it has been paid to M. Valgrand."

Meanwhile the other two ladies in the party were roaming about the dressing-room: Mme. Simone Holbord, wife of a colonel of the Marines who had just covered himself with distinction in the Congo, and the Comtesse Marcelline de Baral.

"How thrilling an actor's dressing-room is!" exclaimed Mme. Holbord, inspecting everything in the room through her glass. "Just look at these darling little brushes! I suppose he uses those in making up? And, oh, my dear! There are actually three kinds of rouge!"

The Comtesse de Baral was fascinated by the photographs adorning the walls.

"'To the admirable Valgrand from a comrade,'" she read in awe-struck tones. "Come and look, dear, it is signed by Sarah Bernhardt! And listen to this one: 'At Buenos Ayres, at Melbourne, and New York, wherever I am I hear the praises of my friend Valgrand!'"

"Something like a globe-trotter!" said Mme. Holbord. "I expect he belongs to the Comédie Française."

Colonel Holbord interrupted, calling to his wife.

"Simone, come and listen to what our friend de Baral is telling me: it is really very curious."

The young woman approached, and the Comte began again for her benefit.

"You have come back too recently from the Congo to be up to date with all our Paris happenings, and so you will not have noticed this little touch, but in the part that he created to-night Valgrand made himself up exactly like Gurn, the man who murdered Lord Beltham!"

"Gurn?" said Mme. Holbord, to whom the name did not convey much. "Oh, yes, I think I read about that: the murderer escaped, didn't he?"

"Well, they took a long time to find him," the Comte de Baral replied. "As usual, the police were giving up all hope of finding him, when one day, or rather one night, they did find him and arrested him; and where do you suppose that was? Why, with Lady Beltham! Yes, really: in her own house at Neuilly!"

"Impossible!" cried Simone Holbord. "Poor woman! What an awful shock for her!"

"Lady Beltham is a brave, dignified, and truly charitable woman," said the Comtesse de Baral. "She simply worshipped her husband. And yet, she pleaded warmly for mercy for the murderer — though she did not succeed in getting it."

"What a dreadful thing!" said Simone Holbord perfunctorily; her attention was wandering to all the other attractions in this attractive room. A pile of letters was lying on a writing-table, and the reckless young woman began to look at the envelopes. "Just look at this pile of letters!" she cried. "How funny! Every one of them in a woman's hand! I suppose Valgrand gets all sorts of offers?"

Colonel Holbord went on talking to the Comte de Baral in a corner of the room.

"I am enormously interested in what you tell me. What happened then?"

"Well, this wretch, Gurn, was recognised by the police as he was leaving Lady Beltham's, and was arrested and put in prison. The trial came on at the Court of Assize about six weeks ago. All Paris went to it, of course including myself! This man Gurn is a brute, but a strange brute, rather difficult to define; he swore that he had killed Lord Beltham after a quarrel, practically for the sake of robbing him, but I had a strong impression that he was lying."

"But why else should he have committed the murder?"

The Comte de Baral shrugged his shoulders.

"Nobody knows," he said: "politics, perhaps, nihilism, or perhaps again — love. There was one fact, or coincidence, worth noting: when Lady Beltham came home from the Transvaal after the war, during which, by the way, she did splendid work among the sick and wounded, she sailed by the same boat that was taking Gurn to England. Gurn also was a bit of a popular hero just then: he had volunteered at the beginning of the war, and came back with a sergeant's stripes and a medal for distinguished conduct. Can Gurn and Lady Beltham have met and got to know each other? It is certain that the lady's behaviour during the trial lent itself to comment, if not exactly to scandal. She had odd collapses in the presence of the murderer, collapses which were accounted for in very various ways. Some people said that she was half out of her mind with grief at the loss of her husband; others said that if she was mad, it was over someone, over this vulgar criminal — martyr or accomplice, perhaps. They even went so far as to allege that Lady Beltham had an intrigue with Gurn!"

"Come! come!" the Colonel protested: "a great lady like Lady Beltham, so religious and so austere? Absurd!"

"People say all sorts of things," said the Comte de Baral vaguely. He turned to another subject. "Anyhow, the case caused a tremendous sensation; Gurn's condemnation to death was very popular, and the case was so typically Parisian that our friend Valgrand, knowing that he was going to create the part of the murderer in this tragedy to-night, followed every phase of the Gurn trial closely, studied the man in detail, and literally identified himself with him in this character. It was a shrewd idea. You noticed the sensation when he came on the stage?"

"Yes, I did," said the Colonel; "I wondered what the exclamations from all over the house meant."

"Try to find a portrait of Gurn in some one of the illustrated papers," said the Comte, "and compare it with — — Ah, I think this is Valgrand coming!"

The Baronne de Vibray had tired of her conversation with the old dresser, Charlot, and had left him to take up her stand outside the dressing-room, where she greeted with nods and smiles the other actors and actresses as they hurried by on their way home, and listened to the sounds at the end of the passage. Presently a voice became distinguishable, the voice of Valgrand singing a refrain from a musical comedy. The Baronne de Vibray hurried to meet him, with both hands outstretched, and led him into his dressing-room.

"Let me present M. Valgrand!" she exclaimed, and then presented the two young women to the bowing actor: "Comtesse Marcelline de Baral, Mme. Holbord."

"Pardon me, ladies, for keeping you waiting," the actor said. "I was deep in conversation with the Minister. He was so charming, so kind!" He turned to the Baronne de Vibray. "He did me the honour to offer me a cigarette! A relic! Charlot! Charlot! You must put this cigarette in the little box where all my treasures are!"

"It is very full already, M. Valgrand," said Charlot deprecatingly.

"We must not keep you long," the Baronne de Vibray murmured. "You must be very tired."

Valgrand passed a weary hand across his brow.

"Positively exhausted!" Then he raised his head and looked at the company. "What did you think of me?"

A chorus of eulogy sprang from every lip.

"Splendid!" "Wonderful!" "The very perfection of art!"

"No, but really?" protested Valgrand, swelling with satisfied vanity. "Tell me candidly: was it really good?"

"You really were wonderful: could not have been better," the Baronne de Vibray exclaimed enthusiastically, and the crowd of worshippers endorsed every word, until the artist was convinced that their praise was quite sincere.

"How I have worked!" he exclaimed: "do you know, when rehearsals began — ask Charlot if this isn't true — the piece simply didn't exist!"

"Simply didn't exist!" Charlot corroborated him, like an echo.

"Didn't exist," Valgrand repeated: "not even my part. It was insignificant, flat! So I took the author aside and I said: 'Frantz, my boy, I'll tell you what you must do: you know the lawyer's speech? Absurd! What am I to do while he is delivering it? I'll make the speech for my own defence, and I'll get something out of it!' And the prison scene! Just fancy, he had shoved a parson into that! I said to Frantz: 'Cut the parson out, my boy: what the dickens am I to do while he is preaching? Simply nothing at all: it's absurd. Give his speech to me! I'll preach to myself!' And there you are: I don't want to boast, but really I did it all! And it was a success, eh?"

Again the chorus broke out, to be stopped by Valgrand, who was contemplating his reflection in a mirror.

"And my make-up, Colonel? Do you know the story of my make-up? I hear they were talking about it all over the house. Am I like Gurn? What do you think? You saw him quite close at the trial, Comte: what do you think?"

"The resemblance is perfectly amazing," said the Comte de Baral with perfect truth.

The actor stroked his face mechanically: a new idea struck him.

"My beard is a real one," he exclaimed. "I let it grow on purpose. I hardly had to make myself up at all; I am the same build, the same type, same profile; it was ridiculously easy!"

"Give me a lock of hair from your beard for a locket," said the Baronne de Vibray impudently.

Valgrand looked at her, and heaved a profound sigh.

"Not yet, not yet, dear lady: I am infinitely sorry, but not yet: a little later on, perhaps; wait for the hundredth performance."

"I must have one too," said Simone Holbord, and Valgrand with great dignity replied:

"I will put your name down for one, madame!"

But the Comte de Baral had looked furtively at his watch, and uttered an exclamation of surprise.

"My good people, it is most horribly late! And our great artiste must be overcome with sleep!"

Forthwith they all prepared to depart, in spite of the actor's courteous protests that he could not hear of letting them go so soon. They lingered at the door for a few minutes in eager, animated conversation, shaking hands and exchanging farewells and thanks and congratulations. Then the sound of their footsteps died away along the corridors, and the Baronne de Vibray and her friends left the theatre. Valgrand turned back into his dressing-room and locked the door, then dropped into the low and comfortable chair that was set before his dressing-table.

He remained there resting for a few minutes, and then sat up and threw a whimsical glance at his dresser who was putting out his ordinary clothes.

"Hang it all, Charlot! What's exhaustion? The mere sight of such jewels as those enchanting women would wake one from the dead!"

Charlot shrugged his shoulders.

"Will you never be serious, M. Valgrand?"

"Heavens, I hope not!" exclaimed the actor. "I hope not, for if there is one thing of which one never tires here below, it is Woman, the peerless rainbow that illuminates this vale of tears!"

"You are very poetical to-night," the dresser remarked.

"I am a lover — in love with love! Oh, Love, Love! And in my time, you know — — " He made a sweeping, comprehensive gesture, and came back abruptly to mundane affairs. "Come, help me to dress."

Charlot offered him a bundle of letters, which Valgrand took with careless hand. He looked at the envelopes one after another, hugely amused.

"Violet ink, and monograms, and coronets, and — perfume. Say, Charlot, is this a proposal? What do you bet?"

"You never have anything else," the dresser grumbled " — except bills."

"Do you bet?"

"If you insist, I bet it is a bill; then you will win," said Charlot.

"Done!" cried Valgrand. "Listen," and he began to declaim the letter aloud: "'Oh, wondrous genius, a flower but now unclosing' — — Got it, Charlot? Another of them!" He tore open another envelope. "Ah-ha! Photograph enclosed, and will I send it back if the original is not to my fancy!" He flung himself back in his chair to laugh. "Where is my collar?" He picked up a third envelope. "What will you bet that this violet envelope does not contain another tribute to my fatal beauty?"

"I bet it is another bill," said the dresser; "but you are sure to win."

"I have," Valgrand replied, and again declaimed the written words: "'if you promise to be discreet, and true, you shall never regret it.' Does one ever regret it — even if one does not keep one's promises?"

"At lovers' perjuries — — " Charlot quoted.

"Drunken promises!" Valgrand retorted. "By the way, I am dying for a drink. Give me a whisky and soda." He got up and moved to the table on which Charlot had set decanters and glasses, and was about to take the glass the dresser offered him when a tap on the door brought the conversation to a sudden stop. The actor frowned: he did not want to be bothered by more visitors. But curiosity got the better of his annoyance and he told Charlot to see who it was.

Charlot went to the door and peered through a narrow opening at the thoughtless intruder.

"Fancy making all this bother over a letter!" he growled. "Urgent? Of course: they always are urgent," and he shut the door on the messenger and gave the letter to Valgrand. "A woman brought it," he said.

Valgrand looked at it.

"H'm! Mourning! Will you bet, Charlot?"

"Deep mourning," said Charlot: "then I bet it is a declaration. I expect you will win again, for very likely it is a begging letter. Black edges stir compassion."

Valgrand was reading the letter, carelessly to begin with, then with deep attention. He reached the signature at the end, and then read it through again, aloud this time, punctuating his reading with flippant comments: "'In creating the part of the criminal in the tragedy to-night, you made yourself up into a most marvellous likeness of Gurn, the man who murdered Lord Beltham. Come to-night, at two o'clock, *in your costume*, to 22 rue Messier. Take care not to be seen, but come. Someone who loves you is waiting for you there.'"

"And it is signed — — ?" said the dresser.

"That, my boy, I'm not going to tell you," said Valgrand, and he put the letter carefully into his pocket-book. "Why, man, what are you up to?" he added, as the dresser came up to him to take his clothes.

"Up to?" the servant exclaimed: "I am only helping you to get your things off."

"Idiot!" laughed Valgrand. "Didn't you understand? Give me my black tie and villain's coat again."

"What on earth is the matter with you?" Charlot asked with some uneasiness. "Surely you are not thinking of going?"

"Not going? Why, in the whole of my career as amorist, I have never had such an opportunity before!"

"It may be a hoax."

"Take my word for it, I know better. Things like this aren't hoaxes. Besides, I know the — the lady. She has often been pointed out to me: and at the trial — — By Jove, Charlot, she is the most enchanting woman in the world: strangely lovely, infinitely distinguished, absolutely fascinating!"

"You are raving like a schoolboy."

"So much the better for me! Why, I was half dead with fatigue, and now I am myself again. Be quick, booby! My hat! Time is getting on. Where is it?"

"Where is what?" the bewildered Charlot asked.

"Why, this place," Valgrand answered irritably: "this rue Messier. Look it up in the directory."

Valgrand stamped impatiently up and down the room while Charlot hurriedly turned over the pages of the directory, muttering the syllables at the top of each as he ran through them in alphabetical order.

"J ... K ... L ... M ... Ma ... Me ... — Why, M. Valgrand — —"

"What's the matter?"

"Why, it is the street where the prison is!"

"The Santé? Where Gurn is — in the condemned cell?" Valgrand cocked his hat rakishly on one side. "And I have an assignation at the prison?"

"Not exactly, but not far off: right opposite; yes, number 22 must be right opposite."

"Right opposite the prison!" Valgrand exclaimed gaily. "The choice of the spot, and the desire to see me in my costume as Gurn, are evidence of a positive refinement in sensation! See? The lady, and I — the counterpart of Gurn — and, right opposite, the real Gurn in his cell! Quick, man: my cloak! My cane!"

"Do think, sir," Charlot protested: "it is absolutely absurd! A man like you — —"

"A man like me," Valgrand roared, "would keep an appointment like this if he had to walk on his head to get there! Good-night!" and carolling gaily, Valgrand strode down the corridor.

Charlot was accustomed to these wild vagaries on his master's part, for Valgrand was the most daring and inveterate rake it is possible to imagine. But while he was tidying up the litter in the room, after Valgrand had left him, the dresser shook his head.

"What a pity it is! And he such a great artiste! These women will make an absolute fool of him! Why, he hasn't even taken his gloves or his scarf!" There was a tap at the door, and the door-keeper looked in.

"Can I turn out the lights?" he enquired. "Has M. Valgrand gone?"

"Yes," said the dresser absently, "he has gone."

"A great night," said the door-keeper. "Have you seen the last edition of the *Capitale*, the eleven o'clock edition? There's a notice of us already. The papers don't lose any time nowadays. They say it is a great success."

"Let's look at it," said the dresser, and, glancing through the notice, added, "yes, that's quite true: 'M. Valgrand has achieved his finest triumph in his last creation.'" He looked casually through the newspaper, and suddenly broke into a sharp exclamation. "Good heavens, it can't be possible!"

"What's the matter?" the door-keeper enquired.

Charlot pointed a shaking finger to another column.

"Read that, Jean, read that! Surely I am mistaken."

The door-keeper peered over Charlot's shoulder at the indicated passage.

"I don't see anything in that; it's that Gurn affair again. Yes, he is to be executed at daybreak on the eighteenth."

"But that is this morning — presently," Charlot exclaimed.

"May be," said the door-keeper indifferently; "yes, last night was the seventeenth, so it is the eighteenth now! Are you ill, Charlot?"

Charlot pulled himself together.

"No, it's nothing; I'm only tired. You can put out the lights. I shall be out of the theatre in five minutes; I only want to do one or two little things here."

"All right," said Jean, turning away. "Shut the door behind you when you leave, if I have gone to bed."

Charlot sat on the arm of a chair and wiped his brow.

"I don't like this business," he muttered. "Why the deuce did he want to go? What does this woman want with him? I may be only an old fool, but I know what I know, and there have been no end of queer stories about this job already." He sat there meditating, till an idea took shape in his mind. "Can I dare to go round there and just prowl about? Of course he will be furious, but suppose that letter was a decoy and he is walking into a trap? One never can tell. An assignation in that particular street, with that prison opposite, and Gurn to be guillotined within the next hour or so?" The man made up his mind, hurriedly put on his coat and hat, and switched off the electric lights in the exquisitely appointed dressing-room. "I'll go!" he said aloud. "If I see anything suspicious, or if at the end of half an hour I don't see M. Valgrand leaving the house — well!" Charlot turned the key in the lock. "Yes, I will go. I shall be much easier in my mind!"

XXXI
Fell Treachery

Number 22 rue Messier was a wretched one-storeyed house that belonged to a country vine-dresser who seldom came to Paris. It was damp, dirty, and dilapidated, and would have had to be rebuilt from top to bottom if it were to be rendered habitable. There had been a long succession of so-called tenants of this hovel, shady, disreputable people who, for the most part, left without paying any rent, the landlord being only too glad if occasionally they left behind them a little miserable furniture or worn out kitchen utensils. He was finding it ever more difficult to let the wretched house, and for weeks together it had remained unoccupied. But one day, about a month ago, he had been astonished by receiving an application for the tenancy from someone who vaguely signed himself Durand; and still further astonished by finding in the envelope bank-notes representing a year's rent in advance. Delighted with this windfall, and congratulating himself on not having gone to the expense of putting the hovel into something like repair — unnecessary now, since he had secured a tenant, and a good one, for at least twelve months — the landlord promptly sent a receipt to this Durand, with the keys, and thought no more about the matter.

In the principal room, on the first floor of this hovel, a little poor furniture had been put; a shabby sofa, an equally shabby arm-chair, a few cane-bottomed chairs, and a deal table. On the table was a tea-pot, a small kettle over a spirit-stove, and a few cups and small cakes. A smoky lamp shed a dim light over this depressing interior, and a handful of coal was smouldering in the cracked grate.

And here, in these miserable surroundings, Lady Beltham was installed on this eighteenth of December.

The great lady was even paler than usual, and her eyes shone with a curious brilliance. That she was suffering from the most acute and feverish nervous excitement was patent from the way in which she kept putting her hands to her heart as though the violence of its throbbing were unendurable, and from the restless way in which she paced the room, stopping at every other step to listen for some sound to reach her through the silence of the night. Once she stepped quickly from the middle of the room to the wall opposite the door that opened on to the staircase; she pushed ajar the door of a small cupboard and murmured "hush," making a warning movement with her hands, as if addressing someone concealed there; then she moved forward again and, sinking on to the sofa, pressed her hands against her throbbing temples.

"No one yet!" she murmured presently. "Oh, I would give ten years of my life to — — ! Is all really lost?" Her eyes wandered round the room. "What a forbidding, squalid place!" and again she sprang to her feet and paced the room. Through the grimy panes of the window she could just see a long row of roofs and chimneys outlined against the sky. "Oh, those black roofs, those horrible black roofs!" she muttered. The already wretched light in the wretched room was burning dimmer, and Lady Beltham turned up the wick of the lamp. As she did so she caught a sound and stopped. "Can that be he?" she exclaimed, and hurried to the door. "Footsteps — and a man's footsteps!"

The next moment she was sure. Someone stumbled in the passage below, came slowly up the stairs, was on the landing.

Lady Beltham recoiled to the sofa and sank down on it, turning her back to the door, and hiding her face in her hands.

"Valgrand!"

Valgrand was a man with a passion for adventure. But invariable success in his flirtations had made him blasé, and now it was only the absolutely novel that could appeal to him. And there could certainly be no question about the woman who had sent him the present invitation being anything but a commonplace one! Moreover, it was not just any woman who had asked him to keep this assignation in the outward guise of Gurn, but the one woman in whose heart the murderer ought to inspire the greatest abhorrence, the widow of the man whom Gurn had murdered. What should his deportment be when he came face to face with her? That was what preoccupied the actor as he left the theatre, and made him dismiss the taxi in which he had started, before he reached his destination.

Valgrand came into the room slowly, and with a trained eye for effect. He flung his cloak and hat theatrically on the arm-chair, and moved towards Lady Beltham, who still sat motionless with her face hidden in her hands.

"I have come!" he said in deep tones.

Lady Beltham uttered a little exclamation as if of surprise, and seemed even more anxious to hide from him.

"Odd!" thought Valgrand. "She seems to be really upset; what can I say to her, I wonder?"

But Lady Beltham made a great effort and sat up, looking at the actor with strained eyes, yet striving to force a smile.

"Thank you for coming, sir," she murmured.

"It is not from you, madame, that the thanks should come," Valgrand answered magnificently; "quite the reverse; I am infinitely grateful to you for having summoned me. Pray believe that I would have been here even sooner but for the delay inevitable on a first performance. But you are cold," he broke off, for Lady Beltham was shivering.

"Yes, I am," she said almost inaudibly, mechanically pulling a scarf over her shoulders. Valgrand was standing, taking in every detail of the squalid room in which he found himself with this woman whose wealth, and taste, and sumptuous home at Neuilly were notorious.

"I must clear up this mystery," he thought, while he moved to the window to see that it was shut, and searched about, in vain, for a little coal to put upon the fire. While he was thus occupied Lady Beltham also rose, and going to the table poured out two cups of tea.

"Perhaps this will warm us, in the absence of anything better," she said, making an effort to seem more amiable. "I am afraid it is rather strong, M. Valgrand; I hope you do not mind?" and, with a hand that trembled as if it held a heavy weight, she brought one of the cups to her guest.

"Tea never upsets me, madame," Valgrand replied as he took the cup. "Indeed, I like it." He came to the table and picked up the basin filled with castor sugar, making first as if to put some in her cup.

"Thanks, I never take sugar in tea," she said.

Valgrand made a little grimace. "I admire you, but I will not imitate you," he said, and unceremoniously tipped a generous helping of the sugar into his own cup.

Lady Beltham watched him with haggard eyes.

While they were sipping their tea, there was silence between them. Lady Beltham went back to the sofa, and Valgrand took a chair quite close to her. The conversation was certainly lacking in animation, he reflected whimsically; would the lady succeed in reducing him to the level of intelligence of a callow schoolboy? And she most certainly did seem to be horribly upset. He raised his eyes to her and found that she was gazing into infinity.

"One has got to draw upon psychology here," Valgrand mused. "It is not me, myself, in whom this lovely creature takes any interest, or she would not have desired me to come in these trappings that make me look like Gurn; it's his skin that I must stop in! But what is the proper attitude to adopt? The sentimental? Or the brutal? Or shall I appeal to her proselytising mania, and do the repentant sinner act? I'll chance it; here goes!" and he rose to his feet.

As he moved, Lady Beltham looked round, uneasy, frightened, almost anguished: it seemed as though she realised that the moment had come for extraordinary things to happen.

Valgrand began to speak as he did upon the stage, restraining his effects at first and controlling his voice of set purpose to give full effect to it later on, modulating it cleverly.

"At your summons, madame, the prisoner Gurn has burst his bonds, broken through the door of his cell, and scaled his prison walls, triumphing over every obstacle with the single object of coming to your feet. He comes —— " and he took a step nearer to her.

Lady Beltham stayed him with a gesture of terror.

"Don't! Don't! Please say no more!" she murmured.

"I've got a bite," Valgrand said to himself. "Let's try another bait," and as if repeating a part he said dramatically: "Has your charitable heart turned towards the guilty soul that you fain would rescue from transgression? Men say you are so great a lady, so good, so near to heaven!"

Again Lady Beltham put up a protesting hand.

"Not that! Not that!" she said imploringly. "Oh, this is torture; go away!"

In her distress she was really superbly beautiful; but Valgrand knew too much about women of every temperament, neurotic, hysterical, and many another kind, not to suppose that here he was merely taking part in a sentimental comedy. He made a rough gesture and laid his hand on Lady Beltham's arm.

"Do you not know me?" he said harshly. "I am Gurn! I will crush you to my heart!" and he tried to draw her close to him.

But this time Lady Beltham threw him off with the violence of despair. "Stand back! You brute!" she cried, in tones that there was no mistaking.

Valgrand recoiled in real dismay, and stood silent in the middle of the room, while Lady Beltham went to the wall farthest from him and leaned for support against it.

"Listen, madame," Valgrand began presently, in dulcet tones that had the effect of making Lady Beltham try to control her emotion and murmur some faint words of apology. "Of course you know I am Valgrand, Valgrand the actor; I will apologise for having come to you like this, but I have some small excuse in your note!"

"My note?" she murmured. "Oh, yes; I forgot!"

Valgrand went on, seeming to pick his words.

"You have overestimated your strength, and now perhaps you find the resemblance too startling? Do not be frightened. But your letter came to me like healing balm upon a quivering wound. For weeks, long weeks — — " The actor stopped, and mechanically rubbed his eyes. "It's odd," he thought to himself, "but I feel ever so much more inclined to go to sleep than to make love." He shook off his real desire for sleep and began again. "I have loved you since the day I saw you first. I love you with an intensity — — "

For some moments Lady Beltham had been looking at him with a calmer air, and eyes that were less hostile. The old amorist observed it, and made a tremendous effort to overcome his most inopportune drowsiness.

"How shall I be silent, when at last kind heaven is about to grant the fondest desire of my heart? When, all afire with love, I am kneeling at your feet?"

Valgrand dropped to his knees. Lady Beltham drew herself up, listening. In the distance a clock struck four.

"Oh, I can bear it no longer!" she cried stammeringly. "I can bear no more! Listen; four o'clock! No, no! It is too much, too much for me!" The woman seemed absolutely frantic. She paced up and down the room like a caged animal. Then she came close to Valgrand, and looked at him with an immense pity in her eyes. "Go, sir; if you believe in God, go away! Go as quickly as you can!"

Valgrand struggled to his feet. His head was heavy, and he had an irresistible desire to hold his tongue and just stay where he was. Partly from gallantry and partly from his desire not to move, he murmured, not without a certain aptness: "I believe only in the god of love, madame, and he bids me remain!"

In vain did Lady Beltham make every effort to rouse the actor and induce him to go away; in vain were all her frantic appeals to him to fly.

"I will stay," was all he said, and he dropped heavily on the sofa by Lady Beltham's side, and mechanically tried to put his arm round her.

"Listen!" she began, freeing herself from him: "in heavens name you must — — And yet, I cannot tell you! Oh, it is horrible! I am going mad! How am I to choose! What am I to do! Which — — ? Oh, go — go — go! There is not a minute to lose!"

"I will stay!" said Valgrand again; this amazing drowsiness was gaining on him so fast that he had but one desire left — for sleep! Surely a strange assignation, this, and a poor kind of lover, too!

Lady Beltham stopped her torrent of appeal, and looked at the actor crumpled up beside her. Suddenly she started and listened: a slight noise became audible, coming from the staircase. Lady Beltham stood erect and rigid: then dropped to her knees upon the floor.

"Oh! It is all over!" she sobbed.

In spite of his overwhelming longing for sleep, Valgrand suddenly started. Two heavy hands fell on his shoulder, and then his arms were pulled behind him and his wrists rapidly bound together.

"Good God!" he cried, in stupefied surprise, turning quickly round. Two men stood before him, old soldiers by the look of them, in dark uniforms relieved only by the gleam of metal buttons. He was going to say more, but one of the men laid his hand over his lips.

"Hush!" he said peremptorily.

Valgrand made frantic efforts to prevent himself from falling.

"What does this mean? Let me go! What right — — "

The two men began to drag him gently away.

"Come along," said one of them in his ear. "Time's up. Don't be obstinate."

"Besides, you know it's quite useless to resist, Gurn," the other added, not unkindly. "Nothing in the world could — — "

"I don't understand," Valgrand protested feebly. "Who are you? And why do you call me Gurn?"

"Let me finish," growled one of the men irritably. "You know we are running an awful risk in getting you out of the prison and bringing you here when you are supposed to be with the chaplain; you swore you would behave squarely with us and go back when you were told. Now you've got to keep your promise."

"The lady paid us well to give you an hour with her," the other man put in, "but you've had more than an hour and a half, and we've got our characters and our situations to look after. So now, come along, Gurn, and don't let us have any nonsense."

Valgrand, fighting hard against his overpowering sleepiness, began to have some vague comprehension of what was happening. He recognised the uniforms, and guessed that the men were prison warders.

"Good God!" he exclaimed thickly, "the fools think I am Gurn! But I am not Gurn! Ask — — " He cast a despairing eye at Lady Beltham who throughout the awful scene remained on her knees in a corner of the room, dumb with anguish, apparently deaf and turned to stone. "Tell them, madame," he implored her. "Oh, God save me!" but still the warders dragged him towards the door. By an herculean effort he swayed them back with him into the middle of the room. "I am not Gurn, I tell you," he shouted. "I am Valgrand, Valgrand the actor. Everybody in the world knows me. You know it too, but — — Search me, I tell you," and he made a sign with his head towards his left side. "Look in my pocket-book; my name's inside; and you'll find a letter too; proof of the trap I've been led into: the letter from that woman over there!"

"Better look and see, Nibet," one warder said to the other, and to Valgrand he added: "Not so much noise, man! Do you mean to get us all caught?"

Nibet passed a quick hand through Valgrand's pockets; there was no note-book there. He shrugged his shoulders.

"Besides, what about it?" he growled. "We brought Gurn here, didn't we? Well, we've got to take Gurn back again. That's all I know. Come on!"

Beaten down by the drowsiness that was quite irresistible, and worn out by his violent but futile efforts to resist the warders, Valgrand was half dragged, half carried out by the two men, his head drooping on his chest, his consciousness failing. But still as they were getting him down the stairs his voice could be heard in the half-dark room above, bleating more weakly and at longer intervals:

158

"I am not Gurn! I am not Gurn!"

Once more silence reigned in the room. After the three men had gone, Lady Beltham rose to her feet, tottered to the window, and stood there listening. She heard their footsteps crossing the street and stopping by the door into the prison. She waited for a few minutes to make sure that they had escaped unnoticed from their amazing adventure, then turned again to the sofa, struggled to unfasten the collar of her dress to get more air, drew a few deep sighs, and swooned.

The door opposite the staircase opened slowly, and noiselessly Gurn emerged from the darkness and went towards Lady Beltham. The murderer flung himself at her feet, covered her face with kisses, and pressed her hands in his.

"Maud!" he called. "Maud!"

She did not answer and he hunted about the room for something to revive her. Presently, however, she recovered consciousness unaided and uttered a faint sigh. Her lover hurried to her.

"Oh, Gurn," she murmured, laying her white hand on the wretch's neck: "it's you, dear! Come close to me, and hold me in your arms! It was too much for me! I almost broke down and told everything! I could have borne no more. Oh, what an appalling time!" She sat up sharply, her face drawn with terror. "Listen: I can hear him still!"

"Try not to think about it," Gurn whispered, caressing her.

"Did you hear him, how he kept on saying 'I am not Gurn! I am not Gurn!' Oh, heaven grant they may not find that out!"

Gurn himself was shaken by the horror of the plot he had contrived with his mistress to effect this substitution of another for himself; it surpassed in ghastliness anything that had gone before, and he had not dared to give the least hint of it to Nibet.

"The warders were well paid," he said to reassure her now. "They would deny everything." He hesitated a second, and then asked: "He drank the drug, didn't he?"

Lady Beltham nodded assent.

"It will take effect. It was acting already: so rapidly, that I thought for a moment he would fall unconscious there, at my feet!"

Gurn drew a deep breath.

"Maud, we are saved!" he exclaimed. "See," he went on, "as soon as it is light, and there are enough people in the street for us to mix with them unobserved, we will go away from here. While you were with — him — — I burned my other clothes, so I will take these to get away in." He picked up the hat and cloak which Valgrand had thrown upon the chair, and wrapped the heavy cloak around himself. "This will conceal me effectively."

"Let us go at once!" Lady Beltham exclaimed, but Gurn stayed her.

"I must get rid of this beard, and my moustache," he said, and he took a pair of scissors from his pocket and was walking towards a looking-glass when suddenly they both heard the distinct sound of footsteps coming slowly and steadily up the stairs. Gurn had no time to get back to his former hiding-place; all he could do was to sink into the one arm-chair that was in the room, and conceal his features as well as he could by turning down the brim of the hat and turning up the collar of the cloak which the actor had forgotten. The man went as white as a sheet, but Lady Beltham appeared to recover all her presence of mind, and strength, and daring, at the approach of danger, and she hurried to the door. But though she tried to keep it shut, it slowly turned upon the hinges, and a timid, hesitating figure appeared in the doorway and advanced towards the retreating woman.

"Who are you? What do you want?" Lady Beltham faltered.

"I beg you to excuse me, madame," the man began, "I came to — — " He caught sight of Gurn and pointed to him. "M. Valgrand knows me well. I am Charlot, his dresser at the theatre, and I came to — I wanted to have a word — stay — — " he took a small square parcel from his pocket. "M. Valgrand went off so hurriedly that he forgot his pocket-book, and so I came to bring it to him." The dresser was trying to get near the murderer, whom he supposed to be his master, but Lady Beltham, in the most acute anxiety, kept between the two men. Charlot misunderstood her intention. "I also came to — — " He stopped again and whispered to Lady

Beltham. "He does not speak: is he very angry with me for coming? I didn't come out of curiosity, or to cause you any trouble, madame; will you ask him not to be very angry with his poor old Charlot?"

Lady Beltham felt like swooning again; she could endure very little of this old man's garrulity. "Go, for goodness' sake, go," she said peremptorily.

"I am going," Charlot said; "I know I am in the way; but I must explain to him," and he raised his voice and spoke to Gurn, who sat quite still, sinking as far as he could into the shadow of the chair. "You are not very angry with me, M. Valgrand, are you?" and getting no reply he looked apologetically at Lady Beltham. "It was all these stories, and then the street, and the prison opposite: but perhaps you do not know; you see, I read in the paper yesterday, or rather to-night, a couple of hours ago, that that man Gurn, who murdered the rich English gentleman, was to be executed this morning. And so I was rather what you might call uneasy; at first I only meant to follow M. Valgrand and wait for him down below, but I lost my way and I have only just arrived; I found the door open, and as I did not know whether he had gone or was still here, I took the liberty to come upstairs. But I am going now, quite easy in my mind, since he is quiet and happy here with you. And I beg your pardon, madame." He threw a last appeal to where Gurn sat. "I hope you will forgive me, M. Valgrand?" He sighed as no answer was forthcoming, and made a pathetic little appeal to Lady Beltham. "You will explain to him, madame, won't you? He is a kind master, and he will understand. One does get fancies like that, you know. But now I will go away easy, quite easy in my mind, since I have seen him."

Charlot turned away slowly, with bent shoulders. As he passed the window he glanced outside and stopped short. Day was just beginning to break, making the wan light of the street lamps still more wan. From the window a view could be obtained of a kind of platform at the corner of the boulevard Arago which was bounded by the high wall of the Santé prison. This spot, usually deserted, was crowded with people; a moving mob, swarming and struggling behind some hastily erected barriers. Charlot stretched a trembling hand towards the spectacle, in sudden comprehension.

"Good heavens!" he cried, "that must be where they are putting up the scaffold. Yes, I can see the planks and uprights; it is the guillotine! The exe — — "

The old man's words ended in a sudden cry, and almost simultaneously there was a heavy thud.

Struck from behind, Charlot fell like a log to the floor, while Lady Beltham recoiled in terror, clenching her fists to prevent herself from screaming.

Seizing the opportunity presented by Valgrand's faithful servant standing so still, hypnotised by the gruesome spectacle being prepared outside, Gurn had drawn a knife from his pocket, and, springing on the unfortunate old man, had driven the blade up to the hilt behind his neck.

Charlot fell prone and rigid, the weapon remaining in the wound and stopping the flow of blood.

Lady Beltham was staring at the victim in horror, but Gurn seized her roughly by the arm.

Without troubling to alter the appearance of his face, but horrified as she was by the tragedies which had succeeded one another in such appalling and rapid succession during this awful night, Gurn drew the half-fainting woman to him, and hurried her away.

"Come quick!" he muttered hoarsely. "Let us get out of this!"

XXXII
On the Scaffold

It was still dark.

In the keen morning air a crowd came hurrying along the pavements, flowing over into the roadways. The boulevards were black with people, all marching briskly towards one common goal. And it was a light-hearted, singing crowd, chanting the choruses of popular songs and swarming into the open restaurants and wine-shops and drinking dens.

And it was noticeable that all these late birds belonged to one of two sharply divided classes. They were either rich, or miserably poor; they either came from the night clubs, or they were the poor devils with no homes or hearths who roam about the city from one year's end to another. There were crooks whose faces shone with the evil excitement of alcohol, out-of-works of all kinds, beggars, and young men — all young men — with sleek oiled hair and shiny boots, in whose eyes and demeanour theft and crime could be seen.

By a curious coincidence the great news seemed to have reached all, toffs and crooks alike, at exactly the same time. About midnight the rumour had run round the town; it was certain, definite this time; the official steps had been taken, and the guillotine was going to raise her blood-stained arms towards the sky; at earliest dawn, Gurn, the man who had murdered Lord Beltham, was to undergo the supreme punishment, and expiate his murder with his life.

No sooner had the great news become known than all prepared, as for a holiday, to go to see the man's head fall. At Montmartre carriages were requisitioned and taxi-cabs were at a premium. Women in gorgeous toilets and sparkling with jewels streamed from the open doors into the carriages which should bear them swiftly towards the Santé prison, and the place of execution. In the faubourgs likewise, the bars were emptied of their customers, and men and women, linked arm-in-arm, set forth on foot, with songs and ribaldries upon their lips, for the spectacle of blood and the boulevard Arago.

Around the Santé prison an atmosphere of pleasure reigned as the people, massed together in tight ranks, produced bottles of wine, and ate sausages, and gaily enjoyed an improvised supper in the open air, while speculating about the details of the sight they had come to see. And so the crowd amused itself, for Gurn's head was going to fall.

Worming his way through the crowd, François Bonbonne, the landlord of the Saint-Anthony's Pig, led a little company of friends who took advantage of his great stature to find the best path to take.

The landlord was half-drunk already in honour of the occasion.

"Come along, Billy Tom," he shouted. "Catch hold of the tail of my coat and then you won't lose us. Where is Hogshead Geoffroy?"

"He's coming along with Bouzille."

"Good! Just fancy if Bouzille had tried to get through here with his train! There are some people about, eh?"

Two men passed the landlord of the market inn just then.

"Come along," said one of them, and as the other caught him up, Juve added: "Didn't you recognise those fellows?"

"No," said Fandor.

Juve told him the names of the men whom they had passed.

"You will understand that I don't want them to recognise me," he said, and as Fandor smiled Juve went on: "It's a queer thing, but it is always the future customers of the guillotine, apaches and fellows like that, who make a point of seeing this ghastly spectacle." The detective stopped and laid a hand upon the journalist's shoulder. "Wait," he said, "we are right in front now: only the men who are holding the line are ahead of us. If we want to get through and avoid the crush we must make ourselves known at once. Here is your pass."

Jérôme Fandor took the card which Juve held out to him, and had got for him as a special favour.

"What do we do now?" he asked.

"Here come the municipal guards," Juve replied; "I can see their sabres flashing. We will get behind the newspaper kiosks and let them drive the crowd back, and then we will go through."

Juve had correctly anticipated the manœuvre which the officer in command of the squadron immediately proceeded to execute. Grave and imposing, and marvellously mounted on magnificent horses, a large number of municipal guards had just arrived on the boulevard Arago, by the side of the Santé prison, and just where the detective and the journalist were standing. A sharp order rang out, and the guards deployed fan-wise and, riding knee to knee, drove the crowd back irresistibly to the end of the avenue, utterly disregarding the angry murmur of protest, and the general crushing that ensued.

The municipal guards were followed by troops of infantry, and these again by gendarmes who, holding hands, moved on all who by some means or other had managed to worm their way between the horses of the guards and the infantry, determined at any cost to keep in the front row of spectators.

Juve and Fandor, armed with their special passes which admitted them to the enclosure where the guillotine actually stood, had no difficulty in getting through the triple line. They found themselves in the centre of a large portion of the boulevard Arago, entirely clear of spectators, and bounded on one side by the walls of the prison, and on the other by those of a convent.

In this clear space about a dozen individuals in black coats and silk hats were walking about, affecting a complete indifference to what was going to happen, although really they were profoundly affected by it.

"Chief detective-inspectors," Juve said, pointing them out: "my colleagues. Some of yours too: do you see them? Chief reporters of the big dailies. Are you aware that you are uncommonly lucky to have been selected, at your extremely youthful age, to represent your paper at this lugubrious function?"

Jérôme Fandor made an odd grimace.

"I don't mind admitting to you, Juve, that I am here because I am like you in wanting to see Gurn's head fall; you have satisfied me beyond all doubt that Gurn is Fantômas, and I want to be sure that Fantômas is really dead. But if it were not the execution of that one particular wretch, — the only thing that can make society safe, — I should certainly have declined the honour of reporting this event."

"It upsets you?"

"Yes."

Juve bent his head.

"So it does me! Just think: for more than five years I have been fighting Fantômas! For more than five years I have believed in his existence, in spite of all ridicule and sarcasm! For more than five years I have been working for this wretch's death, for death is the only thing that can put a stop to his crimes!" Juve paused a moment, but Fandor made no comment. "And I am rather sick and sorry, too: because, although I have reached this certainty that Gurn is Fantômas, and have succeeded in convincing intelligent people, who were ready to study my work in good faith, I have nevertheless not succeeded in establishing legal proof that Gurn is Fantômas. Deibler and the Public Prosecutor, and people generally, think that it is merely Gurn who is going to be decapitated now. I may have secured this man's condemnation, but none the less he has beaten me and deprived me of the satisfaction of having brought him, Fantômas, to the scaffold! I have only consigned Gurn to the scaffold, and that is a defeat!"

The detective stopped. From the boulevard Arago, from the end to which the crowd had been driven back, cheers and applause and joyous shouts broke out; it was the mob welcoming the arrival of the guillotine.

Drawn by an old white horse, a heavy black van arrived at a fast trot, escorted by four mounted police with drawn swords. The van stopped a few yards from Juve and Fandor; the police rode off, and a shabby brougham came into view, from which three men in black proceeded to get out.

"Monsieur de Paris and his assistants," Juve informed Fandor: "Deibler and his men." Fandor shivered, and Juve went on with his explanations. "That van contains the timbers and the knife. Deibler and his men will get the guillotine up in half an hour, and in an hour at the outside, Fantômas will be no more!"

While the detective was speaking, the executioner had stepped briskly to the officer in charge of the proceedings and exchanged a few words with him. He signified his approval of the arrangements made, saluted the superintendent of police of that division, and turned to his men.

"Come along, lads; get to work!" He caught sight of Juve and shook hands with him. "Good morning," he said, adding, as though his work were of the most commonplace kind: "Excuse me: we are a bit late this morning!"

The assistants took from the van some long cases, wrapped in grey canvas and apparently very heavy. They laid these on the ground with the utmost care: they were the timbers and frame of the guillotine, and must not be warped or strained, for the guillotine is a nicely accurate machine!

They swept the ground thoroughly, careful to remove any gravel which might have affected the equilibrium of the framework, and then set up the red uprights of the scaffold. The floor timbers fitted one into another and were joined by stout metal clamps fastened together by a bolt; next the men set the grooved slides, down which the knife must fall, into holes cut for the purpose in the middle of the floor. The guillotine now raised its awful arms to the sky.

Hitherto Deibler had merely watched his men at work. Now he took a hand himself.

With a spirit-level he ascertained that the floor was absolutely horizontal; next he arranged the two pieces of wood, from each of which a segment is cut so as to form the lunette into which the victim's neck is thrust; then he tested the lever, to make sure that it worked freely, and gave a curt order.

"The knife!"

One of the assistants brought a case which Deibler opened, and Fandor instinctively shrank as a flash from the bright steel fell full in his eyes, that sinister triangular knife that presently would do the work of death.

Deibler leant calmly against the guillotine, fitted the shank into the grooves in the two up-rights, and, setting the mechanism to work, hoisted up the knife which glittered strangely; he looked the whole thing over and turned again to his assistants.

"The hay!"

A truss was arranged in the lunette, and Deibler came up to the instrument and pressed a spring. Like a flash the knife dropped down the uprights and severed the truss in two.

The rehearsal was finished. Now for the real drama!

While the guillotine was being set up Juve had stood by Fandor nervously chewing cigarettes.

"Everything is ready now," he said to the lad. "Deibler has only got to put on his coat and take delivery of Fantômas."

The assistants had just arranged two baskets filled with bran along each side of the machine; one was destined to receive the severed head, the other the body when that was released from the plyer. The executioner pulled on his coat, rubbed his hands mechanically, and then strode towards a group of officials who had arrived while the guillotine was being erected, and were now standing by the entrance to the prison.

"Gentlemen," said Deibler, "it will be sunrise in a quarter of an hour. We can proceed to awaken the prisoner."

Slowly, in single file, the officials went inside the prison.

There were present the Attorney General, the Public Prosecutor, his deputy, the Governor of the prison, and behind these, M. Havard, Deibler, and his two assistants.

The little company passed through the corridors to the third floor, where the condemned cells are.

The warder Nibet came forward with his bunch of keys in his hand.

Deibler looked at the Public Prosecutor.

"Are you ready, sir?" and as that gentleman, who was very white, made a sign of assent, Deibler looked at the Governor of the prison.

"Unlock the cell," the Governor ordered.

Nibet turned the key noiselessly and pushed open the door.

The Public Prosecutor stepped forward. He had hoped to find the condemned man asleep, and so have had a moment's respite before announcing the fatal news. But he drew back; for the man was awake and dressed, sitting ready on his bed with mad, haggard eyes.

"Gurn," said the Public Prosecutor. "Be brave! Your appeal has been rejected!"

The others, standing behind him, were all silent, and the words of the Public Prosecutor fell like a knell. The condemned man, however, had not stirred, had not even seemed to understand: his attitude was that of a man in a state of somnambulism. The Public Prosecutor was surprised by this strange impassivity and spoke again, in strangled tones.

"Be brave! Be brave!"

A spasm crossed the face of the condemned man, and his lips moved as though he were making an effort to say something.

"I'm not —— " he murmured.

But Deibler laid his hands upon the man's shoulders and cut the horrid moment short.

"Come now!"

The chaplain came forward in his turn.

"Pray, my brother," he said; "do you wish to hear mass?"

At the touch of the executioner the prisoner had trembled; he rose, like an automaton, with dilated eyes and twitching face. He understood what the chaplain said and took a step towards him.

"I — not —— "

M. Havard intervened, and spoke to the chaplain.

"Really, sir, no: it is time."

Deibler nodded approval.

"Let us be quick; we can proceed; the sun has risen."

The Public Prosecutor was still bleating "Be brave! Be brave!"

Deibler took the man by one arm, a warder took him by the other, and between them they half-carried him to the office for his last toilette. In the little room, dimly lighted by a winking lamp, a chair had been set close to a table. The executioner and his assistant pushed the condemned man into the chair, and Deibler took up a pair of scissors.

The Public Prosecutor spoke to the prisoner.

"Would you like a glass of rum? Would you like a cigarette? Is there anything you wish to have done?"

Maître Barberoux, who had not arrived in time for the awakening of the prisoner, now approached his client; he, too, was ghastly white.

"Is there anything else that I can do for you? Have you any last wish?"

The condemned man made another effort to rise from the chair, and a hoarse groan escaped from his throat.

"I — I —— "

The prison doctor had joined the group, and now drew the Public Prosecutor's deputy aside.

"It is appalling!" he said. "The man has not articulated a single word since he was awakened. He is as though sunk in a stupefied sleep. There is a technical word for his condition: he is in a state of inhibition. He is alive, and yet he is a corpse. Anyhow he is utterly unconscious, incapable of any clear thought, or of saying a word that has any sense. I have never seen such complete stupefaction."

Deibler waved aside the men who were pressing round him.

"Sign the gaol book, please, M. Havard," he said, and while that gentleman affixed a shaky signature to the warrant authorising the delivery of Gurn to the public executioner, Deibler took the scissors and cut a segment out of the prisoner's shirt and cut off a wisp of hair that grew low down on his neck. Meanwhile an assistant bound the wrists of the man who was about to die. Then the executioner looked at his watch and made a half-bow to the Public Prosecutor.

"Come! Come! It is the time fixed by law!"

Two assistants took the wretch by the shoulders and raised him up. There was a horrible, deep, unintelligible rattle in his throat.

"I — I — — "

But no one heard him, and he was dragged away. It was practically a corpse that the servants of the guillotine bore down to the boulevard Arago.

Outside, the first rosy tints of early dawn were waking the birds, and playing on the great triangular knife, drawing gleams from it. The time was ten minutes past five. And now the supreme moment was at hand.

The crowd, momentarily growing denser, was crushed behind the cordon of troops that had difficulty in keeping it at a distance from the guillotine. The soldiers, unheeding the oaths and curses and entreaties with which they were assailed, carried out their orders and permitted no one to take up his stand anywhere in the near neighbourhood of the guillotine, except the few rare individuals who had a special pass.

A sudden murmur ran through the crowd. The mounted police, stationed opposite the guillotine, had just drawn their sabres. Fandor gripped Juve's hand nervously. The detective was very pale.

"Let us get over there," he said, and led Fandor just behind the guillotine, to the side where the severed head would fall into the basket. "We shall see the poor devil get out of the carriage, and being fastened on to the bascule, and pulled into the lunette." He went on talking as if to divert his own mind from the thing before him. "That's the best place for seeing things: I stood there when Peugnez was guillotined, a long time ago now, and I was there again in 1909 when Duchémin, the parricide, was executed."

But he came to an abrupt stop. From the great door of the Santé prison a carriage came rapidly out. All heads were uncovered, all eyes were fixed, and a deep silence fell upon the crowded boulevard.

The carriage passed the journalist and the detective at a gallop and pulled up with a jerk just opposite them, on the other side of the guillotine, and at the very foot of the scaffold. M. Deibler jumped down from the box, and opening the door at the back of the vehicle let down the steps. Pale and nervous, the chaplain got out backwards, hiding the scaffold from the eyes of the condemned man, whom the assistants managed somehow to help out of the carriage.

Fandor was shaking with nervousness and muttering to himself.

But things moved quickly now.

The chaplain, still walking backwards, hid the dread vision for yet a few seconds more, then stepped aside abruptly. The assistants seized the condemned man, and pushed him on to the bascule.

Juve was watching the unhappy wretch, and could not restrain a word of admiration.

"That man is a brave man! He has not even turned pale! Generally condemned men are livid!"

The executioner's assistants had bound the man upon the plank; it tilted upwards. Deibler grasped the head by the two ears and pulled it into the lunette, despite one last convulsive struggle of the victim.

There was a click of a spring, the flash of the falling knife, a spurt of blood, a dull groan from ten thousand breasts, and the head rolled into the basket!

But Juve had flung Fandor aside and sprang towards the scaffold. He thrust the assistants away, and plunging his hands into the bran that was all soaked with blood, he seized the severed head by the hair and stared at it.

Horrified by this scandalous action the assistants rushed upon the detective.

Deibler forced him backwards.

"You must be mad!"

"Get away!"

Fandor saw that Juve was staggering and seemed about to swoon. He rushed towards him. "Good God!" he cried in tones of anguish.

"It isn't Gurn who has just been put to death!" Juve panted brokenly. "This face has not gone white because it is painted! It is made up — like an actor's! Oh, curses on him! Fantômas has escaped! Fantômas has got away! He has had some innocent man executed in his stead! I tell you Fantômas is alive!"